ALSO BY ANNE TYLER

If Morning Ever Comes
(1964)

The Tin Can Tree
(1965)

A Slipping-Down Life
(1970)

The Clock Winder
(1972)

Celestial Navigation
(1974)

Searching for Caleb
(1976)

Earthly Possessions
(1977)

Morgan's Passing
(1980)

THESE ARE BORZOI BOOKS,
PUBLISHED IN NEW YORK BY
ALFRED A. KNOPF

Dinner at the Homesick Restaurant

Anne Tyler

DINNER AT
THE HOMESICK
RESTAURANT

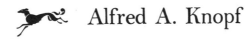 Alfred A. Knopf

New York   1982

THIS IS A BORZOI BOOK
PUBLISHED BY ALFRED A. KNOPF, INC.

Library of Congress Cataloging in Publication Data
Tyler, Anne.
Dinner at the Homesick Restaurant.
I. Title.
PS3570.Y45D5   1982   813'.54   81-13694
ISBN 0-394-52381-4   AACR2

Manufactured in the United States of America

Published March 25, 1982
Second Printing, March 1982

Contents

Contents

Dinner at the
Homesick Restaurant

1

Something You
Should Know

While Pearl Tull was dying, a funny thought occurred to her.
It twitched her lips and rustled her breath, and she felt her son
lean forward from where he kept watch by her bed. "Get . . ."
she told him. "You should have got . . ."

You should have got an extra mother, was what she meant to
say, the way we started extra children after the first child fell
so ill. Cody, that was; the older boy. Not Ezra here beside her
bed but Cody the troublemaker—a difficult baby, born late
in her life. They had decided on no more. Then he developed
croup. This was in 1931, when croup was something serious.
She'd been frantic. Over his crib she had draped a flannel sheet,
and she set out skillets, saucepans, buckets full of water that
she'd heated on the stove. She lifted the flannel sheet to catch
the steam. The baby's breathing was choked and rough, like
something pulled through tightly packed gravel. His skin was
blazing and his hair was plastered stiffly to his temples. Toward
morning, he slept. Pearl's head sagged in the rocking chair and
she slept too, fingers still gripping the ivory metal crib rail.
Beck was away on business—came home when the worst was
over, Cody toddling around again with nothing more than a
runny nose and a loose, unalarming cough that Beck didn't even
notice. "I want more children," Pearl told him. He acted surprised, though pleased. He reminded her that she hadn't felt

she could face another delivery. But "I want some extra," she said, for it had struck her during the croup: if Cody died, what would she have left? This little rented house, fixed up so carefully and pathetically; the nursery with its Mother Goose theme; and Beck, of course, but he was so busy with the Tanner Corporation, away from home more often than not, and even when home always fuming over business: who was on the rise and who was on the skids, who had spread damaging rumors behind his back, what chance he had of being let go now that times were so hard.

"I don't know why I thought just one little boy would suffice," said Pearl.

But it wasn't as simple as she had supposed. The second child was Ezra, so sweet and clumsy it could break your heart. She was more endangered than ever. It would have been best to stop at Cody. She still hadn't learned, though. After Ezra came Jenny, the girl—such fun to dress, to fix her hair in different styles. Girls were a kind of luxury, Pearl felt. But she couldn't give Jenny up, either. What she had now was not one loss to fear but three. Still, she thought, it had seemed a good idea once upon a time: spare children, like spare tires, or those extra lisle stockings they used to package free with each pair.

"You should have arranged for a second-string mother, Ezra," she said. Or she meant to say. "How shortsighted of you." But evidently she failed to form the words, for she heard him sit back again without comment and turn a page of his magazine.

She had not seen Ezra clearly since the spring of '75, four and a half years ago, when she first started losing her vision. She'd had a little trouble with blurring. She went to the doctor for glasses. It was arteries, he told her; something to do with her arteries. She was eighty-one years old, after all. But he was certain it could be treated. He sent her to a specialist, who sent her to someone else . . . well, to make a long story short, they found they couldn't help her. Something had shriveled away behind her eyes. "I'm falling into disrepair," she told the children. "I've outlived myself." She gave a little laugh. To tell the truth, she hadn't believed it. She had made the appropriate sounds of dismay, then acceptance, then plucky cheer; but inwardly, she'd determined not to allow it. She just wouldn't hear of it, that was all. She had always been a strong-willed woman. Once, when Beck was away on business, she'd walked around with a broken arm for a day and a half till he could come stay with the babies. (It was just after one of his transfers. She was a stranger in town and had no one to turn to.) She didn't even hold with aspirin; didn't hold with depending, requesting. "The doctor says I'm going blind," she told the children, but privately, she'd intended to do no such thing.

Yet every day, her sight had faded. The light, she felt, was somehow thinning and retreating. Her son Ezra, his calm face that she loved to linger on—he grew dim. Even in bright sunshine, now, she had difficulty making out his shape. She could barely discern his silhouette as he came near her—that large, sloping body settling into softness a bit in his middle age. She felt his flannel warmth when he sat next to her on the couch, describing what was on her TV or going through her drawer of snapshots the way she liked to have him do. "What's that you've got, Ezra?" she would ask.

"It seems to be some people on a picnic," he would say.

"Picnic? What kind of picnic?"

"White tablecloth in the grass. Wicker basket. Lady wearing a middy blouse."

"Maybe that's Aunt Bessie."

"I'd recognize your Aunt Bessie, by now."

"Or Cousin Elsa. *She* favored middy blouses, I recall."

Ezra said, "I never knew you had a cousin."

"Oh, I had cousins," she said.

She tipped her head back and recollected cousins, aunts, uncles, a grandpa whose breath had smelled of mothballs. It was peculiar how her memory seemed to be going blind with the rest of her. She didn't so much see their faces as hear their fluid voices, feel the crisp ruching of the ladies' shirtwaists, smell their pomades and lavender water and the sharp-scented bottle of crystals that sickly Cousin Bertha had carried to ward off fainting spells.

"I had cousins aplenty," she told Ezra.

They had thought she would be an old maid. They'd grown tactful—insultingly tactful. Talk of others' weddings and confinements halted when Pearl stepped out on the porch. A college education was offered by Uncle Seward—at Meredith College, right there in Raleigh, so she wouldn't have to leave home. No doubt he feared having to support her forever: a millstone, an orphaned spinster niece tying up his spare bedroom. But she told him she had no use for college. She felt that going to college would be an admission of defeat.

Oh, what was the trouble, exactly? She was not bad-looking. She was small and slender with fair skin and fair, piled hair, but the hair was growing dry as dust and the strain was beginning to show around the curled and mobile corners of her mouth. She'd had suitors in abundance, more than she could name; yet they never lasted, somehow. It seemed there was some magical word that everyone knew but Pearl—those streams of girls, years younger than she, effortlessly tumbling into marriage. Was she too serious? Should she unbend more? Lower herself to giggle like those mindless, silly Winston twins? Uncle Seward, *you* can tell me. But Uncle Seward just puffed on his pipe and suggested a secretarial course.

Then she met Beck Tull. She was thirty years old. He was twenty-four—a salesman with the Tanner Corporation, which sold its farm and garden equipment all over the eastern seaboard and where he would surely, surely rise, a smart young fellow like him. In those days, he was lean and rangy. His black hair waved extravagantly, and his eyes were a brilliant shade of blue that seemed not quite real. Some might say he was . . . well, a little extreme. Flamboyant. Not quite of Pearl's class. And certainly too young for her. She knew there were some thoughts to that effect. But what did she care? She felt reckless and dashing, bursting with possibilities.

She met him at a church—at the Charity Baptist Church, which Pearl was only visiting because her girlfriend Emmaline was a member. Pearl was not a Baptist herself. She was Episcopalian, but truthfully not even that; she thought of herself as a nonbeliever. Still, when she went to the Baptist church and saw Beck Tull standing there, a stranger, glossily shaved and wearing a shiny blue suit, and he asked within two minutes if he might be allowed to call, she related it in some superstitious way to the church itself—as if Beck were her reward for attending with the Baptists. She did not dare *stop* attending. She became a member, to her family's horror, and was married at Charity Baptist and went to one Baptist church or another, in one town or another, her entire married life, just so her reward would not be snatched away. (Didn't that maybe, it occurred to her, imply some kind of faith after all?)

Courting her, he brought chocolates and flowers and then—more serious—pamphlets describing the products of the Tanner Corporation. He started telling her in detail about his work and his plans for advancement. He paid her compliments that made her uncomfortable till she could get off alone in her room and savor them. She was the most cultured and refined little lady that he had ever known, he said, and the best mannered, and the daintiest. He liked to place her hand to his, palm to palm, and marvel at its tiny size. Despite the reputation of salesmen, he was respectful to a fault and never grabbed at her the way some other men might.

Then he received his transfer, and after that things sped up so; for he wouldn't hear of leaving her behind but must marry her immediately and take her with him. So they had their Baptist wedding—both of them out of breath, Pearl always pictured later—and spent their honeymoon moving to Newport News. She never even got to enjoy her new status among her girlfriends. She didn't have time to show off a single one of her trousseau dresses, or to flash her two gold rings—the narrow wedding band and the engagement ring, set with a pearl, inscribed *To a Pearl among Women.* Everything seemed so unsatisfying.

They moved, and they moved again. For the first six years they had no children and the moves were fairly easy. She'd gaze at each new town with hopeful eyes and think: This may be where I'll have my son. (For pregnancy, now, took on the luster that marriage had once had—it was the treasure that came so easily to everyone but her.) Then Cody was born, and moving seemed much harder. Children had a way of complicating things, she noticed. There were the doctors and the school transcripts and this, that, and the other. Meanwhile she looked around and saw that somehow, without her noticing, she'd been cut off from most of her relatives. Aunts and uncles had died while she'd been too far away to do more than send a sympathy note. The house where she was born was sold to a man from Michigan; cousins married strangers with last names she'd never heard of; even the street names were changed so she'd be lost if she ever went back. And it struck her once, in her forties, that she really had no notion what had become of that grandpa with the mothball breath. He couldn't still be living, could he? Had he died and no one thought to inform her? Or maybe they'd sent the news to an out-of-date address, three or four years behind times. Or she might have heard but simply forgotten, in the rush of some transfer or other. Anything was possible.

Oh, those transfers. Always there was some incentive—a chance of promotion, or richer territory. But it seldom amounted to much. Was it Beck's fault? He claimed it wasn't, but she didn't know; she really didn't know. He claimed that he was haunted by ill-wishers. There were so many petty people in this world, he said. She pursed her lips and studied him. "Why do you look at me that way?" he asked. "What are you thinking? At least," he said, "I provide for you. I've never let my family go hungry." She admitted that, but still she felt a constant itch of anxiety. It seemed her forehead was always tight and puckered. This was not a person she could lean on, she felt —this slangy, loud-voiced salesman peering at his reflection with too much interest when he tied his tie in the mornings, combing his pompadour tall and damp and frilly and then replacing the comb in a shirt pocket full of pencils, pens, ruler, appointment book, and tire gauge, all bearing catchy printed slogans for various firms.

Over his beer in the evening (but he was not a drinking man; don't get her wrong), Beck liked to sing and pull at his face.

She didn't know why beer made him tug his skin that way—
work it around like a rubber mask, so by bedtime his cheeks had
a stretched-out, slackened look. He sang "Nobody Knows the
Trouble I've Seen"—his favorite song. Nobody knows but
Jesus. She supposed it must be true. What were his private
thoughts, inside his spreading face, under the crest of black
hair? She didn't have the faintest idea.

One Sunday night in 1944, he said he didn't want to stay
married. They were sending him to Norfolk, he said; but he
thought it best if he went alone. Pearl felt she was sinking in at
the center, like someone given a stomach punch. Yet part of
her experienced an alert form of interest, as if this were happening in a story. "Why?" she asked him, calmly enough. He didn't
answer. "Beck? Why?" All he did was study his fists. He looked
like a young and belligerent schoolboy waiting out a scolding.
She made her voice even quieter. It was important to learn the
reason. Wouldn't he just tell her what it was? He'd told her,
he said. She lowered herself, shaking, into the chair across from
him. She looked at his left temple, in which a pulse ticked. He
was just passing through some mood, was all. He would change
his mind in the morning. "We'll sleep on it," she told him.

But he said, "It's tonight I'm going."

He went to the bedroom for his suitcase, and he took his
other suit from the wardrobe. Meanwhile Pearl, desperate for
time, asked couldn't they talk this over? Think it through? No
need to be hasty, was there? He crossed from bureau to bed,
from wardrobe to bed, packing his belongings. There weren't
that many. He was done in twenty minutes. He drew in his
breath and she thought, Now he'll tell me. But all he said was,
"I'm not an irresponsible person. I do plan to send you money."

"And the children," she said, clutching new hope. "You'll
want to visit the children."

(He would come with presents for them and she'd be the one
to open the door—perfumed, in her Sunday dress, maybe wearing a bit of rouge. She'd always thought false color looked
cheap, but she could have been wrong.)

Beck said, "No."

"What?"

"I won't be visiting the children."

She sat down on the bed.

"I don't understand you," she said.

There ought to be a whole separate language, she thought, for words that are truer than other words—for perfect, absolute truth. It was the purest fact of her life: she did not understand him, and she never would.

At the time, they were living in Baltimore, in a row house on Calvert Street. The children were fourteen, eleven, and nine. They were old enough to suspect something wrong, if she didn't take care. She took infinite care. The morning after Beck left she rose and dressed, piled her hair on her head the same as always, and cooked oatmeal for the children's breakfast. Cody and Jenny ate without speaking; Ezra told a long, rambling dream. (He was the only one cheerful in the mornings.) There was some disappointment that the oatmeal lacked raisins. Nobody asked where Beck was. After all, he often left before they woke on a Monday. And there'd been times—many times—when he'd stayed away the whole week. It wasn't so unusual.

When Friday night rolled around, she said he'd been delayed. He'd promised to take them to the Midget Circus, and she told them she would do it instead. Another week passed. She had no close friends, but if she met a chance acquaintance in the grocery store, she remarked that luckily, she wouldn't have to use any meat points today. Her husband was away on business, she said. People nodded, showing no interest. He was almost always away on business. Few had ever met him.

Nights, especially Friday nights, she lay in bed in the dark and listened to the gritty click of heels on the sidewalk. Footsteps would come close and then pass. She would let out her breath. A new set of footsteps approached. Surely *this* was Beck. She knew how hesitantly he would let himself in, expecting the worst—his children's tears, his wife's reproaches. But instead, he'd find everything unchanged. The children would greet him offhandedly. Pearl would peck his cheek and ask if he'd had a good trip. Later, he would thank her for keeping his secret. He would be so easily readmitted, since only the two of them knew he'd left; outsiders would go on believing the Tulls were a happy family. Which they were, in fact. Oh, they'd always been so happy! They'd depended only on each other, because of moving around so much. It had made them very close. He'd be back.

Her Uncle Seward's widow wrote to wish her a happy birthday. (Pearl had forgotten all about it.) Pearl responded immediately, thanking her. *We celebrated at home*, she wrote. *Beck surprised me with the prettiest necklace . . . Say hello to the others*, she added, and she pictured them all in her uncle's parlor; she ached for them, but drew herself up and recalled how they had been so sure no man would marry her. She could never tell them what had happened.

Her old friend Emmaline stopped by, on her way to visit a sister in Philadelphia. Pearl said Beck was out of town; the two of them were in luck; they could talk girl-talk to their hearts' content. She put Emmaline in the double bed with her, instead of in the guest room. They stayed awake half the night gossiping and giggling. Once Pearl almost set a hand on Emmaline's arm and said, "Emmaline. Listen. I feel so horrible, Emmaline." But fortunately, she caught herself. The moment passed. In the morning they overslept, and Pearl had to rush to get the children off to school; so there wasn't much said. "We should do this more often," Emmaline told her as she left, and Pearl said Beck would be sorry he had missed her. "You know he's always liked you," she said. Although actually, Beck used to claim that Emmaline reminded him of a woodchuck.

Easter came, and Jenny had a part in her school's Easter pageant. When the day arrived and Beck was still not home, Jenny cried. Couldn't he *ever* be home? It wasn't his fault, Pearl told her. There was a war on, production speeded up; he couldn't help it if his company needed him more now. They ought to be proud, she said. Jenny dried her tears and told everyone that her daddy had to help with the war effort. The war was so old by now, grinding on; no one was impressed. Still, it made Jenny feel better. Pearl went to the Easter pageant alone, wearing a rakish, visored hat that was patterned after the hats the WACs wore.

When Beck had been gone a month, he sent a note from Norfolk saying he was fine and hoped that she and the kids did not lack for anything. He enclosed a check for fifty dollars. It wasn't nearly enough. Pearl spent a morning pacing the house. First she went over his note in her mind, picking apart his words for underlying meanings. But not much could underlie *right good apartment with hotplate* and *sales manager seems to think well of me*. Then she considered the money. Around lunchtime, she put on her coat and her WACs hat and walked around the corner to Sweeney Bros. Grocery and Fine Produce, where a CASHIER WANTED sign had been yellowing in the window for weeks. They were tickled to death to hire her. The younger Sweeney brother showed her how to work the cash register and said she could start the next morning. When her children came home from school that day, she told them she was taking a job to fill in time. She needed something to keep her busy, she said, now that they were growing up and going off on their own more.

Two months passed. Three months. Fifty dollars a month from Beck. When the second check arrived, no letter came with it. She tore the envelope apart, thinking it must have got stuck inside, but there wasn't a word. With the third check, though, he wrote that he was moving to Cleveland, where the company planned to open a new branch. He said it was a good sign they'd decided on this transfer—or "invite," he called it. He never called it a transfer; he called it an invite. An invite to this important expansion westward. He began the letter, *Dear Pearl & kids*, but Pearl didn't show it to the children. She folded it neatly and put it with the first letter, in a hosiery box in her bureau, where even that meddlesome Cody wouldn't think to look. In the fourth envelope, again, there was only a check. She saw that he was not in *communication* with her (was how she phrased it), but was merely touching base from time to time.

Really, all he was doing was saying, *Please find enclosed.* It didn't occur to her to answer him. Yet she went on saving his letters.

Sometimes she had strange thoughts that surprised her. For instance: At least I have more closet space now. And more drawer space.

At night she dreamed that Beck was new and wonderful again, someone she'd just become acquainted with. He gazed at her adoringly, overturning some unfamiliar center deep inside her. He helped her cross streets, climb steps. His hand cupped her elbow warmly or circled her waist or steadied the small of her back. She felt cherished. When she woke, her only thought was to sink back into her dream. She would keep her eyes shut. Superstitiously, she would play possum, not stirring, trying to persuade the dream that she was still asleep. But it never worked. Finally she would rise, whatever the hour, and go downstairs to make a pot of coffee. Standing at the kitchen window with her cup, watching the sky whiten over the rooftops, she would catch sight of her dark, transparent reflection—her small face and round chin that was taking on a dented look, these past few years; the worried tent of her colorless eyebrows; the pale frazzle of hair that failed to hide the crease across her forehead. That crease was not a wrinkle but a scar, the mark of a childhood accident. Oh, she was not so old! She was not so very old! But then she remembered the accident: she'd been trying to ride a cousin's bicycle, the very first in the family. A "wheel" was what they called it. Trying to ride a wheel. And here it was 1944 and bicycles were everywhere, but so modernized they were hardly the same breed of beast. All three of her children knew how to ride and would, in fact, have had bikes of their own if not for the war. How had she come so far? She had just passed her fiftieth birthday. There was not a hope of Beck's return. He'd found someone younger, someone glamorous and merry, still capable of bearing children. They were laughing at her—at how she'd always been an old maid, really, always an old maid at heart. How she flinched when he turned to her in the dark, still startled, after all these years, by the concreteness of him—by his scratchy whiskers, salty-smelling skin, weighty body. How she had to have things just perfect, the linens on labeled shelves in the cupboard and the shades pulled evenly in the windows. How she'd never learned to let go, to give in, to float on the current of a day, but must always fuss and pull at stray threads and straighten the corners of things; and worst of all, how she *knew* she did that, knew while she was doing it, but still could not stop herself.

He was never coming back.

It was time to tell the children. She was amazed, in fact, that she'd managed to keep it from them for so long. Had they always been this easy to fool? One good thing about telling them: they would rally around her better. She didn't like to admit it but she was losing control of the boys. Instead of supporting her—taking out the garbage, helping her in various manly and protective ways—they seemed to be running wild; yes, even Ezra. They didn't even do the chores they used to do, let alone take on new ones. Cody in fact was hardly ever home. Ezra was dreamy and forgetful and would like as not walk off in the middle of a task. When she told them what was what, she thought, they'd be horrified at how they'd let her down. They'd ask why she'd hidden it all this time, what she could have been thinking of.

Only she couldn't tell them.

She planned how she would do it: she would gather them around her on the sofa, in the lamplight, some evening after supper. "Children. Dear ones," she would say. "There's something you should know." But she wouldn't be able to continue; she might cry. It was unthinkable to cry in front of the children. Or in front of anyone. Oh, she had her pride! She was not a tranquil woman; she often lost her temper, snapped, slapped the nearest cheek, said things she later regretted—but thank the Lord, she didn't expose her tears. She didn't *allow* any tears. She was Pearl Cody Tull, who'd ridden out of Raleigh triumphant with her new husband and never looked back. Even now, even standing at the kitchen window, all alone, watching her tense and aging face, she didn't cry.

Every morning, then, she went off to Sweeney Bros. She continued to wear her hat, giving the impression that she had merely dropped in and was helping out as a favor, in a pinch. As each customer approached (generally someone she knew, at least by sight), she would give a firm nod and then squint, implying a smile. She rang up the purchases efficiently while a boy named Alexander bagged them. "Thank you, and good day," she said at the end, with another shorthand smile. She liked to seem crisp and professional. When neighbors showed up, people she knew more closely, she felt she was dying inside but she didn't lose her composure. With them she was even crisper. She had a little rhythm between the key stabbing and the sliding of groceries along the wooden counter; it kept her mind off things. If she allowed herself to think, she started worrying. Summer had arrived and her children were out of school all day. No telling what they might be up to.

At five-thirty she walked home, past crowds of youngsters playing hopscotch or huddled over marble games, past babies set to air in their carriages, women perched on their stoops fanning themselves in the heat. She'd climb her steps and be met at the door with bad news: "Jenny fell down the stairs today and bit her lower lip clean through and had to go to Mrs. Simmons's house for ice and gauze."

"Oh, Jenny, honey!"

It seemed they greeted her with disaster, saved up all their accidents especially for her. She'd want to take off her hat and shoes and fall back onto the sofa; but no, it was "The toilet's stopped up," and "I tore my pants," and "Cody hit Ezra with the orange juice pitcher."

"Can't you just let me be?" she would ask. "Can't you just give me a minute to myself?"

She'd make supper from tins she'd brought home, nothing fancy. She would listen to the radio while she washed dishes. Jenny was supposed to dry but was off playing tag with the boys. Stepping out the back door to heave her dishpan of water into the yard, Pearl paused to watch them—Cody and Jenny dark and quick, high-pitched, overcome with laughter; Ezra pale, a glimmer in the twilight, slower and more wandery in his movements. Sometimes there'd be neighbor children, too, but more often just the three of them. They stuck together, mostly. She shampooed her hair and rinsed out a slip. Called to Cody to fetch the other two and come inside now.

Nights, she worked on the house. To look at her—an out-of-date kind of woman, frail boned, deep bosomed, as if those pout-fronted gowns of her girlhood had somehow formed her figure—you would never guess it, but Pearl was clever with tools. She patched a crack, glazed a window, replaced two basement stair treads. She mended a lamp switch and painted the kitchen cupboards. Even in the old days, she had done such things; Beck was not very handy. "This whole, entire house is resting on my shoulders," she would tell him, and she meant it as an accusation; but the thought was also reassuring, in a way. She knew that she was competent. From early in their marriage, from the moment she had realized how often they would be moving, she had concentrated on making each house perfect— airtight and rustproof and waterproof. She dropped the effort of continually meeting new neighbors, and she stopped returning (freshly filled) the cake tins they brought over when she arrived. All she cared about was sealing up the house, as if for a hurricane. She woke nights wondering if the basement were dry, and went down barefoot to make sure. She couldn't enjoy their Sunday outings because the house might have burned to the ground in her absence. (How vividly she could picture their return! There'd be an open space where the house used to stand, and a tattered hole for the basement.) Here in Baltimore, she gathered, she was thought to be unfriendly, even spooky— the witch of Calvert Street. What a notion! She'd known such witches in her childhood; she was nothing like them. All she wanted was to be allowed to get on with what mattered: calk the windows; weatherstrip the door. With tools she was her true self, capable and strong. She felt an indulgent kind of scorn for her children, who had not inherited her skill. Cody lacked the patience, Ezra was inept, Jenny too flighty. It was remarkable, Pearl thought, how people displayed their characters in every little thing they undertook.

Hammering down a loose floorboard, with a bristle of nails in her mouth, she would let time slip away from her. It would get to be ten-thirty or eleven. Her children would be standing in the doorway all sweaty and grass stained, blinking in the sudden brightness. "Heavens! Get to bed," she told them. "I thought I called you in hours ago." But a while after they left she'd start to feel deserted, even though they hadn't been much company. She would lay aside her hammer and rise and walk the house, smoothing her skirt, absently touching her hair where it was falling out of its bun. Up the stairs to the hall, past the little room where Jenny slept, and into her own room, with its buckling cardboard wardrobe streaked to look like wood grain, the bare-topped bureau, the cavernous bed. Then out again and up more stairs to the boys' room, a third-floor dormitory that smelled of heat. The trustful sound of her sons' breathing made her envious. She turned and descended the stairs, all the way down to the kitchen. The back door stood open and the screen door fluttered with moths. Neighboring houses rang with someone's laughter, a few cracked notes from a trumpet, an out-of-tune piano playing "Chattanooga Choo-Choo." She closed the door and locked it and pulled down the paper shade. She climbed the stairs once more and took off her clothing, piece by piece, and put on her nightgown and went to bed.

She dreamed he wore that aftershave that he'd used when they were courting. She hadn't smelled it in years, hadn't given it a thought, but now it came back to her distinctly—something pungent, prickled with spice. A swaggery and self-vaunting scent, she had known even then; but catching wind of it, when he arrived on Uncle Seward's front porch to pick her up, she had felt adventurous. She had flung the door open so widely that it banged against the wall, and he had laughed and said, "Well, now. Hey, now," as she stood there, smiling out at him.

She had heard you could not dream a smell, or recall a smell in its absence; so when she woke she was convinced, for a moment, that Beck had let himself into the house and was seated on the edge of the bed, watching while she slept. But there was no one there.

Dance? Oh, I don't think so, she said inside her head. I'm in charge of this whole affair, you see, and all I'd have to do is turn my back one instant for the party to go to pieces, just fall into little pieces. Whoever it was drew away. Ezra turned a page of his magazine. "Ezra," she said. She felt him grow still. He had this habit—he had always had it—of becoming totally motionless when people spoke to him. It was endearing, but also in some ways a strain, for then whatever she said to him ("I feel a draft," or "The paper boy is late again") was bound to disappoint him, wasn't it? How could she live up to Ezra's expectations? She plucked at her quilt. "If I could just have some water," she told him.

He poured it from the pitcher on the bureau. She heard no ice cubes clinking; they must have melted. Yet it seemed just minutes ago that he'd brought in a whole new supply. He raised her head, rested it on his shoulder, and tipped the glass to her lips. Yes, lukewarm—not that she minded. She drank gratefully, keeping her eyes closed. His shoulder felt steady and comforting. He laid her back down on the pillow.

"Dr. Vincent's coming at ten," he told her.

"What time is it now?"

"Eight-thirty."

"Eight-thirty in the morning?"

"Yes."

"Have you been here all night?" she asked.

"I slept a little."

"Sleep now. I won't be needing you."

"Well, maybe after the doctor comes."

It was important to Pearl that she deceive the doctor. She didn't want to go to the hospital. Her illness was pneumonia, she was almost certain; she guessed it from a past experience.

She recognized the way it settled into her back. If Dr. Vincent found out he would send her off to Union Memorial, tent her over with plastic. "Maybe you should cancel the doctor altogether," she told Ezra. "I'm very much improved, I believe."

"Let him decide that."

"Well, I know how my own self feels, Ezra."

"We won't argue about it just now," he said.

He could surprise you, Ezra could. He'd let a person walk all over him but then display, at odd moments, a deep and rock-hard stubbornness. She sighed and smoothed her quilt. It seemed he'd spilled some water on it.

She remembered when Ezra was a child, still in elementary school. "Mother," he had said, "if it turned out that money grew on trees, just for one day and never again, would you let me stay home from school and pick it?"

"No," she told him.

"Why not?"

"Your education is more important."

"Other kids' mothers would let them, I bet."

"Other mothers don't have plans for their children to amount to something."

"But just for one day?"

"Pick it *after* school. Or before. Wake up extra early; set your alarm clock ahead an hour."

"An hour!" he said. "One little hour, for something that happens only once in all the world."

"Ezra, will you let it be? Must you keep at me this way? Why are you so obstinate?" Pearl had asked him.

It only now occurred to her, under her damp quilt, to wonder why she hadn't said yes, he could stay home. If money decided to grow on trees one day, let him pick all he liked! she should have said. What difference would it have made?

Oh, she'd been an angry sort of mother. She'd been continually on edge; she'd felt too burdened, too much alone. And after Beck left, she'd been so preoccupied with paying the rent and juggling the budget and keeping those great, clod-footed children in new shoes. It was she who called the doctor at two a.m. when Jenny got appendicitis; it was she who marched downstairs with a baseball bat the night they heard that scary noise. She'd kept the furnace stoked with coal, confronted the neighborhood bully when Ezra got beaten up, hosed the roof during Mrs. Simmons's chimney fire. And when Cody came home drunk from some girl's birthday party, who had to deal with that? Pearl Tull, who'd never taken anything stronger than a glass of wine at Christmas. She sat him smartly in a kitchen chair, ignored his groans, leaned across the table to him —and couldn't think of a thing to say.

Then Cody graduated from high school, and Ezra was a sophomore, and Jenny was a tall young lady in eighth grade. Beck would not have known them. And they, perhaps, would not have known Beck. They never asked about him. Didn't that show how little importance a father has? The invisible man. The absent presence. Pearl felt a twinge of angry joy. Apparently she had carried this off—made the transition so smoothly that not a single person guessed. It was the greatest triumph of her life. My one true accomplishment, she thought. (What a pity there was no one to whom she could boast of it.) Without noticing, even, she had gradually stopped attending the Baptist church. She stopped referring to Beck in conversation—although still, writing her Christmas cards to relatives in Raleigh, she remarked that Beck was doing well and sent them his regards.

One night, she threw away his letters. It wasn't a planned decision. She was just cleaning her bureau, was all, and couldn't think of any good reason to save them. She sat by her bedroom wastebasket and dropped in *looks like I will be moving up the ladder* and *litle place convenient to the railway station* and *told me I was doing mighty well*. There weren't very many—three or so in the past year. When had she quit ripping open the envelopes with shaking hands and rapidly, greedily scanning the lines? It occurred to her that the man she still mourned, late on sleepless nights, bore no relation whatsoever to the man who sent these tiresome messages. *Ed Ball is retiring in June*, she read with infinite boredom, *and I step into his territory which has*

the highest per capitta income in Delaware. It was a great satisfaction to her that he had misspelled *capita.*

Her children grew up and embarked on lives of their own. Her sons started helping out financially, and Pearl was glad to accept. (She had never been ashamed about taking money—from Uncle Seward in the olden days, or from Beck, or now from the boys. Where she came from, a woman *expected* the men to provide.) And when Cody became so successful, he bought the row house she'd been renting all these years and presented her with the deed one Christmas morning. She could have retired from the grocery store right then, but she put it off till her sight began failing. What else would she do with her time? "Empty nest," they called it. Nowadays, that was the term they used. It was funny, in her old age, to look back and see for how short a period her nest had *not* been empty. Relatively speaking, it was nothing—empty far longer than full. So much of herself had been invested in those children; who could believe how briefly they'd been with her?

When she thought of them in their various stages—first clinging to her, then separating and drifting off—she thought of the hall lamp she used to leave on so they wouldn't be scared in the dark. Then later she'd left just the bathroom light on, further down the hall of whatever house they'd been living in; and later still just the downstairs light if one of them was out for the evening. Their growing up amounted, therefore, to a gradual dimming of the light at her bedroom door, as if they took some radiance with them as they moved away from her. She should have planned for it better, she sometimes thought. She should have made a few friends or joined a club. But she wasn't the type. It wouldn't have consoled her.

Last summer, she'd been half-awakened by a hymn on her clock radio—"In the Sweet Bye and Bye," mournfully sung by some popular singer just before Norman Vincent Peale's sermonette. *We shall meet on that beautiful shore . . .* She'd slipped into a dream in which a stranger told her that the beautiful shore was Wrightsville Beach, North Carolina, where she and Beck and the children had once spent a summer vacation. They were meeting on the shore after changing into swimsuits, for the very first swim of their very first day. Beck was handsome and Pearl felt graceful and the children were still very small; they had round, excited, joyous faces and chubby little bodies. She was astounded by their innocence—by her own and Beck's as well. She stretched her arms toward the children, but woke. Later, speaking to Cody on the phone, she happened to mention the dream. Wouldn't it be nice, she said, if heaven were Wrightsville Beach? If, after dying, they'd open their eyes and find themselves back on that warm, sunny sand, everyone young and happy again, those long-ago waves rolling in to shore? But Cody hadn't entered into the spirit of the thing. *Nice?* he had asked. He asked, was that all she thought of heaven? Wrightsville Beach, where as he recalled she had fretted for two solid weeks that she might have left the oven on at home? And had she taken into account, he asked, his own wishes in the matter? Did she suppose that he wanted to spend eternity as a child? "Why, Cody, all I meant was—" she said.

Something was wrong with him. Something was wrong with all of her children. They were so frustrating—attractive, likable people, the three of them, but closed off from her in some perverse way that she couldn't quite put her finger on. And she sensed a kind of trademark flaw in each of their lives. Cody was prone to unreasonable rages; Jenny was so flippant; Ezra hadn't really lived up to his potential. (He ran a restaurant on St. Paul Street—not at all what she had planned for him.) She wondered if her children blamed her for something. Sitting close at family gatherings (with the spouses and offspring slightly apart, nonmembers forever), they tended to recall only poverty and loneliness—toys she couldn't afford for them, parties where they weren't invited. Cody, in particular, referred continually to Pearl's short temper, displaying it against a background of stunned, childish faces so sad and bewildered that Pearl herself hardly recognized them. Honestly, she thought, wasn't there some statute of limitations here? When was he going to absolve her? He was middle-aged. He had no business holding her responsible any more.

And Beck: well, he was still alive, if it mattered. By now he'd be old. She would bet he'd aged poorly. She would bet he wore a toupee, or false teeth too white and regular, or some flowing, youthful hairdo that made him look ridiculous. His ties would be too colorful and his suits too bold a plaid. What had she ever seen in him? She chewed the insides of her lips. Her one mistake: a simple error in judgment. It should not have had such far-reaching effects. You would think that life could be a little more forgiving.

Once or twice a year, even now, his letters arrived. (Though the money had stopped when Jenny turned eighteen—or two months *after* she turned eighteen, which meant he'd lost track of her birthday, Pearl supposed.) It was typical of him that he lacked the taste to make a final exit. He spent too long at his farewells, chatting in the doorway, letting in the cold. He had retired from the Tanner Corporation, he wrote. He remained at his last place of transfer, Richmond, like something washed up from a flood; but evidently he still traveled some. In 1967 he sent her a postcard from the World's Fair in Montreal, and another in '72 from Atlantic City, New Jersey. He seemed spurred into action by various overblown occasions—when man first walked on the moon, for instance (an event of no concern to Pearl, or to any other serious person). *Well!* he wrote. *Looks like we made it.* His enthusiasm seemed flushed, perhaps alcohol induced. She winced and tore the letter into squares.

Later, when her eyes went, she saved her mail for Ezra. She'd hold up an envelope. "Where's this from? I can't quite make it out."

"National Rifle Association."

"Throw it away. What's this?"

"Republican Party."

"Throw it away. And this?"

"Something in longhand, from Richmond."

"Throw it away."

He didn't ask why. None of her children possessed a shred of curiosity.

She dreamed her uncle hitched up Prince and took her to a medal contest, but she had failed to memorize a piece and stood onstage like a dumb thing with everybody whispering. When she woke, she was cross with herself. She should have done "Dat Boy Fritz"; she'd always been good at dialect. And she knew it off by heart still, too. Her memory had not faded in the slightest. She rearranged her pillow, irritably. Her edges felt uneven, was how she put it to herself. She slept again and dreamed the house was on fire. Her skin dried out from the heat and her hair seemed to sizzle in her ears. Jenny rushed upstairs to save her costume jewelry and her footsteps died away all at once, as if she'd fallen into space. "Stop!" Pearl shouted. She opened her eyes. Someone was sitting next to her, in that leather armchair that creaked. "Jenny?" she said.

"It's Ezra, Mother."

Poor Ezra, he must be exhausted. Wasn't it supposed to be the daughter who came and nursed you? She knew she should send him away but she couldn't make herself do it. "I guess you want to get back to that restaurant," she told him.

"No, no."

"You're like a mother hen about that place," she said. She sniffed. Then she said, "Ezra, do you smell smoke?"

"Why do you ask?" he said (cautious as ever).

"I dreamed the house burned down."

"It didn't really."

"Ah."

She waited, holding herself in. Her muscles were so tense, she ached all over. Finally she said, "Ezra?"

"Yes, Mother?"

"Maybe you could just check."

"Check what?"

"The house, of course. Check if it's on fire."

She could tell he didn't want to.

"For my sake," she told him.

"Well, all right."

She heard him rise and shamble out. He must be in his stocking feet; she recognized that shushing sound. He was gone so long that she began to fear the worst. She strained for the roar of the flames but heard only the horns of passing cars, the clock radio's electric murmur, a bicycle bell tinkling beneath the window. Then here he came, heavy and slow on the stairs. Evidently there was no emergency. He settled into his chair again. "Everything's fine," he told her.

"Thank you, Ezra," she said humbly.

"You're welcome."

She heard him pick up his magazine.

"Ezra," she said, "I've had a thought. Did you happen to check the basement?"

"Yes."

"You went clear to the bottom of the steps."

"Yes, Mother."

"I don't much care for how that furnace sounds."

"It's fine," he told her.

It was fine. She resolved to believe him. She soothed herself by wandering, mentally, from one end of the house to the other, cataloguing how well she'd managed. The fireplace flue was shut against the cold. The drains were clear and the faucets were tight and she'd bled the radiators herself—sightless, turning her key back sharply the instant she heard the hiss of water. The gutters were swept and the roof did not leak and the refrigerator hummed in the kitchen. Everything was proceeding according to instructions.

"Ezra," she said.

"Yes, Mother."

"You know that address book in my desk."

"What address book?"

"Pay attention, Ezra. I only have the one. Not the little red book for telephone numbers but the black one, in my stationery drawer."

"Oh, yes."

"I want everybody in it invited to my funeral."

There was a thrumming silence, as if she had said a bad word. Then Ezra said, *"Funeral,* Mother? You're not dying?"

"No, of course not," she assured him. "But someday," she said craftily. "Just in the eventuality, you see . . ."

"Let's not talk about it," he said.

She paused, assembling patience. What did he expect—that she'd go on forever? It was so tiring. But that was Ezra for you. "All I'm saying," she said, "is I'd like those people invited. Are you listening? The people in my address book."

Ezra didn't answer.

"The address book in my stationery drawer."

"Stationery drawer," Ezra echoed.

Good; he'd got it. He flicked a magazine page, said nothing further, but she knew he'd got it.

She thought of how that address book must have aged by now—smelling mousy, turning brittle. It dated back to long before her sight had started dimming. Emmaline was in it, and Emmaline had been dead for twenty years or more. So was Mrs. Simmons dead, down in St. Petersburg, Florida, and Uncle Seward's widow and perhaps his daughter too. Why, everybody in that book was six feet under, she supposed, except for Beck.

She remembered that he took a whole page—one town after another crossed out. She'd kept it up to date because she'd imagined needing to call him in an emergency. What emergency had she had in mind? She couldn't think of any that would be eased in the slightest by his presence. She'd like to see his face when he received an invitation to her funeral. An "invite," he would call it. "Imagine that!" he would say, shocked. "She left me first, after all. Here's this invite to her funeral." She could hear him now.

She laughed.

The doctor came, stamping his feet. "Is it snowing out?" she asked him.

"Snowing? No."

"You were stamping your feet."

"No," he said, "it's just cold." He settled on the edge of her bed. "Feels like my toes are falling off," he told her. "My knee bones say we're going to have a frost tonight."

She waved away the small talk. "Listen here," she said. "Ezra called you over by mistake."

"Is that so."

"I'm really feeling fine. Maybe earlier I was under the weather, but now I'm much improved."

"I see," he said. He took her wrist in his icy, wrinkled fingers. (He was nearly as old as she was, and had all but given up his practice.) He held it for what seemed to be several minutes. Then he said, "How long has *this* been going on?"

"I don't know what you're talking about."

"Where's the phone?" he asked Ezra.

"Wait! Dr. Vincent! Wait!" Pearl cried.

He had laid down her wrist, but now he set his hand on hers and she felt him leaning over her, breathing pipe tobacco. "Yes?" he said.

"I'm not going to any hospital."

"Of course you're going."

She spoke clearly, maybe a little too loudly, directing her voice toward the ceiling. "Now, I've thought this through," she told him. "I don't want those crank-up beds and professional smells. It would kill me."

"Dear lady—"

"And you know they wouldn't be able to give me penicillin."

"Penicillin, no . . ."

"That's what I took in forty-three."

"Don't tire yourself," the doctor said. "I remember all about it."

Or maybe it was '44. But Beck had not yet left. He'd been away on a business trip, and brought back an archery set for the children. The things he spent his money on! When they were never well off, in the best of times. He took the set on their Sunday drive to a field outside the city—nailed the canvas target to a tree trunk. Oh, he never gave a thought to danger. He was not the type to lie awake nights listing all that could go wrong. Well, anyway. She couldn't say just how it had happened (she was arranging a bouquet of winter grasses at the time, as she no longer partook in sports), but somehow, she got hit. It was Cody who drew the bowstring, but that was incidental; Cody was not the one she had blamed, after the first little flurry. She blamed Beck, who through sheer thoughtlessness if not intention had shot her through the heart; or not the heart exactly but the fleshy part above it, between breast and shoulder. It was the queerest sensation, like being slapped—no sting whatsoever, but a jarring and then a disk of bright blood on her favorite blouse. "Oh!" she said, and she looked down, and went on holding her weeds. Then the pain began. Beck, white faced, pulled the arrow out. Jenny started crying. They drove straight home, forgetting to untack the target from the tree, but by the time they arrived the bleeding had stopped and it appeared there was no real danger. Pearl dressed the wound herself—iodine and gauze. Two days later, she noticed something amiss. The wound was not better but worse, inflamed, and she had a fever. Beck was on another trip, and she had to go to the doctor alone, rushing off breathless and hastily hatted because she wanted to get home again before the children returned from school. In those days, Dr. Vincent was just building up his practice after a tour of duty in the army. She remembered he still had a full head of hair, and he wasn't yet wearing glasses. He gave her a shot of penicillin—a miracle drug he'd first used overseas, he said. Walking home, she felt a tremendous sense of well-being, the way you always do when a doctor has taken upon himself the burden of your illness; but that night, she collapsed. First there was a rash, then chills, then a hazy and swarming landscape. It was Cody who called the ambulance. In the hospital, once the crisis was past, everyone acted stern and reproachful, as if it had been her fault. "You almost died," a nurse told her. But that was nonsense. Of course she wouldn't have died; she had children. When you have children, you're obligated to live. She closed her eyes against the nurse's words. Then two doctors came in and pulled up chairs beside her bed and solemnly, portentously explained about penicillin. She must never, never take it again, and must keep instructions to that effect in her pocketbook at all times. Pearl wasn't paying much heed (she was framing a request to be released, so she could get on home to her children), but she did remember they said, "Once is your limit. Twice will kill you." That impressed her. It was like something in a fairy tale —like a magic potion you could use only once and never again. And here she'd wasted it on such a paltry occurrence: a bow-and-arrow wound. No more miracles! In later years, when penicillin was a household word and her grandchildren took it for every little thing, she would go on and on about it. "Lucky you. Poor me. I'd just better not get an infection, is all I can say, or come down with strep throat or pneumonia."

Pneumonia.

There was a watery, roaring sound in her ears that made it hard to hear her own voice. She had to wait for it to subside before she spoke. "Dr. Vincent," she said.

"I'm here."

His hand was still on hers. It was no longer icy. He had warmed himself on her skin as if she were a stove. She gathered her voice and said, "Tell Ezra I'm staying."

"But—" he said.

"I know what I'm doing."

He was silent.

"Tell him," she said forcefully, "that this is nothing. You understand? I don't want any hospitals. It would kill me, just kill me to hear those loudspeakers paging doctors I have never heard of. This is just a cold. Tell him."

"Well," said Dr. Vincent. He cleared his throat. He removed his hand from hers. "Are you sure?" he asked.

"I'm sure."

He seemed to be thinking. He turned away and said to Ezra, "You hear what she says?"

"Yes," said Ezra, closer than Pearl had expected.

"I suggest we call your brother and sister, though."

Pearl felt a stirring of interest.

"But if it's that serious . . ." Ezra said.

"Let's just see what happens," the doctor told him. He laid a palm on Pearl's forehead.

After that, he must have left. The roar came back to her ears and she didn't quite hear him go. She was dwelling on thoughts of Cody and Jenny; it would be lovely to have all her children together. Then suddenly a heavy chill spread across her chest. Why, she thought. Dr. Vincent is going to allow this! Yes, he's really going to allow it. This is it, then!

Surely not.

She'd been preoccupied with death for several years now; but one aspect had never before crossed her mind: dying, you don't get to see how it all turns out. Questions you have asked will go unanswered forever. Will this one of my children settle down? Will that one learn to be happier? Will I ever discover what was meant by such-and-such? All these years, it emerged, she'd been expecting to run into Beck again. How odd; she hadn't realized. She had also supposed that there would be some turning point, a flash of light in which she'd suddenly find out the secret; one day she'd wake up wiser and more contented and accepting. But it hadn't happened. Now it never would. She'd supposed that on her deathbed . . . deathbed! Why, that was this everyday, ordinary Posturepedic, not the ornate brass affair that she had always envisioned. She had supposed that on her deathbed, she would have something final to tell her children when they gathered round. But nothing was final. She didn't have anything to tell them. She felt a kind of shyness; she felt inadequate. She stirred her feet fretfully and searched for a cooler place on the pillow.

"Children," she had said. This was just before Cody left for college, the day she'd burned Beck's letters. She said, "Children, there's something I want to discuss with you."

Cody was talking about a job. He had to find one in order to help with the tuition fees. "I could work in the cafeteria," he was saying, "or maybe off-campus. I don't know which." Then he heard his mother and looked over at her.

"It's about your father," Pearl said.

Jenny said, "I'd choose the cafeteria."

"You know, my darlings," Pearl told them, "how I always say your father's away on business."

"But off-campus they might pay more," said Cody, "and every penny counts."

"At the cafeteria you'd be with your classmates, though," Ezra said.

"Yes, I thought of that."

"All those coeds," Jenny said. "Cheerleaders. Girls in their little white bobby sox."

"Sweater girls," Cody said.

"There's something I want to explain about your father," Pearl told them.

"Choose the cafeteria," Ezra said.

"Children?"

"The cafeteria," they said.

And all three gazed at her coolly, out of gray, unblinking, level eyes exactly like her own.

She dreamed it was her nineteenth birthday and that devilish John Dupree had brought her a tin of chocolates and a burnt-leather ornament for her hair. "Why, John, how cunning! Have a sweet," she told him. In the dream, it puzzled her to know that John Dupree had been dead for sixty-one years. He was killed in the Argonne Forest by the Huns. She remembered paying a visit of condolence to his mother, who, however, was not receiving guests. "It's all been a mistake, apparently," Pearl told John Dupree. And she fastened up her hair with the burnt-leather ornament.

"There's no question," Jenny said. "We have to call an ambulance. What's got into Dr. Vincent? Is he senile?"

"He does all right, for his age," Ezra said. As usual, he seemed to have missed some central point; even Pearl could see that.

Jenny sighed, or perhaps just made some impatient rustling sound with her clothes.

"It's lucky you called me," she said. "I come and find everything falling apart."

"Nothing's falling apart."

"And why is she lying flat? She's obviously having trouble breathing. Where's that big green cushion Becky made her?"

Pearl had been skidding through time, for a moment—preparing to go by ambulance to have her arrow wound treated. She was braced for the precarious, tilting trip down the stairs on a stretcher. It was mention of Becky that set her straight. Becky was her grandchild, Jenny's oldest daughter. "Jenny?" she said.

"How are you feeling?" Jenny asked.

"Is Cody here too?"

Apparently not. Jenny leaned over the bed to give her a kiss. Pearl patted Jenny's hair and found it badly cut, choppy to the touch, but for once she didn't scold. (Jenny had lovely thick hair that she tended to ignore, to mistreat, as if looks didn't really matter.) "It was nice of you to come," Pearl told her.

"Well, goodness, I was worried," said Jenny. "You're the only mother we have."

Pearl felt she had come full circle. "You should have got an extra," she said.

"Excuse me?"

She didn't repeat it. She turned her face on the pillow and was overtaken by a sudden jolt of anger. Why hadn't they arranged for an extra? All those years when she was the only one, the sole support, the lone tall tree in the pasture just waiting for the lightning to strike . . . well. She seemed to be losing track of her thoughts. "Did you bring the children?" she said.

"Not this time. I left them with Joe."

Joe? Oh, yes, her husband. "Why isn't Cody here?" Pearl asked.

"Well, you know," said Ezra, "it's always so hard to locate him . . ."

"We think you should go to the hospital," Jenny told Pearl.

"Oh, thank you, dear, but I don't believe I care to."

"You're not breathing right. Where's that cushion Becky made when she was little? The one with the uplifting motto," Jenny said. "*Sleep, o faithful warrior, upon thy carven pillow.*" She gave a little snort of laughter, and Pearl smiled, picturing Jenny's habit of covering her mouth with her hand as if overcome, as if struck absolutely helpless by life's silliness. "Anyhow," Jenny said, pulling herself together. "Ezra, *you* agree with me, don't you?"

"Agree?"

"About the hospital."

"Ah . . ." said Ezra.

There was a pause. You could pluck this single moment out of all time, Pearl thought, and still discover so much about her children—even about Cody, for his very absence was a characteristic, perhaps his main one. And Jenny was so brisk and breezy but . . . oh, you might say somewhat opaque, a reflecting surface flashing your own self back at you, giving no hint of *her* self. And Ezra, mild Ezra: no doubt confusedly tugging at the shock of fair hair that hung over his forehead, considering and reconsidering . . . "Well," he said, "I don't know . . . I mean, maybe if we waited a while . . ."

"But how long? How long can we afford to wait?"

"Oh, maybe just till tonight, or tomorrow . . ."

"Tomorrow! What if it's, say, pneumonia?"

"Or it could be only a cold, you see."

"Yes, but—"

"And we wouldn't want her to go if it makes her unhappy."

"No, but—"

Pearl listened, smiling. She knew the outcome now. They would deliberate for hours, echoing each other's answers, repeating and rephrasing questions, evading, retreating, arguing for argument's sake, ultimately going nowhere. "You never did face up to things," she said kindly.

"Mother?"

"You always were duckers and dodgers."

"Dodgers?"
She smiled again, and closed her eyes.

It was such a relief to drift, finally. Why had she spent so long learning how? The traffic sounds—horns and bells and rags of music—flowed around the voices in her room. She kept mislaying her place in time, but it made no difference; all she remembered was equally pleasant. She remembered the feel of wind on summer nights—how it billows through the house and wafts the curtains and smells of tar and roses. How a sleeping baby weighs so heavily on your shoulder, like ripe fruit. What privacy it is to walk in the rain beneath the drip and crackle of your own umbrella. She remembered a country auction she'd attended forty years ago, where they'd offered up an antique brass bed complete with all its bedclothes—sheets and blankets, pillow in a linen case embroidered with forget-me-nots. Two men wheeled it onto the platform, and its ruffled coverlet stirred like a young girl's petticoats. Behind her eyelids, Pearl Tull climbed in and laid her head on the pillow and was borne away to the beach, where three small children ran toward her, laughing, across the sunlit sand.

2

Teaching the Cat
to Yawn

While Cody's father nailed the target to the tree trunk, Cody tested the bow. He drew the string back, laid his cheek against it, and narrowed his eyes at the target. His father was pounding in tacks with his shoe; he hadn't thought to bring a hammer. He looked like a fool, Cody thought. He owned no weekend clothes, as other fathers did, but had driven to this field in his strained-looking brown striped salesman suit, white starched shirt, and navy tie with multicolored squares and circles scattered randomly across it. The only way you could tell this was a Sunday was when he turned, having pounded in the final tack; he didn't have his tie pulled up close to his collar. It hung loose and slightly crooked, like a drunkard's tie. A cockscomb of hair, as black as Cody's but wavy, stood up on his forehead.

"There!" he said, plodding back. He still carried the shoe. He walked lopsided, either smiling at Cody or squinting in the sunlight. It was nowhere near spring yet, but the air felt unseasonally warm and a pale sun poured heat like a liquid over Cody's shoulders. Cody bent and pulled an arrow from a cardboard tube. He laid it against the string. "Wait, now, son," his father said. "You want to do things right, now."

Naturally, this would have to be an educational experience. There were bound to be lectures and criticisms attached. Cody sighed and lowered the bow. His father stooped to put his shoe on, squirming his foot in without undoing the laces, the way Cody's mother hated. The heel of his black rayon sock was worn so thin it was translucent. Cody looked off in another direction. He was fourteen years old—too big to be dragged on family outings any more and definitely too big for bows and arrows, unless of course you'd just leave the equipment to him and his friends, alone, and let them horse around or have themselves a contest or shatter windowpanes and streetlights for the hell of it. How did his father come up with these ideas? This was turning out to be even less successful than most. Cody's mother, who was not the slightest bit athletic, picked dried flowers beside a fence. His little sister buttoned her sweater with chapped and bluish hands. His brother, Ezra, eleven years old, chewed a straw and hummed. He was missing his whistle, no doubt—a bamboo pipe, with six finger holes, on which he played tunes almost ceaselessly. He'd smuggled it along but their father had made him leave it in the car.

At this moment, Cody's two best friends were attending a movie: *Air Force*, with John Garfield and Faye Emerson. Cody would have given anything to be with them.

"Now, your left arm goes like this," his father said, positioning him. "You want to keep your wrist from getting stung, you see. And stand up straight. It was archery gave us our notions of proper posture; says so in the instruction book. Used to be that people slouched around any old how, all except the archers. I bet you didn't know that, did you?"

No, he didn't know that. He stood like something made of clay while his father poked him here and prodded him there, molding him into shape. "In the olden days . . ." his father said.

Cody let go of the bowstring. *Thwack*. The arrow hit the edge of the target, more sidewise than endwise, bounced off harmlessly and fell among the tree roots. "Now! What'd you go and do that for?" his father asked him. "Did I tell you to shoot yet? Did I?"

"It slipped," said Cody.

"Slipped!"

"And anyhow, it couldn't have stuck in the target. Not with that hard fat tree trunk behind it."

"It most certainly could have," his father said. "Like always, you just had to jump on in. Impulsive. Had to have it your way. When are you going to start keeping a better rein on yourself?"

Cody's father (who never kept any sort of rein on himself whatsoever, as Cody's mother constantly reminded him) lunged off toward the target, muttering and grabbing fistfuls of weed heads which he then threw away. Seeds and dry hulls spangled the air around him. "Willful boy; never listens. Don't know why I bother."

Cody's mother shaded her eyes and called, "Did he hit it?"

"*No*, he didn't hit it. How could he; I wasn't even through explaining."

"People have been known to hit a target without a person explaining it beforehand," Cody muttered.

"What say?"

"Let Ezra try," Cody's mother suggested.

His father picked up the arrow and jammed it into the bull's-eye, dead center. "Want to tell me it can't stick?" he asked Cody. He pointed to the arrow, which stayed firm. "Look at that: steel-tipped. Of course it sticks. And spongy bark on the tree. I chose that tree. Of course it sticks. You could have lodged it in easy."

"Ha," said Cody, kicking a clod of earth.

"What say, son?"

"Let Ezra try," Pearl called again. "Beck? Let Ezra try."

Ezra was her favorite, her pet. The entire family knew it. Ezra looked embarrassed and switched the straw to the other side of his mouth. Beck waded back to them. "Oh, I don't know, I don't know. I wonder sometimes," he said.

"Ezra? See if you can hit it, honey," Pearl called.

Beck's glance at Cody might have been sympathy, or else disgust. He pulled another arrow from the cardboard tube. "All right, Ezra, come on and try," he said. "Just don't get carried away like Cody here did."

Ezra came over, still nibbling his straw, and accepted the

bow from Cody. Well, this would be a laugh. There was no one as clumsy as Ezra. When he took his stance he did it all wrong, he just *looked* all wrong, in some way you couldn't put your finger on. His elbows jutted out, winglike; his floppy yellow hair feathered in his eyes. "Now, wait, now," Beck kept saying. "What's the trouble here?" He moved around realigning Ezra's shoulders, adjusting his grip on the bow. Ezra stayed patient. In fact, he might have had his mind on something else altogether; it seemed his attention had been caught by a cloud formation over to the south. "Oh, well," Beck said finally, giving up. "Let her fly, I guess, Ezra. Ezra?"

Ezra's fingers loosened on the string. The arrow sped in a straight, swift path, no arc to it at all. As if guided by an invisible thread—or worse, by the purest and most natural luck— it split the length of the arrow that Beck had already jammed in and it landed at the center of the bull's-eye, quivering. There was a sharp, caught silence. Then Beck said, "Will you look at that."

"Why, Ezra," Pearl said.

"Ezra," their sister Jenny cried. "Ezra, look what you did! What you went and did to that arrow!"

Ezra took the straw from his mouth. "I'm sorry," he told Beck. (He was so used to breaking things.)

"Sorry?" said Beck.

He seemed to be hunting the proper tone of voice. Then he found it. "Well, son," he said, "this just goes to show that it pays to follow instructions. See there, Cody? See what happens? A bull's-eye. I'll be damned. If you'd listened close like Ezra did, and not gone off half-cocked . . ."

He was moving toward the target as he spoke, oaring through the weeds, and Jenny was running to get there first. Cody couldn't take his turn at shooting, therefore, although he was itching to. He was absolutely obligated to split that second arrow as Ezra had split the first. It was unthinkable not to. What were the odds against it? He felt a springy twanging inside, as if he himself were the bowstring. He bent down and pulled a new arrow from the tube and fitted it to the bow. He drew and aimed at a clump of shrubbery, then at his father's dusty blue Nash, and then at Ezra, who was already wandering off again dreamy as ever. Longingly, Cody focused on Ezra's fair, ruffled head. "Zing. *Wham.* Aagh, you got me!" he said. Imagine the satisfaction. Ezra turned slowly and caught sight of him. "No!" he cried.

"Huh?"

Ezra ran toward him, flapping his arms like an idiot and stammering, "Stop, stop, stop! No! Stop!" Did he really think Cody would shoot him? Cody stared, keeping the bow drawn. Ezra took a flying leap with his arms outstretched like a lover. He caught Cody in a kind of bear hug and slammed him flat on his back. It knocked the wind out of Cody; all he could do was gasp beneath Ezra's warm, bony weight. And meanwhile, what had happened to the arrow? It was minutes before he could struggle to a sitting position, elbowing Ezra off of him. He looked across the field and found his mother leaning on his father's arm, hobbling in his direction with a perfect circle of blood gleaming on the shoulder of her blouse. "Pearl, my God. Oh, Pearl," his father was saying. Cody turned and looked at Ezra, whose face was pale and shocked. "See there?" Cody asked him. "See what you've gone and done?"

"Did *I* do that?"

"Gone and done it to me again," Cody said, and he staggered to his feet and walked away.

On a weekday when his father was out of town, his mother shopping for supper, his brother and sister doing homework in their rooms, Cody took his BB gun and shot a hole in the kitchen window. Then he slipped outdoors and poked a length of fishing line through the hole. From the kitchen, he pulled the line until the rusty wrench that he'd tied to the other end was flush against the outside of the glass. He held it there by anchoring the line beneath a begonia pot. When his mother returned from shopping, Cody was seated at the kitchen table coloring a map of Asia.

After their homework was finished, Jenny and Ezra went out back. Ezra had been showing Jenny, all week, how to hit a softball. (It seemed her classmates chose her last whenever they had a game.) As soon as they had walked through, Cody rose and went to the window. He saw them take their places in the darkening yard, bounded on either side by the neighbors' hedges. They were a comically short distance apart. Jenny stood closest to the house and held her bat straight up, gingerly, as if preparing to club to death some small animal. Ezra tossed her a gentle pitch. (He was no great player himself.) Jenny took a whizzing swing, missed, and retrieved the ball from among the trash cans beside the back door. She threw it in a overhand so stiff and deformed that Cody wondered why Ezra bothered. Ezra caught it and pitched again. As the ball arched toward the bat, Cody felt for the fishing line beneath the begonia pot. He gave a quick tug. The windowpane clattered inward, breaking in several pieces. Jenny spun around and stared. Ezra's mouth dropped open. "What was that?" Pearl called from the dining room.

"Just Ezra breaking another window," Cody told her.

One weekend their father didn't come home, and he didn't come the next weekend either, or the next. Or rather, one morning Cody woke up and saw that it had been a while since their father was around. He couldn't say that he had noticed from the start. His mother offered no excuses. Cody, watchful as a spy, studied her furrowed, distracted expression and the way that her hands plucked at each other. It troubled him to realize that he couldn't picture his father's most recent time with them. Trying to find some scene that would explain Beck's leaving, he could only come up with *general* scenes, blended from a dozen repetitions: meals shattered by quarrels, other meals disrupted when Ezra spilled his milk, drives in the country where his father lost the way and his mother snapped out pained and exasperated directions. He thought of once when the Nash's radiator had erupted in steam and his father, looking helpless, had flung his suit coat over it. "Oh, honestly," his mother had said. But that was way back; it was years ago, wasn't it? Cody journeyed through the various cubbies and crannies of the house, hunting up the trappings of his father's "phases" (as his mother called them). There were the badminton racquets, the butterfly net, the archery set, the camera with its unwieldy flashgun, and the shoe box full of foreign stamps still in their glassine envelopes. But it meant nothing that these objects remained behind. What was alarming was his father's half of the bureau: an empty sock drawer, an empty underwear drawer. In the shirt drawer, one unused sports shirt, purchased by the three children for Beck's last birthday, his forty-fourth. And a full assortment of pajamas; but then, he always slept in his underwear. In the wardrobe, just a hanger strung with ties— his oldest, dullest, most frayed and spotted ties—and a pair of shoes so ancient that the toes curled up.

Cody's brother and sister were staggeringly unobservant. They flitted in and out of the house like birds—Ezra playing his whistle, Jenny singing parts of jump-rope songs. Cody had the impression that musical notes filled their heads to over-flowing; they left no room for anything serious. *Auntie Sue got dressed in blue,* Jenny sang, *put on shoes and rubbers too . . .* Her plain, flat voice and heedlessly swinging braids somehow reassured him. After all, what could go so wrong, when she skipped past with her ragged rope? What could go so very wrong?

Then one Saturday she said, "I'm worried about Daddy."

"Why?" Cody asked.

"Cody," she said, in her elderly way, "you can see that he doesn't come home any more. I think he's left us."

"Don't be silly," Cody told her.

She surveyed him for a moment, with a composure that made him uneasy, and when he didn't say any more she turned and went out on the porch. He heard the glider creak as she settled into it. But she didn't start singing. In fact, the house was unusually quiet. The only sound was his mother's heels, clicking back and forth overhead as she put away the laundry. And Ezra wasn't playing his whistle. Cody had no idea where Ezra was.

He went upstairs to his mother's bedroom. She was folding a sheet. "What're you doing?" he asked. She gave him a look. He settled in a ladder-backed chair to watch her work. She was wearing a housedress that he very much disliked, cream colored with deep red streaks across it like paintbrush strokes. The shoulders were shaped by triangular pads that unbuttoned and removed when it was time to wash the dress. Cody had often thought of stealing those pads. With her shoulders broadened, his mother looked powerful and sharp and scary. On her feet were open-toed shoes and short white socks. She traveled rapidly between the laundry basket and the bed, laying out stacks of clothing. There was no stack for his father.

"When is Dad coming home?" he asked.

"Oh," she said, "pretty soon."

She didn't meet his eyes.

Cody looked around him and noticed, for the first time, that there was something pinched and starved about the way this house was decorated. Not a single perfume bottle or china figurine sat upon his mother's bureau. No pictures hung on the walls. Even the bedside tables were completely bare; and in all the drawers in this room, he knew, every object would be aligned and squared precisely—the clothing organized by type and color, whites grading into pastels and then to darks; comb and brush parallel; gloves paired and folded like a row of clenched fists. Who *wouldn't* leave such a place? He straightened, feeling panicky. His mother chose that moment to come over and smooth his hair down. "My," she told him, smiling, "you're getting so big! I can't believe it."

He shrank back in his seat.

"You're getting big enough for me to start relying on," she said.

"I'm only fourteen," Cody told her.

He slipped off the chair and left the room. The bathroom door was closed; he heard the shower running and Ezra singing "Greensleeves." He opened the door just a crack, snaked one arm in, and turned on the hot water in the sink. Then he traveled through the rest of the house, from kitchen to downstairs bathroom to basement, methodically opening every hot water faucet to its fullest. But you couldn't really say his heart was in it.

"Tull?" the man asked.

"Yes."

"Is this the Tull residence?"

"Yes, it is."

"Darryl Peters," the man said, showing a business card.

Cody took a swig of beer and accepted the card. While he was reading it, he sloshed the beer bottle absently to get a good head of suds. He was wearing dungarees and nothing else; it was a blistering day in August. The house, however, was fairly cool—the living room dim, the paper shades pulled all the way down and glowing yellow with the afternoon sun. Mr. Peters looked in wistfully, but remained on the porch with his hat in his hand. He was way overdressed, for August.

"So," said Cody. He nudged the screen door open with his bare foot. Mr. Peters caught hold of it and stepped inside.

"Would your mother be in?" he asked.

"She's taken a job."

"Well, then, your . . . is Ezra Tull your father?"

"He's my brother."

"Brother. Ah."

"*He's* in."

"Well, then," Mr. Peters said.

"I'll go get him."

Cody went upstairs and into Jenny's room. Jenny and Ezra were playing checkers on the floor. Ezra, wearing shorts and a sleeveless undershirt full of holes, stroked his cat, Alicia, and frowned at the board. "Someone to see you," Cody told him.

Ezra looked up. "Who is it?" he asked.

Cody shrugged.

Ezra rose, still hugging the cat. Cody went with him as far as the stairs. He stopped there and leaned over the banister to eavesdrop, grinning. Ezra arrived in the living room. "You want *me?*" Cody heard him ask.

"Ezra Tull?" said Mr. Peters.

"Yes."

"Well, ah . . . maybe there's been a mistake."

"What kind of mistake?"

"I'm from Peaceful Hills Memorial Gardens," Mr. Peters said. "I thought you wished to purchase a resting place."

"Resting place?"

"I thought you filled out this mail-in coupon: Ezra Tull, your signature. *Yes, I would like an eternal home for myself and/or my loved ones. I understand that a sales representative will call.*"

"It wasn't me," said Ezra.

"You didn't fill this out. You're not interested in a plot."

"No, thank you."

"I should have known," said Mr. Peters.

"I'm sorry," Ezra told him.

"Never mind, I can see it's not your doing."

"Maybe when I'm older, or something . . ."

"That's all right, son. Never mind."

Cody climbed to the stuffy, hot third floor, where Lorena Schmidt sat on his bed with her back against the wall. She was new to the neighborhood—a tawny girl with long black hair, one lock of which she was twining around a finger. "Who was that?" she asked Cody.

"A cemetery salesman."

"Ugh."

"He came to see Ezra."

"Who's Ezra?"

"My *brother* Ezra, dummy."

"Well? How should I know?" Lorena said. "You mean that brother downstairs? Blondish kid, good-looking?"

"Good-looking! Ezra?"

"I liked his kind of serious face," Lorena said. "And those pale gray eyes."

"*My* eyes are gray."

"Well. Anyhow," Lorena said.

"Besides," said Cody, "he gets fits."

"He does?"

"He'll fool you. He'll look as normal as anyone else and then all of a sudden, splat! He's flat on the floor, foaming at the mouth."

"I don't believe you," Lorena said.

"Some people think he's dangerous. I'm the only one brave enough to go near him, when he gets that way."

"I don't believe a word of it," Lorena said.

She twisted around to the head of Cody's bed and lifted a corner of the window shade. "I see your mother coming," she said.

"What? Where?"

She turned and flashed him a grin. One of her front teeth was chipped, which made her look unstable, lacking in self-control. "I was teasing," she said.

"Oh."

"You ought to've seen your face. Ha! I haven't even met your mother. How would I know if she was coming?"

"You must have met her," Cody said. "She's a cashier now at Sweeney Brothers Grocery. Folks around this neighborhood call her the Sweeney Meanie."

"Well, we do our shopping at Esmond's."

"So would I," said Cody.

"How come she works? Where's your father?"

"Missing in action," he told her.

"Oops, sorry."

He gave a casual wave of his hand and took a swallow of beer. "She runs the cash register," he said. "Look in Sweeney's window, next time you go past. You'll know her right off. Walk in and say, 'Ma'am, this soup can's dented. Can I have a reduction?' 'Soup's soup,' she'll say. 'Full price, please.' "

"Oh, one of those,' Lorena said.

"Tight little bun on the back of her head. Mouth like it's holding straight pins. Anybody dawdles, tries to pass the time of day, she'll say, 'Move along, please. Please move along.' "

He was smiling at Lorena as he spoke, but inside he felt a

sudden pang. He pictured his mother at the register, with that anxious line like a strand of hair or a faint, fragile dressmaker's seam running across her forehead.

Cody took every blanket and sheet from Ezra's bed and removed the pillow and the mattress. Underneath were four wooden slats, laid across the frame. He lifted them out and stored them in the wardrobe. With great care, he set the mattress back on the frame. He drew a breath and waited. The mattress held. He replaced the bedclothes and he puffed the pillow and laid it delicately at the head. He lugged a pile of magazines from their hiding place in his bureau, opened them, and scattered them on the floor. Then he turned off the light and went to his own bed, across the room.

Ezra padded in barefoot, eating a sandwich. He wore pajama bottoms with a trailing drawstring. "Oh, me," he said, and he sank into bed. There was a crash. The floor shook, and their mother shrieked and came pounding up the stairs. When she turned on the light, Cody raised his head and stared at her with a sleepy, befuddled expression. She had a hand pressed to her heart. She was taking in gulps of air. Jenny shivered behind her, hugging a worn stuffed rabbit. "Good Lord preserve us," their mother said.

Ezra looked like someone in a bathtub full of cloth. He was having trouble disentangling himself from his sheets. One hand, upraised, still clutched the half-eaten sandwich. "Ezra, honey," Pearl said, but then she said, "Why, Ezra." She was looking at the magazines. They were opened to pictures of women in nightgowns, in bathing suits, in garter belts and black lace brassieres, in bath towels, in useless wisps of transparent drapery, or in nothing whatsoever. "Ezra Tull!" she said.

Ezra worked his way up to peer over the edge of his bed frame.

"Truly, Ezra, I never suspected that you would be such a person," she told him. Then she turned and left the room, taking Jenny with her.

Ezra emerged from his bed, flew through the air, and landed on Cody. He grabbed a handful of hair and started shaking Cody's head. All Cody could say was, "Mmf! Mmf!" because he didn't want their mother to hear. Finally he managed to bite Ezra's knee and Ezra rolled off, panting and sobbing. He must have knocked into something at some earlier point, because his left eye was swelling. It made him look sad. Cody got up and showed him where he'd stashed the slats. They fitted them into place, heaved the mattress back on the frame, and attempted to smooth the blankets. Then Cody turned out the light, and they climbed into their beds and went to sleep.

Sometimes Cody dreamed about his father. He would be stepping through the doorway, wearing one of his salesman suits, bringing the afternoon paper as he always did on Friday. His ordinariness was astounding—his thick strings of hair and the tired, yellowish puffs beneath his eyes. (In waking memories, lately, he was not so real, but had blurred and leveled and lost his details.) "How was your week?" he asked, tediously. Cody's mother answered, "Oh, all right."

In these dreams, Cody was not his present self. He had somehow slid backward and become a toddler again, rushing around on tiny, fat legs, feverishly showing off. "See this? And this? See me somersault? See me pull my wagon?" His smallness colored every act; he was conscious of a desperate need to learn to *manage*, to take charge of his surroundings. Waking in the dark, the first thing he did was stretch his long legs and lift his arms, which were becoming veiny and roped with muscle. He thought of how it would be if his father returned some time in the future, when Cody was a man. "Look at what I've accomplished," Cody would tell him. "Notice where I've got to, how far I've come without you."

Was it something I said? Was it something I did? Was it something I didn't do, that made you go away?

*　*　*

School started, and Cody entered ninth grade. He and his two best friends landed in the same homeroom. Sometimes Pete and Boyd came home with him; they all walked the long way, avoiding the grocery store where Cody's mother worked. Cody had to keep things separate—his friends in one half of his life and his family in the other half. His mother hated for Cody to mix with outsiders. "Why don't you ever have someone over?" she would ask, but she didn't deceive him for a moment. He'd say, "Nah, I don't need anybody," and she would look pleased. "I guess your family's enough for you, isn't it?" she would ask. "Aren't we lucky to have each other?"

He only allowed his friends in the house when his mother was at work, and sometimes for no reason he could name he would lead them through her belongings. He would open her smallest top bureau drawer and show them the real gold brooch that his father had given her when they were courting. "He thinks a lot of her," he would say. "He's given her heaps of stuff. Heaps. There's heaps of other stuff that I just don't happen to have on hand." His friends looked bored. Switching tactics, Cody would show them her ironed handkerchiefs stacked so exactly that they seemed encased by an invisible square box. "I mean," he said, "*your* mothers don't do that, do they? Do they? Women!" he said, and then, musing over some mysterious metal clasp or something that was evidently used to hold up stockings, "Who can understand them? Really: can you figure them out? She likes Ezra best, my dumb brother Ezra. Sissy old Ezra. I mean, if it were Jenny, I could see it—Jenny being a girl and all. But Ezra! Who could like Ezra? Can you give me a single reason why?"

His friends shrugged, idly gazing around the room and jingling the loose change in their pockets.

He hid Ezra's left sneaker, his arithmetic homework, his baseball mitt, his fountain pen, and his favorite sweater. He shut Ezra's cat in the linen cupboard. He took Ezra's bamboo whistle to school and put it in the jacket of Josiah Payson, Ezra's best friend—a wild-eyed boy, the size of a full-grown man, who was thought by some to be feebleminded. It was typical of Ezra that he loved Josiah with all his heart, and would even have had him to the house if their mother weren't scared of him. Cody stopped by when Ezra's class was at lunch, and he slipped behind the cloakroom partition and stuck the whistle in the pocket of Josiah's enormous black peacoat. After that there was a stretch of Indian summer and Josiah evidently left his jacket where it hung, so the whistle stayed lost for days. Ezra was very upset about it. "Have you seen my whistle?" he asked everybody. For once, Cody didn't have to listen to "Greensleeves" and "The Ash Grove," played on that breathy little pipe, whose range was so limited that for high notes, Ezra had to blow extra hard and split people's eardrums. "You took it," Ezra told Cody. "Didn't you? I know you did."

"What would I want with a stupid toy whistle?" Cody asked.

He was hoping that when it turned up in Josiah Payson's pocket, Ezra would blame Josiah. But it didn't happen that way. Whatever passed between them was settled without any fuss, and the two of them continued to be friends. Once again, a cracked, foggy "Ash Grove" burbled in every corner of the house.

Their mother went on one of her rampages. "Pearl has hit the warpath," Cody told his brother and sister. He always called her Pearl at such times. "Better look out," he said. "She's dumped all Jenny's bureau drawers."

"Oh-oh," Ezra said.

"She's slamming things around and talking to herself."

"*Oh*, boy," Jenny said.

Cody had met the other two on the porch; they'd stayed late at school. He silently opened the door for them, and they crept up the stairs. Each took a great, lunging stride over the step that creaked—although surely their mother would not have heard them. She was making too much noise in the kitchen. Throwing pots through windowpanes, was what it sounded like.

They tiptoed across the hall to Jenny's room. "What a mess!" Ezra breathed. Heaps of clothing covered the floor. Empty drawers had been hurled everywhere. The wardrobe stood open, its hangers stripped, and Jenny's puff-sleeved dresses lay in a heap. Jenny stared from the doorway. "Jen?" Cody asked her. "What did you do?"

"Nothing," Jenny said in a quavery voice.

"Think! Some little thing, something you've forgotten about . . ."

"Nothing. I promise."

"Well, help me get these drawers back in," he said to Ezra.

It was a two-man job. The drawers were oak, cumbersome and inclined to stick. Cody and Ezra grunted as they fitted them into the bureau. Jenny traveled around the room collecting her clothes. Tears had filled her eyes, and she kept dabbing at her nose with one or another rolled pair of socks. "Stop that," Cody told her. "She'll do it all again, if she finds snot on your socks."

He and Ezra gathered slips and hair ribbons, shook out blouses, tried to get the dresses back on their hangers the way they'd been before. Some were hopelessly wrinkled, and those they smoothed as best they could and hid at the rear of the wardrobe. Meanwhile Jenny knelt on the floor, sniffling and folding undershirts.

"I wish we could just go off," Ezra said, "and not come back till it's over."

"It won't be over till she's had her scene," Cody told him. "You know that. There's no way we can get around it."

"I wish Daddy were here."

"Well, he's not, so shut up."

Ezra straightened a sash.

After they'd put everything in order, the three of them sat in a row on Jenny's bed. The sounds from the kitchen were different now—cutlery rattling, glassware clinking. Their mother must be setting the table. Pretty soon she'd serve supper. Cody had such a loaded feeling in his throat, he never wanted to eat again. No doubt the others felt the same; Ezra kept swallowing. Jenny said, "Let's run away from home."

"We don't have anyplace to run to," Cody said.

Their mother came to the foot of the stairs and called them. Her voice was thin, like the sound of a gnat. "Children."

They filed down, dragging their feet. They stopped at the first-floor bathroom and meticulously scrubbed their hands, taking extra pains with the backs. Each one waited for the others. Then they went into the kitchen. Their mother was slicing a brick of Spam. She didn't look at them, but she started speaking the instant they were seated. "It's not enough that I should have to work till five p.m., no; then I come home and find nothing seen to, no chores done, you children off till all hours with disreputable characters in the alleys or wasting your time with school chorus, club meetings; table not set, breakfast dishes not washed, supper not cooked, floors not swept, mail in a heap on the mat . . . and not a sign of any of you. Oh, I know what's going on! I know what you three are up to! Neighborhood savages, that's what you are, mingling with each and all. How am I supposed to deal with this? How am I expected to cope? Useless daughter, great unruly bruising boys . . . *I* know what people are saying. You think my customers aren't glad to tell me? Coming in simpering, 'Well, Mrs. Tull, that oldest boy of yours is certainly growing up. I saw him with a pack of Camels in the street in front of the Barlow girl's house.' And I have to smile and take it. Have to stand there on exhibit while they're all thinking, 'Poor Mrs. Tull, I don't know how she can hold her head up. It's clear she doesn't have the least ability to handle those children; look at how they're disgracing her.' Sticking potatoes on people's exhaust pipes and letting the air out of tires and shooting at streetlights with BB guns and stealing hubcaps and making off with traffic signs and moving Mrs. Correlli's madonna to Sonny Boy Brown's kitchen stoop and hanging around the hydrants with girls no better than tramps, girls in tight sweaters and ankle chains, oh, I hear about it everywhere . . ."

"But not me, Mama," Jenny said.

"I beg your pardon?"

"I don't do those things."

Well, of course she didn't (only Cody did), but she shouldn't have pointed that out. Now she'd drawn attention to herself. Pearl turned, gathered force, and plunged. "You! I know about you. I couldn't believe my ears. What should I be doing but coming down the church steps Sunday when I see you with that Melanie Miller from your Bible class. 'Oh, Melanie . . .' " She made her voice shrill and prissy, nothing like Jenny's, really. " 'Melanie, I just love your dress. I wish *I* had a dress like that.' Understand," she said, turning to the boys, "this was a cheap little number from Sears. The plaid wasn't matched; there was a ruffle at the hem like a . . . square dance outfit and a bunch of artificial flowers pinned to the waist. A totally inappropriate dress for a nine-year-old, or for anyone. But 'Oh, I wish *I* had that,' your sister says, so everyone thinks, 'Poor Mrs. Tull, she can't even afford a Sears and Roebuck dress with artificial flowers; I don't know how she manages, slaving away at that grocery all day and struggling over her budget at night, cutting here and cutting there, wondering will she scrape by, hoping nobody runs up a doctor bill, praying her children's feet will stop growing . . .'

"And Melanie's mother, well, it's just like opening the door to such a person. First thing you know she'll be walking in here big as life: 'Mrs. Tull, I happen to have the catalogue we ordered Melanie's dress from, if you would care for one for Jenny.' As if I'd want to dress my daughter like an orphan! As if I'd like for her to duplicate some other child! 'No, thank you, Mrs. Miller,' I'll say. 'I may not be able to afford so very much but at least when I do buy, I buy with finished seams. No, Mrs. Miller, you keep your so-called wish book, your quarter-inch hem allowances, smashed felt flowers . . .' What's wrong with us, I'd like to know? Aren't we good enough for my own blood daughter? Doesn't she feel I'm doing my best, my level best, to provide? Does she have to pick up riffraff? Does she have to bring home scum? We're a family! We used to be so close! What happened to us? Why would she act so disloyal?"

She sat down serenely, as if finished with the subject forever, and reached for a bowl of peas. Jenny's face was streaming with tears, but she wasn't making a sound and Pearl seemed unaware of her. Cody cleared his throat.

"But that was Sunday," he said.

Pearl's serving spoon paused, midway between the bowl and her plate. She looked politely interested. "Yes?" she said.

"This is Wednesday."

"Yes."

"It's Wednesday, dammit; it's three days later. So why bring up something from Sunday?"

Pearl threw the spoon in his face. "You upstart," she said. She rose and slapped him across the cheek. "You wretch, you ugly horror." She grabbed one of Jenny's braids and yanked it so Jenny was pulled off her chair. "Stupid clod," she said to Ezra, and she took the bowl of peas and brought it down on his head. It didn't break, but peas flew everywhere. Ezra cowered, shielding his head with his arms. "Parasites," she told them. "I wish you'd all die, and let me go free. I wish I'd find you dead in your beds."

After that, she went upstairs. The three of them washed the dishes, dried them, and put them away in the cupboards. They wiped the table and countertops and swept the kitchen floor. The sight of any crumb or stain was a relief, a pleasure; they attacked it with Bon Ami. They pulled the shades in the windows and locked the back door. Outside, the neighborhood children were organizing a game of hide-and-seek, but their voices were so faint that they seemed removed in time as well as in space. They were like people from long ago, laughing and calling only in memory, or in one of those eerily lifelike dreams that begin on the edge of sleep.

Shortly before Thanksgiving, a girl named Edith Taber transferred to their school. Cody had been new to so many schools himself, he recognized that defiant tilt of her head when she stepped into his homeroom. She carried a zippered notebook that wasn't the right kind at all, and over her skirt she wore what appeared to be a grown man's shirt, which no one had ever heard of doing. But she had thick black hair and the kind of gypsy look that Cody liked; and he was also drawn by the proud and scornful way she walked alone to her classes—as friendless as Cody was, he thought, or at least, as friendless as he felt inside. So that afternoon he walked a short distance behind her (it turned out she lived just one block north of him), and the next afternoon he caught up and walked beside her. She seemed to welcome his company and talked to him nearly nonstop, every now and then clutching her coat collar tight against her throat in a gesture that struck him as sophisticated. Her brother was in the navy, she said, and had promised to bring her a silk kimono if he made it through the war. And she didn't find that Baltimore was very cosmopolitan, and she thought Miss Saunders, the English teacher, resembled Lana Turner. She said she felt it was really attractive when boys didn't slick their hair back but let it fall over their foreheads, straight, the way Cody did. Cody raked his fingers through his hair and said, well, he didn't know about that; he'd always sort of supposed that girls preferred a little wave or curl or something. She said she just despised for a boy to have curls. They walked the rest of the way without speaking, although from time to time Cody whistled parts of the only tune that came to his mind, which happened to be "The Ash Grove."

He couldn't walk her home on Wednesday because he had to stay late for detention, and the following day was Thanksgiving. There wouldn't be any more school till Monday. All Thursday morning, he hung around the front porch in the damp November chill, gazing northward to Edith's street and then wheeling away and taking midair punches at a cushion from the glider. Finally his mother emerged, rosy from the kitchen, and coaxed him inside. "Cody, honey, you'll freeze to death. Come and shell me some pecans." They were having a meager meal—no turkey—but she'd promised to make a pie for dessert. Already the house smelled different: spicier, more festive. Cody would have stayed on the porch forever, though, if he'd thought there was a chance of seeing Edith.

After dinner they all played Monopoly. Generally, Cody's

family didn't allow him in their games; he had this problem with winning. He absolutely insisted on winning any game he played. And he did win too—by sheer fierceness, by caring the most. (Also, he'd been known to cheat.) Sometimes, he would even win when no one else suspected it was a contest. He would eat more peanuts, get his corn shucked the fastest, or finish his page of the comics first. "Go away," his family would say when he approached (nonchalantly shuffling cards or tossing a pair of dice). "You know what we said. Never again!" But this afternoon, they let him play. He tried to hold back, but once he'd bought a hotel on the Boardwalk, things got out of hand. "Oh, my, I should have remembered," his mother said. "What's he doing in this game?" But she was smiling. She wore her blue wool dress and her hair was coming out of its bun, which made her look relaxed. Her token was the flatiron. She skipped right over the Boardwalk, but Ezra was next and he hit it. He didn't have anywhere near enough money. Cody tried to lend him some; he hated it when people just gave up. He liked to get everybody thousands of dollars in debt, struggling to the bitter end. But Ezra said, "No, no, I quit," and backed off, holding up one palm in that old-mannish way he had. So Cody had to go on with just Jenny and his mother, and eventually with just his mother. They played right down to the line, when she landed on the Boardwalk with three dollar bills to her name. As a matter of fact, Cody had a pretty good time.

Then the younger two talked Cody and Pearl into putting on their old skit: "The Mortgage Overdue." "Oh, come on! Please! It wouldn't feel like a holiday without it." Cody and Pearl ended up agreeing to it, even though they were rusty and Cody couldn't remember the dance step that came at the finish. This was something salvaged from his mother's girlhood, the kind of piece performed at amateur recital contests or campfire circles. Pearl played Ivy, the maiden in distress, and Cody was the villain twirling his waxed mustache. "*Ivy, sweet sweet Ivy, lean upon my arm*," he cajoled her with an evil leer, while Pearl rolled her eyes and shrank into a corner. She could have been an actress, her children thought; she had it letter-perfect, the blushing gaze and the old-fashioned singsong of her responses. At the end the hero came and rescued her. Ezra and Jenny always claimed to be too shy, so Cody had to take the hero's part as well. "*I will pay the money for the mortgage on the farm,*" he told the maiden, and he danced her into the dining room. The dance step came back to him after all, but his mother's tongue got twisted and instead of *wedded life* she said *leaded wife* and collapsed in a heap of giggles. Jenny and Ezra gave them three curtain calls.

That evening, Cody went out to the porch and looked northward some more in the twilight. Ezra came too and sat in the glider, pushing back and forth with the heel of one sneaker. "Want to walk toward Sloop Street?" Cody asked him.

"What's on Sloop Street?"

"Nothing much. This girl I know, Edith Taber."

"Oh, yes. Edith," Ezra said.

"You know who she is?"

"She's got this whistle," Ezra said, "that plays sharps and flats with hardly any extra trouble."

"Edith *Taber?*"

"A recorder."

"You're thinking of someone else," Cody told him.

"Well, maybe so."

Cody was silent a moment, leaning on the porch railing. Ezra creaked companionably in the glider. Then Cody said, "A black-haired girl. Ninth-grader."

"New in town," Ezra agreed.

"When'd you see her?"

"Just yesterday," Ezra said. "I was walking home from school, playing my whistle, and she caught up with me and said she liked it and asked if I wanted to see her recorder. So I went to her house and I saw it."

"To her *house?* Did she know you were my brother?"

"Well, no, I don't think so," Ezra said. "She has a parakeet that burps and says, 'Forgive me.' Her mother served us cookies."

"You met her mother?"

"It would be nice to have a recorder, someday."

"She's too old for you," Cody said.

Ezra looked surprised. "Well, of course," he said. "She's fourteen and a half."

"What would she want with a little sixth-grader?"

"She wanted to show me her whistle," Ezra said.

"Shoot," said Cody.

"Cody? Are we going to walk toward Sloop Street?"

"Nah," said Cody. He kicked a pillar.

"If I asked Mother," Ezra said, "do you think she would get me one of those recorders for Christmas?"

"You dunce," said Cody. "You raving idiot. Do you think she's got money to spare for goddamn *whistles?*"

"Well, no, I guess not," Ezra said.

Then Cody went into the house and locked the door, and when Ezra started pounding on it Cody told their mother it was only Mr. Milledge, having one of his crazy spells.

Monday morning, he looked for Edith on the way to school but he didn't see her. As it turned out, she was tardy. She arrived in homeroom just after the bell. He tried to catch her eye but she didn't glance his way; only gazed fixedly at the teacher all during announcements. And when the first bell rang she walked to class with Sue Meeks and Harriet Smith. Evidently, she was no longer friendless.

By third period, it was clear she was avoiding him. He couldn't even get near her; she had a constant bodyguard. But what had he done wrong? He cornered Barbara Pace—a plump, cheerful redhead who served as a kind of central switchboard for ninth-grade couples. "What's the matter with Edith?" he asked.

"Who?"

"Edith Taber. We were getting along just fine and now she won't speak."

"Oh," she said. She shifted her books. She was wearing a

man-sized shirt with the tails out. Come to think of it, so were half the other girls. "Well," she said, "I guess she likes somebody else now."

"Is it my brother?" Cody asked.

"Who's your brother?"

"Ezra. My brother, Ezra."

"*I* didn't know you had a brother," she said, peering at him.

"Well, she liked me well enough last week. What happened?"

"See," she told him patiently, "now she's been to a couple of parties and naturally she's developed new interests. She's got a sort of . . . broader view, and also she didn't realize about your reputation."

"What reputation?"

"Well, you do drink, Cody. And you hung around with that cheap Lorena Schmidt all summer; you smell like a walking cigarette; and you almost got arrested over Halloween."

"Did my brother tell her that?"

"What's this about your brother? Everybody told her. It's not exactly a secret."

"Well, I never claimed to be a saint," Cody said.

"She says you're real good-looking and all but she wants a boy she can respect," said Barbara. "She thinks she might like Francis Elburn now."

"Francis Elburn! That fairy."

"He's really more her type," said Barbara.

"His hair is curly."

"So?"

"Francis Elburn; Jesus Christ."

"There's no need to use profanity," Barbara told him.

Cody walked home alone, long after the others had left, choosing streets where he'd be certain not to run into Edith or her friends. Once he turned down the wrong alley and it struck him that he was still an outsider, unfamiliar with the neighborhood. His classmates had been born and raised here, most of them, and were more comfortable with each other than he could ever hope to be. Look at his two best friends: their parents went to the movies together; their mothers talked on the telephone. *His* mother . . . He kicked a signpost. What he wouldn't give to have a mother who acted like other mothers! He longed to see her gossiping with a little gang of women in the kitchen, letting them roll her hair up in pincurls, trading beauty secrets, playing cards, losing track of time—"Oh, goodness, look at the clock! And supper not even started; my husband will kill me. Run along, girls." He wished she had some outside connection, something beyond that suffocating house.

And his father: he had uprooted the family continually, tearing them away as soon as they were settled and plunking them someplace new. But where was he now that Cody *wanted* to be uprooted, now that he was saddled with a reputation and desperate to leave and start over? His father had ruined their lives, Cody thought—first in one way and then in another. He thought of tracking him down and arriving on his doorstep: "I'm in trouble; it's all your fault. I've got a bad name, I need to leave town, you'll have to take me in." But that would only be another unknown city, another new school to walk into alone. And there too, probably, his grades would begin to slip and the neighbors would complain and the teachers would start to suspect him first when any little thing went wrong; and then Ezra would follow shortly in his dogged, earnest, devoted way and everybody would say to Cody, "Why can't you be more like your brother?"

He let himself into the house, which smelled of last night's cabbage. It was almost dark and the air seemed thick; he felt he had to labor to move through it. He climbed the stairs wearily. He passed Jenny's room, where she sat doing her homework in a tiny dull circle of yellow from the lamp. Her face was thin and shadowed and she didn't bother greeting him. He climbed on up to his own room and flicked on the light switch. He had set his books on the bureau before he realized Ezra was there. Asleep, as usual—curled on his bed with a sheaf of homework papers. Oh, Ezra was so slow and dazed; he could sleep anytime. His lips were parted. His cat, Alicia, lay in the crook of his arm, purring and looking self-satisfied.

Cody knelt beside his bed and pulled from beneath it a half-filled bottle of bourbon, an empty gin bottle, five empty beer bottles, a crumpled pack of Camels, and a box of pretzels. He strewed them around Ezra, arranging them just right. He went to the hall storage closet and took out his father's Six-20 Brownie camera. In the doorway of his room, he aimed and paused and clicked the shutter. Ezra didn't wake, amazingly enough. (The light from the flashgun was so powerful, you'd see swimming blue globes for minutes after being photographed.) But the cat seemed mildly disturbed. She got to her feet and yawned. What a yawn!—huge and disdainful. It would have made a wonderful picture: deadbeat Ezra and his no-account cat, both with gaping mouths. Cody wondered if she'd do it again. "Yawn," he told her, and he advanced the film for another photo. "Alicia? Yawn." She only smirked and settled down again. He yawned himself, demonstrating, but apparently cats didn't find such things contagious. He lowered the camera and came closer to pat her head, scratch beneath her chin, stroke her throat. Nothing worked. "Yawn, dammit," he said, and he tried to pry her teeth apart by force. She drew up sharply, eyes wide and glaring. Ezra woke.

"Your cat is *retarded*," Cody told him.

"Huh?"

"I can't get her to yawn."

Ezra reached over, matter-of-factly, and circled the cat with his arm. She gave a luxurious yawn and nestled down against him, and Ezra went back to sleep. Cody didn't try for another picture, though. He'd never seen anyone take the fun out of things the way Ezra could.

Cody and Ezra and Jenny went shopping for a Christmas present for their mother. Each of them had saved four weeks' allowance, which meant forty cents apiece, and Cody had a dollar extra that he'd taken from Miss Saunders's center desk drawer. That made two dollars and twenty cents—enough for some winter gloves, Cody suggested. Jenny said gloves were boring and she wanted to buy a diamond ring. "That's really stupid," Cody told her. "Even you ought to know you can't buy a diamond ring for two-twenty."

"I don't mean a real one, I mean glass. Or anything, just so it's pretty and not useful."

They were forced to shop in the stores near home, since they didn't want to spend money on carfare. It was mid-December and crowds of other people were shopping too—plowing past with their arms full of packages, breathing white clouds in the frosty air. Further downtown the department store windows would be as rich and bright as the insides of jewel boxes, and there'd be carols and clanging brass bells and festoons of tinsel on the traffic lights, but in this neighborhood the shops were smaller, darker, decorated with a single wreath on the door or a cardboard Santa Claus carrying a carton of Chesterfield cigarettes. Soldiers on leave straggled by in clumps, looking lost. The shoppers had something grim and determined about them —even those with the gaudiest packages. They seemed likely to mow down anyone in their path. Cody took a pinch of Jenny's coat sleeve so as not to lose her.

"I'm serious," she was saying. "I don't want to get her anything warm. Anything necessary. Anything—"

"Serviceable," Ezra said.

They all grimaced.

"If we bought her a ring, though," Ezra said, "she might feel bad about the wastefulness. She might not really enjoy it."

Cody hated the radiant, grave expression that Ezra wore sometimes; it showed that he realized full well how considerate he was being. "What do *you* want for Christmas?" Cody asked him roughly. "World peace?"

"World what? I'd like a recorder," Ezra said.

They crossed an intersection with a swarm of sailors. "Well," said Cody, "you're not getting one."

"I know that."

"You're getting a cap with turn-down earflaps and a pair of corduroy pants."

"Cody!" said Jenny. "You weren't supposed to tell."

"It doesn't matter," Ezra said.

They separated for a woman who had stopped to fit her child's mittens on. "It used to be," Jenny said, "that we got toys for Christmas, and candy. Remember how nice last Christmas was?"

"This one's going to be nice too," Ezra told her.

"Remember down in Virginia, when Daddy bought us a sled, and Mother said it was silly because it hardly ever snowed but December twenty-sixth we woke up and there was snow all over everything?"

"That was fun," Ezra said.

"We had the only sled in town," Jenny said. "Cody started charging for rides. Daddy showed us how to wax the runners and we pulled it to the top of that hill . . . What was the name of that hill? It had such a funny—"

Then she stopped short on the sidewalk. Pedestrians jostled all around her. "Why," she said.

Cody and Ezra looked at her.

"He's really not ever coming home again. Is he," she said.

No one answered. After a minute they resumed walking, three abreast, and Cody took a pinch of Ezra's sleeve, too, so they wouldn't drift apart in the crowd.

Cody sorted the mail, setting aside for his mother a couple of envelopes that looked like Christmas cards. He threw away a department store flyer and a letter from his school. He pocketed an envelope with a Cleveland postmark.

He went upstairs to his room and switched on the goose-necked lamp beside his bed. While the lightbulb warmed, he whistled and stared out the window. Then he tested the bulb with his fingers and, finding it hot enough, wrapped the envelope around it and counted slowly to thirty. After that he pried open the flap with ease and pulled out a single sheet of paper and a check.

. . . says they should be producing to capacity by June of '45 . . . his father wrote. *Sorry the enclosed is a little smaller than expected as I have incurred some . . .* It was his usual letter, nothing different. Cody folded it again and slid it back in the envelope, though it hardly seemed worth the effort. Then he heard the front door slam. "Ezra Tull?" Pearl called. Her cloppy high heels started rapidly up the stairs. Cody tucked the envelope into his bureau and shut the drawer. "Ezra!"

"He's not here," Cody said.

She came to stand in the doorway. "Where is he?" she asked. She was out of breath, untidy-looking. Her hat was on crooked and she still wore her coat.

"He went to get the laundry, like you told him to."

"What do you know about this?"

She bore down on him, holding out a stack of snapshots. The one on top was so blurred and gray that Cody had trouble deciphering it. He took the whole collection from her hand. Ah, yes: Ezra lay in a stupor, surrounded by liquor bottles. Cody grinned. He'd forgotten that picture completely.

"What could it mean?" his mother asked. "I take a roll of film to the drugstore and I come back with the shock of my life. I just wanted to get the camera ready for Christmas. I was expecting maybe some scenes from last summer, or Jenny's birthday cake . . . and here I find Ezra like a derelict! A common drunk! Could this be what it looks like? Answer me!"

"He's not as perfect as you think he is," Cody told her.

"But he's never given me a moment's worry."

"He's done a lot that might surprise you."

Pearl sat down on his bed. She was shaking her head, looking stunned. "Oh, Cody, it's such a battle, raising children," she said. "I know you must think I'm difficult. I lose my temper, I carry on like a shrew sometimes, but if you could just realize how . . . helpless I feel! How scary it is to know that everyone I love depends on me! I'm afraid I'll do something wrong."

She reached up—for the photos, he thought, and he held them out to her; but no, what she wanted was his hand. She took it and pulled him down beside her. Her skin felt hot and dry. "I've probably been too hard on you," she said. "But I look to you for support now, Cody. You're the only person I can turn to; it may be you and I are more alike than you think. Cody, what am I going to do?"

She leaned closer, and Cody drew back. Even her eyes seemed to give off heat. "Uh, well . . ." he said.

"Who took that picture, anyhow? Was it you?"

"Look," he said. "It was a joke."

"Joke?"

"Ezra didn't drink that stuff. I just set some bottles around him."

Her gaze flicked back and forth across his face.

"He's never touched a drop," Cody told her.

"I see," she said. She freed his hand. She said, "Well, all I can say is, that's some joke, young man." Then she stood up and took several steps away from him. "That's some sense of humor you've got," she said.

Cody shrugged.

"Oh, I suppose it must seem very funny, scaring your mother half out of her wits. Letting her babble on like a fool. Slandering your little brother. It must seem hilarious, to someone like you."

"I'm just naturally mean, I guess," Cody said.

"You've been mean since the day you were born," she told him.

After she had walked out, he went to work resealing his father's letter.

Ezra landed on Park Place and Cody said, "Aha! Park Place with one hotel. Fifteen hundred dollars."

"Poor, poor Ezra," Jenny said.

"How'd you do that?" Ezra asked Cody.

"How'd I do what?"

"How'd you get a hotel on Park Place? A minute ago it was mortgaged."

"Oh, I scrimped and saved," Cody said.

"There's something peculiar going on here."

"Mother!" Jenny called. "Cody's cheating again!"

Their mother was stringing the Christmas tree lights. She looked over and said, "Cody."

"What did I do?" Cody asked.

"What did he do, children?"

"He's the banker," Jenny said. "He made us let him keep the bank and the deeds and the houses. Now he's got a hotel on Park Place and all this extra money. It's not fair!"

Pearl set down the box of lights and came over to where they were sitting. She said, "All right, Cody, put it back. Jenny keeps the deeds from now on; Ezra keeps the bank. Is that clear?"

Jenny reached for the deeds. Ezra began collecting the money.

"And I tell you this," Pearl said. "If I hear one more word, Cody Tull, you're out of the game. Forever! Understood?" She bent to help Ezra. "Always cheating, tormenting, causing trouble . . ." She laid the fives beside the ones, the tens beside the fives. "Cody? You hear what I say?"

He heard, but he didn't bother answering. He sat back and smiled, safe and removed, watching her stack the money.

3

Destroyed by Love

I

Supposedly, Jenny Tull was going to be a beauty someday, but the people who told her that were so old they might easily be dead by the time that day arrived, and no one her own age saw much promise in her. At seventeen, she was skinny and severe and studious-looking. Her bones were so sharp, they seemed likely to puncture her skin. She had coarse dark hair that she was always hacking at, much to her mother's disapproval—one week chopping it to a blunt, square shape; the next week cutting bangs that accidentally slanted toward the left; and then, to correct her error, shortening the bangs so drastically that they appeared damaged and painful. While her classmates were wearing (in 1952) bouffant skirts and perky blouses with the collars turned up in back, Jenny's clothes were hand-me-downs from her mother: limp, skimpy dresses fashionable in the forties, with too much shoulder and not enough skirt. And since her mother despised the sloppiness of loafers, Jenny's shoes were the same kind of sturdy brown oxfords that her brothers wore. Every morning she clomped off to school looking uncomfortable and cross. No wonder hardly anyone bothered to speak to her.

She was about to be, for the very first time, the only child at home. Her brother Cody was away at college. Her brother

Ezra had refused to go to college and started instead what his mother openly hoped was a temporary job in Scarlatti's Restaurant, chopping vegetables for salads; but just as he was advancing to sauces, notice came that he'd been drafted. None of his family could envision it: placid Ezra slogging through Korea, tripping over his bayonet at every opportunity. Surely something would be wrong with him, some weakness of spine or eyesight that would save him. But no, he was found to be in perfect health, and in February was ordered off to a training camp down south. Jenny sat on his bed while he packed. She was touched by the fact that he was taking along his little pearwood recorder, the one he'd bought with his first week's wages. It didn't seem to her that he had a very clear idea of what he was getting into. He moved in his cautious, deliberate way, sorting out what he would send to the basement for storage. Since their mother had plans for renting his room, he couldn't just leave things as they were. Already his brother Cody's bed was freshly made up for a boarder, the blankets tight as drumskins on the narrow mattress, and Cody's sports equipment was packed away in cartons.

She watched Ezra empty a drawer of undershirts, most of them full of holes. (Somehow, he always managed to look like an orphan.) He had grown to be a large-boned man, but his face was still childishly rounded, with the wide eyes, the downy cheeks, the delicate lips of a schoolboy. His hair seemed formed of layers of silk in various shades of yellow and beige. Girls were always after him, Jenny knew, but he was too shy to take advantage of it—or maybe even to be aware of it. He proceeded through life absentmindedly, meditatively, as if considering some complex mathematical puzzle from which he was bound to look up, you would think, as soon as he found the solution. But he never did.

"After I leave," he told Jenny, "will you stop in at Scarlatti's Restaurant from time to time?"

"Stop in and do what?"

"Well, talk with Mrs. Scarlatti, I mean. Just make sure she's all right."

Mrs. Scarlatti had been without a husband for years, if she'd ever had one, and her only son had recently been killed in action. Jenny knew she must be lonely. But she was a bleak and striking woman, so fashionably dressed that it seemed an insult to her particular section of Baltimore. Jenny couldn't imagine holding a conversation with her. Still, anything for Ezra. She nodded.

"And Josiah too," Ezra said.

"Josiah!"

Josiah was even more difficult—downright terrifying, in fact: Ezra's friend Josiah Payson, close to seven feet tall, excitable, and incoherent. It was generally understood that he wasn't quite right in the head. Back in grade school, the other children had teased him, and they had teased Ezra too and asked Jenny why her brother hung out with dummies. "Everybody knows Josiah should be sent away," they told her. "He ought to go to the crazy house; everybody says so."

She said, "Ezra, *I* can't talk to Josiah. I wouldn't understand him."

"Of course you'd understand," said Ezra. "He speaks English, doesn't he?"

"He jibbers, he jabbers, he stutters!"

"You must have only seen him when they're picking on him. The rest of the time he's fine. Oh, if Mother'd let me have him to the house once, you would know. He's fine! He's as bright as you or me, and maybe brighter."

"Well, if you say so," Jenny told him.

But she wasn't convinced.

After Ezra was gone, it occurred to her that he'd only mentioned outsiders. He hadn't said anything about taking care of their mother. Maybe he assumed that Pearl could manage on her own. She could manage very well, it was true, but Ezra's leaving seemed to take something out of her. She delayed the renting of his room. "I know we need the money," she told Jenny, "but I really can't face it right now. It still has his smell. Maybe if I aired it a while . . . It still has his shape in it, know what I mean? I look in and the air feels full of something warm. I think we ought to wait a bit."

So they lived in the house alone. Jenny felt even slighter than usual, overwhelmed by so much empty space. In the afternoons when she came home from school, her mother would still be at work, and Jenny would open the door and hesitantly step inside. Sometimes it seemed there was a startled motion, or a stopping of motion, somewhere deep in the house just as she crossed the threshold. She'd pause then, heart thumping, alert as a deer, but it never turned out to be anything real. She'd close the door behind her and go upstairs to her room, turn on her study lamp, change out of her school clothes. She was an orderly, conscientious girl who always hung things up and took good care of her belongings. She would set her books out neatly on her desk, align her pencils, and adjust the lamp so it shone at the proper angle. Then she'd work her way systematically through her assignments. Her greatest dream was to be a doctor, which meant she'd have to win a scholarship. In three years of high school, she had never received a grade below an A.

At five o'clock she would go downstairs to scrub the potatoes or start the chicken frying—whatever was instructed in her mother's note on the kitchen table. Soon afterward her mother would arrive. "Well! I tell you that old Pendle woman is a trial and a nuisance, just a nuisance, lets me ring up all her groceries and then says, 'Wait now, let me see, why, I don't have near enough money for such a bill as this.' Goes fumbling through her ratty cloth change purse while everyone behind her shifts from foot to foot . . ." She would tie an apron over her dress and take Jenny's place at the stove. "Honey, hand me the salt, will you? I see there's no mail from the boys. They've forgotten all about us, it seems. It's only you and me now."

It was only the two of them, yes, but there were echoes of the others all around—wicked, funny Cody, peaceful Ezra, setting up a loaded silence as Jenny and her mother seated themselves at the table. "Pour the milk, will you, dear? Help yourself to some beans." Sometimes Jenny imagined that even her father made his absence felt, though she couldn't picture his face and had little recollection of the time before he'd left them. Of course she never mentioned this to her mother. Their talk was small talk, little dibs and dabs of things, safely skating over whatever might lie beneath. "How is that poor Carroll girl, Jenny? Has she lost any weight that you've noticed?"

Jenny knew that, in reality, her mother was a dangerous person—hot breathed and full of rage and unpredictable. The dry, straw texture of her lashes could seem the result of some conflagration, and her pale hair could crackle electrically from its bun and her eyes could get small as hatpins. Which of her children had not felt her stinging slap, with the claw-encased pearl in her engagement ring that could bloody a lip at one flick? Jenny had seen her hurl Cody down a flight of stairs. She'd seen Ezra ducking, elbows raised, warding off an attack. She herself, more than once, had been slammed against a wall, been called "serpent," "cockroach," "hideous little sniveling guttersnipe." But here Pearl sat, decorously inquiring about Julia Carroll's weight problem. Jenny had a faint, tremulous hope that times had changed. Perhaps it was the boys' fault. Maybe she and her mother—intelligent women, after all—could live without such scenes forever. But she never felt entirely secure, and at night, when Pearl had placed a kiss on the center of Jenny's forehead, Jenny went off to bed and dreamed what she had always dreamed: her mother laughed a witch's shrieking laugh; dragged Jenny out of hiding as the Nazis tramped up the stairs; accused her of sins and crimes that had never crossed Jenny's mind. Her mother told her, in an informative and considerate tone of voice, that she was raising Jenny to eat her.

Cody wrote almost never, and what letters he did write were curt and factual. *I won't be coming home for spring vacation. All my grades are fine except French. This new job pays better than the old one did.* Ezra sent a postcard the moment he arrived in camp, and followed that three days later with a letter describing his surroundings. It was longer than several of Cody's put together, but still it didn't tell Jenny what she wanted to know. *There's somebody two blocks down who's from Maryland too I hear but I haven't had a chance to talk to him and I don't think*

*he's from Baltimore anyway but some other place I wouldn't
know about so I doubt we'd have much to . . .* What was he
saying, exactly? Had he, or had he not, made any friends? If
people lived so close together, you'd think they would have
talked. Jenny pictured the others ignoring him, or worse: tormenting him and making fun of his incompetence. He simply
was not a soldier. But *I have learned right much about my rifle,*
he wrote. *Cody would be surprised.* She tried to imagine his
long, sensitive fingers cleaning and oiling a gun. She understood
that he must be surviving, more or less, but she couldn't figure
out how. She thought of him on his belly, in the dust of the
rifle range, squeezing a trigger. His gaze was so reflective, how
would he hit a target? *They say the whole bunch of us will be
joining the Korean Conflict as soon as we are* . . . Why, they'd
pick him off like a fly! He'd never do more to defend himself
than dodge and shield his head.

*I think a lot about Scarlatti's Restaurant and how nice the
lettuce smelled when I tore it into the bowl,* he wrote—his only
mention of homesickness, if that was what it was. Pearl gave a
jealous sniff. "As if lettuce had a smell!" Jenny was jealous too;
he could have remembered, instead, how he and she used to lie
on the floor in front of the Philco on Monday nights, listening
to the Cities Service Band of America. What did he see in that
restaurant, anyhow? Then a little knob of discomfort started
nudging inside her chest. There was something she hadn't done,
something unpleasant that she didn't want to do . . . Check on
Mrs. Scarlatti. She wondered if Ezra had really meant for her
to keep her promise. He couldn't actually expect that of her,
could he? But she supposed he could. He was a literal-minded
kind of person.

So she folded Ezra's letter and put it in her pocket. Then she
slipped her coat on and walked to St. Paul Street, to a narrow
brick building set in a strip of shops and businesses.

Scarlatti's was the neighborhood's one formal elegant eating
place. It served only supper, mostly to people from better parts
of the city. At this hour—five-thirty or so—it wouldn't even be
open. She went to the rear, where she'd been a couple of times

with Ezra. She circled two garbage cans overflowing with wilted greens, and she climbed the steps and knocked on the door. Then she cupped a hand to the windowpane and peered in.

Men in dirty aprons were rushing around the kitchen, which was a mass of steam and stainless steel, pot lids clattering, bowls as big as birdbaths heaped with sliced vegetables. No wonder they hadn't heard her. She turned the knob, but the door was locked. And before she could knock any harder, she caught sight of Mrs. Scarlatti. She was slouched in the dining room entranceway, holding a lit cigarette—a white-faced woman in a stark black knife of a dress. Whatever she was saying, Jenny couldn't catch it, but she heard the gravelly, careless sound of her voice. And she saw how Mrs. Scarlatti's black hair was swept completely to the right, like one of those extreme Vogue magazine model's, and how she leaned her head to the right as well so that she seemed to be burdened, cruelly misused, bearing up under an exhausting weight that had something to do with men and experience. Imagine Ezra knowing such a person! Imagine him at ease with her, close enough to worry about her. Jenny backed away. She understood, all at once, that her brothers had grown up and gone. Her mental pictures of them were outdated—Ezra playing the bamboo whistle he used to have in grade school, Cody triumphantly rattling his dice over their old Monopoly board. She thought of a faded flannel shirt that Ezra had worn so often, it was like a second skin. She thought of how he would rock back and forth with his hands in his rear pockets when he was lost for something to say, or dig a hole in the ground with his sneaker. And how when Jenny was shattered by one of their mother's rages, he would slip downstairs to the kitchen and fix her a mug of hot milk laced with honey, sprinkled over with cinnamon. He was always so quick to catch his family's moods, and to offer food and drink and unspoken support.

She traveled down the alley and, instead of heading home, took Bushnell Street and then Putnam. It was getting colder; she had to button her coat. Three blocks down Putnam stood a building so weathered and dismal, you'd think it was an abandoned warehouse till you saw the sign: TOM 'N' EDDIE'S BODY SHOP. She had often come here to fetch Ezra home, but she'd only called his name at the drive-in doorway; she had never been inside. Now she stepped into the gloom and looked around her. Tom and Eddie (she assumed) were talking to a man in a business suit; one of them held a clipboard. In the background, Josiah Payson swung a gigantic rubber mallet against the fender of a pickup. Jenny was hit by a piece of memory, a mystifying fragment: Josiah in the school yard, long ago, violently flailing a pipe or a metal bar of some sort, cutting a desperate, whizzing circle in the air and shouting something unintelligible while Ezra stood guard between him and a mob of children. "Everything will be fine; just go away," Ezra was telling the others. But what had happened next? How had it ended? How had it started? She felt confused. Meanwhile Josiah swung his mallet. He was grotesquely tall, as gaunt as the armature for some statue never completed. His cropped black hair bristled all over his head, his skull of a face glistened, and he clenched a set of teeth so ragged and white and crowded, so jumbled together and overlapping, that it seemed he had chewed them up and was preparing to spit them out.

"Josiah," she called timidly.

He stopped to look at her. Or was he looking someplace else? His eyes were dead black—lidless and almost Oriental. It was impossible to tell where they were directed. He heaved the hammer onto a stack of burlap bags and lunged toward her, his face alight with happiness. "Ezra's sister!" he said. "Ezra!"

She smiled and hugged her elbows.

Directly in front of her, he came to a halt and smoothed his stubble of hair. His arms seemed longer than they should have been. "Is Ezra okay?" he asked her.

"He's fine."

"Not wounded or—"

"No."

Ezra was right: Josiah spoke as distinctly as anyone, in a grown man's rumbling voice. But he had trouble finding something to do with his hands, and ended up scraping them together as if trying to rid his palms of dirt or grease, or even of a layer of skin. She was aware of Tom and Eddie glancing over at her curiously, losing track of their conversation. "Come outside," she told Josiah. "I'll let you see his letter."

Outside it was twilight, almost too dark to read, but Josiah took the letter anyway and scanned the lines. There was a crease between his eyebrows as deep as if someone had pressed an ax blade there. She noticed that his coveralls, pathetically well washed, were so short for him that his fallen white socks and hairy shinbones showed. His lips could barely close over that chaos of teeth; his mouth had a bunchy look and his chin was elongated from the effort.

He handed the letter back to her. She had no way of knowing what he had got out of it. "If they'd let me," he said, "I'd have gone with him. Oh, I wouldn't mind going. But they claimed I was too tall."

"Too tall?"

She'd never heard of such a thing.

"So I had to stay behind," he said, "but I didn't want to. I don't want to work in a body shop all my life; I plan to do something different."

"Like what?"

"Oh, I don't know. Find something with Ezra, I guess, once he gets out of the army. Ezra, he would always come to visit me here and look around and say, 'How can you stand it? All the noise,' he'd say. 'We got to find you something different.' But I didn't know where to start hunting, and now Ezra's gone away. It's not the noise that's so bad, but it's hot in summer and cold in winter. My feet get bothered by the cold, get these itchy things all over the toes."

"Chilblains, maybe," Jenny suggested. She felt pleasantly bored; it seemed she had known Josiah forever. She ran a thumbnail down the crease of Ezra's letter. Josiah gazed either at her or straight through her (it was hard to tell which) and cracked his knuckles.

"Probably what I'll do is work for Ezra," he said, "once Ezra opens his restaurant."

"What are you talking about? Ezra's not opening a restaurant."

"Sure he is."

"Why would he want to do that? As soon as he pulls himself together he's going off to college, studying to be a teacher."

"Who says so?" Josiah asked.

"Well, my mother does. He's got the patience for it, she says. Maybe he'll be a professor, even," Jenny told him. But she wasn't so certain now. "I mean, it's not a lifework, restaurants."

"Why isn't it?"

She couldn't answer.

"Ezra's going to have him a place where people come just like to a family dinner," Josiah said. "He'll cook them one thing special each day and dish it out on their plates and everything will be solid and wholesome, really homelike."

"Ezra told you that?"

"Really just like home."

"Well, I don't know, maybe people go to restaurants to get *away* from home."

"It's going to be famous," Josiah said.

"You have the wrong idea entirely," Jenny told him. "How did you come up with such a crazy notion?"

Then without warning, Josiah went back to being his old self —or her old picture of him. He dropped his head, like a marionette whose strings had snapped. "I got to go," he told her.

"Josiah?"

"Don't want those people yelling at me."

He loped away without saying goodbye. Jenny watched after him as regretfully as if he were Ezra himself. He didn't look back.

Cody wrote that he was being interviewed by several corporations. He wanted a job in business after he finished school. Ezra wrote that he could march twenty miles at a go now without much tiring. It began to seem less incongruous, even perfectly natural, that Ezra should be a soldier. After all, wasn't he an enduring sort, uncomplaining, cheerful in performing his duties?

Jenny had worried needlessly. Her mother too seemed to relax somewhat. "Really it's for the best, when you think about it," she said. "A stint in the service is often just the ticket; gives a boy time to get hold of himself. I bet when he comes back, he'll want to go to college. I bet he'll want to teach someplace."

Jenny didn't tell her about his restaurant.

Twice, after her first visit to Josiah, she looked in on him again. She would stop by the body shop after school, and Josiah would come outside a moment to swing his arms and gaze beyond her and speak of Ezra. "Got a letter from him myself, over at the house. Claimed he was marching a lot."

"Twenty miles," Jenny said.

"Some of it uphill."

"He must be in pretty good shape by now."

"He always did like to walk."

The third time she came, it was almost dark. She'd stayed late for chorus. Josiah was just leaving work. He was getting into his jacket, which was made of a large, shaggy plaid in muted shades of navy and maroon. She thought of the jackets that little boys wore in the lower grades of school. "That Tom," Josiah said, jabbing his fists in his pockets. "That Eddie." He strode rapidly down the sidewalk. Jenny had trouble keeping up. "They don't care how they talk to a fellow," he said. "Don't give a thought to what he might feel; feelings just like anyone else . . ."

She dropped back, deciding that he'd rather be alone, but partway down the block he stopped and turned and waited. "Aren't I a human being?" he asked when she arrived at his side. "Don't I feel bad if someone shouts at me? I wish I were out in the woods someplace, none of these people to bother me. Camping out in a dead, dead quiet with a little private tent from L. L. Bean and a L. L. Bean sleeping bag." He turned and rushed on; Jenny had to run. "I've half a mind to give notice," he said.

"Why don't you, then?"

"My mama needs the money."

"You could find something else."

"Oh, no, it isn't easy."

"Why not?"

He didn't answer. They raced past a discount jewelry store, a bakery, a bank of private apartments with inviting yellow windows. Then he said, "Come and have supper at our house."

"What? Oh, I can't."

"Ezra used to come," he said, "back before he worked in the restaurant and couldn't get away. My mama was always glad to set an extra plate out, always, anytime. But *your* mother didn't often let him; your mother doesn't like me."

"Oh, well . . ."

"I wish you'd just have supper with us."

She paused. Then she said, "I'd be happy to."

He didn't seem surprised. (Jenny was astonished, herself.) He grunted and continued to tear along. His whisks of black hair stood out around his head. He led her down a side street, then through an alley that Jenny wasn't familiar with.

From the front, his house must have been very much like hers —a brick row house set in a tiny yard. But they approached it from the rear, where a tacked-on, gray frame addition gave it a ramshackle look. The addition turned out to be an unheated pantry with a cracked linoleum floor. Josiah stopped there to work himself free of his jacket, and then he reached for Jenny's coat and hung them both on hooks beside the door. "Mama?" he called. He showed Jenny into the kitchen. "Got company for supper, Mama."

Mrs. Payson stood at the stove—a small, chubby woman dressed in earth tones. She reminded Jenny of some modest brown bird. Her face was round and smooth and shining. She looked up and smiled, and since Josiah failed to make the introduction Jenny said, "I'm Jenny Tull."

"Oh, any kin to Ezra?"

"I'm his sister."

"My, I'm just so fond of that boy," Mrs. Payson said. She lifted the pot from the stove and set it on the table. "When he was called up I cried, did Josiah tell you? I sat right down and cried. Why, he has been like a son to me, always in and out of the house . . ." She laid three place settings while Josiah poured the milk. "I'll never forget," she said, "back when Josiah's daddy died, Ezra came and sat with us, and fixed us meals, and made us cocoa. I said, 'Ezra, I feel selfish, taking you from your family,' but he said, 'Don't you worry about it, Mrs. Payson.' "

Jenny wondered when that could have been. Ezra had never mentioned Mr. Payson's dying.

Supper was spaghetti and a salad, with chocolate cake for dessert. Jenny ate sparingly, planning to eat again when she got home so her mother wouldn't guess; but Josiah had several helpings of everything. Mrs. Payson kept refilling his plate. "To look at him," she said, "you'd never know he eats so much, would you? Skinny as a fence post. I reckon he's still a growing boy." She laughed, and Josiah grinned bashfully with his eyes cast down—a skeletal, stooped, hunkering man. Jenny had never thought about the fact that Josiah was somebody's son, some woman's greatest treasure. His stubby black lashes were lowered; his prickly head was bent over his plate. He was so certain of being loved, here if no place else. She looked away.

After supper she helped with the dishes, placing each clean plate and glass on open wooden shelves whose edges had grown soft from too many coats of paint. Her mother would be frantic by now, but Jenny lingered over the wiping of each fork. Then Josiah walked her home. "Come back and see us!" Mrs. Payson called from the doorway. "Make sure you're buttoned up!" Jenny thought of . . . was it "Jack and the Beanstalk"? . . . or perhaps some other fairy tale, where the humble widow, honest and warmhearted, lives in a cottage with her son. Everything else—the cold dark of the streets, the picture of her own bustling mother—seemed brittle by comparison, lacking the smoothly rounded completeness of Josiah's life.

They walked up Calvert Street without talking, puffing clouds of steam. They crossed to Jenny's house and climbed the porch steps. "Well," said Jenny, "thank you for inviting me, Josiah."

Josiah made some awkward, jerky motion that she assumed was an effort toward speech. He stumbled closer, enveloped her in a circle of rough plaid, and kissed her on the lips. She had trouble, at first, understanding what was happening. Then she felt a terrible dismay, not so much for herself as for Josiah. Oh, it was sad, he had misread everything; he would be so embarrassed! But how could he have made such an error? Thinking it over (pressed willy-nilly against his whiskery chin, against the knobbiness of his mouth), she saw things suddenly from his viewpoint: their gentle little "romance" (was what he must call it), as seamless as the Widow Payson's fairy tale existence. She longed for it; she wished it were true. She ached, with something like nostalgia, for a contented life with his mother in her snug house, for an innocent, protective marriage. She kissed him back, feeling even through all those layers of wool how he tensed and trembled.

Then light burst out, the front door slammed open, and her mother's voice broke over them. "What? What! What is the meaning of this?"

They leapt apart.

"You piece of trash," Pearl said to Jenny. "You tramp. You trashy thing. So this is what you've been up to! Not so much as notifying me where you are, supper not started, I'm losing my mind with worry—then here I find you! Necking! Necking with a, with a—"

For lack of a word, it seemed, she struck out. She slapped Jenny hard across the cheek. Jenny's eyes filled with tears. Josiah, as if it were he who'd been struck, averted his face sharply and stared away at some distant point. His mouth was working but no sound came forth.

"With a crazy! A dummy! A retarded person. You did it to spite me, didn't you," Pearl told Jenny. "It's your way of making mock of me. All these afternoons that I've been slaving in the grocery store, you were off in some alleyway, weren't you, off with this animal, this gorilla, letting him take his pleasure, just to shame me."

Josiah said, "But-but-but—"

"Just to show me up when I had such great plans for you. Cutting school, no doubt, lying with him in bushes and back seats of cars and maybe this very house, for all I know, while I'm off slaving at Sweeney Brothers—"

"But! But! Aagh!" Josiah shouted, and he sputtered so that Jenny saw white flecks flying in the lamplight. Then he flung out his scarecrow arms and plunged down the steps and disappeared.

She didn't see him again, of course. She chose her routes carefully and never again came near him, never approached any place that he was likely to be found; and she assumed he did the same. It was as if, by mutual agreement, they had split the city between them.

And besides, she had no reason to see him: Ezra's letters stopped. Ezra appeared in person. One Sunday morning, there he was, sitting in the kitchen when Jenny came down to breakfast. He wore his old civilian clothes that had been packed away in mothballs—jeans and a scruffy blue sweater. They hung on him like something borrowed. It was alarming how much weight he had lost. His hair was unbecomingly short and his face was paler, older, shadowed beneath the eyes. He sat slumped, clamping his hands between his knees, while Pearl scraped a piece of scorched toast into the sink. "Jam or honey, which?" she was asking. "Jenny, look who's here! It's Ezra, safe and sound! Let me pour you more coffee, Ezra." Ezra didn't speak, but he gave Jenny a tired smile.

He'd been discharged, as it turned out. For sleepwalking. He had no memory of sleepwalking, but every night he dreamed the same dream: he was marching through an unchanging terrain of cracked mud flats without a tree or a sprig of grass, with a blank blue bowl of sky overhead. He would set one foot in front of the other and march and march and march. In the morning, his muscles would ache. He'd thought it was from his *waking* marches, till they told him differently. All night, they told him, he roamed the camp, plodding between the rows of cots. Soldiers would stir and sit up and say, "Tull? That you?" and he would leave. He wouldn't answer, wouldn't wake, but simply went someplace else. To some of the soldiers, the youngest ones, his silence was frightening. There were complaints. He was sent to a doctor, who gave him a box of yellow pills. With the pills he still walked, but he would fall down from time to time and just lie where he fell until morning. Once he must have landed on his face; when they roused him, his nose was bloody and they thought it might be broken. It wasn't, but for several days he had purple circles under his eyes. Then they sent him to a chaplain, who asked if Ezra had anything particular on his mind. Was there some trouble back home, perhaps? Woman trouble? Illness in his family? Ezra said no. He told the chaplain things were fine; he couldn't for the life of him think what this was all about. The chaplain asked if he liked the army and Ezra said, well, it wasn't something you would like or dislike; it was something you had to get through, was more to the point. He said the army wasn't his style, exactly—what with the shouting, the noise—but still, he was coming along. He guessed he was doing all right. The chaplain said just to try not to sleepwalk again, in that case; but the very next night Ezra walked directly into town, four and a half miles in his olive-drab underwear with his eyes wide open but flat as windows, and a waitress in a diner had to wake him up and get her brother-in-law to drive him back to camp. The next day they called another doctor in, and the doctor asked him a series of questions and signed some papers and sent him home. "So here I am," Ezra said in a toneless voice. "Discharged."

"But honorably," said his mother.

"Oh, yes."

"The thought! All the while this was going on, you never said a word."

"Well, how could you have helped?" he asked.

The question seemed to age her. She sagged.

After breakfast he went upstairs and fell on his bed and slept through the day, and Jenny had to wake him for supper. Even then he could barely keep his eyes open. He sat groggily swaying, eating almost nothing, nodding off in the middle of a mouthful. Then he went back to bed. Jenny wandered through the house and fidgeted with the cords of window shades. Was this how he was going to be, now? Had he changed forever?

But Monday morning, he was Ezra again. She heard his little pearwood recorder playing "Greensleeves" before she was even dressed. When she came downstairs he was scrambling eggs the way she liked, with cheese and bits of green pepper, while Pearl read the paper. And at breakfast he said, "I guess I'll go get my old job back." Pearl glanced over at him but said nothing. "How come you didn't call on Mrs. Scarlatti?" Ezra asked Jenny. "She wrote and said you never came."

Jenny said, "Oh, well, I meant to . . ."

She lowered her eyes and held her breath, waiting. Now was when he would mention Josiah. But he didn't. She looked up and found him buttering a piece of toast, and she let out her breath. She was never going to be certain of what Ezra knew, or didn't know.

I I

By the time Jenny reached college, she'd grown to be the beauty that everyone predicted. Or was it only that she'd come into fashion? Her mirror showed the same face, so far as she could tell, but most of her dormitory's phone calls seemed to be for her, and if she hadn't been working her way through school (waiting tables, folding laundry, shelving books in the library stacks), she could have gone out every night. Away from Baltimore, her looks lost a little of their primness. She let her hair grow and she developed a breathless, flyaway air. But she never forgot about medical school. Her future was always clear to her: a straightforward path to a pediatric practice in a medium-sized city, preferably not too far from a coast. (She liked knowing she could get out anytime. Wouldn't mid-westerners feel claustrophobic?) Friends teased her about her single-mindedness. Her roommate objected to Jenny's study light, was exasperated by the finicky way she aligned her materials on her desk. In this respect, at least, Jenny hadn't changed.

Meanwhile, her brother Cody had become a success—shot ahead through several different firms, mainly because of his ideas for using the workers' time better; and then branched out on his own to become an efficiency expert. And Ezra still worked for Mrs. Scarlatti, but he had advanced as well. He really ran the kitchen now, while Mrs. Scarlatti played hostess out front. Jenny's mother wrote to say it was a shame, a crime and a shame. *I tell him the longer he piddles about in that woman's restaurant the harder he'll find it to get back on track, you know he always intended to go to college . . .*

Pearl still clerked at the grocery store but was better dressed, looking less careworn, since Jenny's scholarship and part-time jobs had relieved the last financial strain. Jenny saw her twice a year—at Christmas and just before the start of school each September. She made excuses for the other holidays, and during the summers she worked at a clothing shop in a small town near her college. It wasn't that she didn't want to see her mother. She often thought of her wiry energy, the strength she had shown in raising her children single-handed, and her unfailing interest in their progress. But whenever Jenny returned, she was dampened almost instantly by the atmosphere of the house—by its lack of light, the cramped feeling of its papered rooms, a certain grim spareness. She almost wondered if she had some kind of allergy. It was like a respiratory ailment; on occasion, she believed she might be smothering. Her head grew stuffy, as it did when she had studied too long without a break. She snapped at people. Even Ezra irritated her, with his calm and his docility.

So she kept her distance, and after missing her family a while began to discard the very thought of them. She grew brisker, busier, more hurried. Ezra's letters—as ponderous as his conversation, just this side of dull—would turn up on the edge of the bathroom sink or crumpled among the bedclothes, where Jenny had laid them aside in midsentence. Her mind just drifted, that was all. And twice, during her first two years in college, Cody stopped to see her while traveling through Pennsylvania on business, and both times she was happy at the prospect (he was so dashing and good-looking, she was proud to show him off), but she felt muffled, gradually, once he'd arrived. It wasn't her fault; it was his. It seemed that everything she said carried, for him, the echo of their mother. She saw him stiffen. She knew exactly what he was thinking. "How are you fixed for money?" he would ask her. "You need a few new dresses?" She would say, "No, thanks, Cody, I'm fine"—really meaning it, needing nothing; but she saw, from his expression, what he had understood her to say: "No, no," in Pearl's thin voice, "never mind me . . ." She could not straighten his tie, or compliment his suit, or inquire about his present life without setting up that guarded look in his face. It made her feel unjustly accused. Did he really imagine she would be so domineering, or reproachful, or meddlesome? "Look," she tried once. "Let's start over. I didn't intend what you think I intended." But his wary, sidelong glance told her that he suspected even this. There was no way to cut themselves out of the tangle. She let him leave. Back in her dorm room she studied her reflection, her swing of dark hair and her narrow-waisted figure. Then she acted gayer than usual, for a while, and had a sense of having clapped her hands to free them of some thick and clinging dust.

Late in her senior year, she fell in love. She had been in love before, of course—once with an English major who'd grown too possessive, bit by bit; and once with a barrel-necked football star who seemed now, when she looked back, to be a symptom of some temporary insanity. But this was different. This was Harley Baines, a genius, a boy of such intelligence that even his smudged tortoiseshell glasses, pure white skin, and adenoidal voice struck awe in his classmates. He was not outside Jenny's group so much as above it, beyond it—a group in himself. It was rumored that he could have had a Ph.D. at twelve but was kept from it by his parents, who wanted him to enjoy a normal childhood. Next year he'd be at Paulham University, outside Philadelphia, doing advanced research in the field of genetics. Jenny was going to Paulham too; she had just been accepted by its medical school. That was what made her notice Harley Baines. Secure in the center of her own noisy group (which would not be hers much longer, which would soon be scattered by graduation, leaving her defenseless), she looked across the campus and saw Harley Baines passing with his stork-like gait, wearing unstylish, pleated flannel trousers and a bulky pullover obviously knitted by his mother. His hair, which could have used a shampoo, was a particularly dense shade of black. She wondered if he knew she was entering Paulham. She wondered if he would care, if he found girls beneath his notice. Was he impervious? Unobtainable? Her friends had to call her name several times, laughing at her bemused expression.

It was the spring of 1957—an unusually late and gradual spring. Professors opened the classroom windows with long, hooked poles, and the smell of lilacs floated in. Jenny wore sleeveless blouses and full skirts and ballerina flats. Harley Baines laid aside his home-knit sweater. Bared, his arms were muscular, thick with black hair. Around his neck he wore a gold or brass disk of some kind. She was dying to know what it was. One day in German class, she asked. He said it was a medal he'd won in a high school science fair, for setting up an experiment on the metabolic rate of white rats. She thought it was a funny thing to go on wearing all this time, but she didn't say so. Instead, she touched the medal lightly with her fingertips. It hung just inside his shirt, and it was almost hot.

She asked him at other times (catching up with him in a corridor, arranging to stand behind him in the cafeteria line) whether he was looking forward to Paulham University, and what sort of housing he would have there, and what he'd heard about Paulham's public transportation system. Offering these questions in an even, noncommittal voice, she felt like one of those circus trainers who take care to present to an animal only the curled-in backs of their hands, showing they pose no threat. She didn't want to alarm him. But Harley didn't act alarmed at all, and answered her courteously, matter-of-factly. (Was that good or bad?) When exams began, she came to him with her genetics notes and asked if he could help her study. They sat outdoors in the grass, in front of the Student Union, on a blue chenille bedspread she'd brought from her room. Their class-mates lounged on other bedspreads all around them—including some of Jenny's friends, who cast her startled, doubtful looks and then glanced quickly past her. She'd been hoping they would stroll over, make Harley a part of the group. But on second thought, she could see that would never happen.

While she framed her queries (acting not so slow-witted as to put him off, but still in need of his assistance), Harley listened and stripped a grass blade. He wore heavy, dressy shoes that seemed out of place on the bedspread. In his probing hands, the grass blade took on the look of a scientific experiment. He answered her levelly, with no question marks after his sentences; he took it for granted that she would understand him. Which she did, in fact, and would have even if she hadn't known her subject ahead of time. His logic proceeded steadily from A to B to C. In his slowness and his thoroughness, he reminded her of Ezra—though otherwise, how different they were! When he finished, he asked if everything was clear now. "Yes, thank you," she said, and he nodded and rose to go. Was that *it?* She rose too, and felt suddenly dizzy—not from standing, she believed, but from love. He had actually managed to bowl her over. She wondered what he would do if she threw her arms around him and collapsed against him, laid her face on his white, white chest, burned her cheek on his scientific medal. Instead she asked, "Will you help me fold the bedspread, please?" He bent to lift one end, and she lifted the other. They advanced. He gave his end to her and then soberly brushed off every wisp of grass, every flower petal and grain of pollen, from his side of the spread. After that he took the spread back again, evidently assuming that she would brush off her side. She looked up into his face. He stepped forward, flipped the spread around him like a hooded cloak, and wrapped her inside its darkness and kissed her. His glasses knocked against her nose. It was an unskillful kiss anyhow, too abrupt, and she couldn't help imagining the picture they made—a blue chenille pillar in the middle of the campus, a twin-sized mummy. She laughed. He dropped the spread and turned on his heel and walked off very fast. A plume of hair bobbed on the back of his head like a rooster's tail.

Jenny returned to her room and took a bath and changed to a ruffled dress. She leaned out her open window, humming. Harley didn't come. Eventually she went to supper, but he wasn't in the cafeteria, either. The next day, after her last exam, she phoned his dormitory. Some sleepy-sounding, gruff boy answered. "Baines has left for home," he said.

"Home? But we haven't had graduation yet."

"He's not planning to go through with that."

"Oh," said Jenny. She hadn't thought of graduation as "going through" with anything, although it was true you could simply have your diploma mailed out. To people like Harley Baines, she supposed, a degree was unimportant. (While Jenny's family was coming all the way to Summerfield for this event.) She said, "Well, thank you anyhow," and hung up, hoping her voice didn't sound as forlorn to Harley's roommate as it did to her.

That summer, after graduation, she worked again at Molly's Togs in the little town near the college. It had always seemed a pleasant job, but this year she was depressed by the studied casualness of married women's clothes—their Bermuda shorts for golfing and their wide-hipped khaki skirts. She gazed away unhelpfully when her customers asked, "Does it suit me? Do you think it's too youthful?" Next year at this time, she would be at Paulham. She wondered how soon she could start wearing a starched white coat.

In July, a letter arrived from Harley Baines, forwarded from home by her mother. When Jenny returned to her boarding-house after work, she found it on the hall table. She stood looking at it a moment. Then she slipped it into her straw purse and climbed the stairs. She let herself into her room, threw her purse on the bed, and opened the window. She took a square tin from a drawer and fed the two goldfish in the bowl on the bureau. All before opening Harley's letter.

Did she guess, ahead of time, what it would say?

Later, she imagined that she must have.

His handwriting was as small and separate as typing. She would have imagined something more headlong from a genius. He used a colon after the greeting, as if it were a business letter.

18 July, 1957

Dear Jenny:

I unreasonably took offense at what was, in fact, a natural reaction on your part. I must have seemed ridiculous.

What I had intended, before our misunderstanding, was that we might become better acquainted over the summer and then marry in the fall. I still find marriage a viable option. I know this must seem sudden—we haven't exactly had a normal American courtship—but after all, we are neither of us frivolous people.

Bear in mind that we will both be at Paulham next year and could share a single apartment, buy groceries in economy lots, etc. Also, I sense that your finances have been something of a problem, and I would be glad to assume that responsibility.

The above sounds more pragmatic than I'd intended. Actually, I find I love you, and am awaiting your earliest reply.

Sincerely, Harley Baines

P.S. I know that you're intelligent. You didn't have to make up all those questions about genetics.

The postscript, she thought, was the most affecting part of the letter. It was written in a looser hand, as if impulsively, while the rest seemed copied and perhaps recopied from a rough draft. She read the letter again, and then folded it and set it on her bed. She went over to study her goldfish, who had left too much food floating on the surface of the water. She would have to cut down on their rations. *Dear Harley*, she practiced. *It was such a surprise to . . .* No. He wouldn't care for gushiness. *Dear Harley: I have considered your terms and . . .* What she was trying to say was "Yes." She was pulled only very slightly by the feelings she'd had for him earlier (which now seemed faded

and shallow, a schoolgirl crush brought on by senior panic).
What appealed to her more was the *angularity* of the situation
—the mighty leap into space with someone she hardly knew.
Wasn't that what a marriage ought to be? Like one of those
movie-style disasters—shipwrecks or earthquakes or enemy pris-
ons—where strangers, trapped in close quarters by circumstance,
show their real strengths and weaknesses.

Lately, her life had seemed to be narrowing. She could pre-
dict so easily the successive stages of medical school, internship,
and residency. She had looked in a mirror, not so long ago, and
realized all at once that the clear, fragile skin around her eyes
would someday develop lines. She was going to grow old like
anyone else.

She took paper from a bureau drawer, sat down on her bed,
and uncapped her fountain pen. *Dear Harley:* she wrote. She
plucked a microscopic hair from the pen point. She thought a
while. Then she wrote, *All right,* and signed her name—the
ultimate in no-nonsense communication. Even Harley couldn't
find it excessive.

The following evening, just before supper, Jenny arrived in
Baltimore. She had burned all her bridges: quit her job, given
away her goldfish, and packed everything in her room. It was
the most reckless behavior she had ever shown. On the Greyhound bus she sat grandly upright, periodically shrugging off
the snoring soldier who drooped against her. When she reached
the terminal she hailed a cab, instead of waiting for a city bus,
and rode home in style.

No one had been told she was coming, so she was puzzled by
the fact that while she was paying off the driver, the front door
of her house opened wide and her mother proceeded across the
porch and down the steps in a flowing, flowered dress, high-
heeled pumps, and a hat whose black net veil was dotted with
what looked like beauty spots. Behind her came Ezra in un-
pressed clothes that were a little too full cut, and last was Cody,
dark and handsome and New Yorkish in a fine-textured, fitted

gray suit and striped silk tie. For a second, Jenny fancied they were headed for her funeral. This was how they would look—formally dressed and refraining from battle—if Jenny were no longer among them. Then she shook the thought away, and smiled and climbed out of the taxi.

Her mother halted on the sidewalk. "My stars!" she said. "Ezra, when you say family dinner, you *mean* family dinner!" She raised her veil to kiss Jenny's cheek. "Why didn't you tell us you were coming? Ezra, did you plan it this way?"

"I didn't know a thing about it," Ezra said. "I thought of writing you, Jenny, but I didn't think you'd come all this distance just for supper."

"Supper?" Jenny asked.

"It's some idea of Ezra's," Pearl told her. "He found out Cody was passing through, maybe spending the night, and he said, 'I want both of you to get all dressed up—' "

"I am *not* spending the *night*," Cody said. "I'm running on a schedule here, when will you see that? I shouldn't even be staying for supper. I ought to be in Delaware."

"Ezra's got something he wants to say," Pearl said, picking a thread off Jenny's sundress, "some announcement he wants to make, and is taking us to Scarlatti's Restaurant. Though hot as it is, I believe a leaf of lettuce is just about all I could manage. Jenny, honey, you're thin as a stick! And what's in this big suitcase? How long are you planning to stay?"

"Oh, well . . . not long," Jenny said. She felt shy about telling her news. "Maybe I ought to change clothes. I'm not as dressed up as the rest of you."

"No, no, you're fine," Ezra told her. He was rubbing his hands together, the way he always did when he was pleased. "Oh, it's working out so well!" he said. "A real family dinner! It's just like fate."

Cody took Jenny's suitcase inside the house. Meanwhile, her mother fussed: smoothing Jenny's hair, clucking at her bare legs. "No stockings! On a public conveyance." Cody came back and opened the door of a shiny blue car at the curb. He helped Pearl in, cupping her elbow. "What do you think of my car?" he said to Jenny.

"It's very nice. Did you buy it new?"

"How else? A Pontiac. Smell that new-car smell," he said. He walked around to the driver's seat. Jenny and Ezra settled in the rear; Ezra's knobby wrists dangled between his knees.

"Of course, it's not yet paid for," Cody said, pulling into traffic, "but it will be very soon."

"Cody Tull!" his mother said. "You didn't go in debt for this."

"Why not? I'm getting rich, I tell you. Five years from now I can walk into an auto dealer, any dealer—Cadillac—and slap cold cash on the counter and say, 'I'll take three. Or on second thought, make that four.' "

"But not now," said Pearl. "Not yet. You know how I feel about buying on time."

"Time is what I deal with," Cody said. He laughed, and shot through an amber light. "What could be more fitting? Ten years more, you'll be riding in a limousine."

"Why would I want to do that?"

"And Ezra can go to Princeton, if he likes. And I can buy Jenny a clinic all her own. I can pay for her to specialize in every field, one by one."

Now was the moment for Jenny to mention Harley, but she watched the scenery and said nothing.

At Scarlatti's, they were shown to a table in the corner, at the end of the long, brocade-draped dining room. It was early evening, not yet dark. The restaurant was almost empty. Jenny wondered where Mrs. Scarlatti was. She started to ask about her, but Ezra was too busy overseeing their meal. He had ordered ahead, evidently, and now wanted it known that four would be eating instead of three. "We have my sister with us too. It's going to be a real family dinner." The waiter, who seemed fond of Ezra, nodded and went to the kitchen.

Ezra sat back and smiled at the others. Pearl was polishing a fork with her napkin. Cody was still talking about money. "I plan to buy a place in Baltimore County," he said, "in the not-too-distant future. There's no particular reason that I should be based in New York. I always did want land, that rolling Maryland farmland. I might raise horses."

"Horses! Oh, Cody, really, that's just not our style," Pearl said. "What would you want with horses?"

"Mother," Cody said, "anything's our style. Don't you see? There's no limit. Mother, do you know who called for my services last week? The Tanner Corporation."

Pearl set her fork down. Jenny tried to remember where she had heard that name before. It rang just the dimmest bell; it was like some lowly household object that you never look at, and only notice when you return after years of absence. "Tanner?" she asked Cody. "What's that?"

"It's where our father worked."

"Oh, yes."

"Where he still may, for all I know. But, Jenny, you should have seen it. Such a nickel-and-dime operation . . . I mean, not small, good Lord, with that mess of branch offices overlapping and conflicting, but so . . . tacky. Really so easily encompassed. And I was thinking: imagine, just like that, I have them in my power. The Tanner Corporation! The great, almighty Tanner Corporation. That afternoon, I went out and ordered my Pontiac."

"There was never," Pearl said, "the slightest thing tacky about the Tanner Corporation."

Their appetizers arrived on chilled plates, along with a slender, pale green bottle of wine. The waiter poured a sip for Ezra, who tasted it as if it were important. "Good," he said. (It was strange to see him in a position of command.) "Cody? Try this wine."

"Never," said Pearl, "was there anything nickel-and-dime, in the smallest, tiniest way, ever in this world, about the Tanner Corporation."

"Oh, Mother, face it," Cody told her. "It's a trash heap. I'm going to strip it to the bones."

You would think he was speaking of something alive—an

animal, some creature that would suffer. Pearl must have thought so, too. She said, "Cody, why must you act toward me in this manner?"

"I'm not acting in any manner."

"Have I ever wronged you, knowingly? Ever done you harm?"

"Please," Ezra said. "Mother? Cody? It's a family dinner! Jenny? Let's have a toast."

Jenny hastily raised her glass. "A toast," she said.

"Mother? A toast."

Pearl's eyes went reluctantly to Ezra's face. "Oh," she said, after a pause. "Thank you, dear, but wine in all this heat would settle on my stomach like a rock."

"It's a toast to *me*, Mother. To my future. A toast," said Ezra, "to the new full partner of Scarlatti's Restaurant."

"Partner? Who would that be?"

"Me, Mother."

Then the double doors to the kitchen opened and in came Mrs. Scarlatti, glamorous as ever, striding on rangy, loose-strung legs and tossing back her asymmetrical hairdo. She must have been waiting for her cue—eavesdropping, in fact. "So!" she said, setting a hand on Ezra's shoulder. "What do you think of my boy here?"

"I don't understand," said Pearl.

"Well, you know he's been my right hand for so long, ever since my son died, really *better* than my son, if the truth be told; poor Billy never cared all that much for the restaurant business . . ."

Ezra was rising, as if something momentous were about to happen. While Mrs. Scarlatti went on speaking in her rasping, used-up voice—telling his own mother what an angel Ezra was, a sweetie, so gifted, such a respect for food, for decent food served decently, such a "divine" (she said) instinct for seasonings—he pulled his leather billfold from his pocket. He peered into it, looked anxious for a moment, and then said, "Ah!" and held up a ragged dollar bill. "Mrs. Scarlatti," he said, "with this dollar I hereby purchase a partnership in Scarlatti's Restaurant."

"It's yours, dear heart," said Mrs. Scarlatti, taking the money.
"What's going on here?" Pearl asked.
"We signed the papers in my lawyer's office yesterday afternoon," Mrs. Scarlatti said. "Well, it makes good sense, doesn't it? Who would I leave this damn place to when I kick off—my chihuahua? Ezra knows it inside out by now. Ezra, pour me a glass of wine."

"But I thought you were going to college," Pearl told Ezra.
"I was?"
"I thought you were planning to be a teacher! Maybe a professor. I don't understand what's happened. Oh, I know it's none of my affair. I've never been the type to meddle. Only let me tell you this: it's going to look very, very peculiar to people who don't have all the facts. Accepting such a gift! And from a woman, to boot! It's a favor; partnerships don't cost a dollar; you'll be beholden all your life. Ezra, we Tulls depend on ourselves, only on each other. We don't look to the rest of the world for any help whatsoever. How could you lend yourself to this?"

"Mother, I like making meals for people," Ezra said.
"He's a marvel," said Mrs. Scarlatti.
"But the obligation!"
Cody said, "Let him be, Mother."
She swung on him so quickly, it was more like pouncing. "I know you're enjoying this," she said.
"It's his life."
"What do you care about his life? You only want to see us break up, dissolve in the outside world."
"Please," said Ezra.
But Pearl rose and marched toward the door. "You haven't eaten!" Ezra cried. She didn't stop. In her straight-backed posture, Jenny saw the first signs of her mother's old age—her stringy tendons and breakable bones. "Oh, dear," Ezra said, "I wanted this to be such a good meal." He tore off after Pearl. Scattered diners raised their heads, thought a moment, and went back to eating.

That left Cody, Jenny, and Mrs. Scarlatti. Mrs. Scarlatti didn't seem particularly distressed. "Mothers," she said mildly. She tucked the dollar bill inside her black linen bosom.

Cody said, "Well? Does that wrap it up? Because I should have been in Delaware an hour ago. Can I give you a lift, Jenny?"

"I guess I'll walk," Jenny said.

The last she saw of Mrs. Scarlatti, she was standing there all alone, surveying the untouched appetizers with an amused expression on her face.

After Cody had driven off, Jenny walked slowly toward home. She didn't see Pearl or Ezra anywhere ahead of her. It was twilight—a sticky evening, smelling of hot tires. As she floated past shops in her sundress, she began to feel like someone's romantic vision of a young girl. She tried out a daydream of Harley Baines, but it didn't work. What did Jenny know about marriage? Why would she even want to get married? She was only a child; she would always be a child. Her wedding plans seemed makeshift and contrived—a charade. She felt foolish. She tried to remember Harley's kiss but it had vanished altogether, and Harley himself was no more real to her than a little paper man in a mail-order catalogue.

In the candy store, two children argued while their mother pressed a hand to her forehead. Next came the pharmacy and then the fortune-teller's—a smudged plate glass window with MRS. EMMA PARKINS—READINGS AND ADVICE arched in curly gold letters that were flaking around the edges. Handmade signs sat propped on the sill like afterthoughts: STRICTEST CONFIDENCE and NO PAYMENT IF NOT FULLY SATISFIED. In the light from a dusty globe lamp, Mrs. Parkins herself paced the room—a fat, drab old woman with a cardboard fan on a Popsicle stick.

Jenny reached the corner, paused, and then turned. She went back to the fortune-teller's door. Should she knock, or just walk on in? She tried the handle. The door swung open and a little bell above it tinkled. Mrs. Parkins lowered her fan and said, "Do tell! A customer."

Jenny hugged her purse to her chest.

"Keeping warm?" Mrs. Parkins asked her.

"Yes," said Jenny. She thought she smelled cough syrup, the bitter, dark, cherry-flavored kind.

"Why don't you have a seat," Mrs. Parkins said.

There were two armchairs, puffy, facing each other across the little round table that held the lamp. Jenny sat in the chair nearest the door. Mrs. Parkins plucked her dress from the backs of her thighs and settled down with a groan, still gripping her fan. "Radio says the weather ought to break tomorrow," she said, "but I don't know if I can last that long. Seems like every year, the heat just hits me harder."

Yet her hand, when she reached for Jenny's, was cool and dry, with tough little pads at the fingertips. She fanned herself while she studied Jenny's palm. It made her work look commonplace. "Long life, good career line . . ." she murmured, as if riffling through a file. Jenny relaxed.

"I suppose there's something special you want to know about," Mrs. Parkins said.

"Oh, well . . ."

"No sense beating around the bush."

Jenny said, "Should I get . . . well . . . married?"

"Married," said Mrs. Parkins.

"I mean, I could. I have this chance. I've been asked."

Mrs. Parkins went on scrutinizing Jenny's hand. Then she beckoned for the other one, which she barely glanced at. Then she sat back and fanned herself some more, gazing at the ceiling.

"Married," she said finally. "Well, I tell you. You could, or you could not. If you don't, you *will* get other offers. Surely. But here is my advice: you go ahead and do it."

"What, get married?"

"If you don't, see," Mrs. Parkins said, "you'll run into a lot of heartbreak. Lot of trouble in your romantic life. From various different people. What I mean to say," she said, "if you don't go on and get married, you'll be destroyed by love."

"Oh," Jenny said.

"That'll be two dollars, please."

Searching through her purse, Jenny had an interesting thought.

By Ezra's rate of exchange, she could have bought a couple of restaurants for the same amount of money.

She married Harley late in August, in the little Baptist church that the Tulls had attended off and on. Cody gave Jenny away and Ezra was the usher. The guests he ushered in were: Pearl, Mr. and Mrs. Baines, and an aunt on Harley's mother's side. Jenny wore a white eyelet dress and sandals. Harley wore a black suit, white button-down shirt, and snub-nosed, dull black shoes. Jenny looked down at those shoes all during the ceremony. They reminded her of licorice jellybeans.

Pearl did not shed a tear, because, she said, she was so glad things had worked out this way, even though certain people might have informed her sooner. It was a relief to see your daughter handed over safely, she said—a burden off. Mrs. Baines cried steadily, but that was the kind of woman she was. She told Jenny after the wedding that it certainly didn't mean she had anything against the marriage.

Then Harley and Jenny took a train to Paulham University, where they'd rented a small apartment. They had no furniture yet and spent their wedding night on the floor. Jenny was worried about Harley's inexperience. She was certain he'd always been above such things as sex; he wouldn't know what to do, and neither would she, and they would end up failing at something the rest of the world managed without a thought. But actually, Harley knew very well what to do. She suspected he'd researched it. She had an image of Harley at a library desk, comparing the theories of experts, industriously making notes in the proper outline form.

III

"On old Olympus's torrid top," Jenny told the scenery rushing past her window, "a Finn and German picked some hops."

This was supposed to remind her of the cranial nerves: olfactory, optic, oculomotor . . . She frowned and checked her textbook. It was 1958—the start of the first weekend in May, but not a weekend she could spare. She was paying a visit to Baltimore when she should have been holed up in Paulham, studying. She had telephoned her mother long-distance. "Could you ask Ezra to meet my train?"

"I thought you had so much work to do."

"I can work down there just as well."

"Are you bringing Harley?"

"No."

"Is anything wrong?"

"Of course not."

"I don't like the sound of this, young lady."

On the telephone, Pearl's voice was dim and staticky, easily dealt with. Jenny had said, "Oh, Mother, really." But now the train was drawing into Baltimore, and the sight of factory smokestacks, soot-blackened bricks, and billboards peeling in the rain—a landscape she associated with home—made her feel less sure of herself. She hoped that Ezra would meet her alone. She rubbed a clean spot on the window and stared out at acres of railroad track, then at the first metal posts flying by, then at slower posts, better defined, and a dark flight of stairs. The train shrieked and jerked to a stop. Jenny closed her book. She stood up, edged past a sleeping woman, and took a small suitcase from the rack overhead.

This station always seemed to be under some kind of construction, she thought. When she arrived at the top of the stairs, she heard the whine of a power tool—an electric drill or saw. The sound was almost lost beneath the high ceiling. Ezra stood waiting, smiling at her, with his hands in his windbreaker pockets. "How was your trip?" he asked.

"Fine."

He took her suitcase. "Harley all right?"

"Oh, yes."

They threaded through a sparse crowd of people in raincoats. "Mother's still at work," Ezra said, "but she ought to be home by the time we get there. And I've put in a call to Cody. I thought we might all have dinner at the restaurant tomorrow night; he's supposed to be passing through."

"How *is* the restaurant?"

Ezra looked unhappy. He guided Jenny through the door, into a dripping mist that felt cool on her skin. "She's not at all well," he said.

Jenny wondered why he called the restaurant "she," as if it were a ship. But then he said, "The treatments are making her worse. She can't keep anything down," and she understood that he must mean Mrs. Scarlatti. Last fall, Mrs. Scarlatti had been hospitalized for a cancer operation—her second, though up until then no one had known of the first. Ezra had taken it very hard. Mournfully trudging down a row of taxis, he said, "She hardly ever complains, but I know she's suffering."

"Are you running the restaurant alone, then?"

"Oh, yes, I've been doing that since November. Everything: the hiring and the firing, bringing in new help as people quit. A restaurant is not all food, you know. Sometimes it seems that food is the least of it. I feel the place is falling apart on me, but Mrs. Scarlatti says not to worry. It always looks like that, she says. Life is a continual shoring up, she says, against one thing and another just eroding and crumbling away. I'm beginning to think she's right."

They had reached his car, a dented gray Chevy. He opened the door for her and heaved her suitcase into the rear, which was already a chaos of *Restaurateur's Weeklys*, soiled clothing, and some kind of tongs or skewers in a Kitchen Korner shopping bag. "Sorry about the mess," he said when he'd slid behind the wheel. He started the engine and backed out of his parking slot. "Have you learned to drive yet?"

"Yes, Harley taught me. Now I drive him everywhere; he likes to be free to think."

They were on Charles Street. The rain was so fine that Ezra hadn't bothered to turn on his windshield wipers, and the glass began to film over. Jenny peered ahead. "Can you see?" she asked Ezra.

He nodded.

"First he wants me to drive," she said, "and then he criticizes every last little thing about how I do it. He's so clever; you don't know how far his cleverness can extend. I mean, it's not just math or genetics he knows all about but the most efficient temperature for cooking pot roast, the best way to organize my kitchen—everything, all charted out in his mind. When I'm driving he says, 'Now, Jennifer, you know full well that three blocks from here is that transit stop where you have to veer left, so what are you doing in the right-hand lane? You ought to plan ahead more,' he says. 'Three blocks!' I say. 'Good grief! I'll get to it when I get to it,' and he says, 'That's exactly what your trouble is, Jenny.' 'Between here and that transit stop,' I tell him, 'anything might happen,' and he says, 'Not really. No, not really. In all three intersections there's a left-turn lane, as you'll recall, so you wouldn't have to wait for . . .' Nothing is unplanned, for Harley. You can see the numbered pages leafing over inside his head. There's never a single mistake."

"Well," Ezra said, "I guess it's like a whole different outlook, being a genius."

"It's not as if I hadn't been warned," said Jenny, "but I didn't realize it was a warning. I was too young to read the signals. I thought he was only like me, you know—a *careful* person; I always was careful, but now compared to Harley I don't seem careful at all. I should have guessed when I went to meet his parents before the wedding, and all the books in his room were arranged by height and blocks of color. Alphabetized I could have understood; or separated by subject matter. But this arbitrary, fixed pattern of things, a foot of red, a foot of black, no hardbacks mingling with the paperbacks . . . it's worse than Mother's bureau drawers. It's out of the frying pan, into the fire! The first time Harley kissed me, he had to brush off this bedspread beforehand that we'd been sitting on. Wouldn't you think that might have told me something? Every night now before he goes to sleep he perches on the edge of the bed and brushes off the soles of his feet. These bare white feet, untouched . . . what could have dirtied them? He wears shoes every waking moment and slippers if he takes one step in the night. But no,

there he sits, so methodical, so exact, everything in its proper
sequence, brush-brush . . . , sometimes I think I'll hit him. I'm
fascinated, I stand there watching him brush his left foot first,
his right foot second, not letting either touch the floor once
he's finished with it, and I think, 'I'm going to bash your head
in for you, Harley.' "

Ezra cleared his throat. "It's the adjustment," he said. "Yes,
that's it: adjustment. The first year of marriage. I'm sure that's
all it is."

"Well, maybe so," Jenny said.

She wished she hadn't talked so much.

When they reached home, therefore—where their mother
had just arrived herself—Jenny said nothing at all about Harley.
(Pearl thought Harley was wonderful, admirable—maybe not
so easy to hold a conversation with but the perfect person to
marry her daughter.) "Now tell me," Pearl said when she'd
kissed her. "How come you didn't bring that husband of yours?
You haven't had some silly kind of quarrel."

"No, no. It's only my work. The strain of work," Jenny
said. "I wanted to come and rest, and Harley couldn't leave his
lab."

It was true that the house seemed restful, suddenly. After
Ezra left for Scarlatti's, her mother led Jenny to the kitchen
and brewed her a cup of tea. One thing Pearl never skimped
on was tea. She moved around the room, heating the speckled
brown teapot, humming some old, wavery hymn. The damp
weather had frizzed her hair into little corkscrews and the steam
had turned her cheeks pink; she looked almost pretty. (What
kind of a marriage had she had? Something must have gone
terribly wrong with it, but Jenny couldn't help imagining it as
perfect, all of a piece, her parents permanently joined. That her
father had left was only a fluke—some misunderstanding still
not cleared up.)

"I thought we'd have a very light supper," said her mother.
"Maybe a salad or something."

"That would be fine," Jenny said.

"Something plain and simple."

Plain and simple was just what Jenny needed. She loosened; she was safe at last, in the only place where people knew exactly who she was and loved her anyhow.

So it was all the odder that after supper, touring the house, she felt a flash of pity for Ezra when she looked in upon his room. Still here! she thought, seeing his boyish tartan blanket on the bed, his worn recorder on the windowsill, the stamped metal tray on his bureau heaped with ancient, green-tinged pennies. How can he bear it? she wondered, and she went back down the stairs, shaking her head and marveling.

This was what Jenny had brought with her: a change of clothes, her anatomy textbook, Harley's letter proposing marriage, and his photo in a sterling silver frame. Unpacking, she set the photo firmly on her desk and examined it. She had brought it not for sentimental reasons but because she planned to think Harley over, to sum him up, and she didn't want distance to alter her judgment. She foresaw that she might be so misguided as to miss him. This picture would remind her not to. He was a stiff and stodgy man; you could see it in the thickened line of his jaw and in the opaque, bespectacled gaze he directed at the camera. He disapproved of her reasoning methods—too rushed and haphazard, he said. He didn't like her chattery friends. He thought her clothes lacked style. He criticized her table manners. "Twenty-five chews per bite," he would tell her. "That's my advice. Not only is it more healthful, but you'll find yourself not eating so much." He was obsessed by the fear that she might grow fat. Since Jenny could count every one of her ribs, she wondered if he had a kind of mad spot—if he were insane not through and through, but in one isolated area. It was the uncontrollability he feared, perhaps: he would not like to see Jenny ballooning, the pounds collecting unrestrained; he wouldn't like to see her *getting out of hand*. That must be it. But she did begin to wonder if she might be gaining weight. She started stepping on the scales every morning. She stood in front of the full-length mirror, sucking in her stomach. Was it possible her hips were widening? Out in public, though, she noticed that the fleshy women were the ones who caught Harley's eye—the burgeoning and dimpled ones, blondes, a little blowzy. It was a mystery, really.

Jenny's grades were not very good. She wasn't failing, or anything like that; but neither was she making A's, and her lab work was often slipshod. Sometimes it seemed to her that she'd been hollow, all these years, and was finally caving in on herself. They'd found her out: at heart, there was nothing to her.

Packing for this trip (which Harley saw as a waste of time and money), she had strode across the bedroom to where his photo sat on the bureau. Harley was standing in front of it. "Move, please," she told him. He looked offended and stepped aside. Then, when he saw what she wanted, his face had . . . well, flown open, you might say. His glare had softened, his lips had parted to speak. He was touched. And *she* was touched that *he* was touched. Nothing was ever simple; there were always these complications. But what he said was, "I don't understand you. Your mother has frightened and mistreated you all your life, and now you want to visit her for no apparent reason."

Probably what he was saying was "Please don't go."

You had to be a trained decoder to read the man.

She shook open his letter of proposal. See how he had dated it: *18 July, 1957*—a form that struck her as pretentious, unless of course he happened to be English. She wondered how she could have overlooked the pompous language, the *American courtship* (as if his superior intelligence placed him on a whole separate continent), and most of all, the letter itself, the very fact that it was written, advancing the project of marriage like a corporation merger.

Well, she *had* overlooked it. She'd chosen not to see. She knew she had acted deviously in this whole business—making up her mind to win him, marrying him for practical reasons. She had calculated, was what it was. But she felt the punishment was greater than the crime. It wasn't such a terrible crime. She'd had no idea (would any unmarried person?) what a serious business she was playing with, how long it lasts, how deep it goes. And now look: the joke was on her. Having got what she was after, she found it was she who'd been got. Talk about calculating! He was going to run her life, arrange it perfectly by height and color. He was going to sit in the passenger seat with that censorious expression on his face and dictate every turn she took, and every shift of gears.

Because she knew it would make Ezra happy, she went to visit the restaurant late in the evening. The rain had stopped, but there was still a mist. She felt she was walking underwater, in one of those dreams where a person can breathe as easily as on land. There were only a few other people out—all of them hurrying, locked in themselves, shrouded by raincoats and plastic scarves. Traffic swished by; reflections of the headlights wavered on the streets.

The restaurant's kitchen seemed overcrowded; it was a miracle that an acceptable plate of food could emerge from it. Ezra stood at the stove, supervising the skimming of some broth or soup. A young girl lifted ladles full of steaming liquid and emptied them into a bowl. "When you're done—" Ezra was saying, and then he said, "Why, hello, Jenny," and came to the door where she waited. Over his jeans he wore a long white apron; he looked like one of the cooks. He took her around to meet the others; sweaty men chopping or straining or stirring. "This is my sister, Jenny," he would say, but then he'd get sidetracked by some detail and stand there discussing food. "Can I offer you something to eat?" he asked finally.

"No, I had supper at home."

"Or maybe a drink from the bar?"

"No, thanks."

"This is our headwaiter, Oakes. And this is Josiah Payson; you remember him."

She looked up and up, into Josiah's face. He was all in white, spotless (how had they found a uniform to fit him?), but his hair still bristled wildly. And it was no easier than ever to see where he was directing his gaze. Not at her; that was certain.

He was avoiding her. He seemed completely blind to the sight of her.

"When the Boyces come," Ezra was saying to Oakes, "tell them we have the cream of mussel soup. There's only enough for the two of them; it's waiting on the back burner."

"How are you, Josiah?" Jenny asked.

"Oh, not bad."

"So you work here now."

"I'm the salad chef. Mostly, I cut things up."

His spidery hands twisted in front of him. The crease in his forehead seemed deeper than ever.

"I've thought of you often," Jenny said.

She didn't mean it, at first. But then she understood, with a rush to her head that was something like illness, that she spoke the truth: she had been thinking of him all these years without knowing it. It seemed he had never once left her mind. Even Harley, she saw, was just a reverse kind of Josiah, a Josiah turned inside out: equally alien, black-and-white, incomprehensible to anyone but Jenny.

"Is your mother well?" she asked him.

"She died."

"Died!"

"A long time ago. She went out shopping and she died. I live in my house all alone now."

"I'm sorry," Jenny said.

But still he wouldn't meet her eyes.

Ezra turned from Oakes and asked, "Are you sure I can't get you a snack, Jenny?"

"I have to leave," she told him.

Going home, she wondered why the walk seemed so long. Her feet felt unusually heavy, and there was some old, rusty pain deep inside her chest.

The ash grove, how graceful, Ezra's recorder piped out, *how sweetly 'tis singing* . . . Waking slowly, still webbed in bits of dreams, Jenny found it strange that a pearwood recorder should put forth plums—perfectly round, pure, plummy notes arriving in a spill on her bed. She sat up and thought for a moment. Then she pushed her blankets back and reached for her clothes.

Ezra was playing "Le Godiveau de Poisson" when she left the house.

Down this street, and then that one, and then another that turned out to be a mistake. She had to retrace her path. It was going to be a beautiful day. The sidewalks were still wet, but the sun was rising in a pearly pink sky above the chimneys. She dug her hands in her coat pockets. She met an old man walking a poodle, but no one else, and even he passed soundlessly and vanished.

When she reached the street she wanted, nothing looked familiar and she had to take the alley. She could only find the house from the rear. She recognized that makeshift gray addition behind the kitchen, and the buckling steps that gave beneath her feet, and the wooden door with most of its paint worn off. She looked for a bell to ring but there wasn't one; she had to knock. There was the scraping of furniture somewhere inside the house—chair legs pushing back. Josiah, when he came, was so tall that he darkened the window she peered through.

He opened the door. "Jenny?" he said.

"Hello, Josiah."

He looked around him, as if supposing she had come to see someone else. She noticed his breakfast on the kitchen table: a slice of white bread spread with peanut butter. In the scuffed linoleum and the sink full of dirty dishes, in his tattered jeans and raveling brown sweater, she read neglect and hopelessness. She pulled her coat tighter around her.

"What are you, what are you here for?" he asked.

"I did everything wrong," she told him.

"What are you talking about?"

"You must feel I'm just like the others! Just like the ones you want to escape from, off in the woods with your sleeping bag."

"Oh, no, Jenny," he said. "I would never believe you're like that."

"You wouldn't?"

"Nobody would; you're too pretty."

"But I mean—" she said.

She set a hand on his sleeve. He didn't pull away. Then she stepped closer and slipped her arms around him. She could feel, even through her coat, how thin and bony his rib cage was, and how he warmed his skimpy sweater. She laid her ear against his chest, and he slowly, hesitantly raised his hands to her shoulders. "I should have gone on kissing you," she said. "I should have told my mother, 'Go away. Leave us alone.' I should have stood up for you and not been such a coward."

"No, no," she heard him say. "I don't think about it. I don't think about it."

She drew back and looked up at him.

"I don't talk about it," he said.

"Josiah," she said, "won't you at least tell me it's all right now?"

"Sure," he said. "It's all right, Jenny."

After that, there was really nothing else to discuss. She stood on tiptoe to kiss him goodbye, and she thought he looked directly at her when he smiled and let her go.

"To everybody's good health," Cody said, raising his glass. "To Ezra's food. To Scarlatti's Restaurant."

"To a happy family dinner," Ezra said.

"Oh, well, that too, if you like."

They all drank, even Pearl—or maybe the little sip she took was only make-believe. She was wearing her netted hat and a beige tailored suit so new that it failed to sit back when she did. Jenny was in an ordinary skirt and blouse, but still she felt dressed up. She felt wonderful, in fact—perfectly untroubled. She kept beaming at the others, pleased to have them around her.

But really, were they all here? In Jenny's new mood, her family seemed too small. These three young people and this shrunken mother, she thought, were not enough to sustain the occasion. They could have used several more members—a family clown, for instance; and a genuine black sheep, blacker than Cody; and maybe one of those managerial older sisters who holds a group together by force. As things were, it was Ezra who had to hold them together. He wasn't doing a very good job. He was too absorbed in the food. Right now he was conferring with the waiter, gesturing toward the soup, which had arrived a touch too cool, he said—though to Jenny it seemed fine. And now Pearl was collecting her purse and sliding back her chair. "Powder room," she mouthed to Jenny. Ezra would be all the more upset, once he noticed she'd gone. He liked the family in a group, a cluster, and he hated Pearl's habit of constantly "freshening up" in a restaurant, just as he hated for Cody to smoke his slim cigars between courses. "I wish just once," he was always saying, "we could get through a meal from start to finish," and he would say it again as soon as he discovered Pearl was missing. But now he was telling the waiter, "If Andrew would keep the china hot—"

"He mostly does, I swear it, but the warming oven's broke."

"What's your opinion?" Cody whispered, setting his face close to Jenny's. "Has Ezra ever slept with Mrs. Scarlatti? Or has he not."

Jenny's mouth dropped open.

"Well?" he asked.

"Cody Tull!"

"Don't tell me it hasn't occurred to you. A lonely rich widow, or whatever she is; nice-looking boy with no prospects . . ."

"That's disgusting," Jenny told him.

"Not at all," Cody said blandly, sitting back. He had a way of surveying people from under half-lowered lids which made him look tolerant and worldly. "There's nothing wrong," he said, "with taking advantage of your luck. And you have to admit Ezra's lucky; *born* lucky. Have you ever noticed what happens when I bring around my girlfriends? They fall all over him. They have ever since we were kids. What do they see in him, anyway? How does he do it? *Is* it luck? You're a woman; what's his secret?"

"Honestly, Cody," Jenny said, "I wish you'd grow out of this."

Ezra finished his conversation with the waiter. "Where's Mother?" he asked. "I turn my back one second and she disappears."

"Powder room," said Cody, lighting a cigar.

"Oh, why does she always do that? More soup is coming, fresh off the stove, piping hot this time."

"Are you having it brought in by barefoot runners?" Cody asked.

Jenny said, "Don't worry, Ezra. I'll go call her."

She made her way between the tables, toward a corridor with an EXIT sign over the archway. But just before the ladies' room, in front of a swinging, leather-covered door, she caught sight of Josiah. He had his white uniform on and was carrying an aqua plastic dishpan full of chicory leaves. "Josiah," she said.

He stopped short and his face lit up. "Hi, Jenny," he said.

They stood smiling at each other, not speaking. She reached out to touch his wrist.

"Oh, no!" her mother cried.

Jenny snatched her hand back and spun around.

"Oh, Jenny. Oh, my God," Pearl said. Her eyes were no longer gray; they were black, and she gripped her shiny black purse. "Well, I understand it all now," she said.

"No, wait," Jenny said. Her heart was beating so fast, it seemed she was vibrating where she stood.

"Visiting for no apparent reason," said Pearl, "and slipping away this morning to meet him like a tramp, some cheap little tramp—"

"Mother, you've got it wrong!" Jenny told her. "It's nothing, don't you see?" She felt she had run out of breath. Gasping for air, she gestured toward Josiah, who merely stood there with his mouth agape. "He just . . . we just met in the hall and . . . it's not that way at all, he's *nothing* to me, don't you see?"

But she had to say this to Pearl's back, hurrying after her through the dining room. Pearl reached their table and said, "Ezra, I cannot stay here."

Ezra stood up. "Mother?"

"I simply cannot," she said. She gathered up her coat and walked away.

"But what happened?" Ezra asked, turning to Jenny. "What's bothering her?"

Cody said, "That lukewarm soup, no doubt," and he rocked back comfortably in his chair with a cigar between his teeth.

"I wish just once," Ezra said, "we could eat a meal from start to finish."

"I don't feel well," Jenny told him.

In fact, her lips were numb. It was a symptom she seemed to remember from before, from some long-forgotten moment, or maybe from a nightmare.

She left her coat behind, and she rushed through the dining room and out to the street. At first, she thought her mother had disappeared. Then she found her, half a block ahead—a militant figure walking briskly. Oh, what if she wouldn't even turn around? Or worse, would turn and lash out, slap, snap, her clawed pearl ring, her knowing face . . . But Jenny ran to catch up with her, anyway. "Mother," she said.

In the light from the liquor store window, she saw her mother reassemble her expression—take on a cool, unperturbed look.

"You've got it all wrong," Jenny told her. "I'm not a tramp! I'm not cheap! Mother, listen to me."

"It doesn't matter," Pearl said politely.

"Of course it matters!"

"You're over twenty-one. If you don't know good from bad by now, there's nothing more I can do about it."

"I felt sorry for him," Jenny said.

They crossed a street and started up the next block.

"He told me his mother had died," Jenny said.

They veered around a gang of teen-aged boys.

"She was all he had—his father's dead too. She was the center of his life."

"Well," said Pearl, "I suppose it can't have been easy for her."

"I don't know how he's going to manage now she's gone."

"I believe I saw her in the grocery once," said Pearl. "A brown-haired woman?"

"Plumpish, sort of."

"Full in the face?"

"Like a wood thrush," Jenny said.

"Oh, Jenny," said her mother, and she gave a little laugh. "The things you come up with, sometimes!"

They passed the candy store, and then the pharmacy. Jenny and her mother fell into step. They passed the fortune-teller's window. The same dusty lamp glowed on the table. Jenny, looking in, thought that Mrs. Parkins had not been much of a prophet. Why, she had even had to listen to the radio for tomorrow's weather! And she should have guessed from the very first instant, from the briefest, most cursory glance, that Jenny was not capable of being destroyed by love.

4

Heart Rumors

The first few times that Mrs. Scarlatti stayed in the hospital, Ezra had no trouble getting in to visit her. But the last time was harder. "Relative?" the nurse would ask.

"No, ah, I'm her business partner."

"Sorry, relatives only."

"But she doesn't have any relatives. I'm all she's got. See, she and I own this restaurant together."

"And what's that in the jar?"

"Her soup."

"Soup," said the nurse.

"I make this soup she likes."

"Mrs. Scarlatti isn't keeping things down."

"I know that, but I wanted to give her something."

This would earn him a slantwise glance, before he was led brusquely into Mrs. Scarlatti's room.

In the past, she had chosen to stay in a ward. (She was an extremely social woman.) She'd sit up straight in her dramatic black robe, a batik scarf hiding her hair, and "Sweetie!" she'd say as he entered. For a moment the other women would grow all sly and alert, till they realized how young he was—way too young for Mrs. Scarlatti. But now she had a private room, and the most she could do when he arrived was open her eyes and then wearily close them. He wasn't even sure that he was welcome any more.

He knew that after he left, someone would discard his soup. But this was his special gizzard soup that she had always loved. There were twenty cloves of garlic in it. Mrs. Scarlatti used to claim it settled her stomach, soothed her nerves—changed her whole perception of the day, she said. (However, it wasn't on the restaurant's menu because it was a bit "hearty"—her word— and Scarlatti's Restaurant was very fine and formal. This hurt Ezra's feelings, a little.) When she was well enough to be home, he had often brewed single portions in the restaurant kitchen and carried them upstairs to her apartment. Even in the hospital, those first few times, she could manage a small-sized bowl of it. But now she was beyond that. He only brought the soup out of helplessness; he would have preferred to kneel by her bed and rest his head on her sheets, to take her hands in his and tell her, "Mrs. Scarlatti, come back." But she was such a no-nonsense woman; she would have looked shocked. All he could do was offer this soup.

He sat in a corner of the room in a green vinyl chair with steel arms. It was October and the steam heat had come on; the air felt sharp and dry. Mrs. Scarlatti's bed was cranked upward slightly to help her breathe. From time to time, without opening her eyes, she said, "Oh, God." Then Ezra would ask, "What? What is it?" and she would sigh. (Or maybe that was the radiator.) Ezra never brought anything to read, and he never made conversation with the nurses who squeaked in and out on their rubber soles. He only sat, looking down at his pale, oversized hands, which lay loosely on his knees.

Previously, he had put on weight. He'd been nowhere near fat, but he'd softened and spread in that mild way that fair-haired men often do. Now the weight fell off. Like Mrs. Scarlatti, he was having trouble keeping things down. His large, floppy clothes covered a large, floppy frame that seemed oddly two-dimensional. Wide in front and wide behind, he was flat as paper when viewed from the side. His hair fell forward in a sheaf, like wheat. He didn't bother pushing it back.

He and Mrs. Scarlatti had been through a lot together, he would have said, if asked—but what, exactly? She had had a bad husband (a matter of luck, she made it seem, like a bad bottle of wine) and ditched him; she had lost her only son, Ezra's age, during the Korean War. But both these events she had suffered alone, before her partnership with Ezra began. And Ezra himself: well, he had not actually been through anything yet. He was twenty-five years old and still without wife or children, still living at home with his mother. What he and Mrs. Scarlatti had survived, it appeared, was year after year of standing still. Her life that had slid off somewhere in the past, his that kept delaying its arrival—they'd combined, they held each other up in empty space. Ezra was grateful to Mrs. Scarlatti for rescuing him from an aimless, careerless existence and teaching him all she knew; but more than that, for the fact that she depended on him. If not for her, whom would he have? His brother and sister were out in the world; he loved his mother dearly but there was something overemotional about her that kept him eternally wary. By other people's standards, even he and Mrs. Scarlatti would not have seemed particularly close. He always called her "Mrs. Scarlatti." She called Ezra her boy, her angel, but was otherwise remarkably distant, and asked no questions at all about his life outside the restaurant.

He knew the restaurant would be fully his when she died. She had told him so, just before this last hospital stay. "I don't want it," he had said. She was silent. She must have understood that it was only his manner of speaking. Of course he didn't *want* it, in the sense of coveting it (he never thought much about money), but what would he do otherwise? Anyway, she had no one else to leave it to. She lifted a hand and let it drop. They didn't mention the subject again.

Once, Ezra persuaded his mother to come and visit too. He liked for the various people in his life to get along, although he knew that would be difficult in his mother's case. She spoke of Mrs. Scarlatti distrustfully, even jealously. "What you see in such a person I can't imagine. She's downright . . . tough, is what she is, in spite of her high-fashion clothes. It looks like her face is not trying. Know what I mean? Like she can't be bothered putting out the effort. Not a bit of lipstick, and those crayony black lines around her eyes . . . and she hardly ever smiles at people."

But now that Mrs. Scarlatti was so sick, his mother kept her thoughts to herself. She dressed carefully for her visit and wore her netted hat, which made Ezra happy. He associated that hat with important family occasions. He was pleased that she'd chosen her Sunday black coat, even though it wasn't as warm as her everyday maroon.

In the hospital, she told Mrs. Scarlatti, "Why, you look the picture of health! No one would ever guess."

This was not true. But it was nice of her to say it.

"After I die," Mrs. Scarlatti said in her grainy voice, "Ezra must move to my apartment."

His mother said, "Now, let's have none of that silly talk."

"Which is silly?" Mrs. Scarlatti asked, but then she was over-taken by exhaustion, and she closed her eyes. Ezra's mother misunderstood. She must have thought she'd asked *what* was silly, a rhetorical question, and she blithely smoothed her skirt around her and said, "Total foolishness, I never heard such rot." Only Ezra grasped Mrs. Scarlatti's meaning. Which was silly, she was asking—her dying, or Ezra's moving? But he didn't bother explaining that to his mother.

Another time, he got special permission from the nurses' office to bring a few men from the restaurant—Todd Duckett, Josiah Payson, and Raymond the sauce maker. He could tell that Mrs. Scarlatti was glad to see them, although it was an awkward visit. The men stood around the outer edges of the room and cleared their throats repeatedly and would not take seats. "Well?" said Mrs. Scarlatti. "Are you still buying every-thing fresh?" From the inappropriateness of the question (none of them was remotely involved with the purchasing), Ezra realized how out of touch she had grown. But these people, too, were tactful. Todd Duckett gave a mumbled cough and then said, "Yes, ma'am, just how you would've liked it."

"I'm tired now," Mrs. Scarlatti said.

Down the hall lay an emaciated woman in a coma, and an old, old man with a tiny wife who was allowed to sleep on a cot in his room, and a dark-skinned foreigner whose masses of visiting relatives gave the place the look of a gypsy circus. Ezra knew that the comatose woman had cancer, the old man a rare type of blood disease, and the foreigner some cardiac problem—it wasn't clear what. "Heart rumor," he was told by a dusky, exotic child who was surely too young to be visiting hospitals. She was standing outside the foreigner's door, delicately reeling in a yo-yo.

"Heart *murmur*, maybe?"

"No, rumor."

Ezra was starting to feel lonely here and would have liked to make a friend. The nurses were always sending him away while they did something mysterious to Mrs. Scarlatti, and much of any visit he spent leaning dejectedly against the wall outside her room or gazing from the windows of the conservatory at the end of the corridor. But no one seemed approachable. This wing was different from the others—more hushed—and all the people he encountered wore a withdrawn, forbidding look. Only the foreign child spoke to him. "I think he's going to die," she said. But then she went back to her yo-yo. Ezra hung around a while longer, but it was obvious she didn't find him very interesting.

Bibb lettuce, Boston lettuce, chicory, escarole, dripping on the counter in the center of the kitchen. While other restaurants' vegetables were delivered by anonymous, dank, garbage-smelling trucks, Scarlatti's had a man named Mr. Purdy, who shopped personally for them each morning before the sun came up. He brought everything to the kitchen in splintery bushel baskets, along about eight a.m., and Ezra made a point of being there so that he would know what foods he had to deal with that day. Sometimes there were no eggplants, sometimes twice as many as planned. In periods like this—dead November, now—nothing grew locally, and Mr. Purdy had to resort to vegetables raised elsewhere, limp carrots and waxy cucumbers shipped in from out of state. And the tomatoes! They were a crime. "Just look," said Mr. Purdy, picking one up. "Vine-grown, the fellow tells me. Vine-*grown*, yes. I'd like to see them grown on anything else. 'But ripened?' I say. 'However was they ripened?' 'Vine-ripened, too,' fellow assures me. Well, maybe so. But nowadays, I don't know, all them taste anyhow like they spent six weeks on a windowsill. Like they was *made* of windowsill, or celluloid, or pencil erasers. Well, I tell you, Ezra: I apologize. It breaks my heart to bring you such rubbage as this here; I'd sooner not show up at all."

Mr. Purdy was a pinched and prunish man in overalls, a white shirt, and a shiny black suit coat. He had a narrow face that seemed eternally disapproving, even during the growing season. Only Ezra knew that inwardly, there was something nourishing and generous about him. Mr. Purdy rejoiced in food as much as Ezra did, and for the same reasons—less for eating himself than for serving to others. He had once invited Ezra to his home, a silver-colored trailer out on Ritchie Highway, and given him a meal consisting solely of new asparagus, which both he and Ezra agreed had the haunting taste of oysters. Mrs. Purdy, a smiling, round-faced woman in a wheelchair, had claimed they talked like lunatics, but she finished two large helpings while both men tenderly watched. It was a satisfaction to see how she polished her buttery plate.

"If this restaurant was just mine," Ezra said now, "I wouldn't serve tomatoes in the winter. People would ask for tomatoes and I'd say, 'What can you be thinking of, this is not the season.' I'd give them something better."

"They'd stomp out directly," Mr. Purdy said.

"No, they might surprise you. And I'd put up a blackboard,

write on it every day just two or three good dishes. Of course! In France, they do that all the time. Or I'd offer no choice at all; examine people and say, 'You look a little tired. I'll bring you an oxtail stew.' "

"Mrs. Scarlatti would just die," said Mr. Purdy.

There was a silence. He rubbed his bristly chin, and then corrected himself: "She'd rotate in her grave."

They stood around a while.

"I don't really want a restaurant anyhow," Ezra said.

"Sure," Mr. Purdy said. "I know that."

Then he put his black felt hat on, and thought a moment, and left.

The foreign child slept in the conservatory, her head resting on the stainless steel arm of a chair like the one in Mrs. Scarlatti's room. It made Ezra wince. He wanted to fold his coat and slide it beneath her cheek, but he worried that would wake her. He kept his distance, therefore, and stood at one of the windows gazing down on pedestrians far below. How small and determined their feet looked, emerging from their foreshortened figures! The perseverance of human beings suddenly amazed him.

A woman entered the room—one of the foreigners. She was lighter skinned than the others, but he knew she was foreign because of her slippers, which contrasted with her expensive wool dress. The whole family, he had noticed, changed into slippers as soon as they arrived each morning. They made themselves at home in every possible way—setting out bags of seeds and nuts and spicy-smelling foods, once even brewing a quart of yogurt on the conservatory radiator. The men smoked cigarettes in the hall, and the women murmured together while knitting brightly colored sweaters.

Now the woman approached the child, bent over her, and tucked her hair back. Then she lifted her in her arms and settled in the chair. The child didn't wake. She only nestled closer and sighed. So after all, Ezra could have put his coat beneath her head. He had missed an opportunity. It was like missing a train —or something more important, something that would never come again. There was no explanation for the grief that suddenly filled him.

He decided to start serving his gizzard soup in the restaurant. He had the waiters announce it to patrons when they handed over the menu. "In addition to the soups you see here, we are pleased to offer tonight . . ." One of the waiters had failed to show up and Ezra hired a woman to replace him—strictly against Mrs. Scarlatti's policy. (Waitresses, she said, belonged in truck stops.) The woman did much better than the men with Ezra's soup. "Try our gizzard soup," she would say. "It's really hot and garlicky and it's made with love." Outside it was bitter cold, and the woman was so warm and helpful, more and more people followed her suggestion. Ezra thought that the next time a waiter left, he would hire a second woman, and maybe another after that, and so on.

He experimented the following week with a spiced crab casserole of his own invention, and then with a spinach bisque, and when the waiters complained about all they had to memorize he finally went ahead and bought a blackboard. SPECIALS, he wrote at the top. But in the hospital, when Mrs. Scarlatti asked how things were going, he didn't mention any of this. Instead, he sat forward and clasped his hands tight and said, "Fine. Um . . . fine." If she noticed anything strange in his voice, she didn't comment on it.

Mrs. Scarlatti had always been a lean, dark, slouching woman, with a faintly scornful manner. It was true, as Ezra's mother said, that she gave the impression of not caring what people thought of her. But that had been part of her charm—her sleepy eyes, hardly troubling to stay open, and her indifferent tone of

voice. Now, she went too far. Her skin took on the pallid look
of stone, and her face began to seem sphinxlike, all flat planes
and straight lines. Even her hair was sphinxlike—a short, black
wedge, a *clump* of hair, dulled and rough. Sometimes Ezra
believed that she was not dying but petrifying. He had trouble
remembering her low laugh, her casual arrogance. ("Sweetie,"
she used to say, ordering him off to some task, trilling languid
fingers. "Angel boy . . .") He had never felt more than twelve
years old around her, but now he was ancient, her parent or
grandparent. He soothed and humored her. Not all she said was
quite clear these days. "At least," she whispered once, "I never
made myself ridiculous, Ezra, did I?"

"Ridiculous?" he asked.

"With you."

"With me? Of course not."

He was puzzled, and must have shown it; she smiled and
rocked her head on the pillow. "Oh, you always were a much-
loved child," she told him. It must have been a momentary
wandering of the brain. (She hadn't known him as a child.)
"You take it all for granted," she said. Maybe she was confusing
him with Billy, her son. She turned her face away from him and
closed her eyes. He felt suddenly anxious. He was reminded of
that time his mother had nearly died, wounded by a misfired
arrow—entirely Ezra's fault; Ezra, the family stumbler. "I'm so
sorry, I'm sorry, I'm sorry," he had cried, but the apology had
never been accepted because his brother had been blamed instead, and his father, who had purchased the archery set. Ezra,
his mother's favorite, had got off scot-free. He'd been left un-
forgiven—not relieved, as you might expect, but forever burdened. "You're mistaken," he said now, and Mrs. Scarlatti's
eyelids fluttered into crepe but failed to open. "I wish you'd get
me straight. See who I *am*, I'm Ezra," he said, and then (for no
logical reason) he bent close and said, "Mrs. Scarlatti. Remember when I left the army? Discharged for sleepwalking? Sent
home? Mrs. Scarlatti, I wasn't really all the way asleep. I mean,
I knew what I was doing. I didn't *plan* to sleepwalk, but part

of me was conscious, and observed what was going on, and could have wakened the rest of me if I'd tried. I had this feeling like watching a dream, where you know you can break it off at any moment. But I didn't; I wanted to go home. I just wanted to leave that army, Mrs. Scarlatti. So I didn't stop myself."

If she had heard (with her only son, Billy, blown to bits in Korea), she would have risen up, sick as she was, and shouted, "Out! Out of my life!" So she must have missed it, for she only rocked her head again and smiled and went on sleeping.

Just after Thanksgiving the woman who'd been in a coma died, and the tiny old man either died or went home, but the foreigner stayed on and his relatives continued to visit. Now that they knew Ezra by sight, they hailed him as he passed. "Come!" they would call, and he would step in, shy and pleased, and stand around for several minutes with his fists locked in his armpits. The sick man was yellow and sunken, hooked to a number of tubes, but he always tried to smile at Ezra's entrance. Ezra had the impression that he knew no English. The others spoke English according to their ages—the child perfectly, the young adults with a strong, attractive accent, the old ones in ragged segments. Eventually, though, even the most fluent forgot themselves and drifted into their native language—a musical one, with rounded vowels that gave their lips a muscled, pouched, commiserative shape, as if they were perpetually tut-tutting. Ezra loved to listen. When you couldn't understand what people said, he thought, how clearly the links and joints in their relationships stood out! A woman's face lit and bloomed as she turned to a certain man; a barbed sound of pain leapt from the patient and his wife doubled over. The child, when upset, stroked her mother's gold wristwatch band for solace.

Once a young girl in braids sang a song with almost no tune. It wandered from note to note as if by accident. Then a man with a heavy black mustache recited what must have been a poem. He spoke so grandly and unselfconsciously that passersby glanced in, and when he had finished he translated it for Ezra. "*O dead one, why did you die in the springtime? You haven't yet tasted the squash, or the cucumber salad.*" Why, even their poetry touched matters close to Ezra's heart.

By December he had replaced three of the somber-suited waiters with cheery, motherly waitresses, and he'd scrapped the thick beige menus and started listing each day's dishes on the blackboard. This meant, of course, that the cooks all left (none of the dishes were theirs, or even their type), so he did most of the cooking himself, with the help of a woman from New Orleans and a Mexican. These two had recipes of their own as well, some of which Ezra had never tasted before; he was entranced. It was true that the customers seemed surprised, but they adjusted, Ezra thought. Or most of them did.

Now he grew feverish with new ideas, and woke in the night longing to share them with someone. Why not a restaurant full of refrigerators, where people came and chose the food they wanted? They could fix it themselves on a long, long stove lining one wall of the dining room. Or maybe he could install a giant fireplace, with a whole steer turning slowly on a spit. You'd slice what you liked onto your plate and sit around in armchairs eating and talking with the guests at large. Then again, maybe he would start serving only street food. Of course! He'd cook what people felt homesick for—tacos like those from vendor's carts in California, which the Mexican was always pining after; and that wonderful vinegary North Carolina barbecue that Todd Duckett had to have brought by his mother several times a year in cardboard cups. He would call it the Homesick Restaurant. He'd take down the old black and gilt sign . . .

But then he saw the sign, SCARLATTI'S, and he groaned and pressed his fingers to his eyes and turned over in his bed.

"You have a beautiful country," the light-skinned woman said. "Thank you," said Ezra.

"All that green! And so many birds. Last summer, before my father-in-law fell ill, we were renting a house in New Jersey. The Garden State, they call it. There were roses everywhere. We could sit on the lawn after supper and listen to the nightingales."

"The what?" said Ezra.

"The nightingales."

"Nightingales? In New Jersey?"

"Of course," she said. "Also we liked the shopping. In particular, Korvette's. My husband likes the . . . how do you say? Drip and dry suits."

The sick man moaned and tossed, nearly dislodging a tube that entered the back of his wrist. His wife, an ancient, papery lady, leaned toward him and stroked his hand. She murmured something, and then she turned to the younger woman. Ezra saw that she was crying. She didn't attempt to hide it but wept openly, tears streaming down her cheeks. "Ah," the younger woman said, and she left Ezra's side and bent over the wife. She gathered her up in her arms as she'd gathered the child earlier. Ezra knew he should leave, but he didn't. Instead he turned and gazed out the window, slightly tilting his head and looking nonchalant, as some men do when they have rung a doorbell and are standing on the porch, waiting to be noticed and invited in.

Ezra's sister, Jenny, sat at the desk in her old bedroom, reading a battered textbook. She was strikingly pretty, even in reading glasses and the no-color quilted bathrobe she always left on a closet hook for her visits home. Ezra stopped at her doorway and peered in. "Jenny?" he asked. "What are you doing here?"

"I thought I'd take a breather," she said. She removed her glasses and gave him a blurry, unfocused look.

"It isn't semester break yet, is it?"

"Semester break! Do you think medical students have time for such things?"

"No, well," he said.

But lately she'd been home more often than not, it appeared to him. And she never mentioned Harley, her husband. She hadn't referred to him once all fall, and maybe even all summer. "It's my opinion she's left him," Ezra's mother had said recently. "Oh, don't act so surprised! It must have crossed your mind. Here she suddenly moves to a new address—closer to the school, she claims—and then can't have us to visit, anytime I offer; always too busy or preparing for some quiz, and when I call, you notice, it's never Harley who answers, never once Harley who picks up the phone. Doesn't that strike you as odd? But I'm unable to broach the subject. I mean, she deflects me, if you know what I mean. Somehow I just never . . . *you* could, though. She always did feel closer to you than to me or Cody. Won't you just ask her what's what?"

But now when he lounged in the doorway, trying to find some way to sidle into a conversation, Jenny put her glasses back on and returned to her book. He felt dismissed. "Um," he said. "How are things in Paulham?"

"Fine," she said, eyes scanning the print.

"Harley all right?"

There was a deep, studious silence.

"It doesn't seem we ever get to see him any more," Ezra said.

"He's okay," Jenny said.

She turned a page.

Ezra waited a while longer, and then he straightened up from the doorway and went downstairs. He found his mother in the kitchen, unpacking groceries. "Well?" she asked him.

"Well, what?"

"Did you talk to Jenny?"

"Ah . . ."

She still had her coat on; she thrust her hands in her pockets and faced him squarely, with her bun slipping down the back of her head. "You promised me," she told him. "You swore you'd talk to her."

"I didn't swear to, Mother."

"You took a solemn oath," she told him.

"I notice she still wears a ring," he said hopefully.

"So what," said his mother. She went back to her groceries. "She wouldn't wear a ring if she and Harley were separated, would she?"

"She would if she wanted to fool us."

"Well, I don't know, if she wants to fool us maybe we ought to *act* fooled. I don't know."

"All my life," his mother said, "people have been trying to shut me out. Even my children. Especially my children. If I so much as ask that girl how she's been, she shies away like I'd inquired into the deepest, darkest part of her. Now, why should she be so standoffish?"

Ezra said, "Maybe she cares more about what *you* think than what outsiders think."

"Ha," said his mother. She lifted a carton of eggs from the grocery bag.

"I'm worried I don't know how to get in touch with people," Ezra said.

"Hmm?"

"I'm worried if I come too close, they'll say I'm overstepping. They'll say I'm pushy, or . . . emotional, you know. But if I back off, they might think I don't care. I really, honestly believe I missed some rule that everyone else takes for granted; I must have been absent from school that day. There's this narrow little dividing line I somehow never located."

"Nonsense; I don't know what you're talking about," said his mother, and then she held up an egg. "Will you look at this? Out of one dozen eggs, four are cracked. Two are *smushed*. I can't imagine what Sweeney Brothers is coming to, these days."

Ezra waited a while, but she didn't say any more. Finally, he left.

He tore down the wall between the restaurant kitchen and the dining room, doing most of the work in a single night. He slung a sledgehammer in a steady rhythm, then ripped away at hunks of plaster till a thick white dust had settled over everything. Then he came upon a mass of pipes and electrical wires and he had to call in professionals to finish off the job. The damage was so extensive that he was forced to stay closed for four straight weekdays, losing a good deal of money.

He figured that while he was at it, he might as well redecorate the dining room. He raced around the windows and dragged down the stiff brocade draperies; he peeled up the carpeting and persuaded a brigade of workmen to sand and polish the floorboards.

By the evening of the fourth day, he was so tired that he could feel the hinging of every muscle. Even so, he washed the white from his hair and changed out of his speckled jeans and went to pay a visit to Mrs. Scarlatti. She lay in her usual position, slightly propped, but her expression was alert and she even managed a smile when he entered. "Guess what, angel," she whispered. "Tomorrow they're letting me leave."

"Leave?"

"I asked the doctor, and he's letting me go home."

"Home?"

"As long as I hire a nurse, he says . . . Well, don't just stand there, Ezra. I need for you to see about a nurse. If you'll look in that nightstand . . ."

It was more talking than she'd done in weeks. Ezra felt almost buoyant with new hope; underneath, it seemed, he must have given up on her. But of course, he was also worried about the restaurant. What would she think when she saw it? What would she say to him? "Everything must go back again, just the way it was," he could imagine. "Really, Ezra. Put up that wall this instant, and fetch my carpets and my curtains." He suspected that he had very poor taste, much inferior to Mrs. Scarlatti's. She would say, "Dear heart, how could you be so *chintzy?*"—a favorite word of hers. He wondered if he could keep her from finding out, if he could convince her to stay in her apartment till he had returned things to normal.

He thanked his stars that he hadn't changed the sign that hung outside.

* * *

It was Ezra who settled the bill at the business office, the following morning. Then he spoke briefly with her doctor, whom he chanced to meet in the corridor. "This is wonderful about Mrs. Scarlatti," Ezra said. "I really didn't expect it."

"Oh," said the doctor. "Well."

"I was getting sort of discouraged, if you want to know the truth."

"Well," the doctor said again, and he held out his hand so suddenly that it took Ezra a second to respond. After that, the doctor walked off. Ezra felt there was a lot more the man could have said, as a matter of fact.

Mrs. Scarlatti went home by ambulance. Ezra drove behind, catching glimpses of her through the tinted window. She lay on a stretcher, and next to her was another stretcher holding a man in two full leg casts. His wife perched beside him, evidently talking nonstop. Ezra could see the feathers on her hat bob up and down with her words.

Mrs. Scarlatti was let off first. The ambulance men unloaded her while Ezra stood around feeling useless. "Oh, smell that air," said Mrs. Scarlatti. "Isn't it fresh and beautiful." Actually, it was terrible air—wintry and rainy and harsh with soot. "I never told you this, Ezra," she said, as they wheeled her through the building's front entrance, "but I really didn't believe I would see this place again. My little apartment, my restaurant . . ." Then she raised a palm—her old, peremptory gesture, directed toward the ambulance men. They were preparing to guide her stretcher through the right-hand door and up the stairs. "Dear fellow," she said to the nearest one, "could you just open that door on the left and let me take a peek?"

It happened so fast, Ezra didn't have time to protest. The man reached back in a preoccupied way and opened the door to the restaurant. Then he resumed his study of the stairs; there was an angle at the top that was going to pose a problem. Mrs. Scarlatti, meanwhile, turned her face with some effort and gazed through the door.

There was a moment, just a flicker of a second, when Ezra dared to hope that she might approve after all. But looking past her, he realized that was impossible. The restaurant was a warehouse, a barn, a gymnasium—a total catastrophe. Tables and upended chairs huddled in one corner, underneath bald, barren windows. Buckling plank footbridges led across the varnished floor, which had somehow picked up a film of white dust, and the missing kitchen wall was as horrifying as a toothless smile. Only two broad, plaster pillars separated the kitchen from the dining room. Everything was exposed—sinks and garbage cans, the blackened stove, the hanging pots with their tarnished bottoms, a calendar showing a girl in a sheer black nightgown, and a windowsill bearing two dead plants and a Brillo pad and Todd Duckett's asthma inhalant.

"Oh, my God," said Mrs. Scarlatti.

She looked up into his eyes. Her face seemed stripped. "You might at least have waited till I died," she said.

"Oh!" said Ezra. "No, you don't understand; you don't know. It wasn't what you think. It was just . . . I can't explain, I went wild somehow!"

But she raised that palm of hers and sailed up the stairs to her apartment. Even lying flat, she had an air of speed and power.

She didn't refuse to see him again—nothing like that. Every morning he paid her a visit, and was admitted by her day nurse. He sat on the edge of the ladylike chair in the bedroom and reported on bills and health inspections and linen deliveries. Mrs. Scarlatti was unfailingly polite, nodding in all the right places, but she never said much in return. Eventually, she would close her eyes as a sign that the visit was finished. Then Ezra would leave, often jostling her bed by accident or overturning his chair. He had always been a clumsy man, but now was more so than usual. It seemed to him his hands were too big, forever getting in the way. If only he could have done something with them! He would have liked to fix her a meal—a sustaining meal, with a depth of flavors, a complicated meal that would require a whole day of chopping things small, and grinding, and blending. In the kitchen, as nowhere else, Ezra came into his own, like someone crippled on dry land but effortlessly graceful once he takes to water. However, Mrs. Scarlatti still wasn't eating. There was nothing he could offer her.

Or he would have liked to seize her by the shoulders and shout, "Listen! Listen!" But something closed-off about her face kept stopping him. Almost in plain words, she was telling him that she preferred he not do such a thing. So he didn't.

After a visit, he would go downstairs and look in on the restaurant, which at this hour was vacant and echoing. He might check the freezer, or erase the blackboard, and then perhaps just wander a while, touching this and that. The wallpaper in the back hall was too cluttered and he ripped it off the wall. He tore away the ornate gilt sconces beside the telephone. He yanked the old-fashioned silhouettes from the restroom doors. Sometimes he did so much damage that there was barely time to cover it up before opening, but everybody pitched in and it always got done somehow or other. By six o'clock, when the first customers arrived, the food was cooked and the tables were laid and the waitresses were calm and smiling. Everything was smoothed over.

Mrs. Scarlatti died in March, on a bitter, icy afternoon. When the nurse phoned Ezra, he felt a crushing sense of shock. You would think this death was unexpected. He said, "Oh, no," and hung up, and had to call back to ask the proper questions. Had the end been peaceful? Had Mrs. Scarlatti been awake? Had she said any words in particular? Nothing, said the nurse. Really, nothing at all; just slipped away, like. "But she mentioned you this morning," she added. "I almost wondered, you know? It was almost like she sensed it. She said, 'Tell Ezra to change the sign.'"

"Sign?"

" 'It's not Scarlatti's Restaurant any more,' she said. Or something like that. 'It isn't Scarlatti's.' I think that's what she said."

From the pain he felt, Mrs. Scarlatti might as well have reached out from death and slapped him across the face. It made things easier, in a way. He was almost angry; he was almost relieved that she was gone. He noticed how the trees outside sparkled like something newly minted.

He was the one who made the arrangements, working from a list that Mrs. Scarlatti had given him months before. He knew which funeral home to call and which pastor, and which acquaintances she had wanted at the service. A peculiar thing: he thought of phoning the hospital and inviting that foreign family. Of course he didn't, but it was true they would have made wonderful mourners. Certainly they'd have done better than those who did come, and who later stood stiffly around her frozen grave. Ezra, too, was stiff—a sad, tired man in a flapping coat, holding his mother's arm. Something ached behind his eyes. If he had cried, Mrs. Scarlatti would have said, "Jesus, Ezra. For God's sake, sweetie."

Afterward, he was glad to go to the restaurant. It helped to keep busy—stirring and seasoning and tasting, stumbling over the patch in the floor where the center counter had once stood. Later, he circulated among the diners as Mrs. Scarlatti herself used to do. He urged upon them his oyster stew, his artichoke salad, his spinach bisque and his chili-bean soup and his gizzard soup that was made with love.

5

The Country Cook

Cody Tull always had a girlfriend, one girl after another, and all the girls were wild about him till they met his brother, Ezra. Something about Ezra just hooked their attention, it seemed. In his presence they took on a bright, sharp, arrested look, as if listening to a sound that others hadn't caught yet. Ezra didn't even notice this. Cody did, of course. He would give an exaggerated sigh, pretending to be amused. Then the girl would collect herself. It was already too late, though; Cody never allowed second chances. He had a talent for mentally withdrawing. An Indian-faced man with smooth black hair, with level, balanced features, he could manage, when he tried, to seem perfectly blank, like a plaster clothing model. Meanwhile, his ragged, dirty, unloved younger self, with failing grades, with a U in deportment, clenched his fists and howled, "Why? Why always Ezra? Why that sissy pale goody-goody Ezra?"

But Ezra just gazed into space from behind his clear gray eyes, from under his shock of soft, fair hair, and went on thinking his private thoughts. You could say this for Ezra: he seemed honestly unaware of the effect he had on women. No one could accuse him of stealing them deliberately. But that made it all the worse, in a way.

Cody half believed that Ezra had some lack—a lack that worked in his favor, that made him immune, that set him apart from ordinary men. There was something almost monkish about him. Women never really managed to penetrate his meditations, although he was unfailingly courteous to them, and considerate. He was likely to contemplate them in silence for an inappropriate length of time, and then ask something completely out of the blue. For instance: "How did you get those little gold circles through your ears?" It was ridiculous—a man reaches the age of twenty-seven without having heard of pierced earrings. However, it must not have seemed ridiculous to the woman he was addressing. She raised a finger to an earlobe in a startled, mesmerized way. She was spellbound. Was it Ezra's unexpectedness? The narrowness of his focus? (He'd passed up her low-cut dress, powdered cleavage, long silky legs.) Or his innocence, perhaps. He was a tourist on a female planet, was what he was saying. But he didn't realize he was saying it, and failed to understand the look she gave him. Or didn't care, if he did understand.

Only one of Cody's girlfriends had not been attracted to his brother. This was a social worker named Carol, or maybe Karen. Upon meeting Ezra, she had fixed him with a cool stare. Later, she had remarked to Cody that she disliked motherly men. "Always feeding, hovering," she said (for she'd met him at his restaurant), "but acting so clumsy and shy, in the end it's *you* that takes care of *them*. Ever notice that?" However, she hardly counted; Cody had so soon afterward lost interest in her.

You might wonder why he went on making these introductions, considering his unfortunate experiences—the earliest dating from the year he turned fourteen, the latest as recent as a month ago. After all, he lived in New York City and his family lived in Baltimore; he didn't really have to bring these women home on weekends. In fact, he often swore that he would stop it. He would meet somebody, marry her, and not mention her even to his mother. But that would mean a lifetime of suspense. He'd keep watching his wife uncomfortably, suspiciously. He'd keep waiting for the inevitable—like Sleeping Beauty's parents, waiting for the needle that was bound to prick her finger in spite of their precautions.

He was thirty years old by now, successful in his business,

certainly ready to marry. He considered his New York apartment temporary, a matter of minor convenience; he had recently
purchased a farmhouse in Baltimore County with forty acres of
land. Weekends, he traded his slim gray suit for corduroys and
he roamed his property, making plans. There was a sunny back-
yard where his wife could have her kitchen garden. There were
bedrooms waiting to be stocked with children. He imagined
them tumbling out to meet him every Friday afternoon when
he came home. He felt rich and lordly. Poor Ezra: all he had
was that disorganized restaurant, in the cramped, stunted center
of the city.

Once, Cody invited Ezra to hunt rabbits with him in the
woods behind the farm. It wasn't a success. First Ezra fell into
a yellowjackets' nest. Then he got his rifle wet in the stream.
And when they paused on a hilltop for lunch, he whipped out
his battered recorder and commenced to tootling "Greensleeves," scaring off all living creatures within a five-mile radius
—which may have been his intention. Cody wasn't even talking to him, at the end; Ezra had to chatter on by himself. Cody
stalked well ahead of him in total silence, trying to remember
why this outing had seemed such a good idea. Ezra sang "Mister
Rabbit." "*Every little soul,*" he sang, blissfully off-key, "*must
shine, shine . . .*"

No wonder Cody was a cuticle chewer, a floor pacer, a hair
rummager. No wonder, when he slept at night, he ground his
teeth so hard that his jaws ached every morning.

Early in the spring of 1960, his sister, Jenny, wrote him a letter.
Her divorce was coming through in June, she said—two more
months, and then she'd be free to marry Sam Wiley. Cody
didn't think much of Wiley, and he flicked this news aside like
a gnat and read on. *Though it looks,* she said, *as if Ezra might
beat me down the aisle. Her name is Ruth but I don't know any
more than that.* Then she said she was seriously considering
dropping out of medical school. The complications of her per-
sonal life, she said, were using up so much energy that she had

none left over for anything else. Also, she had gained three pounds in the last six weeks and was perfectly obese, a whale, living now on lettuce leaves and lemon water. Cody was accustomed to Jenny's crazy diets (she was painfully thin), so he skimmed that part. He finished the letter and folded it.

Ruth?

He opened it again.

... *as if Ezra might beat me down the aisle*, he read. He tried to think of some other kind of aisle—airplane, supermarket, movie house—but in the end, he had to believe it: Ezra was getting married. Well, at least now Cody could keep his own girls. (This gave him, for some reason, a little twinge of uneasiness.) But Ezra! Married? That walking accident? Imagine him in a formal wedding—forgetting license, ring, and responses, losing track of the service while smiling out the window at a hummingbird. Imagine him in bed with a woman. (Cody snorted.) He pictured the woman as dark and Biblical, because of her name: Ruth. Shadowed eyes and creamy skin. Torrents of loose black hair. Cody had a weakness for black-haired women; he didn't like blondes at all. He pictured her bare shouldered, in a red satin nightgown, and he crumpled Jenny's letter roughly and dropped it in the wastebasket.

The next day at work, Ruth's image hung over him. He was doing a time-and-motion study of a power-drill factory in New Jersey, a dinosaur of a place. It would take him weeks to sort it out. *Joining object K to object L: right-hand transport unloaded, search, grasp, transport loaded* ... He passed down the assembly line with his clipboard, attracting hostile glances. Ruth's black hair billowed in the rafters. *Unavoidable delays: 3. Avoidable delays: 9.* No doubt her eyes were plum shaped, slightly tilted. No doubt her hands were heavily ringed, with long, oval fingernails painted scarlet.

When he returned to his apartment that evening, there was a letter from Ezra. It was an invitation to his restaurant this coming Saturday night. *You are cordially invited* was centered on the page like something engraved—Ezra's idea of a joke. (Or maybe not; maybe he meant it in earnest.) Oh, Lord, not another one of Ezra's dinners. There would be toasts and a fumbling, sentimental speech leading up to some weighty announcement—in this case, his engagement. Cody thought of declining, but what good would that do? Ezra would be desolate if a single person was missing. He'd cancel the whole affair and reschedule it for later, and keep on rescheduling till Cody accepted. Cody might as well go and be done with it.

Besides, he wouldn't at all mind meeting this Ruth.

Ezra was listening to a customer—or a one-time customer, from the sound of it. "Used to be," the man was saying, "this place had class. You follow me?"

Ezra nodded, watching him with such a sympathetic, kindly expression that Cody wondered if his mind weren't somewhere else altogether. "Used to be there was fine French cuisine, flamed at the tables and all," said the man. "And chandeliers. And a hat-check girl. And waiters in black tie. What happened to your waiters?"

"They put people off," Ezra said. "They seemed to think the customers were taking an exam of some kind, not just ordering a meal. They were uppish."

"I liked your waiters."

"Nowadays our staff is homier," Ezra said, and he gestured toward a passing waitress—a tall, stooped, colorless girl, open mouthed with concentration, fiercely intent upon the coffee mug that she carried in both hands. She inched across the floor, breathing adenoidally. She proceeded directly between Ezra and the customer. Ezra stepped back to give her room.

The customer said, " 'Nettie,' I said, 'you've just got to see Scarlatti's. Don't knock Baltimore,' I tell her, 'till you see Scarlatti's.' Then we come upon it and even the sign's gone. Homesick Restaurant, you call it now. What kind of a name is that? And the decor! Why, it looks like . . . why, a gigantic roadside diner!"

He was right. Cody agreed with him. Dining room walls lined with home preserves, kitchen laid open to the public,

unkempt cooks milling around compiling their favorite dishes
(health food, street food, foreign food, whatever popped into
their heads) . . . Ever since Ezra had inherited this place—from
a woman, wouldn't you know—he'd been systematically wreck-
ing it. He was fully capable of serving a single entrée all one
evening, bringing it to your table himself as soon as you were
seated. Other nights he'd offer more choice, four or five selec-
tions chalked up on the blackboard. But still you might not get
what you asked for. "The Smithfield ham," you'd say, and up
would come the okra stew. "With that cough of yours, I know
this will suit you better," Ezra would explain. But even if he'd
judged correctly, was that any way to run a restaurant? You
order ham, ham is what you get. Otherwise, you might as well
eat at home. "You'll go bankrupt in a year," Cody had promised,
and Ezra almost did go bankrupt; most of the regular patrons
disappeared. Some hung on, though; and others discovered it.
There were several older people who ate here every night,
sitting alone at their regular tables in the barnlike, plank-floored
dining room. They could afford it because the prices weren't
written but recited instead by the staff, evidently according to
whim, altering with the customer. (Wasn't that illegal?) Ezra
worried about what these older people did on Sundays, when
he closed. Cody, on the other hand, worried about Ezra's account books, but didn't offer to go over them. He would find a
disaster, he was sure—errors and bad debts, if not outright,
naive crookery. Better not to know; better not to get involved.

"It's true there've been some changes," Ezra was telling his
ex-customer, "but if you'll just try our food, you'll see that
we're still a fine restaurant. Tonight it's all one dish—pot roast."

"Pot roast!"

"A really special kind—consoling."

"Pot roast I can get at home," said the man. He clamped a
felt hat on his head and walked out.

"Oh, well," Ezra told Cody. "You can't please everybody, I
guess."

They made their way to the far corner, where a RESERVED

sign sat upon the table that Ezra always chose for family dinners. Jenny and their mother weren't there yet. Jenny, who'd arrived on the afternoon train, had asked her mother's help in shopping for a dress to be married in. Now Ezra worried they'd be late. "Everything's planned for six-thirty," he said. "What's keeping them?"

"Well, no problem if it's only pot roast."

"It's not *only* pot roast," Ezra said. He sat in a chair. His suit had a way of waffling around him, as if purchased for a much larger man. "This is something more. I mean, pot roast is really not the right name; it's more like . . . what you long for when you're sad and everyone's been wearing you down. See, there's this cook, this real country cook, and pot roast is the least of what she does. There's also pan-fried potatoes, black-eyed peas, beaten biscuits genuinely beat on a stump with the back of an ax—"

"Here they come," Cody said.

Jenny and her mother were just walking across the dining room. They carried no parcels, but something made it clear they'd been shopping—perhaps the frazzled, cross look they shared. Jenny's lipstick was chewed off. Pearl's hat was knocked crooked and her hair was frizzier than ever. "What took you so long?" Ezra asked, jumping up. "We were starting to worry."

"Oh, this Jenny and her notions," said Pearl. "Her size eight figure and no bright colors, no pastels, no gathers or puckers or trim, nothing to make her look fat, so-called . . . Why are there five places set?"

The question took them all off guard. It was true, Cody saw. There were five plates and five crystal wineglasses. "How come?" Pearl asked Ezra.

"Oh . . . I'll get to that in a minute. Have a seat, Mother, over there."

But she kept standing. "Then at last we find just the right thing," she said. "A nice soft gray with a crocheted collar, Jenny all the way. 'It's you,' I tell her. And guess what she does. She has a tantrum in the middle of Hutzler's department store."

"Not a *tantrum*, Mother," Jenny told her. "I merely said—"

"Said, 'It isn't a funeral, Mother; I'm not going into mourning.' You'd think I'd chosen widow's weeds. This was a nice pale gray, very ladylike, very suitable for a second marriage."

"Anthracite," Jenny told Cody.

"Pardon?"

"Anthracite was what the saleslady called it. In other words: coal. Our mother thinks it suitable to marry me off in a coal-black wedding dress."

"Uh," said Ezra, looking around at the other diners, "maybe we should be seated now."

But Pearl just stood straighter. "And *then*," she told her sons, "then, without the slightest bit of thought, doing it only to spite me, she goes rushing over to the nearest rack and pulls out something white as snow."

"It was cream colored," Jenny said.

"Cream, white—what's the difference? Both are inappropriate, if you're marrying for the second time and the divorce hasn't yet been granted and the man has no steady employment. 'I'll take this one,' she says, and it's not even the proper size, miles too big, had to be left at the store for alterations."

"I happened to like it," Jenny said.

"You were lost in it."

"It made me look thin."

"Maybe you could wear a shawl or something, brown," said her mother. "That might tone it down some."

"I can't wear a shawl in a wedding."

"Why not? Or a little jacket, say a brown linen jacket."

"I look fat in jackets."

"Not in a short one, Chanel-type."

"I hate Chanel."

"Well," said Pearl, "I can see that nothing will satisfy you."

"Mother," Jenny said, "I'm already satisfied. I'm satisfied with my cream-colored dress, just the way it is. I love it. Will you please just get off my back?"

"Did you hear that?" Pearl asked her sons. "Well, I don't

have to stand here and take it." And she turned and marched back across the dining room, erect as a little wind-up doll.

Ezra said, "Huh?"

Jenny opened a plastic compact, looked into it, and then snapped it shut, as if merely making certain that she was still there.

"Please, Jenny, won't you go after her?" Ezra asked.

"Not on your life."

"*You're* the one she fought with. *I* can't persuade her."

"Oh, Ezra, let's for once just drop it," Cody said. "I don't think I'm up to all this."

"What are you saying? Not have dinner at all?"

"I could only eat lettuce leaves anyhow," Jenny told him.

"But this is important! It was going to be an occasion. Oh, just . . . wait. Wait here a minute, will you?"

Ezra turned and rushed off to the kitchen. From the swarm of assorted cooks at the counter, he plucked a small person in overalls. It was a girl, Cody guessed—a weasel-faced little redhead. She followed Ezra jauntily, almost stiff-legged, wiping her palms on her backside. "I'd like you to meet Ruth," Ezra said.

Cody said, "Ruth?"

"We're getting married in September."

"Oh," said Cody.

Then Jenny said, "Well, congratulations," and kissed Ruth's bony, freckled cheek, and Cody said, "Uh, yes," and shook her hand. There were calluses like pebbles on her palm. "How do," she told him. He thought of the phrase *banty hen*, although he had never seen a banty hen. Or maybe she was more of a rooster. Her brisk, carroty hair was cut so short that it seemed too scant for her skull. Her blue eyes were round as marbles, and her skin was so thin and tight (as if, like her hair, it had been skimped on) that he could see the white cartilage across the bridge of her nose. "So," he said. "Ruth."

"Are you surprised?" Ezra asked him.

"Yes, very surprised."

"I wanted to do it right; I was going to announce it over drinks and then call her in to join the family dinner. But, honey," Ezra said, turning to Ruth, "I guess Mother was overtired. It didn't work out the way I'd planned."

"Shit, that's okay," Ruth told him.

Cody said, "Surely. Certainly. We can always do it later."

Then Jenny started asking about the wedding, and Cody excused himself and said he thought he'd go see how their mother was. Outside in the dark, walking up the street toward home, he had the strangest feeling of loss. It was as if someone had died, or had left him forever—the beautiful, black-haired Ruth of his dreams.

"I knew what that dinner was going to be, tonight," Pearl told Cody. "I'm not so dumb. I knew. He's got himself engaged; he's going to marry the country cook. I knew that anyway but it all came home to me when I walked in the restaurant and saw those five plates and glasses. Well, I acted badly. Very badly. You don't have to tell me, Cody. It was just that I saw those plates and something broke inside of me. I thought, 'Well, all right, if that's how it's got to be, but not tonight, just not tonight, Lord, right on top of buying wedding dress number two for my only daughter.' So then, why, I went and made a scene that caused the dinner to be canceled, exactly as if I'd planned it all ahead of time, which of course I hadn't. You believe me, don't you? I'm not blind. I know when I'm being unreasonable. Sometimes I stand outside my body and just watch it all, totally separate. 'Now, stop,' I say to myself, but it's like I'm . . . elated; I've got to rush on, got to keep going. 'Yes, yes, I'll stop,' I think, 'only let me say this one more thing, just this one more thing . . .'

"Cody, don't you believe I want you three to be happy? Of course I do. Naturally. Why, I wouldn't hold Ezra back for the world, if he's so set on marrying that girl—though I don't know what he sees in her, she's so scrappy and hoydenish; I think she's from Garrett County or some such place and hardly

wears shoes—you ought to see the soles of her feet sometime—
but what I want to say is, I've never been one of those mothers
who try to keep their sons for themselves. I honestly hope
Ezra marries. I truly mean that. I want somebody taking care
of him, *especially* him. You can manage on your own but Ezra
is so, I don't know, defenseless . . . Of course I love you all the
same amount, every bit the same, but . . . well, Ezra is so *good.*
You know? Anyway, now he has this Ruth person and it's
changed his whole outlook; watch him sometime when she
walks into a room, or swaggers, or whatever you want to call
it. He adores her. They get all playful together, like two puppies.
Yes, often they remind me of puppies, snuggling down and
giggling, or bounding about the kitchen or listening to that hill-
billy music that Ruth seems to be so crazy about. But, Cody.
Promise not to tell this to anyone. Promise? Cody, sometimes I
stand there watching them and I see they believe they're completely special, the first, the only people ever to feel the way
they're feeling. They believe they'll live happily ever after, that
all the other marriages going on around them—those ordinary,
worn-down, flattened-in arrangements—why, those are nothing
like what *they'll* have. They'll never settle for so little. And it
makes me mad. I can't help it, Cody. I know it's selfish, but I
can't help it. I want to ask them, 'Who do you think you are,
anyhow? Do you imagine you're unique? Do you really suppose I was always this difficult old woman?'

"Cody, listen. I was special too, once, to someone. I could
just reach out and lay a fingertip on his arm while he was talking
and he would instantly fall silent and get all confused. I had
hopes; I was courted; I had the most beautiful wedding. I had
three lovely pregnancies, where every morning I woke up knowing something perfect would happen in nine months, eight
months, seven . . . so it seemed I was full of light; it was light and
plans that filled me. And then while you children were little,
why, I was the center of your worlds! I was everything to you!
It was Mother this and Mother that, and 'Where's Mother?
Where's she gone to?' and the moment you came in from
school, 'Mother? Are you home?' It's not fair, Cody. It's really

not fair; now I'm old and I walk along unnoticed, just like anyone else. It strikes me as unjust, Cody. But don't tell the others I said so."

At work that next week, charting the steps by which power drills were fitted into their housings, Cody watched the old, dark Ruth fade from the rafters and hallways, until at last she was completely gone and he forgot why she had moved him so. Now a new Ruth appeared. Skinny and boyish, overalls flapping around her shinbones, she raced giggling down the assembly line with Ezra hot on her heels. Ezra's hair was tousled. (He was not immune at all, it appeared, but had only been waiting in his stubbornly trustful way for the proper person to arrive.) He caught her in the supervisor's office and they scuffled like . . . yes, like two puppies. A cowlick bounced on the crown of Ruth's head. Her lips were chapped and cracked. Her nails were bitten into tiny pink cushions and there were scrapes and burns across her knuckles, scars from her country cooking.

Cody called his mother and said he'd be down for the weekend. And would Ruth be around, did she think? After all, he said, it was time he got to know his future sister-in-law.

He arrived on Saturday morning bringing flowers, copper-colored roses. He found Ruth and Ezra playing gin on the living room floor. Ruth's reality, after his week of dreaming, struck him like a blow. She seemed clearer, plainer, harder edged than anybody he'd known. She wore jeans and a shirt of some ugly brown plaid. She was so absorbed in her game that she hardly glanced up when Cody walked in. "Ruth," he said, and he held out the flowers. "These are for you."

She looked at them, and then drew a card. "What are they?" she asked.

"Well, roses."

"Roses? This early in the year?"

"Greenhouse roses. I especially ordered copper, to go with your hair."

"You leave my hair out of this," she said.

"Honey, he meant it as a compliment," Ezra told her.

"Oh."

"Certainly," said Cody. "See, it's my way of saying welcome. Welcome to our family, Ruth."

"Oh. Well, thanks."

"Cody, that was awfully nice of you," Ezra said.

"Gin," said Ruth.

Late that afternoon, when it was time to go to the restaurant, Cody walked over with Ruth and Ezra. He'd had a long, immobile day—standing outside other people's lives, mostly—and he needed the exercise.

It had been raining, off and on, and there were puddles on the sidewalk. Ruth strode straight through every one of them, which was fine since her shoes were brown leather combat boots. Cody wondered if her style were deliberate. What would she do, for instance, if he gave her a pair of high-heeled evening sandals? The question began to fascinate him. He became obsessed; he developed an almost physical thirst for the sight of her blunt little feet in silver straps.

There was no explaining his craving for the gigantic watch—black faced and intricately calibrated, capable of withstanding a deep-sea dive—whose stainless steel expansion band hung loose on her wiry wrist.

Ezra had his pearwood recorder. He played it as he walked, serious and absorbed, with his lashes lowered on his cheeks. "Le Godiveau de Poisson," he played. Passersby looked at him and smiled. Ruth hummed along with some notes, fell into her own thoughts at others. Then Ezra put his recorder in the pocket of his shabby lumber jacket, and he and Ruth began discussing the menu. It was good they were serving the rice dish, Ruth said; that always made the Arab family happy. She ran her fingers through her sprouty red hair. Cody, walking on the other side of her, felt her shift of weight when Ezra circled her with one arm and pulled her close.

In the restaurant, she was a whirlwind. Ezra cooked in a dream, tasting and reflecting; the others (losers, all of them, in Cody's opinion) floated around the kitchen vaguely, but Ruth spun and pounced and jabbed at food as if doing battle. She was in charge of a chicken casserole and something that looked like potato cakes. Cody watched her from a corner well out of the way, but still people seemed to keep tripping over him.

"Where did you learn to cook?" he asked Ruth.

"No place," she said.

"Is this chicken some regional thing?"

"Taste," she snapped, and she speared a piece and held it out to him.

"I can't," he said.

"Why not?"

"I feel too full."

In fact, he felt full of *her*. He'd taken her in all day, consumed her. Every spiky movement—slamming of pot lids, toss of head—nourished him. It came to him like a gift, while he was studying her narrow back, that she actually wore an undershirt, one of those knitted singlets he remembered from his childhood. He could make out the seams of it beneath the brown plaid. He filed the information with care, to be treasured once he was alone.

The restaurant opened and customers began to trickle in. The large, beaming hostess seated them all in one area, as if tucking them under her wing.

"Find a table," Ezra told Cody. "I'll bring you some of Ruth's cooking."

"I'm honestly not hungry," Cody said.

"He's *full*," said Ruth, spitting it out.

"Well, what'll you do, then? Isn't this boring for you?"

"No, no, I'm interested," Cody said.

He could look across the counter and into the dining room,

where people sat chewing and swallowing and drinking, patting their mouths with napkins, breaking off chunks of bread. He wondered how Ezra could stand to spend his life at this.

When the first real flurry was over, Ruth and Ezra settled at the scrubbed wooden table in the center of the kitchen, and Cody joined them. Ezra ate some of Ruth's chicken casserole. Ruth lit a small brown cigarette and tipped back in her chair to watch him. The cigarette smelled as if it were burning only by accident—like something spilled on the floor of an oven, or stuck to the underside of a saucepan. Cody, seated across from her, drank it in. "Eat, Cody, eat," Ezra urged him. Cody just shook his head, not wanting to lose his chestful of Ruth's smoke.

Meanwhile, the other cooks came and went, some of them sitting also to wolf various odd assortments of food while their kettles simmered untended. Ezra's boyhood friend Josiah appeared, metamorphosed into an efficient grown man in starchy white, and he and Ruth had a talk about peeling the apples for her pie. Cody could not have cared less about her pie, but he was riveted by her offhand, slangy style of speech. She held her cigarette between thumb and index finger, with her elbow propped against her rib cage. She hunkered forward to consider some decision, and beneath her knotted brows her eyes were so pale a blue that he was startled.

They left the restaurant before it closed. Josiah would lock up, Ezra said. They took a roundabout route home, down a quiet, one-way street, to drop Ruth off at the house where she rented a room. When Ezra accompanied her up the front steps, Cody waited on the curb. He watched Ezra kiss her good night —a bumbling, inadequate kiss, Cody judged it; and he felt some satisfaction. Then Ezra rejoined him and galumphed along beside him, big footed and blithe. "Isn't she something?" he asked Cody. "Don't you just love her?"

"Mm."

"But there's so much I need to find out from you! I want to take good care of her, but I don't know how. What about life insurance? Things like that! So much is expected of husbands, Cody. Will you help me figure it out?"

"I'll be glad to," Cody said. He meant it, too. Anything: any little crack that would provide him with an entrance.

Eventually, Ezra subsided, although he continued to give the impression of inwardly bubbling and chortling. From time to time, he hummed a few bars of something underneath his breath. And then when they were almost home—passing houses totally dark, where everyone had long since gone to sleep—what should he do but pull out that damned recorder of his and start piping away. It was embarrassing. It was infuriating: "Le Godiveau de Poisson," once again. Depend on Ezra, Cody thought, to have as his theme song a recipe for a seafood dish. He walked along in silence, hoping someone would call the police. Or at least, that they'd open a window. "You there! Quiet!" But no one did. It was so typical: Ezra the golden boy, everybody's favorite, tootling down the streets scot-free.

On Sunday morning, Cody presented himself at Ruth's door— or rather, at the door of the faded, doughy lady who owned the house Ruth stayed in. This lady toyed so fearfully with the locket at her throat that Cody felt compelled to take a step backward, proving he was not a knock-and-rob man. He gave her his most gentlemanly smile. "Good morning," he said. "Is Ruth home?"

"Ruth?"

He realized he didn't know Ruth's last name. "I'm Ezra Tull's brother," he said.

"Oh, *Ezra*," she said, and she stood back to let him enter.

He followed her deep into the interior, past a tumult of over-stuffed furniture and dusty wax fruit and heaps of magazines. In the kitchen, Ruth slouched at the table spooning up corn-flakes and reading a newspaper propped against a cereal box. A pale, pudgy man stood gazing into an open refrigerator. Cody had an impression of inertia and frittered lives. He felt charged with energy. It ought to be so easy to win her away from all this!

"Good morning," he said. Ruth looked up. The pudgy man retreated behind the refrigerator door.

"I hope you're not too far into that cereal," Cody said. "I came to invite you to breakfast."

"What for?" Ruth asked, frowning.

"Well . . . not for any *purpose*. I'm just out walking and I thought you might want to walk with me, stop off for doughnuts and coffee someplace."

"Now?"

"Of course."

"Isn't it raining?"

"Only a little bit."

"No, thanks," she said.

Her eyes dropped back to her newspaper. The landlady slid her locket along its chain with a miniature zipping sound.

"What's going on in the world?" Cody asked.

"What world?" said Ruth.

"The news. What does the newspaper say?"

Ruth raised her eyes, and Cody saw the page she had turned to. "Oh," he said. "The comics."

"No, my horoscope."

"Your horoscope." He looked to the landlady for help. The landlady gazed off toward a cabinet full of jelly glasses. "Well, what . . . um, symbol are you?" Cody asked Ruth.

"Hmm?"

"What astrological symbol?"

"Sign," she corrected him. She sighed and stood up, finally forced to recognize his presence. Snatching her paper from the table, she stalked off toward the parlor. Cody made way for her and then trailed after. Her jeans, he guessed, had been bought at a little boys' clothing store. She had no hips whatsoever. Her sweater was transparent at the elbows.

"I'm Taurus," she said over her shoulder, "but all that's rubbish, anyhow. Total garbage."

"Oh, I agree," Cody said, relieved.

She stopped in the center of the parlor and turned to him. "Look at here," she said, and she jabbed her finger at a line of newsprint. *"Powerful ally will come to your rescue. Accent today on high finance."* She lowered the paper. "I mean, who do they reckon they're dealing with? What kind of business am I supposed to be involved in?"

"Ridiculous," said Cody. He was hypnotized by her eyebrows. They were the color of orange sherbet, and whenever she spoke with any heat the skin around them grew pink, darker than the eyebrows themselves.

"Ignore innuendos from long-time foe," she read, running a finger down the column. "Or listen to this other one: *Clandestine meeting could solve mystery.* Almighty God!" she said, and she tossed the paper into an armchair. "You got to lead quite a life, to get anything out of your horoscope."

"Well, I don't know," Cody said. "Maybe it's truer than you realize."

"Come again?"

"Maybe it's saying you *ought* to lead such a life. Ought to be more adventurous, not just slave away in some restaurant, mope around a gloomy old boardinghouse . . ."

"It's not so gloomy," Ruth said, lifting her chin.

"Well, but—"

"And anyhow, I won't always be here. Me and Ezra, after we marry, we're moving in above the Homesick. Then once we get us some money we plan on a house."

"But still," said Cody, "you won't have anywhere near what those horoscopes are calling for. Why, there's all the outside world! New York, for instance. Ever been to New York?"

She shook her head, watching him narrowly.

"You ought to come; it's springtime there."

"It's springtime here," she said.

"But a different kind."

"I don't see what you're getting at," she told him.

"Well, all I want to say is, Ruth: why settle down so soon, when there's so much you haven't seen yet?"

"Soon?" she said. "I'm pretty near twenty years old. Been rattling around on my own since my sixteenth birthday. Only thing I *want* is to settle down, sooner the better."

"Oh," said Cody.

"Well, have a good walk."

"Oh, yes, walk . . ."

"Don't drown," she told him, callously.

At the door, he turned. He said, "Ruth?"

"What."

"I don't know your last name."

"Spivey," she said.

He thought it was the loveliest sound he had ever heard in his life.

The following weekend, he drove her out to see his farm. "I have seen all the farms I care to," she said, but Ezra said, "Oh, you ought to go, Ruth. It's pretty this time of year." Ezra himself had to stay behind; he was supervising the installation of a new meat locker for the restaurant. Cody had known that before he invited her.

This time he brought her jonquils. She said, "I don't know what I want with *these;* there's a whole mess in back by the walkway."

Cody smiled at her.

He settled her in his Cadillac, which smelled of new leather. She looked unimpressed. Perversely, she was wearing a skirt, on the one occasion when jeans would have been more suitable. Her legs were very white, almost chalky. He had not seen short socks like hers since his schooldays, and her tattered sneakers were as small and stubby as a child's.

On the drive out, he talked about his plans for the farm. "It's where I'd like to live," he said. "Where I want to raise my family. It's a perfect place for children."

"What makes you think so?" she asked. "When I was a kid, all I cared about was getting to the city."

"Yes, but fresh air and home-grown vegetables, and the

animals . . . Right now, the man down the road is tending my livestock, but once I move in full-time I'm going to do it all myself."

"*That* I'd like to see," said Ruth. "You ever slopped a hog? Shoveled out a stable?"

"I can learn," he told her.

She shrugged and said no more.

When they reached the farm he showed her around the grounds, where she stared a cow down and gave a clump of hens the evil eye. Then he led her into the house. He'd bought it lock, stock, and barrel—complete with bald plush sofa and kerosene stove in the parlor, rickety kitchen table with its drawerful of rusted flatware, 1958 calendar on the wall advertising Mallardy's oystershell mixture for layers, extra rich in calcium. The man who'd lived here—a widower—had died upstairs in the four-poster bed. Cody had replaced the bed-clothes with new ones, sheets and a quilt and down pillows, but that was his only change. "I do plan to fix things up," he told Ruth, "but I'm waiting till I marry. I know my wife might like to have a say in it."

Ruth removed a window lock easily from its crumbling wooden sash. She turned it over and peered at the underside.

"I want a wife very much," said Cody.

She put back the lock. "I hate to be the one to tell you," she said, "but smell that smell? Kind of sweetish smell? You got dry rot here."

"Ruth," he said, "do you dislike me for any reason?"

"Huh?"

"Your attitude. The way you put me off. You don't think much of me, do you?" he said.

She gave him an edgy, skewed look, evasive, and moved over to the stairway. "Oh," she said, "I like you a fair amount."

"You do?"

"But I know your type," she said.

"What type?"

"There were plenty like you in my school," she said. "Oh,

sure! Some in every class, on every team—tall and real good-looking, stylish, athletic, witty. *Smooth*-mannered boys that everything always came easy to, that always knew the proper way of doing things, and never dated any but the cheerleader girls, or the homecoming queen, or her maids of honor at the lowest. Passing me in the halls not even knowing who I was, nor guessing I existed. Or making fun of me sometimes, I'm almost certain—laughing at how poor I dressed and mocking my freckly face and my old red hair—"

"Laughing! When have I ever done such a thing?"

"I'm not naming you in particular," she said, "but you sure do put me in mind of a type."

"Ruth. I wouldn't mock you. I think you're perfect," he said. "You're the most beautiful woman I've ever laid eyes on."

"See there?" she asked, and she raised her chin, spun about, and marched down the stairs. She wouldn't answer anything else he said to her, all during the long drive home.

It was a campaign, was what it was—a long and arduous battle campaign, extending through April and all of May. There were moments when he despaired. He'd had too late a start, was out of the running; he'd wasted his time with those unoriginal, obvious brunettes whom he'd thought he was so clever to snare while Ezra, not even trying, had somehow divined the real jewel. Lucky Ezra! His whole life rested on luck, and Cody would probably never manage to figure out how he did it.

Often, after leaving Ruth, Cody would be muttering to himself as he strode away. He would slam a fist in his palm or kick his own car. But at the same time, he had an underlying sense of exhilaration. Yes, he would have to say that he'd never felt more alive, never more eager for each new day. Now he understood why he'd lost interest in Carol or Karen, what's-her-name, the social worker who hadn't found Ezra appealing. She'd made it too easy. What he liked was the competition, the hope of emerging triumphant from a neck-and-neck struggle with Ezra, his oldest enemy. He even liked biding his time, holding himself in check, hiding his feelings from Ruth till the most advantageous moment. (Was *patience* Ezra's secret?) For, of course, this wasn't an open competition. One of the contestants didn't even know he *was* a contestant. "Gosh, Cody," Ezra said, "it's been nice to have you around so much lately." And to Ruth, "Go, go; you'll enjoy it," when Cody invited her anywhere.

Once, baiting Ezra, Cody stole one of Ruth's brown cigarettes and smoked it in the farmhouse. (The scent of burning tar filled his bedroom. If he'd had a telephone, he would have forgotten all his strategies and called her that instant to confess he loved her.) He stubbed out the butt in a plastic ashtray beside his bed. Then later he invited Ezra to look at his new calves, took him upstairs to discuss a leak in the roof, and led him to the night-stand where the ashtray sat. But Ezra just said, "Oh, was Ruth here?" and launched into praise for an herb garden she was planting on top of the restaurant. Cody couldn't believe that anyone would be so blind, so credulous. Also, he would have died for the privilege of having Ruth plant herbs for him. He thought of the yard out back, where he'd always envisioned his wife's kitchen garden. Rosemary! Basil! Lemon balm!

"Why didn't she come to me?" he asked Ezra. "She could always grow her herbs on my farm."

"Oh, well, the closer to home the fresher," said Ezra. "But you're kind to offer, Cody."

Oiling his rifles that night, Cody seriously considered shooting Ezra through the heart.

When he complimented Ruth, she bristled. When he brought her the gifts he'd so craftily chosen (gold chains and crystal flasks of perfume, music boxes, silk flowers, all intended to contrast with the ugly, mottled marble rolling pin that Ezra presented, clumsily wrapped, on her twentieth birthday), she generally lost them right away or left them wherever she happened to be. And when he invited her places, she only came along for the outing. He would take her arm and she'd say, "Jeepers, I'm not some old lady." She would scramble over rocks and through forests in her combat boots, and Cody would follow, bemused and dazzled, literally sick with love. He had lost eight pounds, could not eat—a myth, he'd always thought that was—and hardly slept at night. When he did sleep, he willed himself to dream of Ruth but never did; she was impishly, defiantly absent, and daytimes when they next met he thought he saw something taunting in the look she gave him.

He often found it difficult to keep their conversations going. It struck him sometimes—in the middle of the week, when he was far from Baltimore—that this whole idea was deranged. They would never be anything but strangers. What single interest, even, did they have in common? But every weekend he was staggered, all over again, by her strutting walk, her belligerent chin and endearing scowl. He was moved by her musty, little-boyish smell; he imagined how her small body could nestle into his. Oh, it was Ruth herself they had in common. He would reach out to touch the spurs of her knuckles. She would ruffle and draw back. "What are you doing?" she would ask. He didn't answer.

"I know what you're up to," his mother told him.

"I beg your pardon?"

"I see through you like a sheet of glass."

"Well? What am I up to, then?" he asked. He really did hope to hear; he had reached the stage where he'd angle and connive just to get someone to utter Ruth's name.

"You don't fool me for an instant," said his mother. "Why are you so contrary? You've got no earthly use for that girl. She's not your type in the slightest; she belongs to your brother, Ezra, and she's the only thing in this world he's ever wanted. If you were to win her away, tell me what you'd do with her! You'd drop her flat. You'd say, 'Oh, my goodness, what am I doing with *this* little person?'"

"You don't understand," said Cody.

"This may come as a shock," his mother told him, "but I understand you perfectly. With the rest of the world I might not be so smart, but with my three children, why, not the least little thing escapes me. I know everything you're after. I see everything in your heart, Cody Tull."

"Just like God," Cody said.
"Just like God," she agreed.

Ezra arranged a celebration dinner for the evening before Jenny's wedding—a Friday. But Thursday night, Jenny phoned Cody at his apartment. It was a local call; she said she wasn't ten blocks away, staying at a hotel with Sam Wiley. "We got married yesterday morning," she said, "and now we're on our honeymoon. So there won't be any dinner after all."

"Well, how did all *this* come about?" Cody asked.

"Mother and Sam had a little disagreement."

"I see."

"Mother said . . . and Sam told her . . . and I said, 'Oh, Sam, why not let's just . . .' Only I do feel bad about Ezra. I know how much trouble he's gone to."

"By now, he ought to be used to this," Cody said.

"He was going to serve a suckling pig."

Hadn't Ezra noticed (Cody wondered) that the family as a whole had never yet finished one of his dinners? That they'd fight and stamp off halfway through, or sometimes not even manage to get seated in the first place? Well, of course he must have *noticed*, but was it clear to him as a pattern, a theme? No, perhaps he viewed each dinner as a unit in itself, unconnected to the others. Maybe he never linked them in his mind.

Assuming he was a total idiot.

It was true that once—to celebrate Cody's new business—they had made it all the way to dessert; so if they hadn't ordered dessert you could say they'd completed the meal. But the fact was, they did order dessert, which was left to sag on the plates when their mother accused Cody of deliberately setting up shop as far from home as possible. There was a stiff-backed little quarrel. Conversation fell apart. Cody walked out. So technically, even that meal could not be considered finished. Why did Ezra go on trying?

Why did the rest of them go on showing up, was more to the point.

In fact, they probably saw more of each other than happy families did. It was almost as if what they couldn't get right, they had to keep returning to. (So if they ever did finish a dinner, would they rise and say goodbye forever after?)

Once Jenny had hung up, Cody sat on the couch and leafed through the morning's mail. Something made him feel unsettled. He wondered how Jenny could have married Sam Wiley—a scrawny little artist type, shifty eyed and cocky. He wondered if Ezra would cancel his dinner altogether or merely postpone it till after the honeymoon. He pictured Ruth in the restaurant kitchen, her wrinkled little fingers patting flour on drumsticks. He scanned an ad for life insurance and wondered why no one depended on him—not even enough to require his insurance money if he should happen to die.

He ripped open an envelope marked *AMAZING OFFER!* and found three stationery samples and a glossy order blank. One sample was blue, with *LMR* embossed at the top. Another had a lacy *PAULA*, the *P* entwined with a morning-glory vine, and the third was one of those letters that form their own envelopes when folded. The flap was printed with butterflies and *Mrs. Harold Alexander III, 219 Saint Beulah Boulevard, Dallas, Texas*. He studied that for a moment. Then he took a pen from his shirt pocket, and started writing in an unaccustomed, backhand slant:

Dear Ruth,

Just a line to say hey from all of us. How's the job going? What do you think of Baltimore? Harold says ask if you met a young man yet. He had the funniest dream last night, dreamed he saw you with someone tall, black hair and gray eyes and gray suit. I said well, I certainly hope it's a dream that comes true!

We have all been fine tho Linda was out of school one day last week. A case of "math test-itis" it looked like to me, ha ha! She says to send you lots of hugs and kisses. Drop us a line real soon, hear?

Cody felt he had just found the proper tone toward the end; he was sorry to run out of space. He signed the letter *Luv, Sue (Mrs. Harold Alexander III)*, and sealed, stamped, and addressed it. Then he placed it in a business envelope, and wrote a note to his old college roommate in Dallas, asking if he would please drop the enclosed in the nearest mailbox.

That weekend he didn't go home, and his reward was to dream about Ruth. She was waiting for a train that he was traveling on. He saw her on the platform, peering into the windows of each passenger car as it slid by. He was so eager to reach her, to watch her expression ease when she caught sight of him, that he called her name aloud and woke himself up. He heard it echoing in the dark—not her name, after all, but some meaningless sleep sound. For hours after that he tried to burrow back inside the dream, but he had lost it.

The next morning he began another letter, on the sheet headed *PAULA*. In a curlicued script, he wrote:

Dear Ruthie,

You old thing, don't you keep in touch with your friends any more? I told Mama the other day, Mama that Ruth Spivey has forgotten all about us I believe.

Things here are not going too good. I guess you might have heard that me and Norman are separated. I know you liked him, but you had no idea how tiresome he could be, always so slow and quiet, he got on my nerves. Ruthie stay clear of those pale blond thoughtful kind of men, they're a real disappointment. Go for someone dark and interesting who will take you lots of places you've never been. I'm serious, I know what I'm talking about.

Mama sends you greetings and asks do you want her to sew you anything. She's real crippled now with the arthritis in her knees and can only sit in her chair, has plenty of time for sewing.

See ya, Paula

That letter he mailed from Pennsylvania, when he visited a packing-crate plant the following Tuesday. And on Wednesday, from New York, he sent the blue sheet with *LMR* at the top.

Dear Ruth,

Had lunch with Donna the other day and she told me you were going with a real nice fellow. Was kind of hazy on the particulars but when she said his name was Tull and he came from Baltimore I knew it must be Cody. Everybody here knows Cody, we all just love him, he really is a good man at heart and has been misjudged for years by people who don't understand him. Well, Ruthie, I guess you're smarter than I gave you credit for, I always thought you'd settle for one of those dime-a-dozen blond types but now I see I was wrong.

I'll be waiting for the details.

Love, Laurie May

"You went too far with that last letter," Ruth told him.

"I don't know what you're talking about."

He was sitting on a kitchen stool, watching her cube meat. He'd come directly to the restaurant this Saturday—bypassing home, bypassing the farm—hoping to find her altered somehow, mystified, perhaps tossing him a speculative glance from time to time. Instead, she seemed cross. She slammed her cleaver on the chopping board. "Do you realize," she asked, "that I went ahead and answered that first note? Not wanting someone to worry, I sent it back and said it wasn't mine, there must be some mistake; went out specially and bought a stamp to mail it with. And would've sent the second back, too, only it didn't have a return address. Then the third comes; well, you went too far."

"I tend to do that," Cody said regretfully.

Ruth slung the cleaver with a thunking sound. Cody was afraid the others—only Todd Duckett and Josiah, this early— would wonder what was wrong, but they didn't even look around. Ezra was out front, chalking up tonight's menu.

"Just what is your *problem?*" Ruth asked him. "Do you have something against me? You think I'm some Garrett County hick that you don't want marrying your brother?"

"Of course I don't want you marrying him," Cody said. "I love you."

"Huh?"

This wasn't the moment he had planned, but he rushed on anyway, as if drunk. "I mean it," he said, "I feel driven. I feel pulled. I have to have you. You're all I ever think about."

She was staring at him, astonished, with one hand cupped to scoop the meat cubes into a skillet.

"I guess I'm not saying it right," he told her.

"Saying what? What are you talking about?"

"Ruth. I really, truly love you," he said. "I'm sick over you. I can't even eat. Look at me! I've lost eleven pounds."

He held out his arms, demonstrating. His jacket hung loose at the sides. Lately he'd moved his belt in a notch; his suits no longer fit so smoothly but seemed rumpled, gathered, bunchy.

"It's true you're kind of skinny," Ruth said slowly.

"Even my shoes feel too big."

"What's the matter with you?" she asked.

"You haven't heard a word I said!"

"Over *me*, you said. You must be making fun."

"Ruth, I swear—" he said.

"You're used to New York City girls, models, actresses; you could have anyone."

"It's you I'll have."

She studied him a moment. It began to seem he'd finally broken through; they were having a conversation. Then she said, "We got to get that weight back on you."

He groaned.

"See there?" she asked. "You never eat a thing I offer you."

"I can't," he told her.

"I don't believe you ever once tasted my cooking."

She set the skillet aside and went over to the tall black kettle that was simmering on the stove. "Country vegetable," she said, lifting the lid.

"Really, Ruth . . ."

She filled a small crockery bowl and set it on the table. "Sit down," she said. "Eat. When you've tried it, I'll tell you the secret ingredient."

Steam rose from the bowl, with a smell so deep and spicy that already he felt overfed. He accepted the spoon that she held out. He dipped it in the soup reluctantly and took a sip.

"Well?" she asked.

"It's very good," he said.

In fact, it was delicious, if you cared about such things. He'd never tasted soup so good. There were chunks of fresh vegetables, and the broth was rich and heavy. He took another mouthful. Ruth stood over him, her thumbs hooked into her blue jeans pockets. "Chicken feet," she said.

"Pardon?"

"Chicken feet is the secret ingredient."

He lowered the spoon and looked down into the bowl.

"Eat up," she told him. "Put some meat on your bones."

He dipped the spoon in again.

After that, she brought him a salad made with the herbs she'd grown on the roof and a basketful of rolls she'd baked that afternoon—a recipe from home, she said. Cody ate everything. As long as he ate, she watched him. When she brought him more butter for his rolls, she leaned close over him and he felt the warmth she gave off.

Now two more cooks had arrived and a Chinese boy was sautéing black mushrooms, and Ezra was running a mixer near the sink. Ruth sat down next to Cody, hooking her combat boots on the rung of his chair and hugging her ribs. Cody cut into a huge wedge of pie and gave some thought to food—to its inexplicable, loaded meaning in other people's lives. Couldn't you classify a person, he wondered, purely by examining his attitude toward food? Look at Cody's mother—a nonfeeder, if ever there was one. Even back in his childhood, when they'd depended on her for nourishment . . . why, mention you were hungry and she'd suddenly act rushed and harassed, fretful, out of breath, distracted. He remembered her coming home from work in the evening and tearing irritably around the kitchen. Tins toppled out of the cupboards and fell all over her—pork 'n' beans, Spam, oily tuna fish, peas canned olive-drab. She cooked in her hat, most of the time. She whimpered when she burned things. She burned things you would not imagine it possible to burn and served others half-raw, adding jarring extras of her own design such as crushed pineapple in the mashed potatoes. (Anything, as long as it was a leftover, might as well be dumped in the pan with anything else.) Her only seasonings were salt and pepper. Her only gravy was Campbell's cream of mushroom soup, undiluted. And till Cody was grown, he had assumed that roast beef had to be stringy—not something you sliced, but a leathery dry object which you separated with a fork, one strand from the other, and dropped with a clunk upon your plate.

Though during illness, he remembered, you could count on her to bring liquids. Hot tea: she was good at that. And canned consommé. Thin things, watery things. Then she'd stand in the door with her arms folded while you drank it. He remembered that her expression, when others ate or drank, conveyed a mild distaste. She ate little herself, often toyed with her food; and she implied some criticism of those who acted hungry or over-interested in what they were served. Neediness: she disapproved of neediness in people. Whenever there was a family argument, she most often chose to start it over dinner.

Biting into Ruth's flaky, shattering crust, Cody considered his mother's three children—Jenny, for instance, with her lemon-water and lettuce-leaf diets, never allowing herself a sweet, skipping meals altogether, as if continually bearing in mind that disapproving expression of her mother's. And Cody himself was not much different, when you came right down to it. It seemed that food didn't count, with him; food was something required by others, so that for their sakes—on dates, at business luncheons —he would obligingly order a meal for himself just to keep them company. But all you'd find in his refrigerator was cream for his coffee and limes for his gin and tonics. He never ate break-fast; he often forgot lunch. Sometimes a gnawing feeling hit his stomach in the afternoon and he sent his secretary out for food. "What kind of food?" she would ask. He would say, "Anything, I don't care." She'd bring a Danish or an eggroll or a liverwurst on rye; it was all the same to him. Half the time, he wouldn't even notice what it was—would take a bite, go on dictating, leave the rest to be disposed of by the cleaning lady. A woman he'd once had dinner with had claimed that this was a sign of some flaw. Watching him dissect his fish but then fail to eat it, noticing how he refused dessert and then benignly, tolerantly waited for her to finish a giant chocolate mousse, she had accused him of . . . what had she called it? Lack of enjoyment. Lack of ability to enjoy himself. He hadn't understood, back then, how she could draw so many implications from a single meal. And still he didn't agree with her.

Yes, only Ezra, he would say, had managed to escape all this. Ezra was so impervious—so thickheaded, really; nothing ever touched him. He ate heartily, whether it was his mother's cooking or his own. He liked anything that was offered him, especially bread—would have to watch his weight as he got older. But above all else, he was a feeder. He would set a dish before you and then stand there with his face expectant, his hands clasped tightly under his chin, his eyes following your fork. There was something tender, almost loving, about his attitude toward people who were eating what he'd cooked them.

Like Ruth, Cody thought.

He asked her for another slice of pie.

Mornings, now, he called her from New York, often getting her landlady out of bed; and Ruth when she answered was still creaky voiced from sleep—or was it from bewilderment, even now? Reluctantly, each time, she warmed to his questions, speaking shortly at first. Yes, she was fine. The restaurant was fine. Dinner last night had gone well. And then (letting her sentences stretch gradually longer, as if giving in to him all over again) she told him that this house was starting to wear her down—creepy boarders padding around in their slippers at all hours, no one ever *going* anywhere, landlady planted eternally in front of her TV. This landlady, a widow, believed that Perry Como's eyebrows quirked upward as they did because he was by nature a bass, and singing such high notes gave him constant pain; she had heard that Arthur Godfrey, too, had been enduring constant pain for years, smiling a courageous smile and wheeling about on his stool because the slightest step would stab him like a knife. Yes, everything, to Mrs. Pauling, was a constant pain; *life* was a constant pain, and Ruth had started looking around her and wondering how she stood this place.

Weekends—Friday and Saturday nights—Ruth tore through the restaurant kitchen slapping haunches of beef and whipping egg whites. Ezra worked more quietly. Cody sat at the wooden table. Now and then, Ruth would place some new dish in front of him and Cody would eat it dutifully. Every mouthful was a declaration of love. Ruth knew that. She was tense and watchful. She gave him sideways, piercing glances when he forked up one of her dumplings, and he was careful to leave nothing on his plate.

Then on Sunday mornings, yellow summer mornings at her boardinghouse, he rang her doorbell and pulled her close to him when she answered. Anytime he kissed her, he was visited by the curious impression that some other self of hers was still moving through the house behind her, spunky and lighthearted and uncatchable even yet, checking under pot lids, slamming cupboard doors, humming and tossing her head and wiping her hands on her blue jeans.

"I don't understand," Ezra told them.

"Let me start over," said Cody.

Ezra said, "Is this some kind of a joke? Is that what it is? What is it?"

"Ruth and I—" Cody began.

But Ruth said, "Ezra, honey. Listen." She stepped forward. She was wearing the navy suit that Cody had bought her to go away in, and high-heeled shoes with slender straps. Although it was a glaring day in August, her skin had a chilled, dry, powdery look, and her freckles stood out sharply. She said, "Ezra, we surely never planned on this. We never had the least intention, not me or Cody neither one."

Ezra waited, evidently still not comprehending. He was backed against the huge old restaurant stove, as if retreating from their news.

"It just happened, like," said Ruth.

"You don't know what you're saying," said Ezra.

"Ezra, honey—"

"You would never do this. It's not true."

"See, I don't know how it came about but me and Cody . . . and I should've told you sooner but I kept thinking, oh, this is just some . . . I mean, this is silly; he's so sophisticated, he isn't someone for *me*; this is just some . . . daydream, see . . ."

"There's bound to be an explanation," Ezra said.

"I feel real bad about it, Ezra."

"I'm sure I'll understand in a minute," he said. "Just give me time. Just wait a minute. Let me think it through."

They waited, but he didn't say anything more. He pressed two fingers against his forehead, as if working out some complicated puzzle. After a while, Cody touched Ruth's arm. She said, "Well, Ezra, goodbye, I guess." Then she and Cody left.

In the car, she cried a little—not making any fuss but sniffling quietly and keeping her face turned toward the side window. "Are you all right?" Cody asked.

She nodded.

"You're sure you still want to go on with this."

She nodded again.

They were planning to travel by train—Ruth's idea; she had never set foot on a train—to New York City, where they would be married in a civil ceremony. Ruth's people, she said, were mostly dead or wouldn't much care; so there wasn't any point having the wedding in her hometown. And it went without saying that *Cody's* people . . . well. For the next little bit, they might as well stay in New York. By and by, things would simmer down.

Ruth took off one of her gloves, already gray at the seams, and crumpled it into a ball and blotted both her eyes.

Near Penn Station, Cody found a parking lot that offered weekly rates. It was a good deal of trouble, traveling by train, but worth it for Ruth's sake. She was already perking up. She asked him if he thought there'd be a dining car—an "eating car," she called it. Cody said he imagined so. He accepted the ticket the parking attendant gave him and slid out from behind the steering wheel, grunting a little; lately he'd put on a few pounds around the waist. He took Ruth's suitcase from the trunk. Ruth wasn't used to high heels and she hobbled along unsteadily, every now and then making a loud, scraping sound on the sidewalk. "I hope to get the knack of these things before long," she told Cody.

"You don't have to wear them, you know."

"Oh, I surely *do*," she said.

Cody guided her into the station. The sudden, echoing coolness seemed to stun her into silence. She stood looking around her while Cody went to the ticket window. A lady at the head of the line was arguing about the cost of her fare. A man in a crisp white suit rolled his eyes at Cody, implying exasperation at the wait. Cody pretended not to notice. He turned away as if checking the length of the line behind him, and a plump young woman with a child smiled instantly, fully prepared, and said, "Cody Tull!"

"Um—"

"I'm Jane Lowry. Remember me?"

"Oh, Jane! Jane Lowry! Well, good to see you, how nice to ... and is this your little girl?"

"Yes; say hello to Mr. Tull, Betsy. Mr. Tull and Mommy used to go to school together."

"So you're married," Cody said, moving forward in line. "Well, what a—"

"Remember the day I came to visit you, uninvited?" she asked. She laughed, and he saw, in the tilt of her head, a flash of the young girl he had known. She had lived on Bushnell Street, he remembered now; she had had the most beautiful hair, which still showed its chips of gold light, although she wore it short now. "I had such a crush on you," she said. "Lord, I made a total fool of myself."

"You played a game of checkers with Ezra," he reminded her.

"Ezra?"

"My brother."

"You had a brother?"

"I certainly did; do. You played checkers with him all afternoon."

"How funny; I thought you only had a sister. What was her name? Jenny. She was so skinny, I envied her for years. Anything she wanted, she could eat and not have it show. What's Jenny doing now?"

"Oh, she's in medical school. And Ezra: he runs a restaurant."

"In those days," said Jane, "my fondest wish was to wake up one morning and find I'd turned into Jenny Tull. But I'd forgotten you had a brother."

Cody opened his mouth to speak, but the man in white had moved away and it was Cody's turn at the window. And by the time he'd bought his tickets, Jane had switched to the other line and was busy buying hers.

He didn't see her again—though he looked for her on the train—but it was odd how she'd plunged him into the past. Swaying on the seat next to Ruth, holding her small, rough hand but finding very little to say to her, he was startled by fragments of buried memories. The scent of chalk in geometry class; the balmy, laden feeling of the last day of school every spring; the crack of a baseball bat on the playground. He found himself in a summer evening at a drive-in hamburger stand, with its blinding lights surrounded by darkness, its hot, salty, greasy smell of French fries, and all his friends horsing around at the curb. He could hear an old girlfriend from years ago, her droning, dissatisfied voice: "You ask me to the movies and I say yes and then you change your mind and ask me bowling instead and I say yes to that but you say wait, let's make it another night, as if anything you can have is something it turns out you don't want . . ."

He heard his mother telling Jenny not to slouch, telling Cody not to swear, asking Ezra why he wouldn't stand up to the neighborhood bully. "I'm trying to get through life as a liquid," Ezra had said, and Cody (trying to get through life as a rock) had laughed; he could hear himself still. "Why aren't cucumbers prickly any more?" he heard Ezra ask. And "Cody? Don't you want to walk to school with me?" He saw Ezra aiming a red-feathered dart, his chapped, childish wrist awkwardly angled; he saw him running for the telephone—"I'll get it! I'll get it!" —hopeful and joyous, years and years younger. He remembered Carol, or was it Karen, reciting Ezra's faults—a *motherly* man, she'd said; what had she said?—and it occurred to him that the reason he had dropped her was, she really hadn't understood Ezra; she hadn't appreciated what he was all about. Then Ruth squeezed his hand and said, "I intend to ride trains forever; it's so much better than the bus. Isn't it, Cody? Cody? Isn't it?" The train rounded a curve with a high, thin, whistling sound that took him by surprise. He honestly believed, for an instant, that what he'd heard was music—a tune piped, a burble of notes, a little scrap of melody floating by on the wind and breaking his heart.

6

Beaches on the Moon

Twice or maybe three times a year, she goes out to the farm to make sure things are in order. She has her son Ezra drive her there, and she takes along a broom, a dustpan, rags, a grocery bag for trash and a bucket and a box of cleanser. Ezra asks why she can't just keep these supplies in the farmhouse, but she knows they wouldn't be safe. The trespassers would get them. Oh, the trespassers—the small boys and courting couples and the teen-aged gangs. It makes her mad to think of them. As the car turns off the main road, rattling up the rutted driveway, she already sees their litter—the beer cans tossed among the scrubby weeds, the scraps of toilet paper dangling from the bushes. This land has been let go and the vegetation is matted and wild, bristly, scratchy, no shade at all from the blazing sun. There are little spangles of bottle tops embedded in the dirt of the road. And the yard (which is not truly mown but sickled by Jared Peers, once or twice a summer) is flocked with white paper plates and Dixie cups, napkins, sandwich bags, red-striped straws, and those peculiarly long-lived, accordioned worms of paper that the straws were wrapped in.

Ezra parks the car beneath an oak tree. "It's a shame. A disgrace and a shame," Pearl says, stepping out. She wears a seersucker dress that will wash, and her oldest shoes. On her head is a broad-brimmed straw hat. It will keep the dust from her hair—from all but one faded, blondish frizz bordering each temple. "It's a national crime," she says, and she stands looking around her while Ezra unloads her cleaning supplies. The house has two stories. It is a ghostly, rubbed-out gray. The ridgepole sags and the front porch has buckled and many of the window-panes are broken—more every time she comes.

She remembers when Cody first showed her this place. "Imagine what can be done with it, Mother. Picture the possibilities," he said. He was planning to marry and raise a family here—provide her with lots of grandchildren. He even kept the livestock on, paying Jared Peers to tend it till Cody moved in.

That was years ago, though, and all that remains of those animals now is a couple of ragged hens gone wild, clucking in the mulberry tree out behind the barn.

She has a key to the warped rear door but it isn't needed. The padlock's missing and the rusted hasp hangs open. "Not again," she says. She turns the knob and enters, warily. (One of these days, she'll surprise someone and get her head blown off for her trouble.) The kitchen smells stale and cold, even in the heat of the day. There's a fly buzzing over the table, a rust spot smearing the back of the sink, a single tatter of cloudy plastic curtain trailing next to the window. The linoleum's worn patternless near the counters.

Ezra follows, burdened with household supplies. He sets them down and stands wiping his face on the sleeve of his work shirt. More than once he's told her he fails to see the use of this: cleaning up only to clean again, the next time they come out. What's the purpose, he wants to know. Why go to all this trouble, what does she have in mind? But he's an obliging man, and when she insists, he says no more. He runs his fingers through his hair, which the sweat has turned a dark, streaked yellow. He tests the kitchen faucet. First it explodes and then it yields a coppery trickle of water.

There are half a dozen empty bottles lying on the floor— Wild Turkey, Old Crow, Southern Comfort. "Look! And look," says Pearl. She nudges a Marlboro pack with her toe. She scrapes at a scorch on the table. She discreetly looks away while Ezra

hooks an unmentionable rubber something with the broom
handle and drops it into the trash bag.

"Cody," she used to say, "you could hire a man to come and
haul this furniture off to the dump. Surely you don't want it
for yourself. Cody, there's a Sunday suit in the bedroom closet.
There are shoes at the top of the cellar stairs—chunky, muddy
old garden shoes. You ought to hire a man to come haul them
for you." But Cody paid no attention—he was hardly ever there.
He was mostly in New York; and privately, Pearl had expected
that that was where he would stay. Which of those girlfriends
of his would agree to a life in the country? "You'd just better
watch out who you marry," she had told him. "None of your
dates that *I've* met would do—those black-haired, flashy, beauty-
queen types."

But if only he'd married one of them! If only he'd been satisfied with that! Instead, one afternoon Ezra had come into the
kitchen, had stood there looking sick. "What's wrong?" she'd
asked. She knew it was something. "Ezra? Why aren't you at
work?"

"It's Cody," he said.

"Cody?"

She clutched at her chest, picturing him dead—her most
difficult, most distant child, and now she would never have the
answer to him.

But Ezra said, "He's gone off to get married."

"Oh, married," she said, and she dropped her hand. "Well?
Who to?"

"To Ruth," he said.

"*Your* Ruth?"

"My Ruth."

"Oh, sweetheart," she said.

Not that she hadn't had some inkling. She had seen it coming
for weeks, she believed, though she hadn't exactly seen marriage
—more likely a fling, a flirtation, another of Cody's teases.
Should she have hinted to Ezra? He wouldn't have listened. He
was so gullible, and so much in love. Ruth was the center of his
world, for some reason. And anyway, who would have thought

that Cody would let it get so serious? "He's just doing it to be mean, sweetheart," she told Ezra. She was right, too, as she'd been right the other times she'd said it—oh, those other times! Those inconsequential spats, those childhood quarrels, arguments, practical jokes! "Cody, stop it this instant," she used to tell him. "You think I don't see what you're up to? Let your poor brother alone. Ezra, pay no mind. He's only being mean." Back then, Ezra had listened and nodded, hoping to believe her; he had doted on his older brother. But now he said, "What does it matter why he did it? He did it, that's all. He stole her away."

"If she could be stolen, honey, why, you don't want her anyhow."

Ezra just looked at her—bleak faced, grim, a walking ache of a man. She knew how he felt. Hadn't she been through it? She remembered from when her husband left—a wound, she'd been, a deep, hollow hole, surrounded by shreds of her former self.

She sweeps all the trash to the center of the floor, collects the bottles and the cigarette packs. Meanwhile, Ezra tapes squares of cardboard to the broken windowpanes. He works steadily, doggedly. She looks up once and sees how the sweat has made an eagle-shaped stain across his back. There are other cardboard squares on other panes, broken earlier. In a few more seasons, it occurs to her, they'll be working in the dark. It's as if they're sealing themselves in, windowpane by windowpane.

When Cody came back with Ruth, after the honeymoon, he was better-looking than ever, sleek and dark and well dressed, but Ruth was her same homely self: a little muskrat of a girl with wickety red hair and freckles, her skin that tissue-thin kind subject to lip sores and pink splotches, her twiggish body awkward in a matronly brown suit that must have been bought especially for this occasion. (Though Pearl was to find, in later years, that all Ruth's clothes struck her that way; nothing ever seemed as natural as those little-boy dungarees she used to wear with Ezra.) Pearl watched the two of them sharply, closely, anxious to come to some conclusion about their marriage, but they gave away no secrets. Ruth sat pressing her palms together; Cody kept his arm across the back of the couch, not touching her but claiming her, at least. He talked at length about the farm. They were heading out there directly, settling in that night. It was too late for sowing a garden but at least they could clean the place up, begin to make plans for next spring. Ruth was going to get started on that while Cody went back to New York. Ruth nodded at this, and cleared her throat and fumbled with the pocket of her suit jacket. Pearl thought she was reaching for one of her little cigars, but after a moment she stopped fumbling and placed her palms together again. And in fact, Pearl never saw her smoke another one of those cigars.

Then Ezra arrived—not whistling, oddly quiet, as he'd been since Ruth had left. He stopped inside the door and looked at them. "Ezra," Cody said easily, and Ruth stood up and held out her hand. She seemed frightened. This made Pearl like her, a little. (Ruth, at least, recognized the magnitude of what they'd done.) "How you doing, Ezra," Ruth said, quavering. And Ezra had said . . . oh, something or other, he'd managed something; and stood around a while shifting from foot to foot and answering their small talk. So it looked, on the surface, as if they might eventually smooth things over. Yes, after all, this choosing of mates was such a small, brief stage in a family's history.

But Ezra no longer played tunes on his recorder, and he continued to look limp and beaten, and he went to bed every night with no more than a "Good night, Mother." She grieved for him. She longed to say, "Ezra, believe me, she's nothing! You're worth a dozen Ruth Spiveys! A dozen of both of them, to be frank, even if Cody *is* my son . . ." Though of course she loved Cody dearly. But from infancy, he had batted her away; and his sister had been so evasive, somehow; so whom did that leave but Ezra? Ezra was all she had. He was the only one who would let her in. Sometimes, in his childhood, she had worried that he would die young—one of life's ironic twists, to take what you valued most. She had watched him trudging down the street to school, his duck-yellow head bowed in thought, and she would have a sudden presentiment that this was the last she would see of him. Then when he returned, full of news about friends and

ball games, how solid, how commonplace—even how irritating
—he seemed! And sometimes, long ago when he was small, he
might climb up into her lap and place his thin little arms around
her neck, and she would drink in his smell of warm biscuits and
think, "Really, this is what it's all about. This is what I'm alive
for." Then, reluctantly, she allowed him to slip away again.
(They claimed she was possessive, pushy. Little did they know.)
As a child, he'd had a chirpy style of talking that was so cheerful, ringing through the house like a trill of water . . . when
had that begun to change? As an older boy he grew shy and
withdrawn, gazing out of shining gray eyes and saying next to
nothing. She'd worried when he didn't date. "Wouldn't you
like to bring someone home? Ask someone to Sunday dinner?"
He shook his head, tongue-tied. He blushed and lowered his
long lashes. Pearl wondered, seeing the blush, whether he
thought much about girls and such as that. His father had left
by then and Cody was no help, three years older, off tomcatting
someplace or other. Then as a man, Ezra was . . . well, to be
honest, he was not much different from when he was a boy. In
a way, he was an *eternal* boy, never got boastful and brash like
most men but stayed gentle, somber, contentedly running that
restaurant of his and coming home peaceful and tired.

It was a shock when he introduced her to Ruth. What an
urchin she was! But plainly, Ezra adored her. "Mother, I'd like
you to meet my—meet Ruth." Pearl had stalled a little, at first.
Maybe she had failed to act properly welcoming. Well, who
could blame her? And now, seeing how things had turned out,
who could say she'd been wrong? But she can't help wondering, anyhow . . . If she'd been a little more encouraging, they
might have married sooner. They might have married before
Cody could work his mischief. Or if she had let herself *realize*
. . . Yes, she wonders over and over again: if she'd mentioned
Cody's plot to Ezra, stopped that situation that was not so much
a courtship as a landslide, a kind of gathering and falling of
events . . .

Ridiculous, of course, to imagine that anything she did could
have mattered. What happens, happens. It's no one's fault. (Or

it's only Cody's fault, for he has always been striving and com-
petitive, a natural-born player of games, has had to win absolutely everything, even something he doesn't want like a runty
little redhead far below his usual standards.)

She opens the farmhouse parlor to air it. It smells like skunk.
She leaves the front door ajar, taking care not to step onto the
porch, which could very well give way beneath her. She remembers how, toward the end of that first week after the
honeymoon, she asked Ezra to bring out to Ruth a few odds and
ends for the farm—some extra pans, some linens, a carpet
sweeper she had no use for. Was there an ulterior motive in her
suggestion? If not, why didn't she accompany him, visit the
bride like any good mother-in-law? "Please, I don't want to,"
Ezra said, but she said, "Honey. Go." She hadn't had any conscious design—truly, none at all—but it was a fact that later
that morning, dawdling over the dishes, she'd allowed herself a
little daydream: Ezra coming up behind Ruth, setting his arms
around her, Ruth protesting only briefly before collapsing
against him . . . Oh, shouldn't it be possible to undo what was
done? What all of them had done?

But Ezra when he returned was as subdued as ever, and only
said that Ruth thanked Pearl for the pans and linens but was
sending back the carpet sweeper as the farmhouse had no carpets.

Then Saturday, Cody came storming in with everything Ezra
had taken to Ruth. "What's all this?" he asked Pearl.

"Why, Cody, pots and sheets, as you can surely see."

"How come Ezra brought them out?"

"I asked him to," she said.

"I won't have it! Won't have him hanging around the farm."

"Cody. It was at my request. Believe me," she told him.

"I do," he said.

She tried to get Ezra to go again the following week—taking
the rug from the dining room and the carpet sweeper, once
more—but he wouldn't. "I'm not comfortable there," he said.
"There's no point. What's the point?" She supposed he was
right. Yes, she thought, let Ruth wonder where he'd got to!
People who leave us will be sorry in the end. She imagined

Ruth alone in the farmhouse, roaming from room to room and peering sadly through the bare windows.

The next weekend, Pearl asked Ezra to drive her out. He couldn't very well refuse; he was her only means of transportation. They both, without discussing it, wore Sunday clothing— formal, guestlike clothing. They found the house looking sealed and abandoned. A lone hound nudged at a bone in the yard, but he surely didn't belong there.

Back home, Pearl placed a call to Cody in New York. "Aren't you coming to the farm any more?"

"Things are kind of busy."

"Won't Ruth be there during the week?"

"I want her here with me," he said. "After all, we just did get married."

"Well, when will we see you?"

"Pretty soon, not too long, I'm sure we'll be down in a while . . ."

But they weren't; or if they were, they didn't tell Pearl, and she was too proud to ask again. The summer ended and the leaves turned all colors, but Ezra dragged himself along with no change. "Sweetheart," Pearl told him, as in his boyhood, "isn't there someone you'd like to have home? Some friend to dinner? Anyone," she said. Ezra said no.

From time to time, Pearl called Cody in New York again. He was courteous and noncommittal. Ruth, if she spoke, gave flustered replies and didn't seem to have her wits about her. Then in October, two full weeks went by when no one answered the phone at all. Pearl wondered if they'd gone to the farm, and she begged Ezra to investigate. But when he finally agreed to, he found nobody there. "Someone's shattered four window-panes," he reported. "Threw rocks at them, or shot them out." This made Pearl feel frightened. The world was closing in on them; even here on her own familiar streets, she no longer felt safe. And who knew what might have become of Ruth and Cody? They could be lying dead in their apartment, victims of a burglary or some bizarre, New York–type accident, their bodies undiscovered for weeks. Oh, this was what happened when you broke off all ties with your family! It wasn't right; with your family, if with no one else, you have to keep on trying.

She called frantically, day after day, often letting the phone ring thirty or forty times. There was something calming about that faraway purling sound. She was, at least, connected— though only to an object in Cody's apartment.

Then he answered. It was late in October. She was so taken aback that she didn't know what to say. It seemed the monotonous ring of the phone had grown to be enough for her. "Um, Cody . . ." she said.

"Oh. Mother."

"Cody, where have you *been?*"

"I had a job to see to in Ohio. I took Ruth along."

"You didn't answer the phone for weeks, and we looked for you out at the farm and some of the windows were broken."

"Damn! I thought I was paying Jared to keep that kind of thing from happening."

"You can't imagine how I felt, Cody. When I heard about the windows I felt . . . You're letting that place go to rack and ruin and we never get to see you any more."

"I do have a job to do, Mother."

"I thought that once you married, you were moving down to Baltimore. You were doing over the farmhouse and planting a garden and all."

"Yes, definitely. That's a definite possibility," said Cody. "Get Ezra to tape those windows, will you? And tell him to speak to Jared. I can't have the place depreciating."

"All right, Cody," she said.

Then she asked about Thanksgiving. "Will you be coming down? You know how Ezra likes to have us at the restaurant."

"Oh, Ezra and his restaurant . . ."

"Please. We've hardly seen you," she said.

"Well, maybe."

So in November they returned—Cody looking elegant and casual, Ruth incongruous in a large, ornate blue dress. Her hair was so stubby, her head so small, that the dress appeared to be drowning her. She staggered in her high-heeled shoes. She still would not meet Ezra's gaze.

"What have you two been up to?" Pearl asked Ruth, as they rode in Cody's Cadillac to the restaurant.

"Oh, nothing so much."

"Are you decorating Cody's apartment?"

"Decorating? No."

"We've hardly seen it," Cody said. "I'm taking on longer-term jobs. In December I start reorganizing a textile plant in Georgia, a *big* thing, five or six months. I thought maybe Ruth could come with me; we could rent us a little house of some kind. There's not much point in commuting."

"December? But then you'd miss Christmas," said Pearl.

Cody looked surprised. He said, "Why would we miss it?"

"I mean, would you still make the trip to Baltimore?"

"Oh. Well, no, I guess not," he said. "But we're here for Thanksgiving, aren't we?"

She resolved to say no more. She had her dignity.

They sat at their regular family table, surrounded by a fair-sized crowd. (In those days—the start of the sixties—shaggy young people had just discovered Ezra's restaurant, with its stripped wood and pure, fresh food, and they thronged there every evening.) It was sad that Jenny couldn't come; she was spending the holiday with her in-laws. But Ruth, at least, rounded out their number. Pearl smiled across the table at her. Ruth said, "It feels right funny to be eating where I used to be cooking."

"Would you like to visit the kitchen?" Ezra asked. "The staff would enjoy seeing you."

"I don't mind if I do," she said. It was the first time since her marriage that she'd looked at him directly—or the first that Pearl knew about.

So Ezra scraped back his chair and rose, and guided Ruth into the kitchen. Pearl could tell that Cody wasn't pleased. He stopped in the act of unfolding his napkin and gazed after them, even taking a breath as if preparing to object. Then he must have thought better of it. He shook out the napkin angrily, saying nothing.

"So," said Pearl. "When do you move to the farm?"

"Farm? Oh, I don't know," he said. "Everything's so changed; the whole character of my work has changed." He looked again toward the kitchen.

"But you'd planned on raising a family there. It was all you ever talked about."

"Yes, well, and these long-term contracts," he said, as if he hadn't heard her.

Pearl said, "You had your heart just set on it."

But he continued watching the other two. He was not the least bit interested in what she might be saying. The kitchen was fully exposed, and could not have concealed the smallest secret. So why was Cody nervous? Ezra and Ruth stood talking with one of the cooks, their backs to the dining room. Ezra gestured as he spoke. He lifted both arms wide, one arm behind Ruth but not touching her, not brushing her shoulder, surely not encircling her or anything like that. Even so, Cody rose abruptly from his chair. "Cody!" Pearl said. He strode toward the kitchen, with his napkin crumpled in one fist. Pearl stood up and hurried after him, and arrived in time to hear him say, "Let's go, Ruth."

"Go?"

"I didn't come here to watch you and Ezra chumming it up in the kitchen."

Ruth looked scared. Her face seemed to grow more pointed.

"Come on," said Cody, and he took her elbow. "Goodbye," he told Pearl and Ezra.

"Oh!" said Pearl, running after them. "Oh, Cody, what can you be thinking of? How can you act so foolish?"

Cody yanked Ruth's coat from a brass hook in passing. He opened the front door and pulled Ruth into the street and shut the door behind them.

Ezra said, "I don't understand."

Pearl said, "Why does it always turn out this way? How

come we end up quarreling? Don't we all love each other? Everything else aside," she said, "don't we all want the best for one another?"

"Certainly we do," Ezra said.

His answer was so level and firm that she felt comforted. She knew things were bound to work out someday. She let him lead her back to the table, and the two of them had a forlorn turkey dinner on the wide expanse of white linen.

Upstairs there are four bedrooms, sparsely furnished, musty. The beds are so sunken-looking, evidently even the courting couples have not been tempted by them. They're untouched, the drab, dirty quilts still smooth. But a dead bird lies beneath one window. Pearl calls down the stairwell. "Ezra? Ezra, come here this instant. Bring the broom and trash bag."

He mounts the stairs obediently. She looks down and sees, with a pang, that his lovely fair hair is thinning on the back of his head. He is thirty-seven years old, will be thirty-eight in December. He will probably never marry. He will never do anything but run that peculiar restaurant of his, with its hodge-podge of food, its unskilled waitresses, its foreign cooks with questionable papers. You could say, in a way, that Ezra has suffered a tragedy, although it's a very small tragedy in the eyes of the world. You could say that he and Ruth, together, have suffered a tragedy. Something has been done to them; something has been taken away from them. They have lost it. They *are* lost. It doesn't help at all that Cody in fact is a very nice man—that he's bright and funny and genuinely kind, to everyone but Ezra.

You could almost say that Cody, too, has suffered a tragedy.

In 1964, when she went out to Illinois to visit them, she felt in their house the thin, tight atmosphere of an unhappy marriage. Not a really terrible marriage—no sign of hatred, spitefulness, violence. Just a sense of something missing. A certain failure to connect, between the two of them. Everything seemed so tenuous. Or was it her imagination? Maybe she was wrong. Maybe it was the house itself—a ranch house in a development, rented for the four months or so that Cody would need to reorganize a plastics plant in Chicago. Plainly the place was expensive, with wall-to-wall carpeting and long, low, modern furniture; but there were no trees anywhere nearby, not even a bush or a shrub—just that raw brick cube rising starkly from the flatness. And outside it was so white-hot, so insufferably hot, that they were confined to the house with its artificial, refrigerated air. They were *imprisoned* by the house, dependent upon it like spacemen in a spaceship, and when they went out it was only to dash through a crushing weight of heat to Cody's air-conditioned Mercedes. Ruth, going about her chores every day, had the clenched expression of someone determined to survive no matter what. Cody came home in the evening gasping for oxygen—barely crawling over the doorsill, Pearl fantasized —but did not seem all that relieved to have arrived. When he greeted Ruth, they touched cheeks and moved apart again.

It was the first time Pearl had ever visited them, the first and only time, and this was after years of very little contact at all. They seldom came to Baltimore. They never returned to the farm. And Cody wrote almost no letters, though he would telephone on birthdays and holidays. He was more like an acquaintance, Pearl thought. A not very cordial acquaintance.

Once she and Ezra were driving down a road in West Virginia, on an outing to Harper's Ferry, when they chanced to come up behind a man in jogging shorts. He was running along the edge of the highway, a tall man, dark, with a certain confident, easy swing to his shoulders . . . Cody! Out here in the middle of nowhere, by sheer coincidence, Cody Tull! Ezra slammed on his brakes, and Pearl said, "Well, did you ever." But then the jogger, hearing their car, had turned his face and he wasn't Cody after all. He was someone entirely different, beefy jawed, nowhere near as handsome. Ezra sped up again. Pearl said, "How silly of me, I know full well that Cody's in, ah . . ."

"Indiana," said Ezra.

"Indiana; I don't know why I thought . . ."

They were both quiet for several minutes after that, and in

those minutes Pearl imagined the scene if it really had been Cody—if he had turned, astonished, as they sailed past. Oddly enough, she didn't envision stopping. She thought of how his mouth would fall open as he recognized their faces behind the glass; and how they would gaze out at him, and smile and wave, and skim on by.

Whenever he phoned he was cheerful and hearty. "How've you been, Mother?"

"Why, Cody!"

"Everything all right? How's Ezra?"

Oh, on the phone he was so nice about Ezra, interested and affectionate like any other brother. And on the rare occasions when he and Ruth came through Baltimore—heading somewhere else, just briefly dropping in—he seemed so pleased to shake hands with Ezra and clap him on the back and ask what he'd been up to. At first.

Only at first.

Then: "Ruth! What are you and Ezra talking about, over there?" Or: "Ezra? Do you mind not standing so close to my wife?" When Ezra and Ruth were hardly speaking, really. They were so cautious with each other, it hurt to watch.

"Cody. Please. What are you imagining?" Pearl would ask him, and then he would turn on her: "Naturally, *you* wouldn't see it. Naturally, he can do no wrong, can he, Mother. Your precious boy. Can he."

She had given up, finally, on ever being asked to visit. When Cody called and told her Ruth was pregnant, some two or three years into the marriage, Pearl said, "Oh, Cody, if she'd like it at all, I mean when the baby arrives . . . if she'd like me to come take care of things . . ." But evidently, she wasn't needed. And when he called to say that Luke was born—nine pounds, three ounces; everything fine—she said, "I can't wait to see him. I honestly can't wait." But Cody let that pass.

They sent her photos: Luke in an infant seat, blond and stern. Luke creeping bear-style across the carpet, on hands and feet instead of knees. (Cody had crept that way too.) Luke uncertainly walking, with a clothespin in each fat fist. He had to have the clothespins, Ruth wrote, because then he thought he was holding on to something. Otherwise, he fell. Now that photos were arriving, letters came too, generally written by Ruth. Her grammar was shocking and she couldn't spell. She said, *Me and Cody wrecken Luke's eyes are going to stay blue,* but what did Pearl care about grammar? She saved every letter and put Luke's pictures on her desk in little gilt frames she bought at Kresge's.

I think I ought to come see Luke before he's grown, she wrote. No one answered. She wrote again. *Would June be all right?* Then Cody wrote that they were moving to Illinois in June, but if she really wanted then maybe she could come in July.

So she went to Illinois in July, traveling with a trainload of fresh-faced boy soldiers on their way to Vietnam, and she spent a week in that treeless house barricaded against the elements. It was a shock, even to her, how instantly and how deeply she loved her grandson. He was not quite two years old by then, a beautiful baby with a head that seemed adult in its shape— sharply defined, the golden hair trimmed close and neat. His firm, straight lips seemed adult as well, and he had an unchild-like way of walking. There was a bit of slump in his posture, a little droop to his shoulders, nothing physically wrong but an air of resignation that was almost comical in someone so small. Pearl sat on the floor with him for hours, playing with his trucks and cars. "Vroom. Vroom. Roll it back to Granny, now." She was touched by his stillness. He had a sizable vocabulary but he used it only when necessary; he was not a spendthrift. He was careful. He lacked gaiety. Was he happy? Was this a fit life for a child?

She saw that Cody had a sprinkling of gray in his sideburns, a more leathery look to his cheeks; but that Ruth was still a scrappy little thing in too-short hair and unbecoming dresses. She had not grown fuller or softer with age. She was like certain supermarket vegetables that turn from green to withered without ever ripening. In the evenings, when Cody came home from work, Ruth clattered around the kitchen cooking great quantities of country food that Cody would hardly touch; and Cody had a gin and tonic and watched the news. The two of them asked each other, "How was your day?" and "Everything fine?" but they didn't seem to listen to the answers. Pearl could believe that in the morning, waking in their king-sized bed, they asked politely, "Did you sleep all right?" She felt oppressed and uncomfortable, but instead of averting her gaze she was for some reason compelled to delve deeper into their lives; she sent them out one night to a movie, promising to watch Luke, and then ransacked all the desk drawers but found only tax receipts, and bank statements, and a photo album belonging to the people who really lived here. Anyway, she couldn't have said what it was she was looking for.

Coming home, jouncing on the train amid another group of soldiers, she felt weary and hopeless. She arrived in Baltimore seven hours late, with a racking headache. Then as she entered the station, she saw Ezra walking toward her in his plodding way and she felt such a stab of . . . well, recognition. It was Luke's walk, solemn little Luke. Life was so sad, she thought, that she almost couldn't bear it. But kissing Ezra, she felt her sorrow overtaken by something very like annoyance. She wondered why he put up with this, why he let things go on this way. Could it be that he took some *satisfaction* in his grief? (As if he were paying for something, she thought. But what would he be paying for?) In the car, he asked, "How'd you like Luke?" and she said, "Don't you ever think of just going there and trying to get her back?"

"I couldn't," he said, unsurprised, and he maneuvered the car laboriously from its parking slot.

"Well, I don't see why not," she told him.

"It's not right. It's wrong."

She wasn't given to philosophy, but during the drive home she stared at the grimy Baltimore scenery and considered the question of right and wrong: of theoretical virtue, existing in a vacuum; of whether there was any point to it at all. When they reached home, she got out of the car and entered the house without a word, and climbed the stairs to her room.

Ezra scoops the dead bird onto a piece of cardboard and slides it into the trash bag. Then he tapes the cardboard to the broken windowpane where the bird must have entered. Pearl, meanwhile, sweeps up the shards of glass. She leaves them in a pyramid and goes downstairs for the dustpan. Already, she sees, the house has a bit more life to it—the sunny pattern of leaves shimmering on the parlor floor in front of the open door, the smell of hot grass wafting through the rooms. "It was never all that practical," Cody said on the phone just recently, referring to the farm. "It was only a half-baked idea that I had when I was young." But if he really meant that, why doesn't he go on and sell? No, he couldn't possibly; she has spent so much time sweeping this place, preparing it for him, opening and shutting bureau drawers as if she'd find his secrets there. She can imagine Ruth in this kitchen, Cody out surveying fence lines or whatever it is men do on farms. She can picture Luke running through the yard in denim overalls. He is old enough to go fishing now, to swim in the creek beyond the pasture, maybe even to tend the animals. In August, he'll be eight. Is it eight? Or nine. She's lost track. She hardly ever sees him, and must conquer his shyness all over again whenever he and his parents pass through Baltimore. Each visit, his interests have changed: from popguns to marbles to stamp collecting. Last time he was here, some two or three years back, she got out her husband's stamp album—its maroon, fake-leather cover gone gray with mildew—only to find that Luke had switched to model airplanes. He was assembling a balsa wood jet, he told her, that would actually fly. And he was planning to be an astronaut. "By the time I'm grown," he said, "astronauts will be ordinary. People will be taking rockets like you would take a bus. They'll spend their summers on Venus. They won't go to Ocean City; they'll go to beaches on the moon." "Ah," she said, "isn't that wonderful!" But she was too old for such things.

She couldn't keep up, and the very thought of traveling to the moon made her feel desolate.

And nowadays—well, who can guess? Luke must be involved in something entirely different. It's so long since he was here, and she's not sure he'll ever be back. During that last visit, Ezra got his old pearwood recorder from the closet and showed Luke how to play a tune. Pearl knows very little about recorders, but evidently something happens—the wood dries up, or warps, or something—when they're not played enough; and this one hadn't been played in a decade, at least. Its voice had gone splintery and cracked. How startled she'd been, hearing three ancient notes tumble forth after such a silence! Ezra and Luke walked south on Calvert Street to buy some linseed oil. Not two minutes after they left, Cody asked where they'd got to. "Why, off to buy oil for Ezra's recorder," Pearl told him. "Didn't you see them go?" Cody excused himself and went outside to pace in front of the house. Ruth stayed in the living room, discussing schools. Pearl hardly listened. She could look through the window and see Cody pacing, turning, pacing, his suit coat whipping out behind him. She could tell when Ezra and Luke returned, even before she saw them, by the way that Cody stiffened. "Where have you been?" she heard him ask. "What have you two been doing?"

Luke never did learn how to play the recorder. Cody said they had to go. "Oh, but Cody!" Pearl said. "I thought you were spending the night!"

"Wrong," he told her. "Wrong again. I can't stay here; this place is not safe. Don't you see what Ezra's up to?"

"What, Cody? What is he up to?"

"Don't you see he's out to steal my son?" he asked. "The same way he always stole everybody? Don't you *see?*"

In the end, they left. Ezra wanted to give Luke the recorder for keeps, but Cody told Luke to leave it; he'd get him a newer one, fancier, finer. One that wasn't all dried up, he said.

Pearl believes now that her family has failed. Neither of her sons is happy, and her daughter can't seem to stay married. There is no one to accept the blame for this but Pearl herself, who raised these children single-handed and did make mistakes, oh, a bushel of mistakes. Still, she sometimes has the feeling that it's simply fate, and not a matter for blame at all. She feels that everything has been assigned, has been preordained; everyone must play his role. Certainly she never intended to foster one of those good son/bad son arrangements, but what can you do when one son is consistently good and the other consistently bad? What can the sons do, even? "Don't you *see?*" Cody had cried, and she had imagined, for an instant, that he was inviting her to look at his whole existence—his years of hurt and bafflement.

Often, like a child peering over the fence at somebody else's party, she gazes wistfully at other families and wonders what their secret is. They seem so close. Is it that they're more religious? Or stricter, or more lenient? Could it be the fact that they participate in sports? Read books together? Have some common hobby? Recently, she overheard a neighbor woman discussing her plans for Independence Day: her family was having a picnic. Every member—child or grownup—was cooking his or her specialty. Those who were too little to cook were in charge of the paper plates.

Pearl felt such a wave of longing that her knees went weak.

Ezra has finished taping the glass. Pearl drifts through the other bedrooms, checking the other windows. In the smallest bedroom, a nursery, a little old lady in a hat approaches. It's Pearl, in the speckled mirror above a bureau. She leans closer and traces the lines around her eyes. Her age does not surprise her. She's grown used to it by now. You're old for so much longer than you're young, she thinks. Really it hardly seems fair. And then she thinks, for no earthly reason, of a girl she went to school with, Linda Lou something-or-other—such a pretty, flighty girl, someone she'd always envied. In the middle of their senior year, Linda Lou disappeared. There were rumors, later confirmed—an affair with the school's only male teacher, a married man; and a baby on the way. How horrified her classmates had been! It had thrilled them: that they actually knew such a person, had borrowed her history notes, helped her retie a loose sash, perhaps even brushed her hand accidentally—that hand that may have touched . . . well, who knew what. It occurs to Pearl, peering into the glass, that the baby born of that scandal must be sixty years old by now. He would have gray hair and liver spots, perhaps false teeth, bifocals, a tedious burden of a life. Yet Linda Lou, wearing white, still dances in Pearl's mind, the prettiest girl at the senior social.

"Don't you *see?*" Cody has asked, and Pearl had said, "Honey, I just can't understand you."

Then he shrugged, and his normal, amused expression returned to his face. "Ah, well," he said, "I can't either, I guess. After all, what do I care, now I'm grown? Why should it matter any more?"

She doesn't recall if she managed any reply to that.

She steps away from the mirror. Ezra comes in, bearing the trash bag. "All finished, Mother," he says.

"It looks a lot better, doesn't it?"

"It looks just fine," he tells her.

They descend the stairs, and close the door, and carry their supplies to the car. As they drive away Pearl glances back, like any good housewife checking what she's cleaned, and it seems to her that even that buckling front porch is straighter and more solid. She has a feeling of accomplishment. Others might have given up and let the trespassers take the place over, but never Pearl. Next season she will come again, and the season after, and the season after that, and Ezra will go on bringing her—the two of them bumping down the driveway, loyal and responsible, together forever.

7

Dr. Tull Is Not a Toy

"Whoever's the first to mention divorce has to take the children," Jenny said. "This has kept us together more times than I can count."

She was joking, but the priest didn't laugh. He may have been too young to catch it. All he did was shift uncomfortably in his chair. Meanwhile the children milled around him like something bubbling, like something churning, and the baby dribbled on his shoes. He withdrew his feet imperceptibly, as if trying not to hurt the baby's feelings.

"Yet I believe," he said, appearing to choose his words, "that you yourself have been divorced, have you not?"

"Twice," said Jenny. She giggled, but he only looked worried. "And once for Joe here," she added.

Her husband smiled at her from the sofa.

"If I hadn't had the foresight to keep my maiden name," Jenny said, "my medical diploma would read like one of those address books where people have moved a lot. Names crossed out and added, crossed out and added—a mess! Dr. Jenny Marie Tull Baines Wiley St. Ambrose."

The priest was one of those very blond men with glasslike hair, and his color was so high that Jenny wondered about his blood pressure. Or maybe he was just embarrassed. "Well," he said. "Mrs., um—or Dr.—"

"Tull."

"Dr. Tull, I only thought that the . . . instability, the lack of stability, might be causing Slevin's problems. The turnover in fathers, you might say."

"In fathers? What are you talking about?" Jenny asked. "Slevin's not *my* son. He's Joe's."

"Ah?"

"*Joe* is his father and always has been."

"Oh, excuse me," said the priest.

He grew even pinker—as well he ought, Jenny felt; for slow, plump Slevin with his ashy hair was obviously Joe's. Jenny was small and dark; Joe a massive, blond, bearded bear of a man with Slevin's slanted blue eyes. (She had often felt drawn to overweight men. They made her feel tidy.) "Slevin," she told the priest, "is Joe's by Greta, his previous wife, and so are most of the others you see here. All except for Becky; Becky's mine. The other six are his." She bent to take the dog's bone from the baby. "Anyway . . . but Joe's wife, Greta: she left."

"Left," said the priest.

"Left me flat," Joe said cheerfully. "Cleared clean out of Baltimore. Parked the kids with a neighbor one day, while I was off at work. Hired an Allied van and departed with all we owned, everything but the children's clothes in neat little piles on the floor."

"Oh, my stars," said the priest.

"Even took their beds. Can you explain that? Took the crib and the changing table. Only thing I can figure, she was so used to life with children that she really couldn't imagine; really assumed she would need a crib no matter where she went. First thing I had to do when I got home that night was go out and buy a fleet of beds from Sears. They must've thought I was opening a motel."

"Picture it," Jenny said. "Joe in an apron. Joe mixing Similac. Well, he was lost, of course. Utterly lost. The way we met: he called me at home in the dead of night when his baby got roseola. That's how out of touch he was; it's been twenty years at least since pediatricians made house calls. But I came, I don't know why. Well, he lived only two blocks away. And he was so desperate—answered the door in striped pajamas, jiggling the baby—"

"I fell in love with her the moment she walked in," said Joe. He stroked his beard; golden frizz flew up around his stubby fingers.

"He thought I was Lady Bountiful," Jenny said, "bearing a medical bag instead of a basket of food. It's hard to resist a man who needs you."

"Need had nothing to do with it," Joe told her.

"Well, who admires you, then. He asked if I had children of my own, and how I managed while I worked. And when I said I mostly played it by ear, with teen-aged sitters one minute and elderly ladies the next, my mother filling in when she could or my brother or a neighbor, or Becky sometimes just camping in my waiting room with her math assignment—"

"I could see she wasn't a skimpy woman," Joe told the priest. "Not rigid. Not constricted. Not that super-serious kind."

"No," said the priest, glancing around him. (It hadn't been a day when Jenny could get to the housework.)

Jenny said, "He said he liked the way I let his children crawl all over me. He said his wife had found them irritating, the last few years. Well, you see how it began. I had promised myself I'd never remarry, Becky and I would rather manage on our own, that's what I was best at; but I don't know, there Joe *was*, and his children. And his baby was so little and so recently abandoned that she turned her head and opened her mouth when I held her horizontal; you could tell she still remembered. Anyway," she said, and she smiled at the priest, who really was shockingly young—a wide-eyed boy, was all. "How did we get on this subject?"

"Uh, Slevin," said the priest. "We were discussing Slevin."

"Oh, yes, Slevin."

It was a rainy, blowy April afternoon, with the trees turning inside out and beating against the windowpanes, and the living room had reached just that shade of dusk where no one had realized, quite yet, that it was time to switch on the lights. The air seemed thick and grainy. The children were winding down like little clocks and fussing for their suppers; but the priest, lacking children of his own, failed to notice this. He leaned forward, setting his fingertips together. "I've been concerned," he said, "by Slevin's behavior at C.Y.O. meetings. He's not sociable at all, has no friends, seems moody, withdrawn. Of course it could be his age, but . . . he's fourteen, is he?"

"Thirteen," said Joe, after thinking it over.

"Thirteen years old, naturally a difficult . . . I wouldn't even mention it, except that when I suggested we have a talk he just wrenched away and ran out, and never returned. Now we notice that you, Mr. St. Ambrose, that you drop him off for mass every Sunday, but in fact he's stopped coming inside and simply sits out front on the steps and watches the traffic. He's, you might say, playing hooky, but—"

"Shoot," said Joe. "I get up specially on a Sunday morning to drive him there and he plays *hooky?*"

"But my point is—"

"I don't know why he wants to go anyhow. He's the only one of them that does."

"But it's his withdrawn behavior that worries me," the priest said, "more than his church attendance. Though it might not be a bad idea if, perhaps, you accompanied him to mass sometime."

"Me? Hell, I'm not even Catholic."

"Or I don't suppose *you*, Dr. Tull . . ."

Both men seemed to be waiting for her. Jenny was wondering about the baby's diaper, which bulged suspiciously, but she gathered her thoughts and said, "Oh, no, goodness, I really wouldn't have the faintest—" She laughed, covering her mouth —a gesture she had. "Besides," she said, "it was Greta who was the Catholic. Slevin's mother."

"I see. Well, the important thing—"

"*I* don't know why Slevin goes to church. And to Greta's church, her old one, clear across town."

"Does he communicate with his mother now?"

"Oh, no, she's never been back. Got a quickie divorce in Idaho and that's the last we heard."

"Are there any, ah, step-family problems?"

"Step-family?" Jenny said. "Well, no. Or yes. I don't know. There *would* be, probably; of course these things are never easy . . . only life is so rushed around here, there really isn't time."

"Slevin is very fond of Jenny," Joe told the priest.

"Why, thank you, honey," Jenny said.

"She won him right over; she's got him trailing after her anyplace she goes. She's so cool and jokey with kids, you know."

"Well, I try," Jenny said. "I do make an effort. But you never can be sure. That age is very secretive."

"Perhaps I'll suggest that he stop by and visit me," the priest said.

"If you like."

"Just to gab, I'll say, chew the fat . . ."

Jenny could see that it would never work out.

She walked him to the door, strolling with her hands deep in her skirt pockets. "I hope," she said, "you haven't got the wrong idea about us. I mean, Joe's an excellent father, honestly he is; he's always been good with Slevin."

"Yes, of course."

"Oh, when I compare him with some others I could name!" Jenny said. She had a habit, with disapproving people, of talking a little too much, and she knew it. As they crossed the hall, she said, "Sam Wiley, for instance—my second husband. Becky's father. You'd die if you ever saw Sam. He was a painter, one of those graceful compact *small* types I've never trusted since. Totally shiftless. Totally unreliable. He left me before Becky was born, moved in with a model named Adar Bagned."

She opened the front door. A fine, fresh mist blew in and she took a deep breath. "Oh, lovely," she said. "But isn't that a hilarious name? For the longest time I kept trying to turn it around, thinking it must make more sense if I read it off backward. Goodbye, then, Father. Thanks for dropping in."

She closed the door on him and went off to fix the children's supper.

This would be a very nice house, Jenny was fond of saying, if only the third-floor bathtub didn't drain through the dining room ceiling. It was a tall, trim Bolton Hill row house; she'd bought it back in '64, when prices weren't yet sky-high. In those days, it had seemed enormous; but seven years later, with six extra children, it didn't feel so big any more. It was inconvenient, warrenlike, poorly arranged. There were so many doors and radiators, it was hard to find space for the furniture.

She cooked at a sticky, stilt-legged stove, rinsed greens at a yellowed sink skirted with chintz, set plates on a table that was carved with another family's initials. "Here, children, everyone get his own silver, now—"

"You gave Jacob more peas than me."

"She did not."

"Did too."

"Did not."

"Did too."

"Take them! I don't even like them."

"Where's Slevin?" Jenny asked.

"Who needs Slevin anyhow, the old grouch."

The telephone rang and Joe came in with the baby. "That's your answering service, they want to know—"

"I'm not on; it's Dan's night on. What are they calling *me* for?"

"That's what I thought, but they said—"

He wandered off again, and returned a minute later to settle at the table with the baby in his lap. "Here's her meat," Jenny said, flying past. "Her spoon is on the . . ."

She left the kitchen, climbed the stairs to the second floor and called up to the third. "Slevin?" No answer. She climbed the rest of the way, quickly growing breathless. How out of shape she was! It was true, as her mother was forever telling her, that she had let herself go—a crime, her mother said, for anyone with Jenny's good looks. It was true that she'd become a bit haggard, slackened somewhat, her skin turning sallow and her eyebrows shaggy and her wide, amused mouth a dry brownish color now that she wore no lipstick. "Your hair!" her mother mourned. "Your lovely hair!"—which wasn't lovely at all: a thick, blunt, gray-threaded clump with boxy bangs. "You used to be such a beauty," Pearl would say, and Jenny would laugh. A fat lot of good it had done her! She liked to think that she was wearing her beauty out—using it up, she liked to think. She took some satisfaction in it, like a housewife industriously making her way through a jar of something she did not enjoy, would not buy again, but couldn't just discard, of course.

Panting, clutching a handful of denim skirt, she arrived on the third floor. It was the older children's floor, not her territory, and it had a musty, atticky smell. "Slevin?" she called. She knocked at his door. "Supper, Slevin!"

She opened the door a crack and peered in. Slevin lay on his unmade bed with his forearm over his eyes. A wide strip of blubbery belly showed, as it nearly always did, between jeans and T-shirt. He had his earphones on; that was why he hadn't heard. She crossed the room and lifted the earphones from his head. A miniature Janis Joplin song rang out tinnily: "Me and Bobby McGee." He blinked and gave her a puzzled look, like someone just waking. "Suppertime," she told him.

"I'm not hungry."

"Not hungry! What kind of talk is that?"

"Jenny, honest, I just don't want to get up."

But she was already pulling him to his feet—a burly boy nearly Jenny's height and considerably heavier but still babyish, creamy skinned. She propelled him to the door, pushing from behind with both palms flat on the small of his back. "You're the only one of them that I have to carry bodily to meals," she said. She sang him down the stairs:

*"Oh, they had to carry Harry to the ferry,
And they had to carry Harry to the shore . . ."*

"Seriously, Jenny," Slevin said.

They entered the kitchen. Joe made a trumpet of his hands above the baby's head and said, "Ta-ra! Ta-ra! He approaches!" Slevin groaned. The others didn't look up from their meal.

Sitting in her place next to Joe, gazing around at the tableful of children, Jenny felt pleased. They were doing well, she decided—even the older ones, who'd acted so wary and hostile when she had first met them.

Then she had an unsettling thought: it occurred to her that this would have to be her permanent situation. Having taken on these children, straightened their upturned lives and slowly, steadily won their trust, she could not in good conscience let them down. Here she was, forever. "It's lucky we get along," she said to Joe.

"It's extremely lucky," he said, and he patted her hand and asked for the mustard.

"Isn't it amazing how school always smells like school," Jenny told Slevin's teacher. "You can add all the modern conveniences you like—audiovisual things and computers—it still smells like book glue and that cheap gray paper they used to have for arithmetic and also . . . what's that other smell? There's another smell besides. I know it but I can't quite name it."

"Have a seat, Dr. Tull," the teacher said.

"Radiator dust," said Jenny.

"Pardon?"

"*That's* the other smell."

"I called you in for a purpose," said the teacher, opening the file that lay before her. She was a tiny thing, surely not out of her twenties, perky and freckled with horn-rimmed glasses dwarfing her pointed nose. Jenny wondered how she'd learned to be so intimidating so quickly. "I know you're a busy woman,

Dr. Tull, but I'm genuinely anxious about Slevin's school performance and I thought you ought to be informed."

"Oh, really?" Jenny said. She decided she would feel better if she too wore glasses, though hers were only needed for reading. She dug through her purse and a pink plastic pacifier fell out. She pretended it hadn't happened.

"Slevin is very, very intelligent," the teacher said. She glared at Jenny accusingly. "He goes straight off the top of the charts."

"Yes, I figured that."

"But his English average . . ." the teacher said, flipping through papers. "It's F. Well, maybe D minus."

Jenny clicked her tongue.

"Math: C. History: D. And science . . . and gym . . . He's had so many absences, I finally asked if he'd been cutting school. 'Yes, ma'am,' he said—came right out with it. 'What did you cut?' I asked him. 'February,' he said."

Jenny laughed. The teacher looked at her.

Jenny straightened her glasses and said, "Do you think it might be puberty?"

"*All* these children are going through puberty," the teacher told her.

"Or . . . I don't know; boredom. You said yourself he's intelligent. Why, you ought to see him at home! Monkeying around with machinery, wiring stereos . . . He's got a tape recorder of his own, he worked for it and bought it himself, some superduper model, offhand I can't think of the name. I'm such a dunce about these things, when he talked about head cleaners I thought he meant shampoo; but Slevin knows all about it and—"

"Mr. Davies suggests," said the teacher, "—that's our assistant principal—he suggests that Slevin may be experiencing emotional problems due to the adjustments at home."

"What adjustments?"

"He says Slevin's mother abandoned him and Slevin was moved to your household almost immediately thereafter and had to get used to a brand-new mother and sister."

"Oh, that," said Jenny, waving her hand.

"Mr. Davies suggests that Slevin might need professional counseling."

"Nonsense," Jenny said. "What's a little adjustment? And anyhow, that happened a good six months ago. It's not as if . . . why, look at my daughter! She's had to get used to *seven* new people and she's never said a word of complaint. Oh, we're all coping! In fact my husband was saying, just the other day, we should think about having more children now. We ought to have at least one *joint* child, he says, but I'm not so sure myself. After all, I'm thirty-six years old. It probably wouldn't be wise."

"Mr. Davies suggests—"

"Though I suppose if it means so much to him, it's all the same to me."

"The same!" said the teacher. "What about the population explosion?"

"The what? You're getting me off the subject, here . . . My point is," Jenny said, "I don't see the need to blame adjustment, broken homes, bad parents, that sort of thing. We make our own luck, right? You have to overcome your setbacks. You can't take them too much to heart. I'll explain all that to Slevin. I'll tell him this evening. I'm certain his grades will improve."

Then she bent to pick up the pacifier, and shook hands with the teacher and left.

On the wall in Jenny's office was a varnished wooden plaque: DR. TULL IS NOT A TOY. Joe had made it for her in his workshop. He was incensed by the scrapes and bruises that Jenny gathered daily in her raucous games with her patients. "Make them show some respect," he told her. "Maintain a little dignity." But the sign was all but lost among her patients' snapshots (on beaches, on seesaws, on photographers' blanketed tables, or behind lit birthday cakes) and the crayoned self-portraits they'd brought her. Anyhow, most of them were too young to read. She scooped up Billy Burnham and carried him, squawking and giggling, to the nurse for his tetanus shot. "Now, it's possible," she called back to Mrs. Burnham, "that tonight he'll experience a little soreness in his left—" Billy squirmed, and a button popped off Jenny's white coat.

The Albright baby was due for a DPT shot. The Carroll baby had to have her formula switched. Lucy Brandon's constant sniffle looked like an allergy; Jenny told Mrs. Brandon where she could take her for testing. Both the Morris twins' tonsils were swollen.

She asked the receptionist to order her a sandwich, but the receptionist said, "Aren't you eating out? Your brother's here; he's been waiting half an hour, at least."

"Oh, my Lord, I forgot all about him," Jenny said. She went into the waiting room. Ezra was seated on the vinyl couch, surrounded by pull toys and building blocks and oilcloth picture books. A family of Spanish-speaking children, probably patients of Dr. Ramirez, played at his feet, but you'd never mistake Ezra for a parent. His shaggy yellow hair was soft as a child's; he wore faded work clothes, and his face was wide and expectant.

"Ezra, honey," Jenny told him, "I clean forgot. My next appointment's in twenty minutes; do you suppose we could just grab a hamburger?"

"Oh, surely," Ezra said.

He waited while she took off her white coat and put on a raincoat. Then they rode the elevator down to the marble-paved lobby, and pushed through the revolving door onto a spattery, overcast street. There was a smell like wet coal. Huddled people hurried by and buses wheezed and cathedral bells rang far away.

"I feel dumb," Jenny said, "taking you of all people to a humburger joint."

She was thinking of his restaurant, which always intimidated her a little. Recently, Ezra had remodeled the living quarters above it into a series of tiny, elegant private dining rooms like those in old movies—the velvet-hung compartments where the villain attempts to seduce the heroine. They'd be perfect for anniversary couples, Ezra said. (Like most unmarried men, he was comically, annoyingly sentimental about marriage.) But so far, only business groups and heavily jeweled Baltimore politicians had asked to use the rooms.

Now he said, "A hamburger's fine; I'm crazy about hamburgers." And when they walked through the plate glass doorway, into a slick, tiled area lined with glaring photos of onion rings and milkshakes, he looked around him happily. Secretaries clustered at some tables, construction workers at others. "It's getting like a collective farm," Ezra said. "All these chain places that everyone comes to for breakfast, lunch, sometimes supper . . . like a commune or a kibbutz or something. Pretty soon we won't have private kitchens at all; you just drop by your local Gino's or McDonald's. I kind of like it."

Jenny wondered if there were any eating place he wouldn't like. At a soup kitchen, no doubt, he'd be pleased by the obvious hunger of the customers. At a urine-smelling tavern he'd discover some wonderful pickled eggs that he'd never seen anywhere else. Oh, if it had to do with food, he was endlessly appreciative.

While he ordered for them, she settled herself at a table. She took off her raincoat, smoothed her hair, and scraped at a Pablum spot on her blouse. It felt strange to be sitting alone. Always there was someone—children, patients, colleagues. The empty space on either side of her gave her an echoing, weightless feeling, as if she lacked ballast and might at any moment float upward.

Ezra returned with their hamburgers. "How's Joe?" he asked, sitting down.

"Oh, fine. How's Mother?"

"Doing well, sends her love . . . I brought you something," he said. He set aside his burger to rummage through his windbreaker pockets. Eventually, he came up with a worn white envelope. "Pictures," he said.

"Pictures?"

"Photos. Mother's got all these photos; I just discovered them. I thought maybe you'd be interested in having a few."

Jenny sighed. Poor Ezra: he was turning into the family

custodian, tending their mother and guarding their past and faithfully phoning his sister for lunch. "Why don't you keep them," she said. "You know I'd just lose them."

"But a lot of these are of you," he said. He spilled the envelope onto the table. "I figured the children might like them. For instance, somewhere here . . ." He shuffled various versions of a younger, sterner Jenny. "Here," he said. "Don't you see Becky in this?"

It was Jenny in a plaid tam-o'-shanter, unsmiling. "Ugh," she said, stirring her coffee.

"You were a really nice little girl," said Ezra. He returned to his burger but kept the photo before him. On the back of it, Jenny saw, something had been written in pencil. She tried to make it out. Ezra noticed and said, "Fall, 1947. I got Mother to write the dates down. And I'm going to send Cody some, too."

Jenny could just imagine Cody's face when he got them. "Ezra," she said, "to tell the truth, I wouldn't waste the postage."

"Don't you think he'd like to compare these with how Luke looks, growing up?"

"Believe me," she said, "he'd burn them. You know Cody."

"Maybe he's changed," Ezra said.

"He hasn't," said Jenny, "and I doubt he ever will. Just mention something—one little harmless memory from our childhood—and his mouth turns down. *You* know how his mouth does. I said to him once, I said, 'Cody, you're no better than the Lawsons.' Remember the Lawsons? They moved into our neighborhood from Nashville, Tennessee, and the very first week all four childlren got mumps. Mrs. Lawson said, 'This city is unlucky, I believe.' The next week a pipe in their basement burst and she said, 'Well, that's Baltimore.' Then their daughter broke her wrist . . . When they moved back to Tennessee, I went over to say goodbye. They were loading up their car trunk and they happened to slam the lid down smack on the fingers of their youngest boy. When they drove off he was screaming, and Mrs. Lawson called out, 'Isn't this a fitting way to leave? I always did say Baltimore was unlucky.' "

"Well, now, I'm trying to follow you, here," Ezra said.

"It's whether you add up the list or not," Jenny said. "I mean, if you catalogue grudges, anything looks bad. And Cody certainly catalogues; he's ruining his life with his catalogues. But after all, I told him, we made it, didn't we? We did grow up. Why, the three of us turned out fine, just fine!"

"It's true," said Ezra, his forehead smoothing. "You especially, Jenny. Look at you: a doctor."

"Oh, shoo, I'm nothing but a baby weigher," Jenny said. But she was pleased, and when they rose to go she took along the photographs to make him happy.

Joe said if they did have a baby, he'd like it to be a girl. He'd looked around and noticed they were a little short on girls. "How can you say that?" Jenny asked. She ticked the girls off on her fingers: "Phoebe, Becky, Jane . . ."

When her voice trailed away, he stood watching her. She was expecting him to speak, but he didn't. "Well?" she asked.

"That's only three."

She felt a little rush of confusion. "Have I left one out?"

"*No*, you haven't left one out. Has she left one out," he told the wall. He snorted. "Has she left one out, she asks. What a question! *No*, you haven't left one out. Three is all we have. Three girls."

"Well, there's no need to act so cross about it."

"I'm not cross, I'm frustrated," he said. "I'm trying to have a conversation here."

"Isn't that what we're doing?"

"Yes, yes . . ."

"Then where's the problem?"

He wouldn't say. He stood in the kitchen doorway with his arms folded tight across his chest. He gazed off to one side, scowling. Jenny was puzzled. Were they quarreling, or what? When the silence stretched on, she gradually, imperceptibly returned to slicing the cucumbers for supper. She brought the knife down as quietly as possible, and without a sound scooped the disks of cucumber into a bowl. (When she and Joe had first met, he'd said, "Do you put cucumber on your skin?" "*Cucumbers?*" she'd asked, astonished. "You look so cool," he told her, "I thought of this bottle of cucumber milk my aunt used to keep on her vanity table.")

Two of the children, Jacob and Peter, were playing with the Ouija board in front of the refrigerator. Jenny had to step over them when she went to get the tomatoes. "Excuse me," she told them. "You're in my way." But they ignored her; they were intent on the board. "What will I be when I grow up?" Jacob asked, and he set his fingertips delicately upon the pointer. "Upper middle class, middle middle class, or lower middle class: which?"

Jenny laughed, and Joe glared at her and wheeled and stamped out of the kitchen.

On the evening news, a helicopter crewman who'd been killed in Laos was buried with full military honors. An American flag, folded into a cushiony triangle, was handed to the parents—a gray-haired, square-chinned gentleman and his fragile wife. The wife wore a trim beige raincoat and little white gloves. It was she who accepted the flag. The husband had turned away and was weeping, would not even say a few words to the microphone somebody offered him. "Sir? Sir?" a reporter asked.

One white glove reached out and took the microphone. "What my husband means to say, I believe," the wife declared in a feathery, Southern voice, "is we thank all those who've gathered here, and we know we're just going to be fine. We're strong, and we're going to be fine."

"Hogwash," Slevin said.

"Why, Slevin," said Jenny. "*I* didn't know you were political."

"I'm not; it's just a bunch of hogwash," he told her. "She ought to say, 'Take your old flag! I object! I give up!' "

"My goodness," Jenny said mildly. She was sorting Ezra's photos; she held one out to distract him. "Look," she said. "Your Uncle Cody, at age fifteen."

"He's not my uncle."

"Of course he is."

"He's not my real uncle."

"You wouldn't say that if you knew him. You'd like him," Jenny said. "I wish he'd come for a visit. He's so . . . unbrotherly or something; I don't know. And look!" she said, alighting on another photo. "Isn't my mother pretty?"

"*I* think she looks like a lizard," Slevin said.

"Oh, but when she was a girl, I mean . . . isn't it sad how carefree she was."

"Half the time, she forgets my name," Slevin said.

"Well, she's old," Jenny told him.

"Not that old. What she's saying is, I'm not worth her bother. Old biddy. Sits at the head of the table with a piece of bread on her plate and sets both hands down flat and just stares around at us, stares around, face like one of those rotating fans, waiting for the butter but never asking, never saying a word. Till finally you or Dad says, 'Mother? Could we pass you the butter?' and she says, 'Why, *thank* you,' like she was wondering when you'd realize."

"She hasn't had an easy life," Jenny said.

"I wish just once we'd get all through the meal and nobody offer her the butter."

"She raised us on her own, you know," Jenny told him. "Don't you think it must have been hard? My father walked out and left her when I was nine years old."

"He did?" Slevin asked. He stared at her.

"He left her, absolutely. We never set eyes on him again."

"Bastard," Slevin said.

"Oh, well," said Jenny. She leafed through some more photos. "Jesus! These people! They try to do you in."

"You're overreacting," Jenny told him. "I can't even remember the man, if you want to know the truth. Wouldn't know him if I saw him. And my mother managed fine. It all worked out. Look at this, Slevin: see Ezra's old-fashioned haircut?"

Slevin shrugged and switched the TV channel.

"And see what I was like at your age?" She handed him the picture with the tam-o'-shanter.

He glanced over. He frowned. He said, "Who did you say that was?"

"Me."

"No, it's not."

"Yes, it is. Me at thirteen. Mother wrote the date on the back."

"It's not!" he said. His voice was unusually high; he sounded like a much younger child. "It isn't! Look at it! Why, it's like a . . . concentration camp person, a victim, Anne Frank! It's terrible! It's so sad!"

Surprised, she turned the photo around and looked again. True, the picture wasn't particularly happy—it showed a dark little girl with a thin, watchful face—but it wasn't as bad as all that. "So what?" she asked, and she held it out to him once more. He drew back sharply.

"It's somebody else," he told her. "Not you; you're always laughing and having fun. It's not you."

"Oh, fine, it's not me, then," she said, and she returned to the rest of the photos.

"I want to talk to you about that oldest boy," her mother said on the phone. "What's his name? Kevin?"

"Slevin, Mother. Honestly."

"Well, he stole my vacuum cleaner."

"He did what?"

"Sunday afternoon, when you all came to visit, he slipped into my pantry and made off with my Hoover upright."

Jenny sat down on her bed. She said, "Let me get this straight."

"It's been missing all week," her mother said, "and I couldn't understand it. I knew we hadn't been burglarized, and even if we had, what would anyone want with my old Hoover?"

"But why accuse Slevin?"

"My neighbor told me, just this afternoon. Mrs. Arthur. Said, 'Was that your grandson I saw Sunday? Kind of hefty boy? Loading your Hoover upright into your daughter's car trunk?'"

"That's impossible," Jenny said.

"Now, how do you know that? How do you know what is or is not possible? He's hardly more than a stranger, Jenny. I mean, you got those children the way other people get weekend guests."

"You're exaggerating," Jenny told her.

"Well, all I ask is for you to go check Slevin's bedroom. Just check."

"What, this minute?"

"There's lint specks all over my carpet."

"Oh, all right," Jenny said.

She laid the receiver on her pillow and climbed from the second floor to the third. Slevin's door was open and he wasn't in his room, although his radio rocked with the Jefferson Airplane. She stepped stealthily over Slevin's knapsack, avoided a teetering pile of *Popular Science* magazines, opened his closet door, and found herself staring at her mother's vacuum cleaner. She would know it anywhere: an elderly machine with a gray cloth dust bag. Its cord was coiled neatly and it seemed unharmed. If he'd taken it apart to learn how it worked, she might have understood. Or if he'd smashed it, out of some rage toward her mother. But there it sat, entire. She stood puzzling over it for several seconds. Then she wheeled it out of the closet and lugged it down the stairs, to where her mother's voice was twanging impatiently from the receiver. "Jenny? Jenny?"

"Well, you're right," Jenny said. "I found it in his room."

There was a pause in which Pearl could have said, "I told you so," but kindly did not. Then she said, "I wonder if he might be calling for help in some way."

"By stealing a *vacuum* cleaner?"

"He's really a very sweet boy," Pearl said. "I can see that. Maybe he's asking for a psychologist or some such."

"More likely he's asking for a neater house," Jenny said. "The dust balls on his closet floor have started raising a family."

She pictured Slevin, in desperation, stealing an arsenal of cleaning supplies—this neighbor's broom, that neighbor's Ajax, gathered with the same feverish zeal he showed in collecting Indian head pennies. She was attacked by a sudden sputter of laughter.

"Oh, Jenny," her mother said sadly. "Do you have to see everything as a joke?"

"It's not *my* fault if funny things happen," Jenny said.

"It most certainly is," said her mother, but instead of explaining herself, she all at once grew brisk and requested the return of her vacuum cleaner by tomorrow morning.

Jenny and Joe and every child except the baby were watching television. It was long past bedtime for most of them, but this was a special occasion: the Late, Late Show was *A Taste of Honey*. Everyone in the house had heard of *A Taste of Honey*. It was Jenny's all-time favorite movie. She had seen it once, back in 1963, and never forgotten it. Nothing else had ever measured up to it, she was fond of saying, and after returning from some other movie she was sure to announce, "Well, it was all right, I guess, but it wasn't *A Taste of Honey*." By now, any one of the children could finish that sentence before she got it halfway out. They'd ask as soon as she walked in the door, "Was it *A Taste of Honey*, Jenny? Was it?" and Phoebe was once heard telling Peter, "I like the new teacher okay, I guess, but she isn't *A Taste of Honey*."

When they learned it was coming to television, they had all begged to stay up and watch. The older ones made cocoa and the younger ones set out potato chips. Becky and Slevin arranged a ring of chairs around the TV set in the living room.

"You know what's going to happen," Joe told Jenny. "After

all this time, even *A Taste of Honey* won't be *A Taste of Honey*."

In a way, he was right. Not that she didn't still love it—yes, yes, she assured the children, it was just as she'd remembered—but after all, she was a different person watching it. The movie wrenched her with pity, now, when before it had made her feel hopeful. And wasn't it odd, wasn't it downright queer, that she'd never identified the story with her own? In 1963, she was a resident in pediatrics, struggling to care for a two-year-old born six weeks after her marriage dissolved. Yet she'd watched a movie about an unwed, unsupported pregnant girl with the most detached enjoyment, dreamily making her way through a box of pretzels. (And what had she been doing in a movie theater, anyway? How had she found the time, during such a frantic schedule?)

When it was over, she switched off the TV and shooed the children up the stairs. Quinn, the youngest, who had not been all that impressed with *A Taste of Honey*, was sound asleep and had to be carried by Joe. Even the older ones were groggy and blinking. "Wake up," she told them. "Come on, now," and she tugged at Jacob, who had dropped in a bundle on the topmost step. One by one she guided them to their beds and kissed them good night. How noisy their rooms seemed, even in silence!—that riotous clamor of toys and flung-off clothes, their vibrant, clashing rock star posters and antiwar bumper stickers and Orioles banners. Three of the children wouldn't use sheets but slept in sleeping bags instead—garishly patterned, zippered cocoons sprawled on top of the blankets; and Phoebe didn't like beds at all but curled in a quilt on the floor, most often out in the hall in front of her parents' room. She lay across the doorway like a bodyguard, and you had to watch your step in the dark so as not to trip on her.

"I want that radio *down*," Jenny said, and she kissed the top of Becky's head. Then she peeked into Slevin's room, knocked on the frame of his open door, and entered. He wore his daytime clothes to bed, as always—even his wide tooled belt with the trucker's buckle—and he lay on top of the covers. She had

been kissing him good night every night since she'd married
Joe, but still he acted bashful. All she really did was brush her
cheek against his, allowing him his dignity. "Sleep well," she told
him.

He said, "I see you found the vacuum cleaner."

"Vacuum cleaner," she said, stalling for time.

"I'm sorry I took it," he said. "I guess your mom is pretty
mad, huh? But it wasn't stealing; honest. I just needed to borrow
it for a spell."

She sat on the edge of the bed. "Needed to borrow it for
what?" she asked.

He said, "Well, for . . . I don't know. Just for . . . See, there
it was in the pantry. It was exactly like my mother's. Just exactly. You know how you never think about a thing, or realize
you remember it, and then all at once something will bring it
all back? I forgot how it had that rubber strip around the edge
so it wouldn't scuff the furniture, and that tall, puffy bag I used
to be scared of when I was a kid. It even smelled the same. It
had that same clothy smell, just like my mother's. You know?
So I wanted to take it home. But once I got it here, well, it
didn't work out. It's like I had lost the connection. It wasn't
the same after all."

"That's all right, Slevin," she said. "Heavens, honey, that's
all right." Then she worried her voice had shown too much,
would make him bashful again, so she laughed a little and said,
"Shall we get you a Hoover of your own for your birthday?"

He turned over on his side.

"Or we could have it made up in calico," she told him, giggling. "A tiny stuffed calico vacuum cleaner to take to bed
with you."

But Slevin just closed his eyes, so after a while she wished him
good night and left.

She dreamed she was back with Sam Wiley, her second husband
and the one she'd loved the best. She'd made a fool of herself
over Sam. She dreamed he was twirling on that high wooden

stool they used to have in their kitchen in Paulham. He was preening the scrolls of his handlebar mustache and singing "Let It Be." Which hadn't even existed, at the time.

She opened her eyes and heard "Let It Be" on one of the children's radios, sailing out across the dark hall. How often had she told them? She got up and made her way to Peter's room—barefoot, stepping over Phoebe. Radios late at night sounded so different, she thought—so far away and crackling with static, almost gritty, as if the music had had to travel above miles of railroad tracks and deserted superhighways, past coal yards and auto dumps, oil derricks and factory smokestacks and electrical transformers. She switched off the radio and pulled Peter's sleeping bag up around his shoulders. She checked on the baby in her crib. Then she returned to bed, shivering slightly, and huddled against Joe's hulking back for warmth.

"Mack the Knife," Sam used to sing, and "Greenfields"—yes, that had been around. She remembered how operatic he'd get, rolling his eyes, pounding his chest, trying to make her laugh. (She'd been an earnest young medical student, in those days.) Then she remembered the tender, aching line that the examining table had pressed across the mound of the baby, when Jenny was an intern bending over a patient. Six months pregnant, seven months . . . By her eighth month the marriage was finished, and Jenny was walking around in a daze. She saw that she had always been doomed to fail, had been unlovable, had lacked some singular quality that would keep a husband. She had never known this consciously, before, but the pain she felt was eerily familiar—like a suspicion, long held, at last confirmed.

She wore uniforms designed for male physicians with forty-inch waists; there were no maternity lab coats. On rounds, professors would give her doubtful glances and ask if she were sure she was up to this. Sympathetic nurses brought her so many cups of coffee that she thought she would float away. One of those nurses stayed with her through most of her labor. Other women had their husbands, but Jenny had Rosa Perez, who let her squeeze her fingers as hard as needed and never said a word of complaint.

And what was the name of that neighbor who used to watch the baby? Mary something—Mary Lee, Mary Lou—some fellow intern's wife, as poor as Jenny and the mother of two children under two. She baby-sat for a pittance, but even that was more than Jenny could afford. And the schedule! Months of nights on duty, thirty-six hours on call and twelve off, emergency room, obstetrics, trauma surgery . . . and her residency was not much better. Meanwhile, Becky changed from an infant to a little girl, an outsider really, a lively child with Sam Wiley's snapping black eyes, unrelated to Jenny. Though it was a shock, sometimes, to see her give that level, considering stare so typical of the Tulls. Was it possible, after all, that this small stranger might constitute a family? She learned to walk; she learned to talk. "No!" she would say, in her firm, spunky voice; and Jenny, trying to stay awake at three in the morning or three in the afternoon, whatever bit of time they had together, dropped her head in her hands. "No!" said Becky, and Jenny hauled off and slapped her hard across the mouth, then shook her till her head lolled, then flung her aside and ran out of the apartment to . . . where? (A movie, perhaps?) In those days, objects wobbled and grew extra edges. She was so exhausted that the sight of her patients' white pillows could mesmerize her. Sounds were thick, as if underwater. Words on a chart were meaningless—so many k's and g's, such a choppy language English was, short syllables, clumps of consonants, she'd never noticed; like Icelandic, maybe, or Eskimo. She slammed Becky's face into her Peter Rabbit dinner plate and gave her a bloody nose. She yanked a handful of her hair. All of her childhood returned to her: her mother's blows and slaps and curses, her mother's pointed fingernails digging into Jenny's arm, her mother shrieking, "Guttersnipe! Ugly little rodent!" and some scrap of memory—she couldn't quite place it—Cody catching hold of Pearl's wrist and fending her off while Jenny shrank against the wall.

Was this what it came to—that you never could escape? That certain things were doomed to continue, generation after generation? She failed to see a curb and sprained her ankle, hobbled to work in agony. She misdiagnosed a case of viral pneumonia. She let a greenstick fracture slip right past her. She brought Becky a drink of water in the middle of the night and then suddenly, without the slightest intention, screamed, "Take it! Take it!" and threw the cup into Becky's face. Becky shivered and caught her breath for hours afterward, even in her sleep, though Jenny held her tightly on her lap.

Then her mother called from Baltimore and said, "Jenny? Don't you write your family any more?"

"Well, I've been so busy," Jenny meant to say. Or: "Leave me alone, I remember all about you. It's all come back. Write? Why should I write? You've damaged me; you've injured me. Why would I want to write?"

Instead, she started . . . not crying, exactly, but something worse. She was torn by dry, ragged sobs; she ran out of air; there was a grating sound in her chest. Her mother said, calmly, "Jenny, hang up. You know that couch in your living room? Go lie down on it. I'll be there just as soon as Ezra can drive me."

Pearl stayed two weeks, using all of her vacation time. The first thing she did was call Jenny's hospital and arrange for sick leave. Then she set about putting the world in order again. She smoothed clean sheets on Jenny's bed, brought her tea and bracing broths, shampooed her hair, placed flowers on her bureau. Becky, who had hardly seen her grandmother till now, fell in love with her. Pearl called Becky "Rebecca" and treated her formally, respectfully, as if she were not quite sure how much she was allowed. Every morning she walked Becky to the playground and swung her on the swings. In the afternoon they went shopping together. She bought Becky an old-fashioned dress that made her look solemn and reasonable. She bought picture books—nursery rhymes and fairy tales and *The Little House.* Jenny had forgotten about *The Little House.* Why, she had loved that book! She'd requested it every evening, she remembered now. She'd sat on that homely old sofa and listened while her mother, with endless patience, read it three times, four times, five . . . Now Becky said, "Read it again," and

Pearl returned to page one, and Jenny listened just as closely as Becky did.

Sundays, when his restaurant closed, Ezra drove up from Baltimore. He was not, in spite of his innocent face, an open sort of person, and rather than speak outright of Jenny's new breakability he kept smiling serenely at some point just beyond her. She took comfort from this. There was already too much openness in the world, she felt—everyone raging and weeping and rejoicing. She imagined that Ezra was not subject to the ups and downs that jolted other people. She liked to have him read the papers to her (trouble in Honduras, trouble in Saigon, natural disasters in Haiti and Cuba and Italy) while she listened from a nest of deep blue blankets and a nightgown still warm from her mother's iron.

On the second weekend, Cody blew in from wherever he'd vanished to most recently. He traveled on a breeze of energy and money; Jenny was impressed. He used her telephone for two hours like the wheeler-dealer he always was and arranged to pay for a full-time sitter, a slim young woman named Delilah Greening who turned out to be better help than Jenny would ever have again. Then he slung his suit coat over one shoulder, gave her a little salute, and was gone.

She slept, sometimes, for twelve and fourteen hours straight. She woke dislocated, frightened by the sunlit, tickling silence of the apartment. She mixed up dreams and real life. "How did it happen—?" she might ask her mother, before she remembered that it hadn't happened (the Shriners' parade through her bedroom, the elderly gentleman hanging by his heels from her curtain rod like a piece of fruit). Sometimes at night, voices came vividly out of the dark. "Dr. Tull. Dr. Tull," they'd say, urgently, officially. Or, "Six hundred fifty milligrams of quinine sulfate . . ." Her own pulse thudded in her eardrums. She held her hand toward the light from the streetlamp and marveled at how white and bloodless she had become.

When her mother left and Delilah arrived, Jenny got up and returned to work. For a while, she carried herself as gently as a cup of liquid. She kept level and steady, careful not to spill over. But she was fine, she saw; she really was fine. Weekends, her mother and Ezra paid brief visits, or Jenny took Becky down to Baltimore on the train. They both dressed up for these trips and sat very still so as not to muss their clothes. Jenny felt purified, like someone who had been drained by a dangerous fever.

And the following summer, when she could have accepted more lucrative offers in Philadelphia or Newark, she chose Baltimore instead. She joined two older pediatricians, entered Becky in nursery school, and shortly thereafter purchased her Bolton Hill row house. She continued to feel fragile, though. She went on guarding a trembly, fluid center. Sometimes, loud noises made her heart race—her mother speaking her name without warning, or the telephone jangling late at night. Then she would take herself in hand. She would remind herself to draw back, to loosen hold. It seemed to her that the people she admired (one of her partners, who was a wry, funny man named Dan Charles; and her brother Ezra; and her neighbor Leah Hume) had this in common: they gazed at the world from a distance. There was something sheeted about them—some obliqueness that made them difficult to grasp. Dan, for instance, kept up such a steady, easy banter that you never could ask him about his wife, who was forever in and out of mental institutions. And Leah: she could laugh off the repeated failures of her crazy business ventures like so many pratfalls. How untouched she looked, and how untouchable, chuckling to herself and covering her mouth with a shapely, badly kept hand! Jenny studied her; you could almost say she took notes. She was learning how to make it through life on a slant. She was trying to lose her intensity.

"You've changed," her mother said (all intensity herself). "You've grown so different, Jenny. I can't quite put my finger on what's wrong, but *something* is." She wanted Jenny to remarry; she hoped for a dozen grandchildren, at least; she was always after Jenny to get out and mingle, socialize, make herself more attractive, meet some nice young man. What Jenny didn't tell her was, she simply couldn't be bothered with all that. She felt textureless, so that events just slid right off her with no friction whatsoever; and the thought of the heartfelt conversations required by a courtship filled her with impatience.

Then she met Joe with his flanks of children—his padding, his moat, his barricade of children, all in urgent need of her brisk and competent attention. No conversation *there*—she and Joe had hardly found a moment to speak to each other seriously. They were always trying to be heard above the sound of toy trucks and xylophones. She didn't even have time for thinking any more.

"Of course, the material object is nothing," said the priest. He winced at a squeal from the waiting room. "That's unimportant, the least of my concerns. Though it did have some historical value. It was donated, I believe, by the missionary brother of one of our parishioners."

Jenny leaned back against the receptionist's window and touched a hand to her forehead. "Well, I don't . . ." she said. "*What* did you say this was?"

"A rhinoceros foot," said the priest, "in the shape of an umbrella stand. Or an umbrella stand in the shape of a rhinoceros foot. It was an actual rhinoceros foot from . . . wherever rhinoceri come from."

A naked toddler shot out a door like a stray piece of popcorn, pursued by a nurse with a hypodermic needle. The priest stood back to give them room. "We know it was there in the morning," he said. "But at four o'clock, it was gone. And Slevin was in just previously; I'd asked him to come for a chat. Only I was on the phone when he arrived. By the time I'd hung up he was gone, and so was the rhinoceros foot."

Jenny said, "I wonder if his mother had a rhinoceros foot."

"Pardon?" said the priest.

She realized how this must have sounded, and she laughed. "No," she said, "I don't mean *she* had rhinoceros feet . . . oh, Lord . . ."

The priest said, "Dr. Tull, don't you see this is serious? We have a child in trouble here, don't you see that? Don't you think something ought to be done? Where do you *stand*, Dr. Tull?"

Jenny's smile faded and she looked into his face. "I don't know," she said, after a pause. She felt suddenly bereft, as if something were missing, as if she'd given something up. She hadn't *always* been like this! she wanted to tell him. But aloud she said, "I only meant, you see . . . I believe he steals what reminds him of his mother. Hoovers and umbrella stands. Doesn't that make sense?"

"Ah," said the priest.

"What's next, I wonder," Jenny said. She mused for a moment. "Picture it! Grand pianos. Kitchen sinks. Why, we'll have his mother's whole household," she said, "her photo albums and her grade-school yearbooks, her college roommate asleep on our bed and her high school boyfriends in our living room." She pictured a row of dressed-up boys from the fifties, their hair slicked down wetly, their shirts ironed crisply, perched on her couch like mannequins with heart-shaped boxes of chocolates on their knees. She laughed. The priest groaned. A little blue plastic helicopter buzzed across the waiting room and landed in Jenny's hair.

8

This Really Happened

The summer before Luke Tull turned fourteen, his father had a serious accident at the factory he was inspecting. A girder swung around on its cable, hit Luke's father and the foreman standing next to him, and swept them both off the walkway and down to the lower level of the factory. The foreman was killed. Cody lived, by some miracle, but he was badly hurt. For two days he lay in a coma. There was a question of brain damage, till he woke and, in his normal, crusty way, asked who the hell was in charge around here.

Three weeks later, he came home by ambulance. His thick black hair had been shaved off one side of his head, where a gauze patch covered the worst of his wounds. His face—ordinarily lean and tanned—was swollen across one cheekbone and turning different shades of yellow from slowly fading bruises. His ribs were taped and an arm and a leg were in casts—the right arm and the left leg, so he couldn't use crutches. He was forced to lie in bed, cursing the game shows on TV. "Fools. Jackasses. Who do they think would be watching this crap?"

Luke's mother, who had always been so spirited, lost something important to the accident. First, in the terrible coma days, she drifted around in a wash of tears—a small, wan, pink-eyed woman. Her red hair seemed drained of color. Luke would say,

"Mom?" and she wouldn't hear, would sometimes snatch up her car keys as if mistaking who had called and go tearing off to the hospital again, leaving Luke alone. Even after the coma ended, it didn't seem she came back completely. When Cody was brought home, she sat by his bed for hours saying nothing, lightly stroking one thick vein that ran down the inside of his wrist. She watched the game shows with a tremulous smile. "Jesus, look at them squawk," Cody said disgustedly, and Ruth bent down and laid her cheek against his hand as if he'd uttered something wonderful.

Luke, who had once been the center of her world, now hung around the fringes. It was July and he had nothing to do. They'd only been living here—in a suburb of Petersburg, Virginia—since the end of the school year, and he didn't know any boys his own age. The children on his block were all younger, thin voiced and excitable. It annoyed him to hear their shrieking games of roll-a-bat and the sputtery *ksh! kshew!* of their imaginary rifles. Toddlers were packed into flowered vinyl wading pools which they spent their mornings emptying, measuring cup by measuring cup, till every yard was a sea of mud. Luke could not remember ever being that young. Floating through the icy, white and gold elegance of the rented colonial-style house, he surfaced in various gilt-framed mirrors: someone awkward and unwanted, lurching on legs grown too long to manage, his face past cuteness but not yet solidified into anything better—an oval, fragile face, a sweep of streaky blond hair, a mouthful of braces that made his lips appear irregular and vulnerable. His jeans were getting too short but he had no idea how to go about buying new ones. He was accustomed to relying on his mother for such things. In the old days, his mother had done everything for him. She had got on his nerves, as a matter of fact.

Now he made his own breakfast—Cheerios or shredded wheat —and a sandwich for lunch. His mother cooked supper, but it was something slapped together, not her usual style at all; and mostly she would let Luke eat alone in the kitchen while she and Cody shared a tray in the bedroom. Or if she stayed with

Luke, her *talk* was still of Cody. She never asked Luke about himself, no; it was "your daddy" this and "your daddy" that, never a thing but "your daddy." How well he was bearing up, how he'd always borne up, always been so dependable from the earliest time she had known him. "I was not but nineteen when I met him," she said, "and he was thirty years old. I was a homely chit of a girl and he was the handsomest thing you ever saw, so fine mannered and wearing this perfect gray suit. At the time, I was all set to marry Ezra, your daddy's brother. I bet you didn't know that, did you? Oh, I got around, in those days! Then your daddy stepped in. He was brazen as you please. Didn't care how it looked, didn't have an ounce of shame, just moved right in and claimed me for his own. Well, first I thought he was teasing. He could have had anyone, any girl he liked, somebody beautiful even. Then I saw he meant it. I didn't know which way to turn, for I did love your Uncle Ezra, though he was not so . . . I mean, Ezra was a much plainer person, more like me, you would say. But your daddy'd walk into the room and it seemed like, I don't know, the air just came alive, somehow. He put his hands on my shoulders one day and I told him please, I was engaged to marry Ezra, and he said he knew that. He stepped up close and I said really, Ezra was a good, good man, and he said yes, he was; and we hugged each other like two people sharing some bereavement and I said, 'Why, you're near about my brother-in-law!' and he said, 'Very nearly, yes,' and he kissed me on the lips."

Luke lowered his lashes. He wished she wouldn't talk about such things.

"And if we've had our ups and downs," she said, "well, I just want you to know that it wasn't *his* fault, Luke. Look at me! I'm nothing but a little backwoods Garrett County farm girl, hardly educated. And I'm not so easy to get along with, either. I'm not so easygoing. You mustn't blame him. Why, once—oh, you were in nursery school, I bet you don't remember this—I packed you up and left him. I told him he didn't love me and never had, only married me to spite his brother, Ezra, that he'd always been so jealous of. I accused him of terrible things, just terrible, and then while he was at work I carried you off to the railroad station and . . . this is funny now when I tell it, but it wasn't then: while we were waiting on the bench a Marine threw up in my pocketbook. Came time to board the train and I just couldn't make myself put my fingers in and get out the tickets, assuming they were still usable; and couldn't bear to reach in for the money to buy more tickets, either. So I called your daddy on the telephone, begged a dime from a nun and said, 'Cody, come and get me; this isn't really what I want to be doing. Oh, Cody,' I said, 'we've got so interwoven; even if you didn't love me at all, now we're so entwined. It's you I have to stay with.' And he left off work and drove down to collect me, all steady and sure in his fine gray suit, nothing like the rest of the world. Don't you remember that? You've forgotten all about it," she said. "It's just as well, I reckon. Luke, when you almost lose a person, everything comes so clear! You see how much he matters, how there's no one the least bit like him; he's irreplaceable. How he always puts us first; I mean, has never, in all his days, left you and me behind when he's off on business, but carts us to every new town he's called to because he won't do like his father, he says: travel about forgetting his own relations. It's not true that he brings us along because he doesn't trust me. He really cares for our welfare. When I think now," she said, "about your daddy kissing me that first time—'Very nearly, yes,' he said. 'Yes, very nearly your brother-in-law,' and kissed me so quiet but definite, insisting, like he wouldn't take no for an answer—why, I see now that's when my *life* began! But at the time I had no notion, didn't grasp the importance. I didn't know back then that one person can have such effect on another."

But if she was changed (if even Luke was changed—fading into someone transparent, he imagined), Cody was absolutely the same. After all, Cody hadn't suffered the strain of that coma; he'd been absent from it. He hadn't worried he would die, once he came to, because it wouldn't occur to him that he was the *type* to die. He'd sailed through the whole experience with his usual combination of nonchalance and belligerence, and now he lay thrashing on his bed wondering when he could get up again. "What I mainly am is mad," he told Luke. "This whole damn business has left me mad as hell. I felt that girder hit, you know that? I really felt it hit, and it hurt, and all the time I was flying through the air I wanted to hit it back, punch somebody; and now it seems I'm still waiting for the chance. When do I get to get even? And don't talk to me about lawsuits, compensation. The only thing I want to do is hit that girder back."

"Mom says would you like some soup," said Luke, wiping his palms nervously down his thighs.

"No, I wouldn't like soup. What's she always trying to feed me for? Listen, Luke. If your grandma calls again today, I want you to tell her I've gone back to work."

"To work?"

"I can't stand to hear her fret on the phone any more."

"But all along," Luke said, "you've been telling her you were too sick for company. Yesterday you were too sick and today you've gone back to *work*? What'll she think?"

"It's nothing to me what she thinks," said Cody. He never sounded very fond of Grandma Tull, who had called from Baltimore every day since the accident. Luke enjoyed her, the little he knew of her, but Cody said looks were deceiving. "She puts on a good front," he told Luke. "You don't know what she's like. You don't know what it was like growing up with her."

Luke felt he did know (hadn't he heard it all a million times?) but his father had got started now and wouldn't be stopped. "Let me give you an example," he said. "Listen, now. This really happened." That was the way he always introduced his childhood. "This really happened," he would say, as if it were unthinkable, beyond belief, but then what followed never seemed so terrible to Luke. "I swear it: your grandma had this friend named Emmaline that she hadn't seen in years. Only friend she ever mentioned. And Emmaline lived in . . . I forget. Anyhow, someplace far away. So one Christmas I saved up the money to buy a Greyhound bus ticket to wherever this Emmaline lived. I slaved and borrowed and *stole* the money, and presented my mother with the ticket on Christmas morning. I was seventeen at the time, old enough to take care of the others, and I said, 'You leave tomorrow, stay a week, and I'll watch over things till you get back.' And you know what she said? Listen; you won't believe this. 'But Cody, honey,' she said. 'Day after tomorrow is your brother's birthday.' "

He looked over at Luke. Luke waited for him to go on.

"See," Cody said, "December twenty-seventh was Ezra's birthday."

"So?" Luke asked.

"So she wouldn't leave her precious boy on his birthday! Not even to visit her oldest, dearest, only friend, that her other boy had given her a ticket for."

"I wouldn't like for Mom to leave me on my birthday, either," Luke said.

"No, no, you're missing the point. She wouldn't leave Ezra, her favorite. Me or my sister, she would surely leave."

"How do you know that?" Luke asked him. "Did you ever try giving her a ticket on *your* birthday? I bet she'd have said the same thing."

"My birthday is in February," Cody said. "Nowhere near any occasion for gift giving. Oh, I don't know why I bother talking to you. You're an only child, that's your trouble. You haven't the faintest idea what I'm trying to get across." And he turned his pillow over and settled back with a sigh.

Luke went out in the yard and threw his baseball against the garage. It thudded and bounced back, shimmering in the sunlight. In the old days, his mother had practiced throwing with him. She had taught him to bat and pitch overhand, too. She was good at sports. He saw glimpses in her, sometimes, of the scatty little tomboy she must once have been. But it had always seemed, when they played ball together, that this was only a preparation for the *real* game, with his father. It was like cramming for an exam. Then on weekends Cody came home and pitched the ball to him and said, "Not bad. Not bad at all," when Luke hit it out of the yard. At these moments Luke was conscious of adding a certain swagger to his walk, a certain swing to his shoulders. He imagined he was growing to be more like his father. Sauntering into the house after practice, he'd pass Cody's parked car and ask, "She still getting pretty good mileage?" He would stand in front of the open refrigerator and swig iced tea directly from the pitcher—something his mother detested. Oh, it was time to put his mother behind him now—all those years of following her through the house, enmeshed in her routine, dragging his toy broom after her big one or leaning both elbows on her dressing table to watch, entranced, as she dusted powder on her freckled nose. The dailiness of women's lives! He knew all he cared to know about it. He was exhausted by the trivia of measuring out the soap flakes, waiting for the plumber. High time to move to his father's side. But his father lay on his back in the bedroom, cursing steadily. "What the hell is the matter with this TV? Why bother buying a Sony if there's no one who will fix it?"

"I'll find us a repairman today," Ruth's new, soft voice floated out.

Ruth wore dresses all the time now because Cody said he was tired of her pantsuits. "Everlasting polyester pantsuits," he said, and it was true she didn't look as stylish as most other women, though Luke wasn't so sure that the pantsuits were to blame. Even after she changed to dresses, something seemed to be wrong. They were too big, or too hard-surfaced, or too shiny; they looked less like clothes than . . . housing, Luke thought. "Is this better?" she asked his father, and she stood hopefully in the doorway, flat on her penny loafers because in Garrett County, she said, they had never learned her to walk in high heels. By then, Cody had recovered from his mood. He said, "Sure, honey. Sure. It's fine." He wasn't *always* evil tempered. It was the strain of lying immobile. It was the constant discomfort. He did make an effort. But then, not two hours later: "Ruth, will you explain why I have to live in a place that looks like a candy dish? Is it necessary to rent a house where everything is white and gold and curlicued? You think of that as class?"

It was the nature of Cody's job that he worked alone. As soon as he finished streamlining whatever factory had called him in, he moved on. His partner, a man named Sloan, lived in New York City and invented the devices that Cody determined a need for—sorting racks, folding aids, single hand tools combining the tasks of several. Consequently, there were no fellow workers to pay Cody visits, unless you counted that one edgy call by the owner of the factory where he'd had his accident. And they didn't know any of the neighbors. They were on their own, just the three of them. They might have been castaways. No wonder Cody acted so irritable. The only time Luke and his mother got out was once a week, when they went for groceries. Backing her white Mercedes from the garage, Ruth sat erect and alert, not looking behind her, already anxious about Cody. "Maybe I should've made you stay. If he needs to go to the bathroom—"

"He can good and *wait*," Luke said through his teeth.

"Why, Luke!"

"Let him pee in the bed."

"Luke Tull!"

Luke stared out the window.

"It's been hard on you," his mother said. "We've got to find you some friends."

"I don't need friends."

"Everybody needs friends. We don't have a one, in this town. I feel like I'm drying up. Sometimes I wonder," she said, "if this life is really . . ." But she didn't say any more.

When they returned, Cody was pleasant and cheerful, as if he'd made some resolutions in their absence. Or maybe he'd been refreshed by the solitude. "Talked to Sloan," he told Ruth. "He called from New York. I said to him, soon as I get this cast off I'm going to finish up at the factory and clear on out. I can't take much more of this place."

"Oh, good, Cody, honey."

"Bring me my briefcase, will you? I want to jot down some ideas. There's lots I could be doing in bed."

"I picked out some of those pears you like."

"No, no, just my briefcase, and that pen on the desk in my study. I'm going to see if my fingers are up to writing yet."

He told Luke, "Work is what I need. I've been *starved* for work. It's made me a little snappish."

Luke scratched his rib cage. He said, "That's all right."

"You make sure you get a job you enjoy, once you're grown. You've got to enjoy what you're doing. That's important."

"I know."

"Me, I deal with time," said Cody. He accepted a ball-point pen from Ruth. "Time is my favorite thing of all."

Luke loved it when his father talked about time.

"Time is my obsession: not to waste it, not to lose it. It's like . . . I don't know, an object, to me; something you can almost take hold of. If I could just collect enough of it in one clump, I always think. If I could pass it back and forth and sideways, you know? If only Einstein were right and time were a kind of river you could choose to step into at any place along the shore."

He clicked his pen point in and out, frowning into space. "If they had a time machine, I'd go on it," he said. "It wouldn't much matter to me where. Past or future: just out of my time. Just someplace else."

Luke felt a pang. "But then you wouldn't know *me*," he said.

"Hmm?"

"Sure he would," Ruth said briskly. She was opening the latches of Cody's briefcase. "He'd take you with him. Only mind," she told Cody, "if Luke goes too you've got to bring penicillin, and his hay fever pills, and his fluoride toothpaste, you hear?"

Cody laughed, but he didn't say one way or another about taking Luke along.

That was the evening that Cody first got his strange notion. It came about so suddenly: they were playing Monopoly on

Cody's bed, the three of them, and Cody was winning as usual and offering Luke a loan to keep going. "Oh, well, no, I guess I've lost," said Luke.

There was the briefest pause—a skipped beat. Cody looked over at Ruth, who was counting her deed cards. "He sounds just like Ezra," he told her.

She frowned at Baltic Avenue.

"Didn't you hear what he said? He said it just like Ezra."

"Really?"

"*Ezra* would do that," Cody told Luke. "Your Uncle Ezra. It was no fun beating him at all. He'd never take a loan and he wouldn't mortgage the least little thing, not even a railroad or the waterworks. He'd just cave right in and give up."

"Well, it's only that . . . you can see that I've lost," Luke said. "It's only a matter of time."

"Sometimes it's more like you're Ezra's child, not mine."

"Cody Tull! What a thought," said Ruth.

But it was too late. The words hung in the air. Luke felt miserable; he had all he could do to finish the game. (He knew his father had never thought much of Ezra.) And Cody, though he dropped the subject, remained dissatisfied in some way. "Sit up straighter," he kept telling Luke. "Don't *hunch*. Sit straight. God. You look like a rabbit."

As soon as he could, Luke said good night and went off to bed.

The following morning, everything was fine again. Cody did some more work on his papers and had another talk with Sloan. Ruth cooked a chicken for a nice cold summer supper. Anytime Luke wandered by, Cody said something cheerful to him. "Why so long in the face?" he'd ask, or, "Feeling bored, son?" It sounded funny, calling Luke "son." Cody didn't usually do that.

They all had lunch in the bedroom—sandwiches and potato salad, like a picnic. The telephone, buried among the sheets, started ringing halfway through the meal, and Cody said not to answer it. It was bound to be his mother, he said. They kept perfectly silent, as if the caller could somehow hear them. After the ringing stopped, though, Ruth said, "That poor, poor woman."

"Poor!" Cody snorted.

"Aren't we awful?"

"You wouldn't call her poor if you knew her better."

Luke went back to his room and sorted through his old model airplanes. His parents' voices drifted after him. "Listen," Cody was telling Ruth. "This really happened. For my mother's birthday I saved up all my money, fourteen dollars. And Ezra didn't have a penny, see . . ."

Luke scrabbled through his wooden footlocker, the one piece of furniture that really belonged to him. It had accompanied all their moves since before he could remember. He was hunting the missing wing of a jet. He didn't find the wing but he did find a leather bag of marbles—the kind he used to like, with spritzy bubbles like ginger ale inside them. And a slingshot made from a strip of inner tube. And a tonette—a dusty black plastic whistle on which, for Mother's Day back in first grade, he'd played "White Coral Bells" along with his classmates. He tried it now: *White coral bells, upon a slender stalk* . . . It returned to him, note by note. He rose and went to his parents' room to play it through to the end. *Lilies of the valley deck my—*

His father said, "I can't stand it."

Luke lowered the tonette.

"Are you doing this on purpose?" Cody asked. "Are you determined to torment me?"

"Huh?"

"Cody, honey . . ." Ruth said.

"You're haunting me, isn't that it? I can't get away from him! I spend half my life with meek-and-mild Ezra and his blasted wooden whistle; I make my escape at last, and now look: here we go again. It's like a conspiracy! Like some kind of plot where someone decided, long before I was born, I would live out my days surrounded by people who were . . . nicer than I am, just naturally nicer without even having to try, people that other people preferred; and everywhere I go there's something, just that goddamn forgiving smile or some demented folk song floating out a window—"

"Cody, Luke will be thinking you have lost your senses," Ruth said.

"And you!" Cody told her. "Look at you! Ah, Lord," he said. "Some people fit together forever, don't they? And you haven't a hope in heaven of prying them apart. Married or not, you've always loved Ezra better than me."

"Cody, what are you *talking* about?"

"Admit it," Cody said. "Isn't Ezra the real, true father of Luke?"

There was a silence.

"You didn't say that. You couldn't have," Ruth told him.

"Admit it!"

"You know you don't seriously believe such a thing."

"Isn't it the truth? Tell me! I won't get angry, I promise."

Luke went back to his room and closed the door.

All that afternoon he lay on his bed, rereading an old horse book from his childhood because he didn't have anything else to do. The story struck him as foolish now, although once he'd loved it. When his mother called him for supper, he walked very firmly into the kitchen. He was going to refuse, absolutely, to eat in the bedroom with Cody any more. But his mother had already set two places at the kitchen table. She sat across from him while he ate, not eating much herself. Luke shoveled in various cold foods and refused to meet her eyes. The fact was that she was stupid. He didn't know when he'd seen such a weak and stupid woman.

After supper he went back to his room and listened to a radio show where people called up a tired-sounding host and offered their opinions. They discussed drunken drivers and battered wives. It grew dark, but Luke didn't turn on the light. His mother tapped hesitantly on his door, paused, and left.

Then he must have fallen asleep. When he woke it was darker than ever, and his neck was stiff, and a woman on the radio was saying, "Now, I'm not denying I signed the papers but that was only his fast talk, only him talking me into it. 'Just put your John Doe right here,' he tells me . . ."

"I assume you mean John Hancock," the host said wearily.

"Whatever," said the woman.

Then beneath these voices, murmuring through the wall, came Cody's grumble and Ruth's pale answers. Luke covered his head with his pillow.

He tried to recall his Uncle Ezra. It was several years since they'd met. And even that was such a brief visit, his father taking them away in a huff before they'd got well settled. Finding Ezra was something like hunting through that foot-locker; he had to burrow past a dozen other memories, and more came trailing up along with what he was after. He smelled the burned toast in his grandma's kitchen and remembered Ezra's bedroom, which had once been Ezra's and Cody's to-gether, where boyhood treasures (a football-shaped bookend, a peeling hockey stick) had sat in their places so long that to Ezra, they were invisible. Anything that caught Luke's atten-tion, Ezra had seemed surprised to see. "Oh! Would you like to have that?" he would ask, and when Luke politely declined, not wanting to seem greedy, Ezra said, "Please. I can't think what it's still doing here." His room had been large—a sort of dormi-tory arrangement, occupying the whole third floor—but its stuffy smell of used sheets and twice-worn clothes had made it seem smaller. There was a lock inside the bathroom door down-stairs, Luke recalled, that looked exactly like a little silver cashew; and the bathroom itself was tall and echoing, ancient, cold floored, with a porcelain knob in the tub reading WASTE.

He tried to picture his cousins—Aunt Jenny's children—but only came up with another room: his cousin Becky's ruffled bedroom, with its throng of shabby stuffed animals densely en-circling her bed. How could she sleep? he had wondered. But she told him she had no trouble sleeping at all; and whenever she went away to spend the night, she said, she took the whole menagerie in a giant canvas suitcase and set it out first thing around the new bed, even before unpacking her pajamas; and most of her friends did the same. It was Luke's first inkling that girls were different. He was mystified and charmed, and he treated her protectively for the rest of that short visit—though she was a year older than he and half a head taller.

If Ezra were really his father, Luke thought, then Luke could live in Baltimore where houses were dark and deep and secretive. Relatives would surround him—a loving grandma, funny Aunt Jenny, those rafts of cousins. Ezra would let him help out in his restaurant. He would talk about food and how people need to be fed with care; Luke could hear his ambling way of speaking. Yes, now he had it: the memory homed in. Ezra wore a flannel shirt of soft blue plaid, washed into oblivion. His hair was yellow . . . why! It was Luke's kind of yellow, all streaky and layered. And his eyes were Luke's kind of gray, a full shade lighter than Cody's, and his skin had that same golden cast that caused it to blend into his hair almost without demarcation.

Luke let himself believe in some unimaginable moment between Ruth and Ezra, fourteen years ago. He skipped across it quickly to the time when Ezra would arrive to claim him. "You're old enough to be told now, son . . ."

Knitting this scene in the dark, doubling back to correct a false note or racing forward to a good part, Luke forgot himself and took the pillow off his head. Instantly, he heard Cody's voice behind the wall. "Everything I've ever wanted, Ezra got it. Anything in life I wanted. Even things I thought I had won, Ezra won in the end. And he didn't even seem to be trying; that's the hell of it."

"You won the damn *Monopoly* games, didn't you?" Luke shouted.

Cody said nothing.

The next morning, Cody seemed unusually quiet. Ruth took him into the doctor's to get his walking cast—a moment they'd been waiting for, but Cody didn't act interested now. Luke had to go along to serve as a crutch. He flinched when Cody first laid his heavy arm cast across his shoulders; he felt there was some danger hovering. But Cody was a dead weight, grunting as he walked, evidently thinking about other matters. He heaved himself into the car and stared bleakly ahead of him. In the doctor's waiting room, while Luke and his mother read magazines, Cody just sat empty faced. And after he got his walking cast, he hobbled back to the car unassisted, ignoring Luke's offer of help. He fell into bed as soon as they reached home and lay gazing at the ceiling. "Cody, honey? Remember the doctor said to give that leg some exercise," Ruth told him.

He didn't answer.

Luke went out to the yard and kicked at the grass a while as if he were hunting for something. Next door, a cluster of toddlers in their wading pool stared at him. He wanted to shout, "Turn away! Stop looking at me; you have no business." But instead it was he who turned, wandering out of the yard and down the street. More wading pools; more round-eyed, judging stares. A Welsh corgi, squat and dignified, bustled down the sidewalk, followed by a lady in a flowing caftan. "Toulouse! Toulouse!" she called. The heat was throbbing; it almost breathed. Luke's face became filmed with sweat and his T-shirt stuck to his back. He kept wiping his upper lip. He passed rows of colonial houses similar to his, each with some object featured like a museum piece in the living-room window: a bulbous lamp, a china horse, a vase of stiff-necked marigolds. (And what did his own window have? He couldn't recall. He wanted to say a weeping fig tree, but that was from an apartment they'd rented, three or four towns back.) Sprinklers spun lazily. It was a satisfaction to stop, from time to time, and watch a lawn soak up the spangled water drops.

Now here came some busy lady with her baby in a stroller, small children all around her. He crossed the street to avoid them, took a right turn, and arrived on Willow Bough Avenue with its whizzing traffic, discount drugstores, real estate offices and billboards and service stations. He waited at an intersection, pondering where to go next. One of the things about moving so often was, he never really knew where he was. He believed his sense of direction had been blunted. He couldn't understand how some people seemed to carry a kind of detailed, internal map of the town they lived in.

A Trailways bus zipped past him reading BALTIMORE. Imagine hailing it. (Could you hail a Trailways bus?) Imagine boarding it—assuming he had the money, which he didn't—and riding off to Baltimore, arriving at Ezra's restaurant and strolling in. "Here I am." "*There* you are," Ezra would say. Oh, if only he'd brought his money! Another bus passed, but that was a local. Then a gigantic truck drew up, braking for an amber light. Luke, as if obeying orders, stuck out a thumb. The driver leaned across the seat and opened the door on the passenger side. "Hop on in," he told Luke.

No RIDERS, a label on the window read. None of this was happening. Slowly, like someone being pushed from behind, Luke climbed into the cab. It was filled with loud music and a leathery, sweaty, masculine smell that made him feel instantly comfortable. He slammed the door and settled back. The driver —a knife-faced man, unshaven—squinted up at the traffic light and asked, "Whereabouts you headed, son?"

Luke said, "Baltimore, Maryland."

"Folks know you're going?"

"Sure," said Luke.

The driver shot him a glance.

"Why, my folks . . . *live* in Baltimore," Luke told him.

"Oh, then."

The truck started up again. They rumbled past the shopping mall where Luke's mother went for groceries. A green sign swung overhead, listing points north. "Well," said the driver, adjusting his mirror, "I tell you: I can carry you as far as Richmond. That's where I have to veer west."

"Okay," said Luke.

Even Richmond, after all, was farther than he'd ever meant to go.

On the radio, Billy Swan was singing "I Can Help." The driver hummed along in a creaky voice that never quite hit the right note. His thin gray hair, Luke saw, had recently been combed; it lay close to his skull in damp parallel lines. He held a cigarette between his fingers but he didn't light it. His fingernails were so thick and ridged, they might have been cut from yellow corduroy.

"In the summer of fifty-six," he said, "I was passing along this very road with my wife in a Safeway grocery truck when she commences to go into labor. Not but eight months gone and she proceeds directly into labor. Lord God! I recall to this day. She says, 'Clement, I think it's my time.' Well, I was young then. Inexperienced. I thought a baby came one-two-three. I thought we didn't have a moment to spare. And also, you know what they say: a seven-month baby will turn out good but an eight-month baby won't make it. I can't figure why *that* should be. So anyhow, I put on the brakes. I'm shaking all over. My brake foot is so shaky we're just wobbling down the highway. You see that sign over there? Leading off to the right? See that hospital sign? Well, that is where I taken her. Straight up that there road. I never come by here but what I recall it."

Luke looked politely at the hospital sign, and then swiveled his neck to go on looking after they had passed. It was the only response he could think of.

"Labor lasted thirty-two hours," the driver said. "Safeway thought I'd hijacked their rig."

"Well," said Luke, "but the baby got born okay."

"Sure," the driver told him. "Five-pound girl. Lisa Michelle." He thought a moment. Then he said, "She died later on, though."

Luke cleared his throat.

"Crib death is what they call it nowadays," said the driver. He swerved around a trailer. "Ever hear of it?"

"No, sir, I haven't."

"Sudden crib death. Six months old. Light of my life. Bright as a button, too—loved me to bits. I'd come home and she would just rev right up—wheel her arms and legs like a windmill soon as she set eyes on me. Then she went and died."

"Well, gosh," said Luke.

"Now I got others," the driver said. "Want to see them? Turn down that sun visor over your head."

Luke turned down the visor. A color photo, held in place by a pink plastic clothespin, showed three plain girls in dresses so new and starchy that it must have been Easter Sunday.

"The youngest is near about your age," the driver said. "What are you: thirteen, fourteen?" He honked at a station wagon that had cut too close in front. "They're nice girls," he said, "but I don't know. It's not the same, somehow. Seems like I lost the . . . attachment. Lost the knack of getting attached. I mean, I like them; shoot, I love them, but I just don't have the . . . seems to me I can't get up the energy no more."

A lady on the radio was advertising Chevrolets. The driver switched stations and Barbra Streisand came on, showing off as usual. "But you ought to see my wife!" the driver said. "Isn't it amazing? She loves those kids like the very first one. She just started in all over. I don't know what to make of her. I look at her and I can't believe it. 'Dotty,' I say, 'really it all comes down to nothing. It's not for anything,' I say. 'Dotty, how come you can go *on* like this?' See, me, I never bounced back so good. I pass that hospital road and you know? I halfway believe if I made the turnoff, things would be just like before. Dotty'd be holding my hand, and Lisa Michelle would be waiting to be born."

Luke rubbed his palms on his jeans. The driver said, "Well, now. Listen to me! Just gabbing along; I guess you think I talk too much." And for the rest of the trip he was quiet, only whistling through his teeth when the radio played a familiar song.

He said goodbye near Richmond, going out of his way to leave Luke at a ramp just past a rest center. "You wait right here and you'll get a ride in no time," he said. "Here they're traveling slow anyhow, and won't mind stopping." Then he raised his hand stiffly and drove off. From a distance, his truck looked as bright and chunky as a toy.

But it seemed he took some purpose with him, some atmosphere of speed and assurance. All at once . . . what was Luke *doing* here? What could he be thinking of? He saw himself, alone in the fierce white glare of the sun, cocking his thumb at an amateurish angle on a road in the middle of nowhere. He couldn't even visualize how far he had to go. (He'd never done well in geography.) Although it was hot—the peak of the afternoon, by now—he wished for a windbreaker: protection. He wished for his billfold, not so much for the small amount of money it held as for the i.d. card that had come with it when he bought it. If he were killed on this road, how would they know whom to notify? He wondered if—homeless, parentless—he would have to wear these braces on his teeth for the rest of his life. He pictured himself as an old man, still hiding a mouthful of metal whenever he smiled.

Then an out-of-date, fin-tailed car stopped next to him and the door swung open. "Need a lift?" the driver asked. In the back, a little tow-headed boy bounced up and down, calling, "Come on! Come on! Get in and have a ride. Come on in and ride with us!"

Luke got in. He found the driver smiling at him—a suntanned man in blue jeans, with deep lines around his eyes. "My name's Dan Smollett," he said. "That's Sammy in the back seat."

"I'm Luke."

"We're heading toward D.C. That do you any good?"

"It's fine," said Luke. "I guess," he added, still unsure of his geography. "I'm on my way to Baltimore."

"Baltimore!" said Sammy, still bouncing. "Daddy, can we go to Baltimore?"

"We have to go to Washington, Sammy."

"Don't we know someone in Baltimore too? Kitty? Susie? Betsy?"

"Now, Sammy, settle down, please."

"We're looking up Daddy's old girlfriends," Sammy told Luke.

"Oh," said Luke.

"We just came from Raleigh and saw Carla."

"No, no, Carla was in Durham," his father told him. "It was DeeDee you saw in Raleigh."

"Carla was nice," said Sammy. "She was the best of the bunch. You would've liked her, Luke."

"I would?"

"It's too bad she was married."

"Sammy, Luke doesn't want to hear about our private lives."

"Oh, that's all right," said Luke. He wasn't sure what he was hearing, anyhow.

They were back on the freeway by now, staying in the slow lane—perhaps because of the grinding noise that came whenever Dan accelerated. Luke had never been in a car as old as this one. Its interior was a dusty gray felt, the floors awash in paper cups and Frito bags. The glove compartment—doorless—spilled out maps that were splitting at the seams, along with loose change, Lifesavers, and miniature tractors and dump trucks. In the rear, Sammy bounced among blankets and grayish pillows. "Settle down," his father kept saying, but it didn't do any good. "He gets a little restless, along about afternoon," Dan told Luke.

"How long have you been traveling?" Luke asked.

"Oh, three weeks or so."

"Three weeks!"

"We left just after summer school. I'm a high school English teacher; I had to teach this grammar course first."

"Lookit here," Sammy said, and on his next bounce upward he thrust a wad of paper into Luke's face. Evidently, someone had been chewing on it. It was four sheets, mangled together, bearing typed columns of names and addresses. "Daddy's old girlfriends," Sammy said.

Luke stared.

"They are not," said his father. "Really, Sammy." He told Luke, "That's my graduating class in high school. Boys *and* girls. Last year they had a reunion; I didn't go but they sent us this address list."

"Now we're looking up the girls," Sammy said.

"Not all the girls, Sammy."

"The girls that you went out with."

"My wife is divorcing me," Dan told Luke. He seemed to think this explained everything. He faced forward again, and Luke said, "Oh." Another rest center floated by, a distant forest of Texaco and Amoco signs. A moving van honked obligingly when Sammy gave the signal out the window. Sammy squealed and bounced all the harder—a spiky mass of bones and striped T-shirt, flapping shorts, torn sneakers.

"What year are you in school?" Dan asked Luke.

"I'm going into ninth grade."

"Read any Hemingway? *Catcher in the Rye?* What are they giving you to read?"

"I don't know yet. I'm new," said Luke.

He could easily picture Dan as a teacher. He would wear his jeans in the classroom. He'd be one of those casual, comradely types that Luke had never quite trusted. Better to have him in suit and tie; at least then you knew where you stood.

"In Washington," Sammy said, "there's *two* girls, Patty and Lena."

"Don't say girls, say women," Dan told him.

"Patty Sears and Lena Sparrow."

"I'm better on the S's," Dan said to Luke. "They were in my homeroom."

"Lena we hear is separated," Sammy said.

Luke said, "But what do you do when you visit? What is there to do?"

"Oh, sit around," Sammy said. "Stay a few days if they ask us. Play with their dogs and their cats and their kids. Most of them do have kids. And husbands."

"Well, then," said Luke. "If they've got husbands . . ."

"But we don't know that till we get there. Do we," Sammy said.

"Sammy's a little mixed up," Dan said. "It's not as though we're hunting replacements. We're just traveling. This divorce has come as a shock and I'm just, oh, traveling back. I'm visiting old friends."

"But only *girl* friends," Sammy pointed out.

"They're girls I used to get along fine with. Not sweethearts, necessarily. But they liked me; they thought I was fine. Or at least, they seemed to. I assumed they did. *I* don't know. Maybe they were just acting polite. Maybe I was a mess all along."

Luke couldn't think what to say.

"So listen!" Dan told him. "You read *The Great Gatsby* yet?"

"I don't think so."

"How about *Lord of the Flies*? You get to *Lord of the Flies*?"

"I haven't read anything," said Luke. "I've been moved around a lot; anyplace I go they're doing *Silas Marner*."

This seemed to throw Dan into some kind of depression. His shoulders sagged and he said no more.

Sammy finally stopped bouncing and sat back with a *Jack and Jill*. Pages turned, rattling in the hot wind that blew through the car. On the seat between Dan and Luke, Dan's address list fluttered. It didn't seem very long. Four or five sheets of paper, two columns to a sheet; it would be used up in no time. Luke said, "Um . . ."

Dan looked over at him.

"You must have gone to college," Luke said.

"Yes."

"Or even graduate school."

"Just college."

"Don't you have some addresses from there?"

"College isn't the same," said Dan. "I wouldn't be going far enough back. Why," he said, struck by a thought, "college is where I met my wife!"

"Oh, I see," Luke said.

Outside Washington, Dan stopped the car to let him off. On the horizon was a haze of buildings that Dan said was Alexandria. "Alexandria, Virginia?" Luke asked. He didn't understand what that had to do with Washington. But Dan, who seemed in a hurry, was already glancing in his side-view mirror. Sammy hung out the window calling, "Bye, Luke! When will I see you again? Will you come and visit when we find a place? Write me a letter, Luke!"

"Sure," said Luke, waving. The car rolled off.

By now it must be four o'clock, at least, but it didn't seem to Luke that he felt any cooler. His eyes ached from squinting in the sunlight. His hair had grown stringy and stiff. Something about this road, though—the foreign smells of tar and diesel fuel, or the roar of traffic—made him believe for the first time that he really was getting somewhere. He was confident he'd be picked up sooner or later. He thumbed a while, walked a few yards, stopped to thumb again. He had turned to begin another walk when a car slammed on its brakes, veering to the shoulder in front of him. "For God's sake," a woman called. "Get in this instant, you hear?"

He opened the door and got in. It was a Dodge, not nearly as old as Dan's car but almost as worn-looking, as if it had been used a great deal. The woman inside was plump and fortyish. Her eyes were swollen and tears had streaked her cheeks, but he trusted her anyhow; you'd think she was his mother, the way she scolded him. "Are you out of your mind? Do you want to get killed? Do you know the kind of perverts in this world? Make sure your door's shut. *Lock* it, dammit; we're not in downtown Sleepy Hollow. Fasten your seat belt. Hook up your shoulder harness."

He was happy to obey. He adjusted some complicated kind of buckle while the woman, sniffling, ground the gears and shot back into traffic. "What's your name?" she asked him.

"Luke."

"Well, Luke, are you a total idiot? Does your mother know you're hitching rides? Where are your parents in all of this?"

"Oh, ah, Baltimore," he said. "I don't guess you would be going there."

"God, no, what would I want with Baltimore?"

"Well, where *are* you going?"

"I don't know," she told him.

"You don't know?"

He looked at her. The tears were streaming down her cheeks again. "Um, maybe—" he said.

"Oh, relax. Never mind, I'll take you on to Baltimore."

"You will?"

"It's better than circling the Beltway forever."

"Golly, thanks," he said.

"They're letting infants out on their own these days."

"I'm not an infant."

"Don't you read the papers? Sex crimes! Muggings! Murders! Things that make no sense."

"So what? I've been traveling on my own a *long* time. Years," he said. "Ever since I was born, almost."

"For all you know," she told him, "I could be holding you for ransom."

This startled a laugh out of him. She glanced over and gave a sad smile. There was something reassuring about the comfortable mound of her stomach, the denim skirt riding up her stocky legs, the grayish-white tennis shoes. Periodically, she swabbed at the tip of her nose with her knuckles. He noticed that she wore a wedding ring, and had worn it for so long it looked embedded in her finger.

"Just two or three miles ahead, not a month ago," she said, "a boy in a sports car stopped to pick up a girl and she smashed in his skull with a flashlight, rolled him down an embankment, and drove away in his sports car."

"That proves it's you doing something dangerous, not me," he pointed out. (How easy it was to fall into the bantering, argumentative tone reserved for mothers!) "What did you pick me up for? I could be planning to kill you."

"Oh, indeed," she said, sniffling again. "You wouldn't happen to have a Kleenex on you, by any chance?"

"No, sorry."

"I'd never stop for just anyone," she told him. "Only if they're in danger—I mean young girls alone, or infants like you."

"I am not an—"

"Yesterday it was a girl in short shorts, can you believe it? I told her; I said, 'Honey, you're inviting trouble, dressed like that.' Day before, it was a twelve-year-old boy. He said he'd been robbed of his bus fare and had to get home as best he could. Day before that—"

"What, you drive here every day?"

"Most days."

He looked out the window at the vans and oil tankers, interstate buses, cars with their overloaded luggage racks. "I had sort of thought this was a long-*range* highway," he said.

"Oh, no. Heavens, no. No, I live right nearby," she told him.

"Then what are you driving around for?"

Her chin crumpled in. "None of your business," she said.

"Oh."

"What it is, you see, I generally do this from two or three in the afternoon till suppertime. Sometimes I go to Annapolis, sometimes off in Virginia someplace. Sometimes just round and round the Beltway. It all depends," she said. She tossed him a look, as if expecting him to ask what it all depended on, but he had been insulted and said nothing. She sighed. "Two or three o'clock is when my daughter wakes up. My daughter is four-teen years old. Just about your age, right? How old are you?"

He drummed his fingers and looked out the window.

"In the summer, she sleeps forever. My husband says, 'Jeepers, Mag.' He says, 'Why do you let her sleep so late?' Well, I'll tell you why. It's because she's impossible. Truly impossible. I mean, it isn't believable that she could be so awful. She comes downstairs in her bathrobe, yawning. Finds me in the kitchen. Says, 'Well, Ma, I see you're wearing your insecticide perfume again. DDT Number Five.' Then she floats away. Leaving me sniffing my wrists and wondering. I say, 'Liddie, are you going to clean your room today?' and she says, 'Listen to you, sniping and griping; you sound exactly like your mother.' I make a little joke; she says, 'Very funny, Ma. Ha ha. The big comedian.' I find she's stolen my best lace bra that I only wear on my anni-versary and she flings it back all grimy at the seams: 'Take it, who wants it, it's too flat-chested anyhow.' To my face, she calls me a bitch, says I'm fat and homely, says she hates me, and I say, 'Listen here, young lady, it's time we got a few things straight,' but all she does is yawn and start chewing one of those plastic price-tag strings off the sleeve of her blouse. I tell my husband, 'Speak to her,' so he says, 'Liddie, *you* know how your mother gets. Why do you upset her?' I say, 'How I get? What do you mean, how I get?' and before you know, it's him and me fighting, which may have been her plan all along. Division. Disruption. Chaos. That's what she enjoys. She's got this boy- friend, treats him terribly. Finally he broke up with her, and she cried all night and asked a hundred times, 'Why did I act like I did? What can I do to change his mind?' I told her to be honest, just phone him and say she didn't know what had got into her; so next morning she phoned, and they made up, and everything was wonderful and she came and thanked me for my good advice. Her life was back in order, it looked like. So she sat at the table a while, calm as I've seen her. Then she started swinging her foot. Then she started picking her fingernails. Then she went and phoned her boyfriend again. Said, 'Roger, I didn't want to tell you this but I thought it's time you knew. The doctor says I'm dying of leukemia.' "

Luke laughed. She looked over at him innocently, but he noticed a wry, proud twist at the corners of her mouth. "Around two or three o'clock," she said, "I get in my car and start driving. At first, I'm talking out loud. You ought to see me. 'I'm never coming back,' I say. I'm cursing through my teeth; I'm honking at crippled old ladies. 'That little wretch, that pest, that spoiled brat,' I say. 'She'll be sorry!' I speed along—oh, you ought to see my traffic record! One more point on my license and I'll have to take that Saturday course on the evils of reckless driv- ing; have to watch that movie where the lady ends up de- capitated. Well, at least it'll get me out of the house. I sling the car around and don't let other cars ahead of me and I picture how my husband will come home and say, 'Liddie? Where is your mother? What did you *do* to her, Liddie?' and Liddie will feel just awful . . . but then I think of my husband. I have a really nice husband. It's not him I want to leave. And I wonder if I could sneak back home at night and tell him, 'Psst! Let's *both* leave. Let's elope,' I'll say. But I know he wouldn't do it. He's not as much involved. She annoys him but he's not around enough to make any serious mistakes with her. That's what kills me: making mistakes. Overreacting, letting her get to me . . . oh, I can think of so many! You could say that what I'm leaving behind is my own poor view of me, right? So then I start driving slower. I start remembering things. I think of Liddie when she was small: she always stood so straight. You could pick her out of a crowd by her straight little back. And for one whole year she would only eat with chopsticks. Click-click against her plate . . . you ought to have seen the mess! But I didn't mind. In those days, she liked me a lot. I was a really good mother, and she liked me."

"Maybe she *still* likes you," Luke said doubtfully.

"No," said the woman. "She doesn't."

They passed a sign for Baltimore. The countryside seemed endlessly the same—fields of high grass, then the backsides of housing developments with clotheslines and motorcycles and aboveground, circular swimming pools, then fields of high grass again, as if the scenery came around regularly on a giant conveyor belt.

"What it is," said the woman, "it's like I'm driving till I find her past self. You know? And *my* past self. Then mile by mile, I simmer down. I let up on the gas a bit more. So by suppertime, I'm ready to come home again."

Luke checked the clock on her dashboard. It was four thirty-five.

"Tonight I'll just fix a tuna salad," she said.

"Well, I appreciate your doing this."

"It's nothing," she said, and she gave a final swipe to her nose.

By five o'clock, they had reached the outskirts of Baltimore. It was something like entering a piece of machinery, Luke thought—all sooty and cluttered and churning. The woman seemed used to it; she drove without comment. "Now, tell me what to do after Russell Street," she said.

"Ma'am?"

"How do I find your house?"

"Oh," he said, "why don't you just drop me off downtown."

"Where downtown?"

"Anyplace will do."

She looked over at him.

He said, "I live so near, I mean . . ."

"Near to where?"

"Why, to anywhere."

"Now, listen, Luke," she said. "I'm getting a very odd feeling here. I want to know exactly where your parents are."

He wondered what she would do if he told her he had to look them up in the telephone book. He'd been away so long, he would say, at summer camp or someplace, the address had just slipped his . . . no. But the fact was, he had never known Ezra's street address. It was just a house they arrived at, Cody driving, Luke sitting in back.

"The thing of it is," he said, "they're both at work. They own this restaurant, the Homesick Restaurant. Maybe you could drop me off at the restaurant."

"Where is that?"

"Ah . . ."

"There is no such place, is there," she said. "I knew it! Homesick Restaurant, indeed."

"There is! Believe me," he said. "But it's new. They just did buy it, and I haven't been there yet."

"Look it up," she told him.

She stopped so suddenly, he was glad he'd fastened his seat belt. A telephone booth stood beside them. "Go on! Look it up," she told him. She must have thought she was calling his bluff.

Luke said, "All right, I will."

Then in the phone booth—the old, fully enclosed kind, a glass and aluminum boxful of heat—he ran a finger past *Homeland Racquet Club, Homeseekers Realty*, and found himself so surprised by *Homesick Restaurant* that it might have been a bluff after all. "It's on St. Paul Street," he said when he came back to the car. "You can drop me off anywhere; I'll find the number."

But no, she had to take him to the doorstep, though it meant a good deal of doubling back because St. Paul, it turned out, was one-way and she kept miscalculating the cross streets. When she parked in front of the restaurant, she said, "Well, I'll be! It exists."

"Thank you for the ride," Luke said.

She peered at him. "Are you going to be all right, Luke?" she asked.

"Of course I am."

"And you're certain your parents are here."

"Of course they are."

But she waited, anyhow. (It reminded him of the grade-school parties given by his classmates—his mother making sure he got in before she drove away.) He tried the restaurant's door and found it locked. He would have to go around to the rear. The woman leaned out her window and called, "What's the trouble, Luke?"

"I forgot, I have to use the kitchen entrance."

"What if that's locked, too?"

"It isn't."

"You listen, Luke," she called to him. "Everything is changing; things aren't safe like in the old days. Every alley in this city is full of muggers, are you hearing what I say? Every doorway and vacant building, Luke, every street in Baltimore."

He waved and disappeared. A moment later he heard her car take off again—but reluctantly, without its usual verve, as if she were still absorbed in her catalogue of dangers.

He knew the restaurant so well, he must have carried its image constantly within him: its clatter of pans and crash of china, smell of cut celery simmering in butter, broom-shaped bundles of herbs dangling from the rafters, gallon jars of wrinkly Greek olives, bushel baskets of parsley, steaming black kettles watched devotedly by a boy no older than Luke. Beyond the kitchen, hardly separate from it, stretched the dining room with its white-draped tables and dusty sunbeams. There were so many decorations in the dining room—gifts and mementos, accumulated over the years—that Luke was always reminded of someone's home, one of those teeming family houses where kindergarten drawings are taped above the mantel and then forgotten. He recognized the six-foot collage of Ezra's hearts-of-palm salad, presented by an artist who often ate here, and he saw the colored paper chain that he and his cousins had festooned around a light fixture for some long-ago Christmas dinner. (Ezra had never taken it down, though the dinner had broken off in a quarrel and the chain was now brittle and faded.) Luke knew that in one corner, out of his line of vision, sat a heavy antique bicycle that Ezra had bought in a Timonium flea market. MERCURIO'S CULINARY DELICACIES was lettered importantly across its wooden basket, which was filled with frosty glass pears and bananas contributed by a customer. Astride the bicycle stood a cardboard Marilyn Monroe with her dress blowing up—the prank of unknown persons, but no one had ever removed her and Marilyn rode on, her neck creased nearly to the breaking point, her smile growing paler season by season and her accordion-pleated skirt curling at the edges.

Hot, flushed workers darted around the kitchen, intent on their private tasks, weaving between the others like those Model T's in silent comedies—*zip!*, just missing, never once colliding, their paths crisscrossing but miraculously slipping past disaster. Luke stood in the doorway unnoticed. His trip had been such a process in itself; he had almost lost sight of his purpose. What was he doing here, anyhow? But then he saw Ezra. Ezra was piling biscuits in a crude rush basket. He wore not the blue plaid shirt that Luke remembered—which was flannel, after all, unsuitable for summer—but a chambray shirt with the sleeves rolled up. He thoughtfully set each biscuit in its place, his large, blunt hands deliberate. Luke made his way across the kitchen. He was surprised by a flash of shyness. His heart was beating too fast. He arrived in front of Ezra and said, "Hi."

Ezra looked up, still thoughtful. "Hi," he said.

He didn't know who this was.

Luke was stricken, at first. Then he began to feel pleased. Why, he must have changed immeasurably! He'd shot up a foot; his voice was getting croaky; he was practically a man. And there was some safety, a kind of shield, in Ezra's flat gaze. Luke rearranged his plans. He squared his shoulders. "I'd like a job," he said firmly.

Ezra grew still. "Luke?" he said.

"If that boy over there can tend the kettles—" Luke was saying. He stopped. "Pardon?"

"It's Cody's Luke. Isn't it."

"How'd you guess?"

"I could tell when you did your shoulders that way, just like your dad, just exactly like your dad. How funny! And something about the tone of your voice, all set to do battle . . . well, Luke!" He shook Luke's hand very hard. His fingers had a sandy feel from the biscuits. "Where are your parents? Back at the house?"

"I'm here on my own."

"On your own?" Ezra said. He was smiling genially, uncertainly, like someone hoping to understand a joke. "You mean, with nobody else?"

"I wanted to ask if I could stay with you."

Ezra stopped smiling. "It's Cody," he said.

"Excuse me?"

"Something's happened to him."

"Nothing's happened."

"I should have gone down; I knew I should. I shouldn't have let him stop me. The accident was worse than they let on."

"No! He's fine."

Ezra surveyed him for a long, silent moment.

"He's already got his walking cast," Luke told him.

"Yes, but his other wounds, his head?"

"Everything's okay."

"You swear it?"

"Yes! Gosh."

"See, I don't have any other brothers," Ezra said.

"I swear. I cross my heart," said Luke.

"Then where is he?"

"He's in Virginia," said Luke. "I left him there. I ran away."

Ezra thought this over. A waitress sidled past him with a tray of delicately clinking, trembling glasses.

"I didn't plan to," Luke told him. "But he said to me . . . see, he said . . ."

Oh, there was no point in telling Ezra what Cody had said.

It was nonsense, one of those remarks that pop up out of no-where. And here was Luke, much too far from home, faltering under his uncle's kindly gaze. "I can't explain," he said.

But just as if he *had* explained, Ezra said, gently, "You mustn't take it to heart. He didn't mean it. He wouldn't hurt you for anything in the world."

"I know that," Luke said.

On the telephone with Ruth, Ezra was jocular and brotherly, elaborately casual, playing down what had happened. "Now, Ruth, I'm sitting here looking straight at him and he's perfectly all right . . . police? What for? Well, call them back, tell them he's safe and sound. A lot of fuss over nothing, tell them."

Luke listened, smiling anxiously as if his mother could see him. He laced the spirals of the telephone cord between his fingers. They were in Ezra's little office behind the kitchen. Ezra sat at a desk piled with cookbooks, bills, magazines, a pot of chives, a copper pan with a cracked enamel lining, and a framed news photo of two men in aprons holding an entire long fish on a platter.

Then evidently, Cody took over the phone. Ezra sounded more serious now. "We could maybe keep him a while," he said. "We'd like to have him visit. I hope you'll let him." In the directness and soberness of his tone, even in his short sentences, Luke read a kind of caution. He worried that Cody was shouting on the other end of the line; he dropped the cord and wandered away, pretending to be interested in the books in Ezra's bookcase. He felt embarrassed for his father. But there must not have been any shouting after all; for Ezra said serenely, "All right, Cody. Yes, I can understand that."

When he'd hung up, he told Luke, "They'll be here as soon as possible. He'd rather come get you now, he said."

Luke felt a little notch of dread beginning in his stomach. He wondered how angry his father was. He wondered how he could have thought of doing this—coming all this distance! So alone! It seemed like something he had floated through in a dream.

His grandmother's house still had its burned-toast smell, its dusky corners, its atmosphere of secrecy. If you moved in here, Luke thought, wouldn't you go on finding unexpected cubby-holes and closets for weeks or even months afterward? (Yes, imagine moving in. Imagine sharing the cozy living room, Grandma's peaceful kitchen.) His grandmother skittered around him, adding tiny dishes of food to what was already on the table. Ezra kept telling her, "Mother, take it easy. Don't fuss so." But Luke enjoyed the fuss. He liked the way she would stop in the midst of preparing something to come running over and cup his face. "Look at you! Just look!" She was shorter than he was, now. And she had aged a great deal, or else he'd been too young before to notice. There was something scratchy and fly-away about her little screwed-tight topknot, once blond but now colorless, and her face sectioned deeply by pockets of lines and her wrinkled, spotted hands. He saw how much she loved him, purely from her hungry touch on his cheeks, and he wondered how his father could have misjudged her so.

"It's not right that your parents just come and take you back," she told him. "We'll make them stay. We'll just make them. I'll change the sheets in Jenny's old room. You can have the guest room. Oh, Luke! I wouldn't have known you. I wouldn't have dreamed it was you if I'd seen you on the street; it's been that long. Though I would have said . . . yes, I would have thought to myself as I passed, 'My, that child reminds me of my Cody years ago; doesn't he? Just fairer haired, is all.' I would have had this little pang and then forgotten, and then later maybe, making tea at home, I'd think, 'Wait now, something was disturbing me back there . . .' "

She tried to pour a bowl of leftover green beans into a saucepan but missed, and slopped most of the liquid onto the counter, and swabbed it with wads of paper towels while laughing at herself. "What an old lady! What a silly old lady, you're thinking. My eyesight isn't what it used to be. No, no, Ezra, I can manage, dear."

"Mother, why don't you let me take over?"

"I can certainly manage in my own kitchen, Ezra," she said. "Wouldn't you like to go back to the restaurant? No telling what those people of yours are up to."

"You just want to have Luke to yourself," Ezra teased her.

"Oh, I admit it! I admit it!"

She turned on the flame beneath the saucepan. "Everything is coming together," she told Luke. "I've been so worried, just sick with worry, picturing Cody in pain and longing to go to him, and of course he wouldn't let me; he's been like that ever since he was a baby, so . . . thorny, so bristly, just always has his back up. And now a little trouble or something—no, don't look so uneasy! I won't ask any questions, I promise; Ezra told me; it's none of our business, but . . . a little trouble of some kind brings you here to us, I don't know, maybe an argument? One of Cody's tempers?"

"*Mother*," said Ezra.

"And so," she went on hastily, "we get to see him after all. He's really going to show himself. But, Luke. Be truthful. He isn't, he's not . . . scarred or anything, is he? His face, I mean. He hasn't got any disfiguring scars."

"Just bruises," said Luke. "Nothing that'll last. In fact," he added, "they're mostly gone by now."

It surprised him to find that he had held on to the picture of a broken Cody all this time, when really the bruises had faded, come to think of it, and the swellings had disappeared and the hair had almost completely grown over his head wound.

"He always was so handsome," Pearl said. "It was part of his identity."

Ezra moved around the table, setting out plates and silverware. The saucepan hissed on the stove. Luke sat down on a kitchen chair and tipped back against a radiator. Its sharply sculptured ribs and tall pipes made him think of old-fashioned, comforting places—a church he'd visited with a kindergarten friend, for instance, or his second-grade classroom, where once, when a snowstorm started during lunch hour, he had imagined a blizzard developing and keeping all the children snugly marooned for days, drinking cups of soup sent up from the cafeteria.

After supper, he and Pearl watched TV while Ezra went back to check the restaurant. Pearl kept the living room completely dark, lit only by the flickering blue TV screen. Both the front windows were open and they could hear the noises from the street—a game of prisoner's base, a Good Humor bell, a woman calling her children. Around nine o'clock, when the twilight had finally given way to night and the stuffy air had cooled some, Luke caught the distinctive, tightly woven hum of a Mercedes drawing up to the curb. He tensed. Pearl, who wouldn't have recognized the sound, went on placidly watching TV. "Who's that, dear?" she asked him, but it was some actor she referred to; she was peering at the television set. There were footsteps across the porch. "Eh?" she said. "Already?" She rose, fumbling first for the arms of her chair in two or three blind passes. She opened the front door and said, "Cody?"

Cody stood looming, larger than Luke had expected, his arm and leg casts glowing whitely in the dark. "Hello, Mother," he said.

"Why, Cody, let me look at you! And Ruth: hello, dear. Cody, are you all right? I can't make out your face. Are you really feeling better?"

"I'm fine," Cody told her. He kissed her cheek and then limped in.

"Hey, Dad," Luke said, rising awkwardly.

Cody said, "May I ask what you thought you were up to?"

"Well, I don't know . . ."

"Don't know! Is that all you have to say? You scared the hell out of us! Your mother's been beside herself."

"Oh, honey, we were so worried!" Ruth cried. She pulled him close and kissed him. Her dress—a magenta polyester that she wore on special occasions—crumpled its sharp ruffles against his chest. He smelled her familiar, grassy smell that he'd never really noticed before.

"We near about lost our minds," Ruth told Pearl. "I believe I must've aged a quarter-century. I felt if I looked out that same front window one more time I'd go mad, go stark, raving mad —same old curve in the road, same old sidewalk, empty. You just don't know."

"I do know. I do know," said Pearl.

She was feeling for the switch to a lamp that sat on a table. The silk shade rustled and tilted. Then Ezra arrived in the door. "Cody?" he said. "Is that you?" He strode in fast and first encountered Ruth—almost ran her down—and seized her hand and pumped it. "Good to see you, Ruth," he said. Meanwhile, Cody found the switch for his mother and turned the lamp on. It was coincidental; he was only being helpful, but Luke felt he'd turned on the lamp to *examine* them: Ruth and Ezra, face to face. Ezra blinked in the sudden light and then gave Cody a bear hug. Cody stood unresisting. "How's your arm? How's your leg?" Ezra asked. "What, no crutches?"

Cody went on studying Ruth and Ezra. "He says he can't use them," said Ruth. "He says with his opposite arm in a cast . . ." She reached out and smoothed Luke's T-shirt, which didn't need smoothing. She pushed his hair off his forehead. "And now that he's got this walking cast . . ." she said absently. "Oh, Luke, sweetheart, didn't you think you'd be missed?"

Cody turned away and sank into an armchair. "Would you two like some iced tea?" Pearl asked.

"No, thanks," said Cody.

"Or coffee? A nice cup of coffee?"

"No! God. Nothing," said Cody.

Luke expected Pearl to look hurt, but she only gave Cody a curiously satisfied smile. "You always were a grump when you weren't feeling well," she told him.

In fact, how surprising this whole visit was!—low-keyed and uneventful, even boring. Luke started out sitting rigidly erect, but gradually he relaxed and let his attention drift to a variety show on TV. The grown-ups murmured around him without any emphasis, discussing money. Cody wanted Pearl to get a new furnace; he would pay for it, he said. Pearl said she had a little savings, but Cody kept insisting, as if there were something gratifying, something triumphant in buying a person a furnace. Oh, money, money, money. You'd think they could come up with some more interesting subject.

Luke pressed a lever in his armchair and found himself flung back, his feet raised suddenly on some sort of footrest. Now Pearl was asking where they would go after Petersburg, and Cody was saying he didn't know; Sloan and he were hoping to take on this cosmetics firm down in . . . His reasonable tone of voice made Luke feel hoodwinked, betrayed. Why, all this time he'd been hearing such terrible tales! He'd been told of such ill will and bitterness! But Cody and Pearl conversed pleasantly, like any civilized adults. They discussed whether the North or the South was a better place to live. They had a mild, dull, uninvested sort of argument about it, till it emerged that Pearl was assuming Baltimore was North and Cody was assuming it was South. She asked if this new factory might be as dangerous as the last one. "*Any* place is dangerous," said Cody, "if idiots are running it."

"Cody, I worry so," she told him. "If you knew how frantic I've been! Hearing my oldest, my firstborn son is in critical condition and I'm not allowed to come see him."

"Critical condition! I'm walking around, aren't I?"

"The walking *wounded*," she said, and she threw her hands up. "Isn't it ironic? I'd always thought disasters were . . . lower class. I would read these hard-luck stories in the paper: lady evicted when she's trying to raise the seven children of her daughter who was shot to death in a bar, and one of the children's retarded and another has to be taken for dialysis so many times per week by city bus, transferring twice . . . well, of course I feel sorry for such people but also, I don't know, impatient, as if they'd brought it on themselves some way. There's a limit, I want to tell them; only so much of life is luck. But now look:

my eyesight's poorly and my oldest son's had a serious accident and *his* son's run away from home for reasons we're not told, and I haven't seen my daughter in weeks because she's all tied up with her little girl who's got that disease, what's it called, Anor Exia—"

"How's Becky doing, anyhow?" Cody asked, and Luke had an image of Cody's reaching into a wild snarl of strings and tugging on the one short piece that wasn't all tangled with the others.

"No one knows," Pearl said, rocking.

Ruth massaged her forehead, which had the strained, roughened look it always got after a difficult day. Ezra laughed at something on TV. Cody, who was watching the two of them, sighed sharply and turned back to his mother.

"We'd better be going," he told her.

She straightened. "What?" she said. "You're leaving?"

"We've got a long drive."

"But that's exactly why you're staying!" she told him. "Rest tonight. Start fresh in the morning."

"We can't," said Cody.

"Why can't you?"

"We have to . . . ah, feed the dog."

"I didn't know you had a dog."

"A Doberman."

"But Dobermans are vicious!"

"That's why we better hurry back and feed him," Cody said. "Don't want him eating up the neighbors."

He reached out a hand toward Luke, and Luke clambered off the reclining chair to help him to his feet. When Cody's fingers closed on his, Luke imagined some extra tightness—a secret handshake, a nudge at the joke they'd put over on Pearl. He kept his face deliberately expressionless.

"Listen, all," Ezra said. "It isn't long till Thanksgiving, you know."

Everybody stared at him.

"Will you come back here for Thanksgiving? We could have a family dinner at the restaurant."

"Oh, Ezra, no telling where we'll be by then," said Cody.

"What," said Pearl. "You never heard of airplanes? Amtrak? Modern transportation?"

"We'll talk about it when the time gets closer," Cody said, patting her shoulder. "Ruth, you got everything? So long, Ezra, let me know how it's going."

There was a flurry of hugs and handshakes. Later, Luke wasn't sure he'd said thank you to Ezra—though what did he want to thank him for, exactly? Something or other . . . They made their way down the sidewalk and into Cody's car, which still had the stale, blank smell of air-conditioned air. Everyone called out parts of sentences, as if trying to give the impression that they had so much left to say to each other, there wasn't room to fit it all in. "Now, you be sure to—" "It sure was good to—" "Tell Jenny we wish—" "And drive defensively, hear?"

They pulled away from the curb, waving through the window. Pearl and Ezra fell behind. Luke, sitting in back, faced forward and found his father at the wheel. Ruth was in the passenger seat. "Mom?" Luke said. "Don't you think you ought to drive?"

"He insisted," Ruth said. "He drove all the way here, too." She turned and looked at Luke meaningfully, over the back of the seat. "He said he wanted it to be him that drove to get you."

"Oh," said Luke.

What was she waiting for? She went on looking at him for some time, but then gave up and turned away again. Trying his best, Luke sat forward to observe how Cody managed.

"Well, I guess it wouldn't be all that hard," he said, "except for shifting the gears."

"Shifting's easy," Cody told him.

"Oh."

"And luckily there's no clutch."

"No."

They passed rows and rows of houses, many with their porches full of people rocking in the dark. They turned down a block where there were stoops instead of porches, white stoops set close to the street. On one of these a whole family perched, with a beer cooler and an oscillating fan and a baby in a mesh crib on the sidewalk. A TV sat on a car hood at the curb so if you happened by on foot, you'd have to cross between TV and audience, muttering, "Excuse me, please," just as if you'd walked through someone's living room. Luke gazed back at that family as long as they were in sight. They were replaced by a strip of bars and cafés, and then by an unlit alley.

"Isn't it funny," Luke told his father, "no one's ever asked you to reorganize anything in Baltimore."

"Very funny," Cody said.

"We could live with Grandma then, couldn't we?"

Cody said nothing.

They left the city for the expressway, entering a world of high, cold lights and a blue-black sky. Ruth slid slowly against the window. Her small head bobbed with every dip in the road.

"Mom's asleep," Luke said.

"She's tired," said Cody.

Perhaps he meant it as a reproach. Was this where the scolding started? Luke kept very quiet for a while. But what Cody said next was, "It wears her out, that house. Your grandma's so difficult to deal with."

"Grandma's not difficult."

"Not for you, maybe. For other people she is. For your mother. Grandma believes your mother is 'scrappy.' She told me that, once. Called her 'scrappy and hoydenish.' " He laughed, recalling something, so that Luke started smiling expectantly. "One time," Cody said, "—I bet you don't remember this—your mother and I had this silly little spat and she packed you up and ran off to Ezra. Then as soon as she got to the station, she started thinking what life would be like with your grandma and she called and asked me to come drive her home."

Luke's smile faded. "Ran off to *where?*" he asked.

"To Ezra. But never mind, it was only one of those—"

"She didn't run to Ezra. She was planning to go to her folks," Luke said.

"What folks?" Cody asked him.

Luke didn't know.

"She's an orphan," Cody said. "What folks?"

"Well, maybe—"

"She was planning to go to Ezra," Cody said. "I can see it now! I can picture how they'd take up their marriage, right where ours left off. Oh, I believe I've always had the feeling it wasn't my marriage, anyhow. It was someone else's. It was theirs. Sometimes I seemed to enjoy it better when I imagined I was seeing it through someone else's eyes."

"Why are you *telling* me this?" Luke asked him.

"All I meant was—"

"What are you, crazy? How come you go on hanging *on* to these things, year after year after year?"

"Now, wait a minute, now . . ."

"Mom?" Luke shook her shoulder. "Mom! Wake up!"

Ruth's head sagged over to the other side.

"Let her rest," Cody said. "Goddammit, Luke—"

"Wake up, Mom!"

"Hmm," said Ruth, not waking.

"Mom? I want to ask you. Mom? Remember when you packed me up and left Dad?"

"Mm."

"Remember?"

"Yes," she murmured, curling tighter.

"Where were we going to go, Mom?"

She raised her head, with her hair all frowsy, and gave him a blurry, dazed stare. "What?" she said. "Garrett County, where my uncle lives. Who wants to know?"

"Nobody. Go back to sleep," Cody told her.

She went back to sleep. Cody rubbed his chin thoughtfully.

They sped through a corridor of light that was bounded on both sides by the deepest darkness. They met and passed solitary cars that disappeared in an instant. Luke's eyelids drooped.

"What I mean to say," Cody said. "What I drove all this way to say . . ."

But then he trailed off. And when he started speaking again, it was on a whole different subject: time. How time was underestimated. How time was so important and all. Luke felt relieved. He listened comfortably, lulled by his father's words. "Everything," his father said, "comes down to time in the end— to the passing of time, to changing. Ever thought of that? Anything that makes you happy or sad, isn't it all based on minutes going by? Isn't happiness expecting something time is going to bring you? Isn't sadness wishing time back again? Even *big* things—even mourning a death: aren't you really just wishing to have the time back when that person was alive? Or photos— ever notice old photographs? How wistful they make you feel? Long-ago people smiling, a child who would be an old lady now, a cat that died, a flowering plant that's long since withered away and the pot itself broken or misplaced . . . Isn't it just that time for once is stopped that makes you wistful? If only you could turn it back again, you think. If only you could change this or that, undo what you have done, if only you could roll the minutes the other way, for once."

He didn't seem to expect an answer, which was lucky. Luke was too sleepy to manage one. He felt heavy, weighted with other people's stories. He imagined he was slipping or falling. He believed he was gliding away, streaming down a great, wide, light-filled river of time along with all the people he had met today. He let his head nod over, and he closed his eyes and slept.

9

Apple Apple

One morning Ezra Tull got up and shaved, brushed his teeth, stepped into his trousers, and encountered a lump in the bend of his right thigh. His fingers glanced over it accidentally and faltered and returned. In the bedroom mirror, his broad, fair face had a frozen look. The word cancer came on its own, as if someone had whispered it into his ear, but what caused his shocked expression was the thought that flew in after it: All right. Let it happen. I'll go ahead and die.

He shook that away, of course. He was forty-six years old, a calm and sensible man, and later he would make an appointment with Dr. Vincent. Meanwhile he put on a shirt, and buttoned it, and unrolled a pair of socks. Twice, without planning to, he tested the lump again with his fingertips. It was nearly the size of an acorn, sensitive but not painful. It rolled beneath his skin as smoothly as an eyeball.

It wasn't that he really wanted to die. Naturally not. He was only giving in to a passing mood, he decided as he went downstairs; this summer hadn't been going well. His mother, whose vision had been failing since 1975, was now (in 1979) almost totally blind, but still did not fully admit it, which made it all the harder to care for her; and his brother was too far away and his sister too busy to offer him much help. His restaurant was floundering even more than usual; his finest cook had quit because her horoscope advised it; and a heat wave seemed to be stupefying the entire city of Baltimore. Things were so bad that the most inconsequential sights served to confirm his despair—the neighbor's dog panting on the sidewalk, or his mother's one puny hydrangea bush wilting and sagging by two o'clock every afternoon. Even the postman signified catastrophe; his wife had been murdered in a burglary last spring, and now he lugged his leather pouch through the neighborhood as if it were heavy beyond endurance, as if it would eventually drag him to a halt. His feet went slower and slower; his shoulders bent closer to the ground. Every day the mail arrived later.

Ezra stood with his coffee at the window and watched the postman moping past and wondered if there were any point to life.

Then his mother came downstairs, planting her feet just so. "Oh, look," she said, "what a sunny morning!" She could feel it, he supposed—warming her skin in squares when she stood next to him at the window. Or perhaps she could even see it, since evidently she still distinguished light from dark. But her dress was done up wrong. She had drawn her wispy gray-blond hair into its customary bun, and deftly applied a single spark of pink to the center of her dry, pursed lips, but one side of her collar stuck up at an angle and the flowered material pouched outward, showing her slip in the gap between two buttons.

"It's going to be another scorcher," Ezra told her.

"Oh, poor Ezra, I hate to see you go to work in this."

All she said carried references to sight. He couldn't tell if she planned it that way.

She let him bring her a cup of coffee but she turned down breakfast, and instead sat beside him in the living room while he read the paper. This was their only time together—morning and noon, after which he left for the restaurant and did not return till very late at night, long past her bedtime. He had trouble imagining what she did in his absence. Sometimes he telephoned from work and she always sounded so brisk—"Just fixing myself some iced tea," she would say, or "Sorting through my stockings." But in the background he would hear the ominous, syrupy strains of organ music from some television soap opera, and he suspected that she simply sat before the TV much of the day, with a cardigan draped graciously over her shoulders even in this heat and her chilled hands folded in her lap. Certainly she saw no friends; she had none. As near as he could recall, she had never had friends. She had lived through her children; the gossip they brought was all she knew of the outside world, and their activities provided her only sense of motion. Even back when she worked at the grocery store, she had not consorted with the customers or the other cashiers. And now that she had retired, none of her fellow workers came to visit her.

No, this was the high point of her day, no doubt: these slow midmorning hours, the rustling of Ezra's paper, his spotty news reports. "Another taxi driver mugged, it says here."

"Oh, my goodness."

"Another shoot-out down on the Block."

"Where will it all end?" his mother wondered.

"Terrorist bomb in Madrid."

Newspapers, letters, photos, magazines—those he could help her with. With those she let herself gaze straight ahead, blank eyed, while he acted as interpreter. But in all other situations, she was fiercely independent. What, exactly, was the nature of their understanding? She admitted only that her sight was not what it had once been—that it was impaired enough to make reading a nuisance. "She's blind," her doctor said, and she reported, "He thinks I'm blind," not arguing but managing to imply, somehow, that this was a matter of opinion—or of will, of what you're willing to allow and what you're not. Ezra had learned to offer clues in the casual, slantwise style that she would accept. If he were to say, for instance, "It's raining, Mother," when they were setting out for somewhere, she would bridle and tell him, "Well, *I* know that." He learned to say, "Weatherman claims this will keep up. Better bring your umbrella." Then her face would alter and smooth, adjusting to the information. "Frankly, I don't believe him," she would say, although it was one of those misty rains that falls without a sound, and he knew she hadn't detected it. She concealed her surprise so well that only her children, accustomed to her stubborn denial of anything that might weaken her, could have seen what lay behind that challenging gray stare.

Last month, Ezra's sister had reported that their mother had called to ask a strange question. "She wanted to know if it were true," she said, "that lying on her back a long time would give her pneumonia. 'What for?' I asked her. 'Why do you care?' 'I was only curious,' she said."

Ezra lowered his paper, and he cautiously placed two fingertips at the bend of his thigh.

After they'd finished their coffee, he washed out the cups and straightened the kitchen, which nowadays had an unclean look no matter what he did to it. There were problems he didn't know how to handle—the curtains graying beside the stove, and the lace doily growing stiff with dust beneath the condiment set on the table. Did you actually launder such things? Just throw them in the machine? He could have asked his mother, but didn't. It would only upset her. She would wonder, then, what else she'd missed.

She came out to him, testing her way so carefully that her small black pumps seemed like quivering, delicate, ultrasensitive organs. "Ezra," she said, "what are your plans for this morning?"

"No plans, Mother."

"You're certain, now."

"What is it you want to do?"

"I was thinking we could sort through my desk drawers, but if you're busy—"

"I'm not busy."

"You just say so if you are."

"I'll be glad to help."

"When you were little," she said, "it made you angry to see me sick or in need of aid."

"Well, that was when I was little."

"Isn't it funny? It was you that was the kindest, the closest, the sweetest child; the others were always up to something, off with their own affairs. But when I fell sick, you would turn so coldhearted! 'Does this mean we don't get to go to the movies?' you'd ask. It was your brother who'd take over then—the one I'd least expect it of. I would say, 'Ezra, could you just fetch me an afghan, please?' and you would turn stony and pretend not to hear. You seemed to think I'd done something *to* you— got a headache out of malice."

"I was very young then," Ezra said.

Although it was odd how clenched he felt, even now—not so much angry as defenseless; and he'd felt defenseless as a child, too, he believed. He had trusted his mother to be everything for him. When she cut a finger with a paring knife, he had felt defeated by her incompetence. How could he depend on such a person? Why had she let him down so?

He took her by the upper arm and led her back to the living room. (He was conscious, suddenly, of his height and his solid, comfortable weight.) He seated her on the couch and went over to the desk to remove the bottom drawer.

This was something he had done many times before. It wasn't, certainly, that the drawer needed cleaning, although to an outsider it might appear disorganized. Cascades of unmounted photos slid about as he walked; others poked from the moldy, crumbling albums stacked to one side. There was a shoe box full of his mother's girlhood diaries; an incomplete baby book for Cody; and a Schrafft's candy box containing old letters, all with the stamps snipped off the envelopes. There was a dim, lavender-colored corsage squashed as stiff and hard as a dried-up mouse carcass; a single kid glove hardened with age; and a musty-smelling report card for Pearl E. Cody, fourth year, 1903, with the grades entered in a script so elegant that someone might have laid A-shaped tendrils of fine brown hair next to every subject. Ezra was fond of these belongings. He willingly went over them again and again, describing them for his mother. "There's that picture of your Aunt Melinda on her wedding day."

"Ah?"

"You are standing next to her with a fan made out of feathers."

"We'll save it," said his mother. She was still pretending they were merely sorting.

But soon enough, she forgot about that and settled back, musing, while he recited what he'd found. "Here is a picture of someone's porch."

"Porch? Whose porch?"

"I can't tell."

"What does it look like?"

"Two pillars and a dark floor, clay pot full of geraniums . . ."

"Am I in it?"

"No."

"Oh, well," she said, waving a hand, "maybe that was Luna's porch."

He had never heard of Luna.

To tell the truth, he didn't believe that relatives were what his mother was after. Ladies and gentlemen drifted by in a blur; he did his best to learn their names, but his mother dismissed them airily. It was herself she was hunting, he sensed. "Do you see me, at all? Is that the dinner where I wore the pale blue?" Her single-mindedness sometimes amused him, sometimes annoyed him. There was greed in the forward jutting of her chin as she waited to hear of her whereabouts. "Am *I* in that group? Was *I* on that picnic?"

He opened a maroon velvet album, each of its pulpy gray pages grown bright yellow as urine around the edges. None of the photos here was properly glued down. A sepia portrait of a bearded man was jammed into the binding alongside a Kodachrome of a pink baby in a flashy vinyl wading pool, with SEPT '63 stamped on the border. His mother poked her face out, expectant. He said, "Here's a man with a beard. I think it's your father."

"Possibly," she said, without interest.

He turned the page. "Here's a group of ladies underneath a tree."

"Ladies?"

"None of them look familiar."

"What are they wearing?"

"Long, baggy dresses," he told her. "Everything seems to be sagging at the waist."

"That would be nineteen-ten or so. Maybe Iola's engagement party."

"Who was Iola?"

"Look for me in a navy stripe," she told him.

"There's no stripes here."

"Pass on."

She had never been the type to gaze backward, had not filled his childhood with "When I was your age," as so many mothers did. And even now, she didn't use these photos as an excuse for reminiscing. She hardly discussed them at all, in fact—even those in which she appeared. Instead, she listened, alert, to any details he could give her about her past self. Was it that she wanted an outsider's view of her? Or did she hope to solve some mystery? "Am I smiling, or am I frowning? Would you say that I seemed happy?"

When Ezra tried to ask *her* any questions, she grew bored. "What was your mother like?" he would ask.

"Oh, that was a long time ago," she told him.

She hadn't had much of a life, it seemed to him. He wondered what, in all her history, she would enjoy returning to. Her courtship, even knowing how it would end? Childbirth? Young motherhood? She did speak often and wistfully of the years when her children were little. But most of the photos in this drawer dated from long before then, from back in the early part of the century, and it was those she searched most diligently. "The Baker family reunion, that would be. Nineteen-o-eight. Beulah's sweet sixteen party. Lucy and Harold's silver anniversary." The events she catalogued were other people's; she just hung around the fringes, watching. "Katherine Rose, the summer she looked so beautiful and met her future husband."

He peered at Katherine Rose. "She doesn't look so beautiful to *me*," he said.

"It faded soon enough."

Katherine Rose, whoever she was, wore a severe and complicated dress of a type not seen in sixty years or more. He was judging her rabbity face as if she were a contemporary, some girl he'd glimpsed in a bar, but she had probably been dead for decades. He felt he was being tugged back through layers of generations.

He flipped open tiny diaries, several no bigger than a lady's compact, and read his mother's cramped entries aloud. "*December eighth, nineteen-twelve. Paid call on Edwina Barrett. Spilled half-pint of top cream in the buggy coming home and had a nice job cleaning it off the cushions I can assure you . . .*" "*April fourth, nineteen-o-eight. Went into town with Alice and weighed on the new weighing machine in Mr. Salter's store. Alice is one hundred thirteen pounds, I am one hundred ten and a half.*" His mother listened, tensed and still, as if expecting something momentous, but all he found was *purchased ten yards heliotrope brilliantine*, and *made chocolate blanc-mange for the Girls' Culture Circle*, and *weighed again at Mr. Salter's store.* During the summer of 1908—her fourteenth summer, as near as he could figure—she had weighed herself about every two days, hitching up her pony Prince and riding clear downtown to do so. "*August seventh*," he read. "*Had my measurements taken at the dressmaker's and she gave me a copy to keep. I have developed in every possible sense.*" He laughed, but his mother made an impatient little movement with one hand. "*September ninth*," he read, and then all at once had the feeling that the ground had rushed away beneath his feet. Why, that perky young girl was this old woman! This blind old woman sitting next to him! She had once been a whole different person, had a whole different life separate from his, had spent her time *swinging clubs with the Junior Amazons* and *cutting up with the Neal boys something dreadful* and *taking first prize at the Autumn Recital Contest. (I hoped that poor Nadine would win*, she wrote in a chubby, innocent script, *but of course it was nice to get it myself.)* His mother sat silent, absently stroking the dead corsage. "Never mind," she told him.

"Shall I stop?"
"It wasn't what I wanted after all."

On his way to the restaurant, Ezra ducked into a bookstore and located a Merck Manual in the Family Health section. He checked the index for *lump*, but all he found was *lumpy jaw (actinomycosis)*. Evidently you had to know the name of your disease first—in which case, why bother looking it up? He thought through what he remembered of his high school biology course, and decided to check under *lymph gland*. The very phrase was reassuring; lymph glands swelled all the time. He had a couple in his neck that grew pecan sized anytime he developed a sniffle. But there were no lymph glands listed in the index, and it stopped him cold to see *lymphatic leukemia* and *lymphohematogenous tuberculosis*. He shut the book quickly and replaced it on the shelf.

Josiah had already opened the restaurant, and two helpers were busy chopping vegetables in the kitchen. A salesman in a plaid suit was trying to interest Josiah in some new product. "But," Josiah kept saying. "But I don't think—" Josiah was so gawky and confused-looking—an emaciated giant in white, with his black and gray hair sticking out in frenzied tufts as if he'd grabbed handfuls in desperation—that Ezra felt a rush of love for him. He said, "Josiah, what's the problem?" and Josiah turned to him gratefully. "Uh, see, this gentleman here—"

"Murphy's the name. J. R. Murphy," said the salesman. "I sell soy sauce, private brand. I sell it by the case."

"We could never manage a case," said Ezra. "We hardly ever use it."

"You will, though," the salesman told him. "Soy sauce is the coming thing; better get it while you can. This here is the antidote for radiation."

"For what?"

"Nucular accidents! Atom bums! Just take a look at the facts: those folks in Hiroshima didn't get near as many side effects as expected. Want to know why? It was all that Japanese food with soy sauce. Plain old soy sauce. Keep a case of this around and you'll have no more worries over Three Mile Island."

"But I don't even like soy sauce."

"Who says you've got to like it?"

"Well, maybe just a few bottles . . ." Ezra said.

He wondered if there were some cryptic, cultish mark on his door that told all the crazy people he'd have trouble saying no.

He went to check on the dining room. Two waitresses were shaking out tablecloths and spreading them with a crisp, ripping sound. Josiah was lugging in bales of laundered napkins. There was always a moment, this early in the day, when Ezra found his restaurant disheartening. He was chilled by the empty tables, the looming, uncurtained windows, the bitter smell of last night's cigarettes. What kind of occupation was this? People gulped down his food without a thought, too busy courting or arguing or negotiating to notice what they ate; then they went home and forgot it. Nothing amounted to anything. And Ezra was a middle-aged man with his hair growing transparent at the back of his head; but here he was, where he'd been at twenty, living with his mother in a Calvert Street row house and reading himself to sleep with cookbooks. He had never married, never fathered children, and lost the one girl he had loved out of sheer fatalism, lack of force, a willing assumption of defeat. (*Let it be* was the theme that ran through his life. He was ruled by a dreamy mood of acceptance that was partly the source of all his happiness and partly his undoing.)

Josiah came to stand before him. "See my boots?" he asked.

Ezra surfaced and looked down at Josiah's boots. They poked from beneath the white uniform—gigantic, rubber-coated canvas boots that could weather a flood, a snowstorm, an avalanche.

"L. L. Bean," Josiah said.

"Ah."

L. L. Bean was where Josiah got his mystery gifts. Once or twice a year they arrived: a one-man tent; a goose-down sleeping bag; hunting shoes in his unwieldy, hard-to-find size; an olive-drab poncho that could see him through a monsoon; a pocket survival kit containing compass, flint, signal mirror, and metallic blanket. All this for a man who'd been born and reared in the city and seemed inclined to stay there. There was never any card or note of explanation. Josiah had written the company, but L. L. Bean replied that the donor preferred to stay anonymous. Ezra had spent hours helping Josiah think of possibilities. "Remember that old lady whose walk you used to shovel? Maybe it's her."

"She'd be dead by now, Ezra."

"Remember Molly Kane, with her wheelchair? You used to wheel her to Algebra One."

"But she said, 'Let go my chair, you big ree-tard!' "

"Maybe now she regrets it."

"Oh, no. Not her. Not Molly Kane."

"Maybe just someone you changed a tire for and never gave it another thought. Someone you opened a door for. Maybe . . . I don't know . . ."

Ordinarily he enjoyed these speculations, but now, looking down at Josiah's mammoth boots, he was struck by the fact that even Josiah—lanky, buck-toothed, stammering Josiah—had a human being all his own that he was linked to, whether or not he knew that person's name, and lived in a nest of gifts and secrets and special care that Ezra was excluded from.

"*New Year's Day, nineteen-fourteen,*" Ezra read aloud. "*I hope this little diary will not get lost as last year's did. I hope I will not put anything foolish in it as I have been known to do before.*"

His mother hid a smile, unsuccessfully. What foolishness could she have been up to so long ago? Ezra's eyes slipped down the page to a line that had been crossed out. "There's something here I can't read," he said.

"I never was known for my penmanship."

"No, I mean you scribbled over it with so many loops and things—"

"Apple apple," his mother said.

"Excuse me?"

"That's what we wrote over words that we wanted kept secret. *Appleappleapple* all joined together, so no one could guess what was written underneath."

"Well, it certainly worked," Ezra said.

"Move on," his mother told him.

"Oh. Um . . . *put a flaxseed poultice on my finger . . . started some gartlets of pale pink ribbon . . . popped some popcorn and buttered half, made cracker-jack of the rest . . .*"

His mother sighed. Ezra skimmed several pages in silence.

How plotless real life was! In novels, events led up to something. In his mother's diaries, they flitted past with no apparent direction. Frank brought her perfumed blotters and a box of "cocoa-nut" candy; Roy paid quite a call and couldn't seem to tear himself away; Burt Tansy took her to the comic opera and afterward presented her with a folio of the songs; but none of these people was ever mentioned again. Someone named Arthur wrote her a letter that was *the softest thing*, she said. *I didn't know he could be so silly. It was all in form though and I am not very mad.* A certain Clark Allensby promised to visit and did not; *I suppose it is all for the best*, she said, *but I can't understand his actions as to-morrow he is leaving.* And while she was stretching the curtains, she said, *the darkie announced a young man come to visit. I looked like a freak but went in anyhow and there sat Hugh McKinley. He was heading for the seed store so just HAPPENED to stop by, and staid some while . . .*

Ezra began to see that for his mother (or for the young girl she had been), there was a plot, after all. She had imagined a perfectly wonderful plot—a significance to every chance meeting, the possibility of whirlwind courtships, grand white weddings, flawless bliss forever after. *James Wrayson came to call most shockingly late*, she wrote. *Stole my picture off the piano and put it in his pocket. Acted too comical for words. I'm sure I don't know what will come of this.*

Well, nothing had come of it. Nothing came of anything. She married a salesman for the Tanner Corporation and he left her and never came back. "Ezra? Why aren't you reading to me?" his mother asked.

"I'm tired," he said.

He took her to an afternoon ball game. In her old age, she had become a great Orioles fan. She would listen on the radio if she couldn't attend in person, even staying up past her bedtime if the game went into extra innings. Baseball was the only sport that made sense, she said: clear as Parcheesi, clever as chess. She looked pleased with herself for thinking of this, but Ezra suspected that it had something in common too with those soap operas she enjoyed. Certainly she viewed each game as a drama, and fretted over the gossip that Ezra culled for her from the sports pages—players' injuries, rivalries, slumps, mournful tales of young rookies so nervous they flubbed their only chances. She liked to think of the Orioles as poverty-stricken and virtuous, unable to simply *buy* their talent as richer teams did. Players' looks mattered to her as deeply as if they were movie stars: Ken Singleton's high, shining cheekbones, as described by one of her granddaughters, sent her into a little trance of admiration. She liked to hear how Al Bumbry wiggled his bat so jauntily before a hit; how Stanhouse drove people crazy delaying on the mound. She wished Doug DeCinces would shave off his mustache and Kiko Garcia would get himself a haircut. She thought Earl Weaver was not fatherly enough to be a proper manager and often, when he replaced some poor sad pitcher who'd barely had a chance, she would speak severely into the radio, calling him "Merle Beaver" for spite and spitting out her words. "Just because he grows his own tomatoes," she said, "doesn't necessarily mean a person has a heart."

Sometimes Ezra would quote her to his friends at the restaurant, and halfway through a sentence he would think, Why, I'm making her out to be a . . . character; and all he'd said would feel like a lie, although of course it had happened. The fact was that she was a very strong woman (even a frightening one, in his childhood), and she may have shrunk and aged but

her true, interior self was still enormous, larger than life, powerful. Overwhelming.

They got to the stadium early so his mother could walk at
her own pace, which was so slow and halting that by the time
they were settled, the lineup was already being announced.
Their seats were good ones, close to home plate. His mother
sank down gratefully but then had to stand, almost at once, for
the national anthem. For *two* national anthems; the other team
was Toronto. Halfway through the second song, Ezra noticed
that his mother's knees were trembling. "Do you want to sit
down?" he asked her. She shook her head. It was a very hot
day but her arm, when he took hold of it, was cool and almost
unnaturally dry, as if filmed with powder.

How clear a green the grass was! He could see his mother's
point: precise and level and brightly colored, the playing field
did have the look of a board game. Players stood about idly
swinging their arms. Toronto's batter hit a high fly ball and the
center fielder plucked it from the sky with ease, almost absentmindedly. "Well!" said Ezra. "That was quick. First out in no
time."

There was a knack to his commentary. He informed her without appearing to, as if he were making small talk. "Gosh. Look
at that change-up." And "Call that a ball? Skimmed right past
his knees. Call that a ball?" His mother listened, face uplifted
and receptive, like someone at a concert.

What did she get out of this? She'd have followed more
closely, he thought, if she had stayed at home beside her radio.
(And she'd never *bring* a radio; she worried people might think
it was a hearing aid.) He supposed she liked the atmosphere,
the cheering and excitement and the smell of popcorn. She even
let him buy her a Styrofoam cup of beer, which was allowed to
grow warm after one sip; and when the bugle sounded she
called, "Charge," very softly, with an embarrassed little half-
smile curling her lips. Three men were getting drunk behind her
—booing and whistling and shouting insults to passing girls—but
Ezra's mother stayed untroubled, facing forward. "When you
come in person," she told Ezra, "you direct your own focus,

you know? The TV or the radio men, they might focus on the pitcher when you want to see what first base is doing; and you don't have any choice but to accept it."

A batter swung at a low ball and connected, and Ezra (eyes in every direction) saw how the field came instantaneously alive, with each man following his appointed course. The shortstop, as if strung on rubber bands, sprang upward without a second's preparation and caught the ball; the outfield closed in like a kaleidoscope; the second-base runner pivoted and the shortstop tagged him out. "Yo, Garcia!" a drunk yelled behind them, in that gravelly, raucous voice that some men adopt in ball parks; and he sloshed cold beer down the back of Ezra's neck. "Well . . ." Ezra said to his mother. But he couldn't think how to encompass all that had happened, so finally he said, "We're up, it looks like."

She didn't answer. He turned to her and found her caving in on herself, her head falling forward, the Styrofoam cup slipping from her fingers. "Mother? Mother!" Everyone around him rose and milled and fussed. "Give her air," they told him, and then somehow they had her stretched out on her back, lying where their feet had been. Her face was paper white, immobile, like a crumpled rock. One of the drunks stepped forward to smooth her skirt decorously over her knees, and another stroked her hair off her forehead. "She'll be all right," he told Ezra. "Don't worry. It's only the heat. Folks, make room! Let her breathe!"

Ezra's mother opened her eyes. The air was bright as knife blades, shimmering with a brassy, hard light, but she didn't even squint; and for the first time Ezra fully understood that she was blind. It seemed that before, he hadn't taken it in. He reeled back, squatting at the feet of strangers, and imagined having to stay here forever: the two of them, helpless, flattened beneath the glaring summer sky.

That night he dreamed he was walking among the tables in his restaurant. A long-time customer, Mr. Rosen, was dithering over the menu. "What do you recommend?" he asked Ezra. "I see you've got your stroganoff, but I don't know, that's a little heavy. I mean I'm not so very hungry, just peckish, got a little weight on my stomach right here beneath my rib cage, know what I mean? What do you think might be good for that? What had I ought to eat?"

This was how Mr. Rosen behaved in real life, as well, and Ezra expected it and always responded kindly and solicitously. But in the dream, he was overtaken by a most untypical panic. "I have nothing! Nothing!" he cried. "I don't know what you want! I don't have anything! Stop asking!" And he wrung his hands at the thought of his empty, gleaming refrigerator and idle stove.

He woke sweating, tangled in damp sheets. There was a certain white quality to the darkness that made him believe it was close to dawn. He climbed out of bed, hitching up his pajama bottoms, and went downstairs and poured a glass of milk. Then he wandered into the living room for a magazine, but the only ones he found were months old. Finally he settled on the rug beside his mother's desk and opened the bottom drawer.

A recipe for marmalade cake: *From the kitchen of* . . . with no name filled in. Someone's diploma, rolled and secured with a draggled blue ribbon. A clipping from a newspaper: *Bristlecone pines, in times of stress, hoard all their life in a single streak and allow the rest to die.* A photo of his sister in an evening dress with gardenias looped around her wrist. A diary for 1909, with a violet pressed between its pages. *Washed my yellow gown, made salt-rising bread, played Basket Ball,* he read. *Bought a hat shape at Warner's and trimmed it with green grosgrain. Preserved tomatoes. Went to Marching Drill. Learned progressive jackstraws.*

Her vitality hummed in the room around him. She was forever doing something to her "waists," which Ezra assumed to be blouses. Embroidering waists or mending waists or buying goods for a waist or sewing fresh braid on a waist, putting insertion on a waist, ripping insertion *off* a waist, tucking her red plaid waist until the tucker got out of fix, attaching new sleeves to a waist—even, for one entire week, attending a course called "Fashioning the Shirtwaist." She pressed a bodice, sewed a corset cover, darned her stockings, altered a girdle, stitched a comforter, monogrammed a handkerchief, cut outing flannel for skirts. (Yet in all the time he'd known her, Ezra had never seen her so much as hem a dish towel.) She went to hear a lecture entitled "Thunder Tones from the Guillotine." She pestered the vet about Prince's ailment—an injured stifle, whatever that was. She sold tickets to socials, amateur theatricals, and Mission Society picnics. She paid a call on her uncle but found his door double-locked and only a parlor window open.

In Ezra's slumbering, motionless household, the loudest sound came from fifteen-year-old Pearl, hitching up her underskirts to clamber through that long-ago window.

Daily, in various bookstores, he proceeded from the Merck Manual to other books, simpler to use, intended for laymen. Several were indexed by symptoms, including *lump*. He found that his lump could indeed be a lymph node—a temporary swelling in reaction to some minor infection. Or it could also be a hernia. Or it could be something worse. *Consult your doctor*, he read. But he didn't. Every morning, still in his pajamas, he tested the lump with his fingers and resolved to call Dr. Vincent, but later he would change his mind. Suppose it did turn out to be cancer: why would he want to endure those treatments— the radiation and the toxic drugs? Better just to die.

He noticed that he thought of dying as a kind of adventure, something new that he hadn't yet experienced. Like an unusual vacation trip.

His sister, Jenny, stopped by with her children. It was a Wednesday, her morning off. She took over the house with no trouble at all. "Where's your ironing? Give me your ironing," she said, and "What do you need in the way of shopping?" and "Quinn, get down from there." She had so much energy; she spent herself with such recklessness. In her worn-looking clothes, run-down shoes, with her dark hair lifting behind her, she flew around the living room. "I think you should buy an air-conditioner, Mother. Have you heard the latest pollution count? For someone in your state of health . . ."

Her mother, bleakly speechless, withstood this storm of words and then lifted one white hand. "Come closer so I can see your hair," she said.

Jenny came closer and submitted to her touch. Her mother stroked her hair with a dissatisfied expression on her face. "I don't know why you can't take better care of your looks," she said. "How long since you've been to a beauty parlor?"

"I'm a busy woman, Mother."

"How much time would you need for a haircut? And you're not wearing makeup, are you. Are you? In this light, it's hard to tell. Oh, Jenny. What must your husband think? He'll think you're not trying. You've let yourself go. I expect I could pass you on the street and not know you."

Her favorite expression, it seemed to Ezra: I wouldn't know you if I saw you on the street. She used it when referring to Jenny's poor grooming, to Cody's sparse visits, to Ezra's tendency to put on weight. Ezra caught a sudden glimpse of a wide, vacant sidewalk and his various family members strolling down it, their faces averted from one another.

Jenny's children ambled through the house, looking bored and disgusted. The baby chewed on a curtain pull. Jane, the nine-year-old, perched on Ezra's knee as casually as if he were a piece of furniture. She smelled of crayons and peanut butter—homely smells that warmed his heart. "What are you fixing in your restaurant tonight?" she asked.

"Cold things. Salads. Soups."

"Soups are hot," she said.

"Not necessarily."

"Oh."

She paused, perhaps to store this information in some tidy filing cabinet inside her head. Ezra was touched by her willingness to adjust—by her amiable adaptability. Was it possible, he sometimes wondered, that children *humored* grown-ups? If grown-ups insisted on toilet training, on *please* and *thank you* —well, all right, since it seemed to mean so much to them. It wasn't important enough to argue about. This is a transitive verb, some grown-up would say, and the children would go along with it; though to them it was immaterial, frankly. Transitive, intransitive, who cared? What difference did it make? It was all a foreign language anyhow.

"Maybe you could invite me to your restaurant for supper," Jane told Ezra.

"I'd be delighted to invite you for supper."

"Maybe I could bring a friend."

"Certainly."

"I'll bring Barbie."

"That would be wonderful," Ezra said.

"You bring a friend, too."

"All my friends work in the restaurant."

"Don't you ever date?"

"Of course I date."

"I don't mean just some one of those lady cooks you pal around with."

"Oh, I've dated in my time."

She filed that away also.

Jenny was criticizing their mother's doctor. She said he was too old, too old-fashioned—too general, she said. "You need a good internist. I happen to know a man on—"

"I've been going to Dr. Vincent as long as I've lived in Baltimore," her mother said.

"What's that got to do with it?"

"We don't all just change for change's sake."

Jenny rolled her eyes at Ezra.

Ezra said, "Maybe *you* could be her doctor."

"I'm her relative, Ezra."

"So much the better," Ezra said.

"Besides, my field is pediatrics."

"Jenny," said Ezra. "What would you say—"

He stopped. Jenny raised her eyebrows.

"What would you say is your patients' most common disease?"

"Mother-itis," she told him.

"Oh."

"Why do you ask?"

"It's not, um, cancer or anything."

"Why do you ask?" she said again.

He only shrugged.

After she'd collected the ironing, and made a shopping list, and rounded up the children, she said that she had to be off. She brushed her cheek against her mother's and patted Ezra's arm. "I'll walk you to the car," he said.

"Never mind."

He walked her anyway, relieving her of the laundry bag while she carried the baby astride her hip. They passed the mailman. He was bent so low to the ground that he didn't even notice them.

Out by the car, Ezra said, "I've got this lump."

"Oh?" said Jenny. "Where?"

He touched his groin. "In the morning it starts out small," he said, "but by evening it's so big, it's like a rock or something in my trouser pocket. I'm wondering if it's, you know. Cancer."

"It's not cancer. More likely a hernia, from the sound of it," she said. "Go see a doctor." She got in the car and buckled the baby into her carrier. Then she leaned out the open window. "Do I have all the children?" she asked.

"Yes."

She waved and drove off.

Back in the house, his mother was hovering at the window exactly as if she could see. "That girl has too big a family," she said. "I suppose her looks must be ruined by now."

"No, I haven't noticed it."

"And her hair. Honestly. Ezra, tell me the truth," she said. "How does Jenny seem to you?"

"Oh, the same as always."

"I mean, don't you think she's let herself go? What about what she was wearing, for instance?"

He tried to remember. It was something faded, but perfectly acceptable, he guessed. Was it blue? Gray? He tried to picture her hairdo, the style of her shoes, but only came up with the chiseled lines that had always, even in her girlhood, encircled her neck—rings of lines that gave her a lush look. For some reason, those lines made him sad now, and so did Jenny's olive hands with the ragged, oval fingernails, and the crinkles at the corners of her eyes, and the news that his life would, after all, go on and on and on.

"February sixth, nineteen-ten," Ezra read aloud. *"I baked a few Scottish Fancies but they wouldn't do to take to a tea."*

His mother, listening intently, thought that over a while. Then she made her gesture of dismissal and started rocking again in her rocker.

"I hitched up Prince and rode downtown for brown silk gloves and an ice bag. Then got out my hat frames and washed my straw hat. For supper fixed a batch of—"

"Move on," his mother said.

He riffled through the pages, glimpsing *buttonhole stitch* and *watermelon social* and *set of fine furs for $22.50.* *"Early this morning,"* he read to his mother, *"I went out behind the house to weed. Was kneeling in the dirt by the stable with my pinafore a mess and the perspiration rolling down my back, wiped my face on my sleeve, reached for the trowel, and all at once thought, Why I believe that at just this moment I am absolutely happy."*

His mother stopped rocking and grew very still.

"The Bedloe girl's piano scales were floating out her window," he read, *"and a bottle fly was buzzing in the grass, and I saw that I was kneeling on such a beautiful green little planet. I don't care what else might come about, I have had this moment. It belongs to me."*

That was the end of the entry. He fell silent.

"Thank you, Ezra," his mother said. "There's no need to read any more."

Then she fumbled up from her chair, and let him lead her to

the kitchen for lunch. He guided her gently, inch by inch. It seemed to him that he had to be very careful with her. They were traversing the curve of the earth, small and steadfast, surrounded by companions: Jenny flying past with her children, the drunks at the stadium sobering the instant their help was needed, the baseball players obediently springing upward in the sunlight, and Josiah connected to his unknown gift giver as deeply, and as mysteriously, as Ezra himself was connected to this woman beside him.

10

Dinner at the
Homesick Restaurant

When Pearl Tull died, Cody was off on a goose hunt and couldn't be reached for two days. He and Luke were staying in a cabin owned by his business partner. It didn't have a telephone, and the roads were little more than logging trails.

Late Sunday, when they returned, Ruth came out to the driveway. The night was chilly, and she wore no sweater but hugged herself as she walked toward the car, her white, freckled face oddly set and her faded red hair standing up in the wind. That was how Cody guessed something was wrong. Ruth hated cold weather, and ordinarily would have waited inside the house.

"It's bad news," she said. "I'm sorry."

"What happened?"

"Your mother's passed away."

"Grandma *died?*" asked Luke, as if correcting her.

Ruth kissed Luke's cheek but kept her eyes on Cody, maybe trying to gauge the damage. Cody himself, wearily closing the car door behind him, was uncertain of the damage. His mother had been a difficult woman, of course. But even so . . .

"She died in her sleep, early yesterday," Ruth said. She took Cody's hand in both of hers and gripped it, tightly, so that the pain he felt right then was purely physical. He stood for a while, allowing her; then he gently pulled away and went to open the car trunk.

They had not bagged any geese—the hunt had been a lame excuse, really, to spend some time with Luke, who was now a senior in high school and would not be around for much longer. All Cody had to unload was the rifles in their canvas cases and a duffel bag. Luke brought the ice chest. They walked toward the house in silence. Cody had still not responded.

"The funeral's tomorrow at eleven," said Ruth. "I told Ezra we'd be there in the morning."

"How is he taking it?" Cody asked.

"He sounded all right."

Inside the front door, Cody set down the duffel bag and propped the rifles against the wall. He decided that he felt not so much sad as heavy. Although he was lean bodied, still in good shape, he imagined that he had suddenly sunk in on himself and grown denser. His eyes were weighty and dry, and his step seemed too solid for the narrow, polished floorboards in the hall.

"Well, Luke," he said.

Luke seemed dazed, or perhaps just sleepy. He squinted palely under the bright light.

"Do you want to go to the funeral?" Cody asked him.

"Sure, I guess," said Luke.

"You wouldn't have to."

"I don't mind."

"Of course he's going," said Ruth. "He's her grandson."

"That doesn't obligate him," Cody told her.

"Of course it obligates him."

This was where they differed. They could have argued about it all night, except that Cody was so tired.

For their journey south, Cody drove Ruth's car because his own was still spattered with mud from the goose hunt. He supposed they would have to ride in some shiny, formal funeral procession. But when he happened to mention this to Ruth, halfway down the turnpike, she told him that Ezra had said their mother had requested cremation. ("Golly," Luke breathed.) There would only be the service, therefore—no cemetery trip and no burial. "Very sensible," Cody said. He thought of the tidy framework of his mother's bones, the crinkly bun on the back of her head. Did that fierce little figure exist any more? Was it already ashes? "Ah, God, it's barbaric, however you look at it," he told Ruth.

"What, cremation?" she asked.

"Death."

They sped along—Cody in his finest gray suit, Ruth in stiff black beside him. Luke sat in the rear, gazing out the side window. They were traveling the Beltway now, approaching Baltimore. They passed trees ablaze with red and yellow leaves and shopping malls full of ordinary, Monday morning traffic. "When I was a boy, this was country," Cody said to Luke.

"You told me."

"Baltimore was nothing but a little harbor town."

There was no answer. Cody searched for Luke in the rearview mirror. "Hey," he said. "You want to drive the rest of the way?"

"No, that's all right."

"Really. You want to?"

"Let him be," Ruth whispered.

"What?"

"He's upset."

"What about?"

"Your mother, Cody. You know he always felt close to her."

Cody couldn't figure how anyone could feel close to his mother—not counting Ezra, who was thought by some to be a saint. He checked Luke's face in the mirror again, but what could you tell from that impassive stare? "Hell," he said to Ruth, "all I asked was did he want to drive."

The city seemed even more ruined than usual, tumbling under a wan, blue sky. "Look at there," Cody said. "Linsey's Candy and Tobacco. They sold cigarettes to minors. Bobbie Jo's Barbecue. And there's my old school."

On Calvert Street, the row houses stood in two endless lines. "I don't see how you knew which one was home," Luke had told him once, and Cody had been amazed. Oh, if you lived here you knew. They weren't alike at all, not really. One had dozens of roses struggling in its tiny front yard, another an illuminated madonna glowing night and day in the parlor window. Some had their trim painted in astonishing colors, assertively, like people with their chins thrust out. The fact that they were *attached* didn't mean a thing.

He parked in front of his mother's house. He slid from the car and stretched, waiting for Ruth and Luke.

By now, Pearl would have been out the door and halfway down the steps, reaching for the three of them with those eager, itchy fingers of hers.

"Is that your sister's car?" Ruth asked him.

"*I* don't know what kind of car she drives."

They climbed the steps. Ruth had her hand hooked in the back of Luke's belt. He was too tall for her to cup the nape of his neck, as she used to do.

When Cody first left home, he would knock when he returned for a visit. It was a deliberate, planned act; it was an insult to his mother. She had known that and objected. "Can't you walk straight in? Do you have to act like company?" "But company is what I am," he'd said. She had started outwitting him; she had lain in wait, rushing to meet him at the very first sound of his shoes on the sidewalk. (So it was, perhaps, not solely love that had sent her plunging down the steps.) Now, crossing the porch, Cody didn't know whether to knock or just open the door. Well, he supposed this house belonged to Ezra now. He knocked.

Ezra looked sad and exhausted, loosely filling a lightweight khaki suit that only he would have thought appropriate. As always, he seemed whiskerless, boy faced. There was a space between his collar and the knot of his tie. A handkerchief bunched messily out of his jacket pocket. "Cody. Come in," he said. He touched Cody's arm in that tentative way he had— something more than a handshake, less than a hug. "Ruth? Luke? We were starting to worry about you."

From the gloomy depths of the house, Jenny stepped forward to kiss everyone. She smelled of some complicated perfume but had her usual hastily assembled look—her tailored coat unbuttoned, her dark hair rough and tossed. Her husband ambled behind her, fat and bearded, good-natured. He clapped Cody on the shoulder. "Nice to see you. Too bad about your mother."

"Thank you, Joe."

"We're supposed to be starting for the church this very minute," Jenny said. "We have to leave early because we're picking up some of the children on the way."

"*I'm* all set," Cody said.

Ezra asked, "But don't you want coffee first?"

"No, no, let's get going."

"See," Ezra said, "I had planned on coffee and pastries before we started out. I'd assumed you'd be coming earlier."

"We've already had breakfast," Cody told him.

"But everything's on the table."

Cody felt his old, familiar irritation beginning. "Ezra—" he said.

"That was thoughtful of you," Ruth told Ezra, "but really, we're fine, and we wouldn't want to hold people up."

Ezra checked his watch. He glanced behind him, toward the dining room. "It's only ten-fifteen," he said. He walked over to a front window and lifted the curtain.

Now that it was apparent he had something on his mind, the others stood waiting. (He could be maddeningly slow, and all the slower if pushed.)

"It's like this," he said finally.

He coughed.

"I was kind of expecting Dad," he said.

There was a blank, flat pause.

"Who?" Cody asked.

"Our father."

"But how would he know?"

"Well, ah, I invited him."

"Ezra, for God's sake," Cody said.

"It wasn't *my* idea," Ezra said. "It was Mother's. She talked about it when she got so sick. She said, 'Look in my address book. Ask everybody in it to my funeral.' I wondered who she meant, at first. You know she never wrote anyone, and most of her relatives are dead. But as soon as I opened the address book I saw it: Beck Tull. I didn't even realize she knew where he had run off to."

"He wrote her; that's how she knew," Cody said.

"He did?"

"From time to time he sent these letters, boasting, bragging. *Doing fine . . . expecting a raise . . .* I peeked inside when Mother wasn't looking."

"I never even guessed," said Ezra.

"What difference would it have made?"

"Oh, I don't know . . ."

"He ditched us," Cody said, "when we were kids. What do you care about him now?"

"Well, I don't," said Ezra. And Cody, who had so often been exasperated by Ezra's soft heart, saw that in this case, it was true: he really didn't care. He looked directly at Cody with his peculiarly clear, light-filled eyes, and he said, "It was Mother who asked; not me. All I did was call him up and say, 'This is Ezra. Mother has died and we're holding her funeral Monday at eleven.'"

"That was *all?*" Cody said.

"Well, and then I told him he could stop by the house first, if he got here early."

"But you didn't ask, 'How are you?' or 'Where've you been?' or 'Why'd you go?'"

"I just said, 'This is Ezra. Mother has died and—'"

Cody laughed.

"At any rate," Jenny said, "it doesn't seem he's coming."

"No," said Cody, "but think about it. I mean, don't you get it? First he leaves and Mother pretends he hasn't. Out of pride, or spite, or *some*thing, she never says a word about it, makes believe to all of us that he's only on a business trip. A thirty-five-year business trip. Then Ezra calls him on the phone and does the very same thing. 'This is Ezra,' he says, as if he'd seen Dad just yesterday—"

Jenny said, "Can we get started now? My children will be freezing to death."

"Oh, surely," Ruth told her. "Cody, honey, her children are waiting on us."

"Mother would have done that, just exactly," Cody said. "If Dad had walked in she would have said, 'Ah, yes, there you are. Can you tell me if my slip is showing?'"

Joe gave a little bark of laughter. Ezra smiled, but his eyes filmed over with tears. "That's true," he said. "She would have. You know? She really would have."

"Fine, then, she would have," Jenny said. "Shall we go?"

She had been so young when their father left, anyhow. She claimed to have forgotten all about him.

At the funeral, the minister, who had never met their mother, delivered a eulogy so vague, so general, so universally applicable that Cody thought of that parlor game where people fill in words at random and then giggle hysterically at the story that results. Pearl Tull, the minister said, was a devoted wife and a loving mother and a pillar of the community. She had lived a long, full life and died in the bosom of her family, who grieved for her but took comfort in knowing that she'd gone to a far finer place.

It slipped the minister's mind, or perhaps he hadn't heard, that she hadn't been anyone's wife for over a third of a century; that she'd been a frantic, angry, sometimes terrifying mother; and that she'd never shown the faintest interest in her community but dwelt in it like a visitor from a superior neighborhood, always wearing her hat when out walking, keeping her doors tightly shut when at home. That her life had been very long indeed but never full; *stunted* was more like it. Or crabbed. Or . . . what was the word Cody wanted? Espaliered. Twisted and flattened to the wall—all the more so as she'd aged and wizened, lost her sight, and grown to lean too heavily on Ezra. That she was not at all religious, hadn't set foot in this church for decades; and though in certain wistful moods she might have mentioned the possibility of paradise, Cody didn't take much comfort in the notion of her residing there, fidgeting and finding fault and stirring up dissatisfactions.

Cody sat in the right front pew, the picture of a bereaved and dutiful son. But skeptical thoughts flowed through his head so loudly that he almost believed they might be heard by the congregation. He was back to his boyhood, it seemed, fearing that his mother could read his mind as unhesitatingly as she read the inner temperature of a roasting hen by giving its thigh a single, contemptuous pinch. He glanced sideways at Ruth, but she was listening to the minister.

The minister announced the closing hymn, which Pearl had requested in her funeral instructions: "We'll Understand It All By and By." Raising his long, boneless face to lead the singing, Reverend Thurman did appear bewildered—perhaps less by the Lord's mysterious ways than by the unresponsive nature of this group of mourners. Most were just staring into open hymnbooks, following each stanza silently. And there were so few of them: a couple of Ezra's co-workers, some surly teen-aged grandchildren sulking in scattered pews, and five or six anonymous old people, who were probably there as church members but gave the impression of having wandered in off the streets for shelter, dragging their string-handled shopping bags.

When the service was finished, the minister descended from the pulpit and stopped to offer Cody, as firstborn, a handshake and condolences. "All my sympathy . . . know what a loss . . ."

"Thank you," said Cody, and he and Ruth and the minister proceeded down the aisle. Jenny and Joe followed, and last came Ezra, blowing his nose. By rights the grandchildren should have risen too, but if they had there would have been hardly any guests remaining.

Outside, the cold was a relief, and Cody was grateful for the lumbering noise of the traffic in the street. He stood between Jenny and Ruth and accepted the murmurs of strangers. "Beautiful service," they told him.

"Thank you," he said.

He heard a woman say to Ezra, over by the church doorway, "I'm so sorry for your trouble," and Ezra said, kindly, "Oh, that's all right"—although for Ezra alone, of the three of them, this death was clearly *not* all right. What would he fill his life with now? He had been his mother's eyes. Lately, he had been her hands and feet as well. Now that she was gone he would come home every night and . . . do what? What would he do? Just sit on the couch by himself, Cody pictured; or lie on his bed, fully dressed, staring into the swarming, brownish air above his bed.

Jenny said, "Did Ezra tell you we're meeting at his restaurant afterward?"

Cody groaned. He shook an old man's hand and said to Jenny, "I knew it. I just knew it." Hadn't he told Ruth, in fact? In the car coming down, he'd said, "Oh, God, I suppose there'll be one of those dinners. We'll have to have one of those eternal family dinners at Ezra's restaurant."

"He's probably too upset," Ruth said. "I doubt he'd give a dinner now."

This showed she didn't know Ezra as well as she'd always imagined. Certainly he would give a dinner. Any excuse would do—wedding or engagement or nephew's name on the honor roll. "Dinner at the Homesick Restaurant! Everyone in the family! Just a cozy family gathering"—and he'd rub his hands together in that annoying way he had. He no doubt had his staff at work even at this moment, preparing the . . . what were they called? The funeral baked meats. Cody sighed. But he suspected they would have to attend.

The old man must have spoken; he was waiting for Cody to answer. He tilted his flushed, tight-skinned face beneath an elaborate plume of silver hair that let the light shine through. "Thank you," Cody said. Evidently, this was the wrong response. The old man made some disappointed adjustment to his mouth. "Um . . ." said Cody.

"I said," the old man told him, "I said, 'Cody? Do you know me?' "

Cody knew him.

It shouldn't have taken him so long. There were clues he should have picked up at once: that fan-shaped pompadour, still thick and sharply crimped; the brilliant blue of his eyes; the gangsterish air of his pinstriped, ill-fitting navy blue suit.

"Yes," the old man said, with a triumphant nod. "It's your father speaking, Cody."

Cody said to Jenny, "I'm not sure if Ezra remembered to set a place for Dad."

"What?" Jenny said. She looked at Beck Tull. "Oh," she said.

"At the restaurant. Did he remember?"

"Oh, well, probably," she said.

"Nothing fancy," Cody told Beck.

Beck gaped at him.

"Just a light repast at the Homesick."

"What are you talking about?" Beck asked.

"Dinner afterward, of course, at the Homesick Restaurant."

Beck passed a hand across his forehead. He said, "Is this here Jenny?"

"Yes," Jenny told him.

"Jenny, last time I set eyes on you you were just about eight years old," said Beck. "Was it eight? Or nine. Your favorite song was 'Mairzy Doats.' You babbled that thing night and day."

"Oh, yes," Jenny said distantly. "And little lambs eat ivy."

Beck, who had drawn a breath to go on speaking, paused and shut his mouth.

"*You* remember Ruth," said Cody.

"Ruth?"

"My wife."

"Why should I remember her? I've been away! I haven't been here!"

Ruth stepped forward to offer her hand. "So Cody's married," said Beck. "Fancy that. Any children?"

"Well, Luke, of course," Cody said.

"I'm a grandfather!" He turned to Jenny. "How about you? Are you married?"

"Yes, but he's left to pick up the little ones," Jenny said. She waved goodbye to somebody.

"And Ezra?" Beck asked. "Where's Ezra?"

"Over there by the steps," Cody said.

"Ah."

Beck set off jauntily, running a hand through his crest of hair. Jenny and Cody gazed after him.

"If I just saw him on the street," Jenny said, "I would have passed him by."

"We *are* just seeing him on the street," Cody told her.

"Well. Yes."

They watched Beck arrive before Ezra with a bounce, like a child presenting some accomplishment. Ezra bent his head courteously to hear Beck's words, then gave him a mild smile and shook his hand.

"Imagine!" they heard Beck say. "Look at you! Both my sons are bigger than I am."

"Dinner is at my restaurant," Ezra told him calmly.

Beck's expression faltered once again, but recovered itself. "Wonderful!" he said. He moved toward the teen-agers, who had got wind of what was going on and stood in a clump nearby —silent, staring, hostile as usual. Beck seemed not to notice. "I'm your grandpa," he told them. "Your Grandpa Tull. Ever heard of me?" Probably they hadn't, unless they'd thought to inquire. He moved down the line, beaming. "I'm your long-lost grandpa. And you are—? What a handsome young fellow!"

He pumped the hand of the tallest teen-ager, who unfortunately was not a grandson at all but one of Ezra's salad boys.

Cody and Ruth and Jenny led the way to the restaurant on foot. The others lagged behind untidily. The first group turned onto St. Paul Street and passed various bustling little buildings —a dry cleaner's and a drugstore and a florist. All the other pedestrians were black; most held jangling radios to their ears, so that scraps of songs about love and jealousy and hardhearted women kept approaching and fading away. Then Ezra's wooden sign swung overhead, and the three of them climbed the steps and walked in.

In the chilly light from the windows, the restaurant seemed glaringly empty. One long table was covered with white linen, set with crystal and china. Thirteen places, Cody counted; for Jenny's Joe would be bringing more children, those too small to have sat through the service. A sweet-faced, plump waitress in a calico smock was drawing up a high chair for the baby. When she saw them come in, she stopped to give Jenny a hug. "I'm so sorry for your trouble," she said. "You and all your family, hear?"

"Thank you, Mrs. Potter," Jenny said. "Do you know my brother Cody? And this is Ruth, his wife."

Mrs. Potter clicked her tongue. "It's a terrible day for you," she said.

Cody turned toward the door in time to see Beck and Ezra enter, trailed by teen-agers. Ezra had obviously relaxed and grown talkative; he never could be cool to anyone for long. "So I tore out that wall there . . ." he was saying.

"Very nice. Very classy," said Beck.

"Stripped down these floors . . ."

"I hope you don't serve that kind of food a fellow can't identify."

"Oh, no."

"A *mish*mash of food, one thing not separate from another."

"No, never," Ezra said.

Cody watched with interest. (Ezra very often served such food.) Ezra led Beck through the room, waving an arm here and there. "See, these tables can be moved together if anyone should . . . and this is the kitchen . . . and these are two of my cooks, Sam and Myron. They've come in especially for our dinner. At night I have three more: Josiah, Chenille, and Mohammad."

"Quite an operation," said Beck.

The others, meanwhile, hung around their table. No one took a seat. Cody's son, Luke, and Jenny's son Peter—both unnaturally formal in white shirts and ties—wrestled together in an aimless, self-conscious way, tossing hidden glances at Beck. Probably these children saw him as a brand-new chance—a fresh start, someone to appreciate them at last. Yet when they finally sat down, no one chose a place near Beck. It was shyness, maybe. Even Ezra settled some distance away. Since Joe and the younger ones had still not arrived, this meant that Beck found himself flanked by several empty chairs. He didn't seem to notice. Kinglike, he sat alone, folding his hands before his plate and beaming around at the others. A tracery of red veins, distinct as mapped rivers and tributaries, showed in his cheeks. "So," he said. "My son owns a fancy restaurant."

Ezra looked pleased and embarrassed.

"And my daughter's a doctor," said Beck. "But Cody? What about you?"

Cody said, "Why, *you* know: I'm an efficiency consultant."

"A, how's that?"

Cody didn't answer. Ezra said, "He checks out factories. He tells them how to do things more efficiently."

"Ah! A time-study man."

"He's one of the very best," said Ezra. "He's always getting written up in articles."

"Is that so. Well, I sure am proud of you, son."

Cody had a sudden intimation that tomorrow, it would be more than he could manage to drag himself off to work. His success had finally filled its purpose. Was this all he had been striving for—this one brief moment of respect flitting across his father's face?

"I often wondered about you, Cody," Beck said, leaning toward him. "I often thought about you after I went away."

"Oh?" said Cody, politely. "Have you been away?"

His father sat back.

"*Any*how," Ezra said. He cleared his throat. "Well. Dad. Are you still working for the Tanner Corporation?"

"No, no, I'm retired. Retired in sixty-five. They gave me a wonderful banquet and a sterling silver pen-and-pencil set. Forty-two years of service I put in."

Ruth murmured—an admiring, womanly sound. He turned to her and said, "To tell you the truth, I kind of miss it. Miss the contacts, miss the life . . . A salesman's life has a lot of action, know what I mean? Lot of activity. Oftentimes now it doesn't seem there's quite enough to keep me busy. But I do a bit of socializing, cardplaying. Got a few buddies at my hotel. Got a lady friend I see." He peeked around at the others from under his tufted eyebrows. "I bet you think I'm too old for such things," he said. "I know what you're thinking! But this is a really fine lady; she puts a lot of stock in me. And you understand I mean no disrespect to your mother, but now that she's gone and I'm free to remarry . . ."

Somehow, it had never occurred to Cody that his parents were still married. Jenny and Ezra, too, blinked and drew back slightly.

"Only trouble is this lady's daughter," Beck told them. "She's got this daughter, no-good daughter, thirty-five years old if she's a day but still residing at home. Eustacia Lee. No good whatsoever. Lost two fingers in a drill press years ago and never worked since, spent her compensation money on a snowmobile. I'm not too sure I want to live with her."

No one seemed able to think of any comment.

Then Joe arrived. He burst through the door, traveling in an envelope of fresh-smelling air, carrying the baby and towing a whole raft of children. Really there were only three, but it seemed like more; they were so chattery and jumbled. "Mrs. Nesbitt almost didn't let me out of school," and "You'll never guess what the baby ate," and "Phoebe had to stay in for being prejudiced in math." "Who's this?" a child asked, facing Beck.

"Your Grandpa Tull."

"Oh," she said, taking a seat. "Do us kids get wine?"

"Joe, I'd like you to meet my father," Jenny said.

"Really?" said Joe. "Gosh." But then he had to figure out the high-chair strap.

The last two children slipped into the empty chairs on either side of Beck. They twined their feet through the rungs, set pointy elbows on the table. Surrounded, Beck gazed first to his left and then to his right. "Will you look at this!" he said.

"Pardon?" Jenny asked.

"This group. This gathering. This . . . assemblage!"

"Oh," said Jenny, taking a bib from her purse. "Yes, it's quite a crowd."

"Eleven, twelve . . . thirteen . . . counting the baby, it's fourteen people!"

"There would have been fifteen, but Slevin's off at college," Jenny said.

Beck shook his head. Jenny tied the bib around the baby's neck.

"What we've got," said Beck, "is a . . . well, a crew. A whole crew."

Phoebe, who was religious, started loudly reciting a blessing. Mrs. Potter set a steaming bowl of soup before Beck. He sniffed it, looking doubtful.

"It's eggplant soup," Ezra told him.

"Ah, well, I don't believe . . ."

"Eggplant Soup Ursula. A recipe left behind by one of my very best cooks."

"On this day of death," Phoebe said, "the least some people could do is let a person pray in silence."

"She cooked by astrology," Ezra said. "I'd tell her, 'Let's have the endive salad tonight,' and she'd say, 'Nothing vinegary, the stars are wrong,' and up would come some dish I'd never thought of, something I would assume was a clear mistake, but it worked; it always worked. There might be something *to* this horoscope business, you know? But last summer the stars advised her to leave, and she left, and this place has never been the same."

"Tell us the secret ingredient," Jenny teased him.

"Who says there's a secret ingredient?"

"Isn't there always a secret ingredient? Some special, surprising trick that you'd only share with blood kin?"

"Well," said Ezra. "It's bananas."

"Aha."

"Without bananas, this soup is nothing."

"On this day of death," Phoebe said, "do we have to talk about food?"

"It is not a day of death," Jenny told her. "Use your napkin."

"The thing is," Beck said. He stopped. "What I mean to say," he said, "it looks like this is one of those great big, jolly, noisy, rambling . . . why, *families!*"

The grown-ups looked around the table. The children went on slurping soup. Beck, who so far hadn't even dipped his spoon in, sat forward earnestly. "A clan, I'm talking about," he said. "Like something on TV. Lots of cousins and uncles, jokes, reunions—"

"It's not really that way at all," Cody told him.

"How's that?"

"Don't let them mislead you. It's not the way it appears. Why, not more than two or three of these kids are even related to you. The rest are Joe's, by a previous wife. As for me, well, I haven't been with these people in years—couldn't tell you what that baby's name is. Is it a boy or a girl, by the way? Was I even informed of its birth? So don't count *me* in your clan. And Becky down there, at the end of the table—"

"Becky?" said Beck. "Does she happen to be named for me, by any chance?"

Cody stopped, with his mouth open. He turned to Jenny.

"No," said Jenny, wiping the baby's chin. "Her name's Rebecca."

"You think we're a family," Cody said, turning back. "You think we're some jolly, situation-comedy family when we're in particles, torn apart, torn all over the place, and our mother was a witch."

"Oh, Cody," Ezra said.

"A raving, shrieking, unpredictable witch," Cody told Beck. "She slammed us against the wall and called us scum and vipers, said she wished us dead, shook us till our teeth rattled, screamed in our faces. We never knew from one day to the next, was she all right? Was she not? The tiniest thing could set her off. 'I'm going to throw you through that window,' she used to tell me. 'I'll look out that window and laugh at your brains splashed all over the pavement.' "

The main course was set before them, on tiptoe, by Mrs.

295

Potter and another woman who smiled steadily, as if determined not to hear. But nobody picked up his fork. The baby crooned softly to a mushroom button. The other children watched Cody with horrified, bleached faces, while the grown-ups seemed to be thinking of something else. They kept their eyes lowered. Even Beck did.

"It wasn't like that," Ezra said finally.

"You're going to deny it?" Cody asked him.

"No, but she wasn't *always* angry. Really she was angry very seldom, only a few times, widely spaced, that happened to stick in your mind."

Cody felt drained. He looked at his dinner and found pink-centered lamb and bright vegetables—a perfect arrangement of colors and textures, one of Ezra's masterpieces, but he couldn't take a bite.

"Think of the other side," Ezra told him. "Think of how she used to play Monopoly with us. Listened to Fred Allen with us. Sang that little song with you—what was the name of that song you two sang? *Ivy, sweet sweet Ivy* . . . and you'd do a little soft-shoe. The two of you would link arms and soft-shoe into the kitchen."

"Is that right!" said Beck. "*I* didn't remember Pearl could soft-shoe."

Mrs. Potter poured wine into Cody's glass. He set his fingers around the stem but then couldn't lift it. He was conscious of Ruth, to his right, watching him with concern.

Then Ezra said, "So! What do you think of this wine, Dad?"

"Oh, afraid I'm not much for wine, son," said Beck.

"This is a really good one."

"Little shot of bourbon is more my style," said Beck.

"And best of all's the dessert wine. They make it with these grapes that have suffered from a special kind of mold, you see—"

"Well, wait now," Beck said. "Mold?"

"You're going to love it."

"And what is this here whitish stuff?"

"It's kasha."

"I don't believe I've heard of that."

"You'll love it," Ezra said.

Beck shook his head, but he looked gratified, as if he liked to think that Ezra had traveled so far beyond him.

Then Cody pushed his plate away. "I've got this partner, Sloan," he said. "A bachelor all his life. He never married."

Everyone took on an exaggerated attentiveness—even the children.

"Last year," Cody said, "Sloan ran into some old girlfriend, a woman he'd known years ago, and she had her little daughter with her. They were celebrating the daughter's birthday. Sloan asked which birthday it was, just making conversation, and when the woman told him, something rang a bell. He calculated the dates, and he said, 'Why! My God! She must be mine!' The woman looked over at him, sort of vaguely, and then she collected her thoughts and said, 'Oh. Yes, she is, as a matter of fact.' "

They waited. Cody smiled and gave them a little salute, implying that they could go back to their food.

"Well. What a strange lady," Beck said finally.

"Not at all," Cody told him.

"You'd think she'd at least have—"

"What she was saying was, the man had nothing to do with them. He wasn't ever there, you see, so he didn't count. He wasn't part of the family."

Beck drew back sharply. His eyes no longer seemed so blue; they had darkened to a color nearer navy.

Then Joe said, "The baby!"

The baby was struggling soundlessly, convulsively, mouth open and face going purple. "She's strangling," Jenny said. Several people leapt up and a wineglass overturned. Joe was trying to pull the baby from the high chair, but Jenny stopped him. "Never mind that! Let me at her!" It seemed the tray was strapped in place and they couldn't get the baby out from under it. An older child started crying. Something crashed to the floor. Jenny punched the baby in the midriff and a mushroom button shot onto the table. The baby wailed and turned pink. Hiccuping, she was dragged from the high chair and placed on her mother's lap, where she settled down cheerfully and started pursuing a pea around the rim of Jenny's plate.

"Will I live to see them grown?" Jenny asked the others.

"He's gone," said Ezra.

They knew instantly whom he meant. Everyone looked toward Beck's chair. It was empty. His napkin was tossed aside, one corner dipping into his plate and soaking up gravy.

"Wait here," Ezra said.

They not only waited; they suspended talk, suspended movement, while Ezra rushed across the dining room and out the front door. There was a pause, during which even the baby said nothing. Then Ezra came back, running his fingers distractedly through his hair. "He's nowhere in sight," he said. "But it's only been a minute. We can catch him! Come on, all of you."

Still, no one moved.

"Please!" said Ezra. "Please. For once, I want this family to finish a meal together. Why, every dinner we've ever had, something has gone wrong. Someone has left in a huff, or in tears, everything's fallen apart . . . Come on! Everybody out, cover the area, track him down! We could gather back here when we find him and take up where we left off."

"Or," Cody pointed out, "we could finish the meal *without* him. That's always a possibility."

But it wasn't; even he could see that. One empty place at the table ruined everything. The chair itself, with its harp-shaped wooden back, had a desolate, reproachful look. Slowly, people rose. The children grouped around Ezra, who was issuing directives like a military strategist. "You and the little ones try Bushnell Street . . . rendezvous with Joe on Prima . . ." Then Ruth stood up too, to take the baby while Jenny put her coat on. They headed for the door. "Good hunting!" Cody called, and he tipped his chair back expansively and asked Mrs. Potter for another glass of wine.

Inwardly, though, he felt chastened. He thought of times in grade school when he'd teased some classmate to tears, taken things a little too far, and then looked around to find that all of his friends had stopped laughing. Wasn't there the same hollow silence in this dining room, among these sheeted tables? Mrs. Potter replaced the wine bottle upon a silver-rimmed coaster. She stepped back and folded her hands across her stomach.

"I believe I'll just go check on how they're doing," Cody told her.

Outside, the sky had deepened to a blue that was almost gaudy. A weak sun lit the tops of the buildings, and it didn't seem so cold. Cody stood with his hands at his hips, his feet spread wide—unperturbed, to all appearances—and looked up and down the street. One section of the search party was just disappearing around a corner: Joe and the teen-agers. A stately black woman with her head wrapped in bandannas had stopped to redistribute the contents of two grocery bags.

Cody took the alley to the right of the doorway, a narrow strip of concrete lined with old packing crates and garbage cans battered shapeless. He passed the restaurant's kitchen window, where an exhaust fan blew him a memory of Ezra's lamb. He skirted a spindly, starved cat with a tail as matted as a worn-out bottlebrush. The back of his neck took on that special alertness required on Baltimore streets, but he walked at an easy, saunter-ing pace with his hands in his trouser pockets.

"Always have a purpose," his father used to tell him. "Act like you're heading someplace purposeful, and none of the low-life will mess with you." He had also said, "Never trust a man who starts his sentences with 'Frankly,' " and "Nine tenths of a good sidearm pitch is in the flick of the wrist," and, "If you want to sell a person something, look off elsewhere as you're speaking, not straight into his eyes."

"All we have is each other," Ezra would say, justifying one of his everlasting dinners. "We've got to stick together; nobody else has the same past that we have." But in that meager handful of advice offered by Beck Tull—truly the sole advice Cody could remember from him—there didn't seem much of a past to build on. From the sound of it, you would imagine that the three of them shared only a purposeful appearance, a mistrust of frankness, a deft wrist, and an evasive gaze.

Cody suddenly longed for his son—for Luke's fair head and

hunched shoulders. (He would rather die than desert a child of his. He had promised himself when he was a boy: anything but that.) He thought back to their goose hunt, where they hadn't had much to say to each other; they had been shy and stand-offish together. He wondered whether Sloan would lend him the cabin again next weekend, so they could give it another try.

He came out on Bushnell—sunnier than the alley and almost empty. He shaded his eyes with his hand and looked around him and—why! There was Luke, as if conjured up, sitting for some reason on the stoop of a boarded-over building. Cody started toward him, walking fast. Luke heard his footsteps and raised his head as Cody arrived. But it wasn't Luke. It was Beck. His silver hair appeared yellow in the sunlight, and he had taken off his suit coat to expose his white shirt and his sharp, cocked shoulders so oddly like Luke's. Cody came to a halt.

"I was just looking for the Trailways station," Beck told him. "I thought I could make it walking, but now I'm not so sure."

Cody took out his handkerchief to wipe his forehead.

"See, Claudette will be expecting me," said Beck. "That's the lady friend I mentioned. I figured I better go on and find a bus. Sorry to eat and run, but you know how it is with women. I told her I'd be home before supper. She's depending on me."

Cody replaced the handkerchief.

"I guess she'll want to get married, after this," said Beck. "She knows about Pearl's passing. She's sure to be making plans."

He held up his jacket, as if inspecting it for flaws. He folded it carefully, inside out, and laid it over his arm. The lining was something silky, faintly rainbow hued, like the sheen on aging meat.

"To tell the truth," Beck said, "I don't much want to marry her. It's not only that daughter; it's me. It's really me. You think I haven't had girlfriends before? Oh, sure, and could have married almost any one of them. Lots have begged me, 'Write your wife. Get a divorce. Let's tie the knot.' 'Well, maybe in a while,' I'd tell them, but I never did. I don't know, I just never did."

"You left us in her clutches," Cody said.

Beck looked up. He said, "Huh?"

"How could you do that?" Cody asked him. "How could you just dump us on our mother's mercy?" He bent closer, close enough to smell the camphorish scent of Beck's suit. "We were kids, we were only kids, we had no way of protecting ourselves. We looked to you for help. We listened for your step at the door so we'd be safe, but you just turned your back on us. You didn't lift a finger to defend us."

Beck stared past Cody at the traffic.

"She wore me out," he told Cody finally.

"Wore you out?"

"Used up my good points. Used up all my good points."

Cody straightened.

"Oh, at the start," Beck said, "she thought I was wonderful. You ought to have seen her face when I walked into a room. When I met her, she was an old maid already. She'd given up. No one had courted her for years; her girlfriends were asking her to baby-sit; their children called her Aunt Pearl. Then I came along. I made her so happy! There's my downfall, son. I mean with anyone, any one of these lady friends, I just can't resist a person I make happy. Why, she might be gap-toothed, or homely, or heavyset—all the better! I expect that if I'd got that divorce from your mother I'd have married six times over, just moving on to each new woman that cheered up some when she saw me, moving on again when she got close to me and didn't act so pleased any more. Oh, it's closeness that does you in. Never get too close to people, son—did I tell you that when you were young? When your mother and I were first married, everything was perfect. It seemed I could do no wrong. Then bit by bit I guess she saw my faults. I'd never hid them, but now it seemed they mattered after all. I made mistakes and she saw them. She saw that I was away from home too much and not enough support to her, didn't get ahead in my work, put on weight, drank too much, talked wrong, ate wrong, dressed wrong, drove a car wrong. No matter how hard I tried, seemed like everything I did got muddled. Spoiled. Turned into an accident. I'd bring home a simple toy, say, to cheer you all up when I came, and it would somehow start a fight—your mother saying it was too expensive or too dangerous or too difficult, and the three of you kids bickering over who got to play with it first. Do you recall the archery set? I thought it would be such fun, bring us all together—a family drive to the country, where we'd set up a target on a tree trunk and shoot our bows and arrows. But it didn't work out like I'd planned. First Pearl claims she's not athletic, then Jenny says it's too cold, then you and Ezra get in some kind of, I don't know, argument or quarrel, end up scuffling, shoot off an arrow, and wing your mother."

"I remember that," said Cody.

"Shot her through the shoulder. A disaster, a typical disaster. Then next week, while I'm away, something goes wrong with the wound. I come home from a sales trip and she tells me she nearly died. Something, I don't know, some infection or other. For me, it was the very last straw. I was sitting over a beer in the kitchen that Sunday evening and all at once, not even knowing I'd do it, I said, 'Pearl, I'm leaving.' "

Cody said, "You mean *that* was when you left?"

"I packed a bag and walked out," said Beck.

Cody sat down on the stoop.

"See," said Beck, "what it was, I guess: it was the grayness; grayness of things; half-right-and-half-wrongness of things. Everything tangled, mingled, not perfect any more. I couldn't take that. Your mother could, but not me. Yes sir, I have to hand it to your mother."

He sighed and stroked the lining of his jacket.

"I'll be honest," he said, "when I left I didn't think I'd ever care to see you folks again. But later, I started having these thoughts. 'What do you suppose Cody's doing now? What's Ezra up to, and Jenny?' 'My family wasn't so much,' I thought, 'but it's all there really is, in the end.' By then, it was maybe two, three years since I'd left. One night I was passing through Baltimore and I parked a block away, got out and walked to the house. Pretty near froze to death, standing across the street and waiting. I guess I was going to introduce myself or something, if anybody came out. It was you that came. First I didn't even know you, wondered if someone else had moved in. Then

I realized it was just that you had grown so. You were almost a man. You came down the walk and you bent for the evening paper and as you straightened, you kind of flipped it in the air and caught it again, and I saw that you could live without me. You could do that carefree a thing, you see—flip a paper and catch it. You were going to turn out fine. And I was right, wasn't I? Look! Haven't you all turned out fine—leading good lives, the three of you? She did it; Pearl did it. I knew she would manage. I turned and walked back to my car.

"After that, I just stuck to my own routine. Had a few pals, a lady friend from time to time. Somebody'd start to think the world of me and I would tell myself, 'I wish Pearl could see this.' I'd even write her a note, now and then. I'd write and give her my latest address, anyplace I moved to, but what I was really writing to say was, 'There's this new important boss we've got who regards me very highly.' Or, 'There's a lady here who acts extremely thrilled when I drop by.' Crazy, isn't it? I do believe that all these years, anytime I had any success, I've kind of, like, held it up in my imagination for your mother to admire. Just take a look at *this*, Pearl, I'd be thinking. Oh, what will I do now she's gone?"

He shook his head.

Cody, searching for something to say, happened to look toward Prima Street and see his family rounding the corner, opening like a fan. The children came first, running, and the teen-agers loped behind, and the grown-ups—trying to keep pace—were very nearly running themselves, so that they all looked unexpectedly joyful. The drab colors of their funeral clothes turned their faces bright. The children's arms and legs flew out and the baby bounced on Joe's shoulders. Cody felt surprised and touched. He felt that they were pulling him toward them—that it wasn't they who were traveling, but Cody himself.

"They've found us," he told Beck. "Let's go finish our dinner."

"Oh, well, I'm not so sure," Beck said. But he allowed himself to be helped to his feet. "Oh, well, maybe this one last course," he said, "but I warn you, I plan to leave before that dessert wine's poured."

Cody held on to his elbow and led him toward the others. Overhead, seagulls drifted through a sky so clear and blue that it brought back all the outings of his boyhood—the drives, the picnics, the autumn hikes, the wildflower walks in the spring. He remembered the archery trip, and it seemed to him now that he even remembered that arrow sailing in its graceful, fluttering path. He remembered his mother's upright form along the grasses, her hair lit gold, her small hands smoothing her bouquet while the arrow journeyed on. And high above, he seemed to recall, there had been a little brown airplane, almost motionless, droning through the sunshine like a bumblebee.

Anne Tyler was born in Minneapolis, Minnesota, in 1941 but grew up in Raleigh, North Carolina, and considers herself a Southerner. She was graduated at nineteen from Duke University, where she twice won the Anne Flexner Award for creative writing, and became a member of Phi Beta Kappa. She has done graduate work in Russian studies at Columbia University and worked for a year as the Russian bibliographer at the Duke University Library. This is Miss Tyler's ninth novel, and her stories have appeared in such magazines as *The New Yorker*, *The Saturday Evening Post*, *Redbook*, *McCall's*, *Harper's*, *The Southern Review*, and *Quest*. She is married to a psychiatrist, Taghi Modarressi, and she and her huband now live in Baltimore, Maryland, with their two daughters.

A NOTE ON THE TYPE

The text of this book was set on the Linotype in Janson, a recutting made direct from type cast from matrices long thought to have been made by the Dutchman Anton Janson, who was a practicing type founder in Leipzig during the years 1668–87. However, it has been conclusively demonstrated that these types are actually the work of Nicholas Kis (1650–1702), a Hungarian, who most probably learned his trade from the master Dutch type founder Dirk Voskens. The type is an excellent example of the influential and sturdy Dutch types that prevailed in England up to the time William Caslon developed his own incomparable designs from them.

The book was composed by Maryland Linotype Composition Co. Inc., Baltimore, Maryland. It was printed and bound by R. R. Donnelley & Company, Harrisonburg, Virginia.

Typography and binding design by
Dorothy Schmiderer